No NOVEL that Kathleen Norris has ever written is likely to find more readers than BREAD INTO ROSES.

It is the story of Susannah Farjeon, from the dreadful moment in the Far East when her dreams of happiness seemed shattered, through days of wealth and power, to the time when she found love and peace at last. Susannah had had far from a usual life. At the time of her father's death, in Peking, she was one of the most flattered and courted young women of the American colony; she was beautiful, full of the enthusiasm of youth, and had a sincerity which distinguished her in the superficial life around her. And on the boat returning to America, trying to forget the blow of a broken engagement, she met Alec, whom she would marry . . .

Then came the fear that was to haunt Susannah, fear because Alec had turned out to be not the unimportant mining engineer she thought, but something entirely different. And she was afraid for her marriage . . . that it would not be an *always* marriage, the only kind her love and sincerity could ever accept.

How Alec did forget his marriage vows; how another man, understanding, charming, came into her life and she grew to love him; all this, together with the problems which beset any young new-married couple, the small joys, the great tragedies, make up this new romance. It is a story rich in emotion, and in the appealing details of real life.

Like *The American Flaggs,* Mrs. Norris' last book, BREAD INTO ROSES is a distinguished novel of our people and our times.

BREAD INTO ROSES

KATHLEEN NORRIS

Bread Into Roses

THE SUN DIAL PRESS, INC.
New York

PRINTED AT THE *Country Life Press*, GARDEN CITY, N. Y., U. S. A.

1938
THE SUN DIAL PRESS, INC.

FOR KATE

You so small, do you bring anew to me
 Joys of the happiest years of them all?
Soften everything time could do to me,
 Make life true to me, you so small?

You so grand, in the royal way of you
 Holding firm in your petal hand
Loves that lived long before the day of you,
 What to say of you, you so grand!

You so sweet, as you grasp the whole of it,
 Keep the happy old law complete,
Sandbox, high chair, and spoon and bowl of it,
 And the soul of it, you so sweet!

BREAD INTO ROSES

❧ CHAPTER I ❧

THE GLARE OF BURNING MIDAFTERNOON lay over the world and over the ship and poured in through the western port to flicker blinding reflections from the restless water across the crowded and cluttered cabin. Eva Farjeon lay stretched flat and straight on her bed, with her eyes shut against the trying light, and an expression of weary endurance upon her pretty, middle-aged face. Susannah stood at the porthole, looking out at the scene which lay below it.

At four o'clock on a July day the steamer Queen Augusta was pulling herself free of the waters of the Whangpoo and starting her long journey back to San Francisco. The usual excitement of departure was over; a few bored deck stewards were sweeping mashed flowers and torn telegrams from the decks and dropping them overboard into the littered, dirty water; a few inexperienced travelers were making meticulous arrangements regarding deck chairs. But most of the passengers had disappeared into their cabins for a welcome interval of unpacking and rest and settling down generally to the tedium of the trip. Stewards' bells were ringing busily; trunks rocked and banged as they were bumped along the narrow passages.

The Farjeons were seasoned travelers. Mother and daughter, they had slipped away from the cheering and waving crowd upstairs as soon as the little tender had brought them to the ship half an hour earlier. Eva had taken two aspirin tablets, had jerked bags and flowers and coats from one of the beds to stretch herself there; Susannah had scarcely changed her position at the porthole.

"The last of the Bund, Mother. I wonder when we shall see it again," Susannah said, not turning her head.

"I don't care if we never see it again!" Eva said.

Her daughter looked at her, moved her lips as if she were about to speak, thought better of it, and again resumed her study of the sluggish waters of the Whangpoo. This was the busiest hour on the river; steamboats, junks, barges were jumbled upon it in mad confusion; whistles and screams tore the hot lifeless air; between the narrow banks the shipping of all the world plowed, drifted, paddled to and fro.

The long waterfront, its go-downs and warehouses heaped with bales and barrels, boxes and crates, was fringed with black barges, upon whose dark unsavory decks every activity known to Chinese ignorance and poverty was in full swing. Fighting, washing, laughing, cooking, sleeping, tending babies, tending ducks or dogs, combing hair, combing rope, and always and above all and through all drinking tea, the dark-skinned mysterious men and women lived their appointed lives in complete indifference to watching eyes or to any possible reminder of contrast. Their laughter cackled above the lazy splash of water and the scraping of city feet.

"They're probably as happy as we are," Susannah Farjeon said.

"I didn't hear you," Eva said ungraciously.

"It was nothing."

Back of the eternal agitation of the piers and the fringe of countless little food stalls, black with dirt and age, that were today steaming in the heat, the low silhouette of the city of Shanghai arose; into the narrow black mouths of its streets rickshas drawn by bent and running men vanished like morsels of food sucked into a hopper.

It was all disappearing now; it was all merging into an indistinguishable haze. The lower banks of the river, clustered thick with black labyrinths of houses that had been tangled together for hundreds of years like the filthy heart of an old hive, were beginning to slide by. Destroyers lay at anchor, trim in brass and paint; the flag of America, the flags of England and Japan, hung limp in the heat. Odorous small craft moved about like black rats swimming in the dirt of the river.

"Frightful days in the Old City when it's as hot as this," Susannah said musingly.

"Frightful days anywhere," her mother added promptly. "Do freshen up, Sanna," she added in a gentle complaining voice, "and go upstairs! Your white crape is there somewhere—Amah brought it after the trunks had gone. I think I stuck it into the brown hatbox."

"It's so hot, Mother," the daughter said. "I think I'll stay down here and read until it's time to dress, and then maybe slip up and write some thank-you notes. No one's on deck now."

She had spoken dreamily, as if half to herself. Her mother opened suspicious eyes.

"Where's Johnny?"

"I don't know," Susannah answered briefly. She crossed the little stateroom, pulled out the upper drawer of a wardrobe trunk and looked into it vaguely. "There are packages of books here," she said. "I'm going to open them. Some are from darling old Woodsey, I think, and the Palmers sent books, and Jean brought me the new Marie Antoinette."

"Keep the cards from the flowers," Eva commanded, closing her eyes again. Presently she spoke clearly, seriously, in the silence:

"Sanna, is anything wrong between you and Johnny?"

"How d'you mean wrong? Oh, Lord, look! Candy from old Joe Potter," Susannah said, opening packages. "And we've been so indecently rude to that poor man. Here are almonds from your beau, Mother. 'Compliments of J. J. Sweet, R.N.'"

"The idea!" Eva said, flattered, and smiling feebly at the card Susannah put into her hand. "Poor old fool! He had the girl in the shop write the card," she commented.

"Probably sent the chit boy down for it and had it all wrapped. Don't look gift horses in the face, darling. Daisies from Phyllis. 'Just a breath from my Hung-jao garden.' Wouldn't you know that Phyllis, who could buy up the whole city and never know it, would send us a handful of withered daisies!"

"Gift horses, ahem!" Eva observed.

"Well, of course. I take that back. It's awfully decent of people to pay any attention to our comings and goings at all; we never entertain, and we're eternally arriving and departing." Susannah pushed an open trunk like a little closet back against a wall, put a handful of toilet articles on the shelves of the little washstand, tossed books to the unoccupied bed. She sighed as she did so; they would be sixteen days on the steamship, and with all that the little cabin held and must hold, she knew there would be small chance of order ever being established in that time. Three trunks, two hatboxes, five bags, the roll of rugs, the typewriter, her mother's extra coat, her own fox scarf, the roped box that had winter underwear and cloth dresses in it, all these and the incidental scattering of books and ash trays and candy boxes and small possessions generally would keep the place in a state of incurable confusion.

"What's Johnny doing?" her mother asked presently.

"I don't know."

"You saw him when you went upstairs?"

"Oh yes."

"Where's his cabin, Sanna?"

"I don't know, Mother. I don't even know the number of it. I'm all turned round, anyway. When I started downstairs I was making off for the second cabin."

"If it wasn't for Johnny that's where we'd be this minute, in the second cabin," Eva Farjeon said. "And I'd be in my good hundred and fifty dollars."

"The rooms in the second cabin are exactly as good as any of these on D deck," Susannah observed. She looked out of the port again. "Getting down the river," she observed encouragingly. "Paddies and water buffalo and marshes. We're almost to the Fort."

"I can begin to feel the motion. The light, jumping about that way, makes me feel horrid," Eva complained.

"You know you can't feel any motion yet!" Susannah had extracted two gowns; she put them on hangers and placed them where they swayed to and fro gently with the motion of the laboring great ship. "We don't have to dress tonight; we can wear these," she said.

"I don't want to wear my yellow, Sanna."

"Why not?"

"Because it's the only decent sport dress I have for Kobe and Yokohama. We shan't have time to do any laundry work between here and there. I'd much rather get into my old crape—it always looks decent—and save the yellow."

"Well, why don't you, Mother? Or the coffee lace; that's always nice. Why don't you do what you want to do?"

"Because I don't want people to think I haven't sense enough not to know that you don't dress on sailing night."

Susannah laughed briefly and a little mirthlessly.

"You've been practically commuting on this line for thirty-seven years," she observed amusedly. "Everyone's aware that you know the ropes, that you were brought up in China, and that your husband was the late Captain Lynn Lorimer Farjeon, U.S.A. All Shanghai knows it!"

"Yes, and my father was naval attaché for seventeen years," Eva completed it in quiet complacency. "But everyone on *board* doesn't know it," she added.

"But what do you care what these people think, darling? It looked to me like the dullest crowd I ever saw. Not a person we know."

"Well, you and Johnny 'll pick up some young people. You always do."

"Ha!" It was an oddly unsatisfactory monosyllable. Susannah had finished the superficial settling-in now, had taken off her wilted white tennis silk, her shoes and hat, and had stretched herself out on her own bed, her forehead wet with perspiration, a pile of books slipping against her elbow.

Somehow the worst hours she and her mother ever knew were spent in their rooms at this time of the afternoon. Mornings took care of themselves; in the evenings there always were other persons about, there was always something to do. But in the dull quiet afternoon, when they came in to lie down and rest and talk, it was as if the masks they always wore slipped a little, or perhaps as if the mask the future always wore slipped a little, and what they saw frightened them. Susannah was twenty-seven now, Eva just twenty years older; increasingly of late years both mother and daughter had had reason to fear that beyond that bright mask of their plans, their visits and invitations and pleasant opportunities, there was no future at all.

Just of late, however, Eva's misgivings had been laid to rest. Feeling this keenly, it was with real reluctance that Sanna presently came out of a few moments of somber reflection to say:

"Mother, listen. You've got to know this, and you might as well know it now. It's all off between me and Johnny."

Mrs Farjeon received this blow without the movement of a muscle. Susannah had turned on her side; one hand cupped her cheek against the pillow; she had evidently settled herself for a talk. Her mother lay motionless, her eyes fixed upon the girl's face, her whole being one stunned interrogation.

"It's been off since last night at Bernardine's," Susannah added and was silent, expectant in her turn.

The storm broke with only a few faint drops.

"How do you mean, Sanna?" her mother asked gently.

"We had a talk last night, and it's—well, *off*," Susannah persisted, trying to laugh.

There was a pause. Susannah's cheeks were very red.

"I don't know what you mean," her mother said then, in nervous disapproval of her flippancy.

"I mean my engagement to Mr John Ashburton Wardell," the girl said.

"You've had a quarrel? Sanna, how can you be so foolish as to take chances now, when you're on your way home actually to be married!"

"I didn't take them," Susannah murmured, with a faint accent on the first word. "He did."

"Johnny?"

"Yes. You see, Mother," the girl said, speaking carefully, as if her throat were a little sore, "his ladylove has been in Shanghai for ten days. She got in on the President Hoover."

Eva Farjeon had raised herself to a sitting position, had dropped her feet to the floor. Her face was keenly anxious.

"Susannah, let me understand you," she said. "Has there really been a break between you and Johnny?"

"Absolutely. He's going to marry Ethel Mallock."

Mrs Farjeon fell back upon the pillow again, her eyes closed. She spoke in a whisper, as if to some unseen listener above.

"Oh, this is what I get for going up to Peking for three weeks! Oh, fool that I am! But I thought of course you were safe with Helen. I've no one to blame but myself! Sanna," she added sharply, jerking herself up to a sitting

position again, "you say you've broken your engagement!
Well, you *haven't*. This can't go any further! I'll see Johnny
right away."

"What to say, Mother?"

"A great deal!" Eva answered, with a trembling angry
laugh. "He can't get away with any nonsense like this! I've
already written your aunt Nona that you're to be married.
It's sheer nonsense—I simply can't understand—why, it's un-
thinkable! Is a man calmly to say that he's tired—that he's
gone back to an old love—a girl who married another man
only a few years ago——"

"Listen, Mother darling. Calm down. There's no use making a fuss about something we can't help. Johnny's on board
this ship; we'll see him every day for sixteen days. She's on
board, too, in the cabin de luxe, of course. She's beautiful,
she's rich, she's twenty-five, and she wants Johnny!".

"Why, but this is sheer nonsense, Sanna," her mother
said, actually pale.

"He doesn't think so, and she doesn't think so, and if
we have any pride at all we won't let them see that *we* think
so."

"But you're not just going to give up! Johnny Wardell
asked you to marry him fifty times, and you were engaged.
Doesn't that mean *anything*?" Eva demanded pathetically.
"I'm bewildered; I don't understand. What on earth happened?"

"Nothing sensational. She got here ten days ago; you
weren't here, but the papers all spoke of the beautiful Mrs
Mallock, who was going to be so much entertained. I met
her at a woman's luncheon at Lil's. But I didn't know until
Johnny told me that she was the Ethel Nye he'd been so
much in love with five years ago. He said he wasn't even
going to see her, that she'd made him too unhappy—said it
was all over and no use raking in cold ashes."

"Go on!"

"Well, of course he did meet her—at Hope's, I think. They had a housewarming; there were about thirty of us there. I saw Johnny talking to this Ethel Mallock in the garden for a few minutes, but then he came in again, and we danced; they had pencil games, and Johnny acted quite naturally. She kept away from him, and he kept away from her; I didn't pay much attention. He told me, when he was taking me home, that she was divorced and that her husband's mother had the little girl, and that she was going to marry one of the richest railway men in America, Parsons or Pennant or some such name. He said dozens of men were after her."

"Ha! They always say that," Eva commented scornfully.

"Well, anyway, it was broiling hot this last week, and we'd all go out to the club in the mornings and loaf there all day, and she was always there. And last night, at Bernardine's, he said he wanted to talk to me, and we walked down the lawn to the tennis court, and he said that he was sorry, but that Ethel and he had found each other again and he wanted to be free."

"I hope you said, 'Nonsense!' " Eva said, trembling.

"I couldn't. I told him I thought it was——" Susannah stopped short, frowning a little as if in pain.

"Was what?"

"Well—unexpected."

"And then he said he was going to be on this boat?"

"Yes, he said that she was coming back on this boat—I knew that, anyway. And he said he had made arrangements to come along, too."

"But I thought he was going the other way, to meet his mother in Paris?"

"He was. That was the original arrangement. But quite suddenly—yesterday or the day before—he decided to come this way. He cabled his mother to meet him in New York."

Mrs Farjeon considered the situation. She was still breathing fast, but her first burst of anger had died away; she was biting her lip and looking into space through narrowed eyelids.

"Is she pretty, Sanna?"

"Mrs Mallock? Yes. Or, anyway, she's quite striking. Platinum, with very black eyes and white skin. And she has —well, *clothes!*" Susannah said eloquently. "You never saw such clothes! At the garden party on Sunday she had a gown as fine as an evening handkerchief, tumbling and dragging on the grass, and an old-fashioned frilled parasol to match. White—all white, but with a line of black and blue here and there. Paris."

Eva Farjeon brought her eyes back from far spaces. Her little fair face looked haggard and worn in the glaring, unbecoming afternoon light.

"What are we going to do?" she demanded forlornly.

"I don't see what we can do. Just grin and bear it, I suppose."

"That," Eva said definitely, almost viciously, "I *won't* do! Are we supposed to sit back quietly—dressing for dinner, and playing races and Bingo, and drinking soup up on deck at eleven o'clock—and let this sort of thing go on? Meet him, and chat with him, and the whole thing off? Why, I would have stayed in Shanghai first; I wouldn't have come home at all! It was only your aunt Nona being so anxious to have you married in her house—and Johnny's parents being right there in Philadelphia—two hours away . . ."

She sat on, soliloquizing, an ineffectual little figure in her tumbled white gown, with her mussed, graying fair hair. Susannah, sending her mother an occasional sympathetic glance, noticed that her face looked blotched and pale. She herself said little; she lay listening, her expression very thoughtful.

"It's a horrible mess, and I don't see quite how we are going to go through with it," she admitted presently, in a puzzled tone. "Believe me, Mother, I don't like it one bit better than you do! But there seems to be no help for it."

"But, Sanna, we can't just *take* it!"

"For the moment we can't very well do anything else. Once we're off the boat—in San Francisco——"

"Once we're off the boat in San Francisco we'll lose him completely!" Eva said despairingly.

"Well, and isn't that what we want to do?" Susannah asked simply.

"Well, no, of course not. I mean—after all, he owes—— I mean, what on earth would we have left, Sanna? What could we *do?* Visit your aunt Nona for a little while, perhaps. But there's Lola and Anita apt to come home with children any time; we couldn't *stay* there, even if Nona wanted us, which she wouldn't! I mean I think Johnny Wardell has acted like a perfect fool—and I think in some ways he *is* a perfect fool—but after all he's *something.* A great many marriages have queer beginnings, but people settle down and forget that there ever was any nonsense like this!"

"You can't exactly call it nonsense, Mother, when a man of twenty-five tells you flatly that he's through!"

"I don't believe he did!" Eva said stubbornly. "And if he does come to his senses I beg of you—I *beg* of you—to forgive him. It's maddening, I can see that, but it's the best way out! And considering that at the last moment I changed to the first-class passage, all on his account . . ."

❧ CHAPTER II ❧

THE VOICE FLOWED ON AND ON, Eva talking herself quiet after her outburst. Susannah listened in a sort of dream; after a while she was hardly conscious of hearing anything at all, or seeing the cabin with the lights wheeling and slipping about on its white ceiling. Her thoughts were far away.

But it was a strange dream, and one from which she wished that she might awaken, even though Johnny's extraordinary conduct had not caused her, she had honestly to admit, the bitter hurt of rejected love. She did not love him —not as he loved her; he had said a hundred times he did not care whether she did or not, he would do the loving. But even without heartbreak involved the situation was bad enough.

Susannah and Johnny had planned an autumn wedding in her aunt's handsome Park Avenue apartment in New York. Her friends had seen her off from Shanghai today with barely veiled allusions to the engagement that was still supposedly a profound secret; they had made her good-by presents that were tacit tributes to the beauty and cleverness of the girl who was about to make a brilliant match. Her future had been based upon marriage to Johnny; there was no other future. And there was the almost insufferable present, when she must be incessantly in Johnny's neighborhood, watching as a discarded sweetheart the triumph of the pretty, younger, more audacious woman who would certainly permit none of the savor of the situation to escape her.

Outrageous of him insolent of him, to engage passage on the very ship that was taking the interloping Ethel back to America! But there was no use in abusing Johnny; whether he'd been within his rights or outside them was not really the question. The question was how to meet the problem now—tonight and tomorrow—when she would have to dress and go down to dinner, drift into the big lounge after dinner and listen to the music, take her share in the life of the ship.

A great weariness came over her; and she felt discouraged, unequal to the demand of this hot, sticky afternoon hour of glare and gentle motion, and of all the hours to come.

"Look here, we've had a swell run for our money, and you're not in love with me and I'm not with you!" Johnny had said laughingly, in Bernardine's garden last night. Bernardine lived out near the golf club; it had been cool and moonwashed out there in the black night; music had been sounding faintly from the house. Johnny had had cocktails and wine and one or two brandies; he had been carried on to a sort of false courage by the excitement of food and drink, moonlight and dancing; he had taken a chummy sort of attitude toward Susannah, a sort of "let's-be-sensible-and-admit-it" position. "Listen," he had said, "I was cracked about Ethel Nye five years ago, and I'm just as cracked about her now."

"Does she know we're engaged?" Susannah had asked, too dazed to know why it had seemed to matter, or indeed what she was saying at all.

"No, she doesn't. She knows I like you a lot better than any other girl out here; I told her so. But I didn't say anything about being engaged."

"Didn't?"

"Nope. Because—look here, everything's changed, see?
I mean I think everything ought to be changed, because,
look—it wouldn't be fair to her, nor to me, nor to you
either, to go on with this while we all feel . . ."

Thus Johnny, flushed and laughing, and not quite sure
that the whole thing was not a good joke on them, all three.
Susannah, after the first unbelievable minute, had listened
almost without comment. Fair! Somewhere deep down in
her soul she had been laughing at his earnest use of that
word. When they were going to be flagrantly, brutally selfish, how men did love to talk of being fair!

"Ethel is one wonderful little sport," Johnny had presently
been saying seriously. "She doesn't know you and I were
engaged, but she knows that you and I've meant a lot to
each other, and her one worry is that you'll get the small
end of it, see? She says she doesn't want to cut anyone out;
she was regularly mad about it. So that's why I'm clearing
the whole thing up this way, and that's why I'm sailing for
America sooner than I expected to. See? It all works out."

It had not worked out at all in Susannah's mind. But
there had been nothing appropriate to say. She had had to let
him go last night after a while without comment or reproach;
she had lain awake through the short summer night wondering what to do, wondering if there was anything she could
do.

That night she had slept at Hope's house; her mother had
come down from Peking the next morning, but before Susannah even joined her at the modest apartment where they
were to pack their trunks and say good-by to the friends who
kept coming and going, Eva had heard that Johnny Wardell
was to sail with them on the Queen Augusta, and had
changed her second-cabin tickets for first-cabin reservations.
Susannah had had no opportunity to explain that everything was changed, that what Johnny did didn't concern

them now. She had found her mother in a constantly changing group of women friends. Presently they had all gone
over to the Cathay for luncheon, and had chatted and
smiled with more friends. No chance for confidences! It had
been indeed a typical Shanghai day, with a general excitement of parties, races, boating and love affairs stirring in
the air, and smart frocks and uniforms on exhibition in the
big airy upstairs hotel dining room high above the crowded
Bund and the lazily moving, muddy Whangpoo. Visiting
girls, newcomers to the Orient, always found luncheon at
the Cathay a thrilling experience; the food was novel and
delicious, and everyone in town who was anybody at all
came through the dining rooms sooner or later.

But Susannah no longer thought it exciting. She had
been an eager little girl of fourteen, with a mane of fair
hair falling on her shoulders, when she and Mother and
Dad had lunched here first; Dad had come out to his post
in Peking; everything had amused and pleased and delighted
them then; just to be in China had been a wonderful thing!
Honolulu had been lovely, Japan a great adventure, but to
be actually househunting in Peking, after visits in Shanghai,
this was to live on heights quite unbelievable to a little girl
who had to remember the background of only a dull army
post or two by way of contrast. Susannah had been at the
diary-writing age; she hated the look of those battered little
old leather "Line-a-Day" books now. The oldest of them
was a dreadful thirteen years old; thirteen years, and they
seemed not more than so many months!

In those first books Susannah had recorded enthusiastically the descriptions of the walled houses in Peking, the
Legation teas, the races at Pao-Machang. Always a lamen-
table speller, she had boasted of her "poney" who did not
"bight", of the other girls being "peeked" because he had
won the race, of the mafoo who almost "dyed" of joy.

Those were years in which Eva had enjoyed a real social

position in diplomatic circles, and when she and Susannah had made occasional trips to the United States only for pleasure, or for the daughter's education. Susannah had had three half-terms in a California boarding school, had returned to the Orient to take her place beside her mother in society.

After that, where had the years slipped to? They had vanished like mist; eighteen, twenty-one, twenty-three had rushed upon Susannah with bewildering speed, or rathei with no consciousness on her part that there was time at all, and that it was passing.

But at twenty-three had come a change and an awakening; in the bad winter when everyone was ill and when so many died, Captain Lynn Lorimer Farjeon had gotten a chill, and within three days the bewildered widow and the stunned girl had had to face life without him.

This had been the Friendship Dynasty, Susannah said long after, looking back at those days. For the popularity of Lynn Farjeon had been a very real thing; his charm, his hospitality, his humor and affection and generosities had combined to leave to his womenfolk a legacy of devotion and sympathy. In their dark hour somebody's little house had been empty, and at their command; somebody else had undertaken to sell at top prices the club memberships, the ponies, the old crystals and tapestries. When the two women, in their fresh black, had presently decided to go home, for a while anyway, they had found that their passage was paid, their stateroom filled with flowers. Everyone had been only too kind—too kind—too kind.

Susannah had been having love affairs for some years at this point. They had been the brief love affairs of this exciting world, carried on at races, dances, receptions, regimental band concerts, picnics, theatricals. They had usually ended with mutual promises and heartaches when the visitor departed for home, wherever home was, or when the officer was removed to some other station. Men coming to China fell in love with Susannah at first sight; possibly because she was different, in her sober, sensible, amused fashion, from the other women they met there. Susannah did not drink, she did not smoke, she did not gossip. She liked books and horses, charades and games and picnics, dogs and cooking. Her feeling for her father was the one love of her life; for the rest, she laughed at the men who flattered her and courted her, enjoyed dancing with them, and was always rather embarrassed when they carried the friendship on into deeper waters.

At twenty she had been engaged to Pat Lilienthal; her father had persuaded her to break the engagement. Looking back, Susannah had never been able to recall quite why she had fancied herself in love with the fascinating "Irish Jew" whose charms had taken all Peking society by storm, or why she had fancied herself not in love with him. Many a girl had married with much less affection, she knew, than that which she had felt for Pat; a man as rich, as handsome, as affectionate and gay and likable usually had no trouble in finding a wife. It had been springtime when Pat came to Peking; everyone had been in white; meals had been out of doors; the dreaming old Chinese city had supplied an incomparably romantic background for their romance, as for a score of others that had been going on at that particular moment. The fragrance of roses, the deep shade of the trees about the old building at the Ministries, the sound of regimental bands came back to her when she remembered that time. Everyone had been in and out of everyone else's house; everywhere had been teacups, platters of cold ham, iced glasses, voices, laughter. And always she herself in thin white ruffles had been laughing up at handsome Pat. . . .

"You don't love him, Missy," her father had said.

"I'm mad about him!"

"That's just talk, Sanna. Examine into your own soul and

heart. You don't love Pat. Remember what you told me about Captain Rodgers, three years ago."

"Dad, that was my first crush. That—waked me up. Every girl has a first crush that shows her—proves to her how she *can* feel. Don't remind me of Noel Rodgers! I used to lie awake nights hoping his wife would die a swift and painless death. I writhed over it for hours whenever I heard him call her 'Sweet.' "

"Exactly. Don't you think you ought to feel at least as much for Pat?"

"And what makes you think I don't, Cap?" But even as she had said it she had known that her father was right, that she was taking complete adoration from Pat and returning a good deal less.

So when Pat went away Susannah had had an honest talk with him. Dad had stipulated for a year's trial of their devotion; they would write, they wouldn't consider the break final at all, but they must wait and see just what a twelve-month would do to their feelings. And long before that twelvemonth was ended, Pat, in Minneapolis, and Susannah, in Peking, had been deep into new loves and off with the old forever.

After her father's death everything had been very different. Eva's financial resources were slender indeed; she and Susannah had become almost professional visitors. They had gone to America and visited the Randalls at the Presidio, when Marie-Thérèse and Susannah had renewed their little-girl friendship; they had gone to New York and stayed with Aunt Nona, and Susannah had been bridesmaid at Lola's marriage to Jere Pope. In Honolulu they had always found some old army friend to entertain them; in Chicago they always had lunched or dined or stayed overnight with the Pritchetts. They had gone back to Shanghai in the season when low traveling rates were available, and everyone there had duly welcomed them. They had visited, and Susannah had gone with beaus to lunch at the Cathay and had smiled and nodded at friends all up and down the room. The big smooth-faced headwaiter had remembered her, of course, and had asked, "Scrambled eggs with finnan haddie for Miss Farjeon?" and Susannah had laughed joyously and said, "Now imagine that!"

But still these later China days had not had quite the savor of the old days. Well past twenty-six, and traveling with an almost penniless, gay, pretentious little mother, had not been the same thing at all as arriving eager and enthusiastic and fourteen with a dad who had legitimate reasons for living in China and who made friends as soon as he smiled. Susannah had not ever felt herself exactly unwelcome or superfluous, but she had felt ages older than the new crop of laughing, dancing, smartly dressed girls who came out on every steamer, and she had rather wished herself married and off the market. Simple enough in sound, truly, for a woman who was beautiful and young, this plan of marriage, but not quite so simple to accomplish. The nicest men, as usual, were married. They paid her the most extravagant compliments, their wives warned her that she would be poisoned in a teacup one of these days, but that didn't, after all, get one very far.

Susannah and Eva had been home again, had come back again, had been rather aimlessly drifting about Shanghai three months before this hot afternoon when she was lying in her stateroom on the Queen Augusta thinking the situation over, when two important events had changed the current of their lives. Eva had had an offer of a free trip all the way to New York, and five hundred dollars to boot, in return for discharging a real favor to the Palmers. It was rather a tiresome favor, this accompanying a broken, irritable old man all the way from Peking to the home of a daughter in Pennsylvania, but somebody had had to do it, and the only other members of the family were a husband

and a son, both of whom were held to their duties in the American Consulate.

Eva had departed upon this friendly service, and Susannah had gone to a tea at the German Minister's, to encounter Johnny Wardell. The rest was history; the usual history of a beautiful, amused and flattered woman, a completely captivated man a few years younger, a watchful and appreciative group of friends. Everyone had loyally played Susannah's game; she had found herself carried again to the peak of popularity and success, for Johnny was very rich, altogether eligible in every other discernible way, and quite the ideal match for poor darling Susannah. Eva, returning two months later, had found the affair practically settled, Shanghai's smartest set only waiting the announcement to overwhelm both principals with congratulations; in short, had returned to find her fondest dream for her daughter only a few months short of realization.

Johnny must meet his mother in Paris and take her back to Philadelphia for his wedding. Well, of course! He was an only son; his mother and grandmother and married sister would naturally want to have a share in his marriage plans. Susannah had a New York aunt and cousins who would perhaps want to give her her entire trousseau, Eva had said, holding up her side of the situation with what had seemed to Susannah a rather pathetic pride. They would all go home; Johnny by way of Suez; Susannah and Eva the quicker way, meeting him in New York when his ship docked there in October.

This had been the position until ten days earlier. It had been only then that Johnny had mentioned Ethel Mallock, the fascinating little blonde who had broken his heart five years ago. Ethel was arriving in Shanghai on the President Hoover.

"You'll like her," Johnny had predicted with a grin.

"She sounds fascinating."

"She's a tramp. God, she's a devil. She's always had her own way; she's always had too much money. She's rough, I mean to say the girl's *rough*," Johnny had said, over a deep interior chuckle.

"She sounds kind of cute just the same," Susannah had said, over a jab at the heart.

"She's cute all right!" Johnny had fallen into a muse, and when they had spoken again it had not been of Ethel Nye Mallock.

CHAPTER III

THE HEAT BURNED ON AND ON over the flat water meadows, and the forts that had been bombed in many wars. The ship plowed gallantly through the last of the river waters and reached the sea, and still there was no air to breathe, and the odors of oil and cooking lingered in the long passages. It was twilight, and the bell gong rang up and down the stairways and halls; the decks were deserted now, their long, clean stretches empty under floods of light.

"I'm *sick*," Eva said despairingly, sitting broken and forlorn on the edge of her bed.

"I know. It's a rotten situation."

"He'd be ostracized from decent society if people knew this."

"Not Johnny, with his looks and the Ashburton money."

"To have them right on the boat with us!"

"Yep, that's the rub. I feel as if I'd like to crawl into a hole somewhere and lick my wounds," Susannah said, with a shred of rueful laughter. "Instead, I suppose we shall presently be wearing paper caps at the captain's dinner. Well—it's twenty minutes to eight."

"I honestly don't feel as if I could go through it," Eva said. "Could we pretend that we're sick, Sanna?"

"Not for sixteen days, darling. No, we'll manage it somehow, and get to San Francisco, and we can plan on from
there!"

"But I've written your aunt, and she'll probably have a
letter in San Francisco all full of wedding plans. She's terribly excited about it; I could tell that from her cable. Of
course I didn't dare say anything definite, since the War-
dells in Philadelphia hadn't been told, but I did mention his
name, and she cared enough to cable me, 'Delighted with
news, depend on me for details.' "

"Yes, I know. I saw the cable." Susannah sat up, feeling
fuzzy and warm. "I'm going to glide down the passage for
a shower," she said. "It won't really cool me off, but I'll
pretend it does."

"What shall you do if you see them, Sanna—Johnny and
this—this Ethel person?" Eva asked fearfully.

"Smile, I suppose, and say that it seems good to see so
many of the old staff on the Augusta."

"I'd cut him dead."

"I don't believe you would. Girls have a perfect right
to break engagements; I don't see why men shouldn't.
I wish," Susannah added, but this was only in her own
thoughts, as she went about the business of bath and dressing, "that I had a profession. There's something very dignified in work. I wish I were 'S. L. Farjeon, M.D.' I wish I'd
had newspaper training or knew something about the me-
chanics of theatricals. But I'm old-fashioned, I guess. Waiting about for some man to marry me. All very well if it
works, but horribly flat if it doesn't. I wonder if Mother
would consent to living in some little place like—well, Carmel, for example. Marie-Thérèse and I rented a darling place
there for almost nothing once; we could live there on fifteen
hundred a year. She's borrowed a thousand from Aunt
Nona for this trip," Susannah's thoughts ran on. "I could
pay that off, if I opened a little school, or sold Chinese

things. There are nice shops there—there's Del Monte and Monterey to draw on for customers . . ."

She was back in the cabin now, looking at herself somberly in the gently tipping mirror. The reflection that looked back was that of a beautiful woman, albeit there were circles under her eyes, and the ivory-smooth cheeks were unusually pale. The warm brown of the thick soft hair had red lights in it; there was brown in Susannah's fine skin; there were red lights in her brown eyes. Thickly lashed, and spaced far apart, there was a look of childish candor and childish curiosity in these round deep-set eyes, but the mouth was chiseled and firm and sophisticated, and the aristocratic clean line of the chin lent definiteness to the face. Long cheekbones, a long, rounded throat, a low forehead against which the warm silky lights of the hair made a sort of mist, flat small ears well set back, and decorated now by a pair of strange long jade earrings; Susannah could not but feel satisfaction in her appearance. But it was a rather bitter satisfaction, and there was an ironic twist to her smile as she put on a striped silk frock, plain and straight, with a green belt to match her earrings, and picked up a green cotton coat. The coat had been Hope's; the frock had originally been made at a smart shop in Fifty-seventh Street for her cousin Lola Pope. Susannah's handsomest clothes were all given her at secondhand; she didn't mind. She did not even think of it tonight, as she went slowly upstairs through the familiar narrow ship corridors, smelling the familiar smell of sea water and bilge water, wet linoleum, hot tar, rubber floor coverings, soup with onions in it, baking. Reaching the promenade deck, she fitted a pleasantly expectant smile to her face, peeping into the writing room, where several women who did not like to be quite the first to go down to dinner were writing post cards, peeping into the lounge and the Venetian Ballroom, nodding at the inevitable children coasting on the shining floor. CINEMA TONIGHT, 9 P.M., the chart outside the purser's office read; stewards were already aligning chairs for the audience.

Her mother was talking earnestly with one of the ship's officers in the Palm Bar. Susannah joined them; the officer, immediately brightening, began to take an interest in the conversation.

"Sanna, Doctor Fretz," said Eva, who was always scrupulous at getting names. "My big daughter, Doctor."

"Doctor Fretz and I met at the races yesterday," Susannah said, with her slow, considering smile. Yesterday! She had not known then what she knew now. She had not dreamed yesterday that Johnny was anything except the devoted admirer he had seemed to be, while they sat in the Burts's box, and watched the horses, and laughed, and when everyone was lamenting her departure on the next afternoon and warning her that if she did not come back there would be an American-Chinese war.

"Of course we did," said Arnold Fretz. "You gave me a good tip. I got twenty-two dollars for my two."

"It's too bad my mother has had to consult you so soon, Doctor. Will she live through the night?"

"Well," said the doctor, narrowing his eyes, "with care, yes. But we must keep up the nourishment."

"Doctor, who's sitting at your table tonight?" Susannah could presently ask, with her friendly smile. Before he could answer in words she read his politely regretful expression and wished that she could take the question back. But it was too late. Ah, his table was full; some friends of friends of his had come through from Europe; he didn't know them at all—they seemed extremely nice people . . .

Susannah and her mother went down alone to the dining room at a quarter before eight and had a small table to themselves. The head steward, bowing politely, asked them if they would not like a table to themselves, and they answered graciously that they would. Just why they decided thus, neither one could have said at the moment; any company would have been good company tonight. But Eva appeared a little confused, and Susannah, only conscious of wondering if Johnny and Ethel had come down earlier and were watching them, was carrying things off with what smoothness she could muster. So they found themselves dining together, and chatted smilingly, and were silent, and chatted easily again in the fashion of traveling mothers and daughters for an uncomfortable forty minutes, and then went upstairs again, after the waiter had drawn out both their chairs and had received little nods of recognition.

They had coffee in the lounge. Just as they reached it a cheerful party arose from a table, upon which cocktail glasses were scattered, and started down for the dining room. Ethel Mallock and party. Susannah saw a stout old bald man who was laughing heartily, a thin dark younger man, a redheaded woman, middle-aged and stout and overdressed, especially for sailing night, with great diamonds on her hands and an emerald brooch at her breast, and Johnny and Ethel. Ethel still wore her hat and the checked silk and smart white coat she had worn all day; she looked like a person much too busy and happy to bother about dress. She did not see Susannah. Her small arms hooked on either side into an arm of Johnny and of the dark young man, she was progressing by little jumps, her head bent and her eyes on the carpet.

"Come on, let's eat, I'm starved!" Susannah heard her say. And in answer to some remark from a man, "Ah, is there a picture? But we don't have to go to it, do we?"

Johnny, laughing, looked away and saw Susannah and nodded his handsome head. If he was embarrassed he showed nothing of it; he and the others disappeared, and Susannah and her mother had their coffee. Afterward they went to see the picture, which was not very good partly because the music was much too loudly reproduced, and partly because the night was so airless. It was good to get out on the deck at about half-past ten, and walk about under the lights, and breathe as much of sea coolness as an unusually humid night permitted. The deck steward, sweating in his white duck, asked if they would like chairs.

"I don't think we do, do you, Mother? We never use them."

"I don't think so, thank you. You're being kept pretty busy, aren't you, getting in only today?"

"We certainly are, meddam. We didn't get the larst of the beggage off much before one o'clock."

"Imagine!"

"Really, they do remarkable things to amuse one on these boats," Eva said. "We're just up from dinner, and here they are passing sandwiches."

"It's nearly eleven, Mother. And people eat continually at sea."

"Well, I believe I'll go down. Are you coming?"

"I'm going up to the boat deck and take a turn around. Perhaps there's some air up there. I warn you the cabin will be awful."

"I know. But it's all right once one gets to sleep. Sanna," little Eva said, catching at her daughter's arm, as Sanna turned toward the companionway, "you're not feeling too badly? You wouldn't—you wouldn't do anything—you're all I have, you know!"

"Mother, you idiot!" Susannah stooped to kiss her in the gloom of the iron stairway. "Go downstairs and go to sleep," she commanded, her brief laugh half impatient and half touched. "Do you think I'd give anyone in the world the satisfaction of thinking that I jumped overboard for love of him!"

"You're such a comfort, darling," Eva whimpered, going

on her way. Susannah mounted the stairs alone and stepped out into the darkness and quiet of the boat deck. As she paced slowly about it, suiting her step to the gentle motion of the boat, looking in vain toward the black silken sea and the bright spangling of the stars for any breath of freshness, she could see an occasional muffled form in a deck chair or pass an occasional solitary figure walking like herself. But the music, the crowd, the voices were all far below.

She went to the rail just below the bridge and leaned on it and looked down at the water that was churning away in a great fan, milky with phosphorus. Where beams from the ports fell against the sea it had a smooth molten appearance, like flowing metal; there was almost no wake tonight; there were little coins of light swimming on the water, appearing and disappearing, always the same, never the same. They fascinated her eyes and drugged her thoughts; she fell into a sort of stupor watching them, not thinking, not feeling, suspended between the black night sea and the starry night sky, and seeming to belong to both, to the boundless dark of the moving mysterious world and the great cosmic pattern overhead. Susannah felt her heart swell with a sort of world pain. "How little we are!" she murmured half aloud, leaning her back against a white-painted girder, looking up at the stars, seeing the ropes and davits and the bulk of the canvased lifeboats moving slowly up and down.

"Hello!" a voice said at her elbow. She came to her full sense with a shock. It was Johnny, of course, facing her, close beside her. The light was in her eyes as she half turned; she made herself smile. "I knew you'd be out here somewhere," he said, carrying off the situation determinedly, gaily. "I wanted to see how you were!"

Susannah seemed to find nothing to say. She withdrew a little into the shadow, one elbow resting on the high rail. Her bright eyes never faltered from his.

"Sanna," he said, "are you angry at me?"

"Angry?" she echoed in a whisper. "No. No, of course not."

"I mean—everything came in such a rush," Johnny said, on a note of apology. "Come on, talk to me!"

Again Susannah, against her desperate effort to think of something appropriate to say, was silent.

"You see, I had no more idea than the dead that—— I mean to say I didn't know Ethel was coming to China!" Johnny blundered on.

"I know you didn't."

"Well, you see? You could have knocked me down when she walked up to me at the tea at the Barracks. 'Johnny,' she said, 'I don't expect you to forgive me. But I want you to know I'm sorry!' Well, whoops!" Johnny finished eloquently. "For Ethel, you know, that was some *come*down! I was knocked for a *loop*."

He was a tall, loosely built young man, with wildly waving fair hair, a big nose, a big hard jaw, big hard hands. As always, his clothes indicated Bond Street, his accent New York, his manner all the country clubs, the racecourses, the roulette tables, the yachts and hunts and golf courses that had helped to make him the elegant young idler he was. He was rich, Johnny, and he was nice, too. He always wanted everyone to be happy. He had come up here to the boat deck to find her tonight because he had been afraid she was unhappy.

He looked at her, expectant and smiling, and Susannah had to speak.

"If you felt that way, Johnny, of course you had to say so."

"Well, exactly!" he said eagerly. "But I mean—our all being on this boat—that's the catch. Ethel was coming back anyway," he hastened to explain; "she didn't change *her* plan. But my jumping into it—I don't know why I didn't think of it's putting the screws on you. See?"

"It's a rather sudden change of plan for me," was all Susannah could think to say. Her words sounded stiff.

"Yes, I know. And what I want you to know is that I wouldn't hurt you for anything in the world," Johnny said. "You're one of the great sports of the world—Ethel thinks so, too—and you and I are always going to be friends. Why, Sanna, if you ever were in trouble and didn't come to me I'd be terribly hurt—no kidding, I would! Get me?"

His arm had been so recently about her, that big hard jaw of his had so recently been pressed against her own, that she felt a little confused by this rush of generous promise; she could not adjust the relationship that had been theirs with this new relationship of loyal friendship; she felt chilled and bewildered.

"You know what a fool I am!" Johnny went on. "If I do a rotten thing I'm the one that knows it! I think perhaps it was kind of rotten to change this whole thing around and then ship on this same boat. I mean I didn't *mean* it rotten, but it was. I mean you might think it was! But you understand how it was, don't you? I was cracked about Ethel, and when she showed up—*sorry*—why, it just knocked me over. For five days I've just been spinning around like a top, not knowing what it was all about! However, if you're not mad at me——?"

He stopped on an interrogative note, and Susannah said lifelessly:

"No, I'm not mad at you, Johnny."

"Well, then everything's swell! Give my love to your mother, and if I've been stupid forgive me—you know what a fool I am! I'll see you both tomorrow. I was cut out of a fivesome, and I've got to go down again. You're swell, Sanna."

His arms were about her for a second, and he kissed her

lightly on her hair. Then he was gone. Susannah stood motionless for a long time where he had left her, looking up at the stars and the faintly moving outline of the lifeboats and ropes and davits against them.

When she went down the cabin was insufferably stuffy. Eva, quite nude under the thin stretch of the sheet, was sound asleep. The electric fan hummed and whirred; an empty dress hanger clicked against the wall, was silent, clicked again. Susannah began to undress, going through motions slowly but with meticulous care. She rubbed cold cream on her face; brushed her thick silky mop; put the trees into her shoes. She looked at her dress critically; could it be worn again with pressing, or must it be cleaned? The stewardess had reminded her that electric irons were not permitted in the cabins, but had added that she would gladly press anything the ladies needed. That meant a larger tip; no help for it. Money would be short from now on. There was no haven of a brilliant marriage at the end of the trip; Mother owed money, she had borrowed on her pension in a lavish fashion that would cripple her for months to come.

Carmel. The Miss Farjeon who had lived in China and had tried to open a children's school, and who now was working in the Giftie Shoppe, or was it the Devonshire Tea Potte? Devoted to her mother. The father had been an army man, or a navy man, or something. Nice people. Miss Farjeon had played Prossy in *Candida* at the Community Theater and had really been awfully good.

But perhaps a garden, with roses and delphinium in it, and always for comfort the sand dunes and the glorious sea. And no longer the cruel watching eyes at races and clubs, at the Cathay for luncheon. No longer the little complacent rouged women saying, "She must be getting on for thirty, isn't she, Marian?" and the men feeling free to be carelessly affectionate with her, because, after all, Sanna Farjeon was not quite a girl any longer.

"I'll have a dog," Susannah said half aloud, stretching her young smooth body against the cool linen, looking patiently at the port through which no air seemed to come and the blurred fan that seemed to have nothing to stir. And suddenly she began to laugh and then to cry. Johnny was upstairs, doubling five diamonds, leaning to the man nearest him with an aside, "I'll high-spade you for five bucks," muttering, "You crook!" when Ethel put down a strong dummy against him. Spoiled, bold, lawless, there was something dashing about Johnny, something that all women liked. Susannah missed him; for two months now he had been openly her slave, following her about, paying her ricksha man, buying her tickets for the races, escorting her from one box to another, from teas to cocktail parties and on to dinners and dances.

"Ah, you don't love me at all, you iceberg!" he had told her more than once. Susannah had only looked at him with her serious, cryptic smile when he said it. It suited her to have him give more than she did in the matter of love. But tonight, in her loneliness and hurt, she told herself that she did love him; she had built a plan of life upon the thought of marrying him; she felt jarred and shamed that it should be torn asunder.

The night life of the big ship went on. After a while the faint far throbbing of the orchestra stopped; voices and laughter and the sound of elaborately hushed good nights in the passages died away. The creaking of wood continued; once the great horn, caught in a moment's summer fog, belched forth a hoarse protest; always the idle slap of satin waters sounded against the ship's side.

Susannah had silenced the ticking dress hanger; she got up to silence jingling trunk keys. One o'clock. Lying on her back, feeling the endless gentle sway and twist of the ship beneath her, she stared wide-eyed into the darkness. She felt as if she never would sleep again.

"I'm not immoral, I'm not even unmoral," said Ethel. "I'm amoral. That's awful, isn't it? I tell you it's true. I have no character!"

"I don't know the distinctions between them," Susannah said amiably. "No, no more tea, but bring me some hot water, please," she said to the lounge steward.

The steward bent attentively.

"Hot water!" he murmured, as one discovering a lode of pure gold. He was off; Ethel said languidly that she would like a bacardi cocktail—if he ever came back.

"You shan't have it," said Johnny. "You walk your mile, ride the gee-gee in the gym, take a salt plunge, and then you spoil it all with bacardi cocktails at five o'clock! It's nonsense."

"How did you acquire your character, Sanna? I seem to feel that you have character," Ethel said.

"The poor always have character. It's the rich who are always short on morals," Susannah answered, nodding at the steward in acknowledgment.

"Sanna's unique. Charlie Larkin told me, the night he met her, that she only had one serious fault—she was straight," Johnny said.

It was the eighth day out; the voyage was halfway done. Long before this, Sanna had encountered Ethel a score of times; Ethel had given a dinner in a private dining room, and Susannah had been a guest; they had had tea with the captain in his quarters next the bridge. Now they were Ethel and Sanna to each other, warily, with an occasional touch or triumph on Ethel's side and an occasional impulse of sheer hate on Susannah's. She had moments of hating herself as heartily as she hated Ethel; it did not matter, the wretched experience would be over in sixteen days, much better keep

it meanwhile as surface-serene as one might, and show as
little hurt as was possible.

She and Eva breakfasted in bed; they were in for a big
tip to the stewardess, anyway; they might as well let her
earn it. After an hour or two of idling and reading they
dressed, and came up on deck just as the fragrant hot bouillon was being wheeled about. Susannah would be in the
pink of morning freshness and beauty now, greeting a new
friend or two, watching deck tennis or shuffleboard, walking about the deck with the English officer or the young
Danish diplomat. If she encountered Johnny and Ethel it
was simplest, it was easiest all round to stop and chat, to
discuss the weather and who won the pool, to wander with
them into the bar for the hour before luncheon. Eva by this
time was usually playing bridge fast and furiously; sometimes Susannah went in and sat on the arm of her chair
to watch a few hands, when Eva always said abstractedly,
"That's right, ducky, bring me good luck!"

After luncheon there were Bingo and races and tea, and
after tea the bad hour, the grim hour of hot airless twilight,
when the cabin on Deck D was stuffy, when there seemed to
be no particular object in living. Just to dress, presently, and
descend to say indifferently, "I think I'll have the iced bouillon, Miller, and the usual cold chicken and salad," somehow lacked thrill. Sometimes she and Eva were asked to
cocktail parties, which only meant that dinner was in-
ordinately delayed and they were late for the movie, and
twice they went up to have tea with the captain. Captain
Broderick was a fine stalwart Britisher of sixty; a widower
for eighteen years, he would gladly have accepted a little
encouragement from the beautiful Miss Farjeon, but Susannah, during the sixteen days of the voyage, was never
for one single second aware of his existence.

It was after dinner on the third or fourth night, when her
mother was well started at a bridge game, that Susannah

felt suddenly that she must get away from the voices and
the lights and the music; somehow the smooth procedure
of the evening's social program was nothing short of unen-
durable. She couldn't stand it!

She walked through the salty warm airs of the hallways,
went through the library. The librarian was there between
eight and nine; several women were earnestly discussing
with him the merits of novels bound in brown and red.
Their first sea trip, evidently. Older passengers knew that
ship's novels were only those that happened to be left in the
cabins, abandoned as worthless by their original owners.
Well, perhaps these ladies would like them, at that!

Bored, Susannah went on to the brightly lighted deck.
Couples hung on the rail in rapt contemplation of stars and
sea, or rather, rapt in the absorbing business of developing
ship's friendships, and permitting the stars and sea to form
the background. It was all so usual, so absurd, somehow,
so futile!

She stood undecided at a companionway. She could
mount, of course, to the boat deck; that was always com-
paratively deserted, because always dark, at night. Or she
could go down to the deck of the second cabin, to find
complete solitude among the shadows of the hatch-heads
and the capstans and the oddly shaped big lockers and
cranes and ladders of thick painted ropes that so cluttered
it. Everyone who was awake in the second cabin was on the
forward deck now, dancing. There was to be an entertainment tonight.

The boat deck—the second-cabin deck? Susannah saw
some women her mother knew approaching, and made a
hasty decision. She opened the little rope gate that was
marked TOURIST ONLY and descended steep iron stairs. It
should be the second cabin.

And as she made her choice her Fate leaned forward to
touch her with an approving hand.

⚜ CHAPTER IV ⚜

"It seems all wrong not to have it enough that one is in perfect health and traveling on a big ship from one fascinating port to another. My only responsibility is to decide between chicken salad and salmon aspic!" Susannah said with an ashamed laugh.

"It *is* wrong," her companion said, with a sidewise glance that showed her a glint of his eyes in the dark. "You'll get the gods down on you!"

"Oh, they're that already!" Susannah assured him lightly.

It was night; several long days had gone by since first she had slipped away from the first cabin's efforts at entertainment, and had found her way down to this special little eyrie on the second-cabin deck. Tourist-cabin passengers were not permitted to go up to the first-cabin decks, but there was nothing to prevent Susannah from coming down here, and on her first night's investigation she had discovered that by coming through the little gate and down the steep companionway, crossing an open deck space and passing the windows of the second-cabin dining room, and mounting three narrow steps guarded by a rail, she could take possession of a sheltered little deck completely hidden away behind lifeboats, delightfully near the rush of the wake, and safe from observation.

Here, seated on a wide flat box with a heavily canvased cover, and leaning on the rail, she could watch the eternal racing away of the waters, watch the last of the sunset fade from the western sky and the first silvering of the moon steal through the summer dusk. As soon as Eva was happily established at the card table Susannah would escape to this blessed little eyrie of peace and solitude. A tall, squarely built man in a gray coat, with fairish thick hair blown about by the wind, sometimes would be standing at the rail near by, but she paid small attention to him; one of those prosperous sensible business men who traveled second class for choice as well as for economy, perhaps, he did not matter at all.

But on the third night that found her establishing herself in her sanctuary, he spoke to her quite casually. His name was Hazeltyne, Alexander Hazeltyne. Susannah said that she thought that quite a movie name, and he returned pleasantly that Susannah Farjeon was also an unusual title.

"Your name isn't on the second-cabin list; I looked for it," she told him at their second meeting.

"No. I'm on rather a special mission, and I didn't want it to appear. It's 'Carey' on the list."

"The second-cabin appointments seem to me just as nice as the first," Susannah said tactfully.

"Absolutely. Quieter, and less of a crowd. The orchestra comes down here twice a day; there are movies every night —there's really no difference, except perhaps that the meals aren't quite so elaborate. But as a matter of fact I know one of the stewards of this line," Alexander Hazeltyne said, "and the quality of the supplies is exactly the same for all the cabins. My wife and I," he added, "said years ago that we would always travel second."

"Some of these cabins," Susannah said, with a rueful little laugh, "look pleasanter to me than those on Deck D."

"They are!" he agreed quickly. Perhaps he had also

reached the point that she had reached, of enjoying their quiet chat at the end of each of the ship's empty days; at all events Susannah found herself escaping to it with a pleasant little quickening of the heart, as time went by, and even though she was sometimes quite early at the meeting place, she never failed to find him there.

They sat on the flat, canvas-covered box and leaned an elbow each on the rail, squared about to face each other. Sometimes the moon shone in the man's face and glinted on the glasses that he wore; sometimes starlight gleamed in Susannah's eyes and burnished the tips of her loosely waved hair. From ship talk, talk of weather and Shanghai and Peking, which he had never seen, and Vladivostok, which she had never seen, they went on to personalities.

"Engineering? And what is the name of the place?"

"Baguio, in the Philippine Islands."

"Do you know some people named Marshall Morris there?"

"Very well."

"They were on the ship when we went out. We loved them."

"Both fine. She's very brilliant. But you've not been there?"

"Manila, no. And now where do you go, Mr Hazeltyne?"

"I must be three or four days in San Francisco. Then I fly to Gary and spend three or four days there. Then New York. And what's your itinerary?"

"New York eventually, I suppose. I've an aunt and some married cousins there. We wish now—Mother and I—that we hadn't left China at all," Susannah confessed, on a rueful little laugh. "We've wonderful friends there, and somehow —somehow one seems of more use to one's friends in China. They need someone to stay with a mother, or manage a dinner, or run a bazaar or theatricals, or manage a house through a hospital siege. I don't know New York very well, but it doesn't seem to me you need your friends there."

"You're quite right. But then why did you start for home?"

The question came with so much real interest, and in so friendly a voice, and the need for sympathy was so strong in her at the moment that Susannah could answer quite simply:

"I was going home to be married."

"Ah?"

"I was to marry a Philadelphia man. As a matter of fact he's on this boat. But now the engagement's off, and he's going to marry someone else. He's going to marry a Mrs Mallock."

"Mrs Mallock? I know who she is. She was in Manila last year. But you don't mean that she—he didn't——"

"Yes, he did. That's exactly what happened." Odd that it seemed to ease her heart to tell him about it! "They had been friends years ago, and when she got her divorce this year she came straight after him."

A pause.

"I see," Alexander Hazeltyne said thoughtfully then. "That was Johnny Wardell, then?" he asked.

"You know him?"

"One hears everything in the Orient. I knew his firm in Manila. Ethel Nye she was, wasn't she? Very pretty woman. But how does it happen that they're both on this boat?"

"Ethel had engaged her passage back on it before ever she left the States," Susannah explained. "Mother and I were coming on it, only we were coming second cabin for economical reasons. It's all rather mixed. Johnny was going home the other way—his mother is in Europe and he was to meet her. But quite suddenly he decided to sail on the Augusta. Mother, not knowing in the least what it was all about, promptly changed our reservations to first class, on

Johnny's account. So I'm having a nice trip," Susannah ended, on a little drawl.

"You're not traveling second cabin!" the man ejaculated.

"No, no. We're on Deck D."

"I'm not, either," he said, and they both laughed.

"I've been saving your feelings all the way along!" the girl confessed.

"And I yours, while both of us were reiterating that it was just as nice as first."

"But I don't see you in the dining room or the lounge or anywhere, Mr Hazeltyne."

"I'm not much about. I usually have a swim before breakfast. But I'm working. One of the members of the firm is with me, and we've got a lot of tabulating to do. And we usually have our meals late, upstairs."

"In the little grill? We went up there for scrambled eggs last night. But I thought," Susannah said, "that you told me that your wife and you had decided always to travel second?"

"It was just something she said, not seriously. I lost my wife nearly three years ago," the man said, after a moment.

A strange odd leap at her heart; her eyes came to his, and he could see the deep shine in them, like the light in star sapphires.

"I'm sorry."

"She was injured, riding. I got there in time to talk to her; there was nothing they could do."

"Children?"

"One boy. He's only a baby. He spends most of his time with my mother. Betty, my wife, had no father or mother. Phil's—well, he'll be three in January," the father said.

Susannah nodded, reconstructing his whole position, and hers toward him, as they talked. He was no longer the shadowy square figure of a second-cabin passenger, just one more casual, indifferent acquaintance in her life, with an unknown wife somewhere, an unimportant man who had engineering interests in the Philippine Islands. He had become something quite changed: Alexander Hazeltyne.

"I don't do much walking about the promenade deck," he told her. "It wouldn't be very serious now if I were identified, but it's going to be better if I can get the San Francisco and Gary end of things settled before anyone knows what I'm after. But I do walk the boat deck. I suppose you wouldn't come up tomorrow, say about twelve, and take a constitutional with me?"

"I might," she said. It was oddly amusing to be managing this little affair right under the eyes, as it were, of Johnny and Ethel; it brought back somehow her interest in life. On the next morning she dressed herself with rather more care than she had shown for a week; when she met him on the boat deck he said at once: "You're—if you'll excuse me— a far more beautiful woman than I had any idea!"

"We've only seen each other by moonlight," Susannah reminded him, laughing. The color was high on her smooth cheeks, the pale green of her plain silk frock and stitched silk hat infinitely becoming to her russet-tinged hair and the warm lights in her eyes.

"You don't mind my saying that as you came up over the top of the companion then you looked exactly like the cover of a July magazine. I mean, blue sea and the white boats and the wind pulling at your hair," Alexander said.

"I expect you to say things like that," she assured him. After a while, as they walked to and fro she said: "Isn't this nice?" and he answered quickly and seriously: "It's— *extraordinarily*—nice."

She found her companion very attractive. He was not exactly handsome, but he had a fine face, with eyes always ready to laugh and a good mouth. He must be clever, Susannah thought, for he had an air of being sure of himself; his speech was definite and quick; he had been to almost every place in the world that they chanced to mention, and he talked well. His clothes, although not as aggressively new as Johnny's always seemed to be, were correct; she liked the cut of his coats and caps, the way his shoes fitted, the shabby gloves that had once been expensive and that fitted his hands so well.

On the third morning that they walked the deck together he said quite simply:

"You know, I suppose, that I've fallen in love with you?"

They walked on. Susannah found her throat thick.

"Do I?"

"Yes," he said, "I think you do. You let me put my arm about you down at the rail last night. I've thought of it ever since. What did you think it meant?"

"That was last night," the girl said, with an oblique glance.

"I know it was. But what did you think it meant?"

"That, perhaps," she admitted.

They paced the narrow space between the ports and the boats in silence for a full minute. Then the man asked simply:

"Any chance?"

"We've known each other ten days."

"So what?" Alexander said, and she laughed.

"So nothing."

"It's one o'clock, your mother 'll be waiting. But you'll think about this? Would you and she come in before dinner tonight and have sherry or whatever you like with me?"

"I think she might love it."

"About seven? And you'll be downstairs as usual somewhere around nine?"

Susannah did not answer, except with a look straight into his eyes. But she was radiant when she joined her mother five minutes later, and, settling at luncheon, Eva remarked curiously upon the bright color in her cheeks.

"Hot up on the boat deck, darling?"

"No; lovely. There was quite a breeze. . . . I'll have Seven and Eight and Fifteen, and afterward Twenty-six," Susannah said to the white-clad Chinese waiter. Eva ordered; the Oriental pattered away.

"See anyone?" the mother asked.

"I didn't hear you, Mother."

"See anyone? See Johnny or Mrs Mallock?"

"They don't usually show up until afternoon. No, there was nobody up there except kids playing tennis and shuffleboard. Mother, Mr Carey wants us to have cocktails or something with him this afternoon."

"Who's he?"

"He's the man I told you about—his real name is Hazeltyne, but because of some business deal that he's putting through he's calling himself Carey."

"The second-cabin man?"

"No; I told you about that. He thought I was and I thought he was. But he's in Cabin A, on Deck B."

"Cabin A? Oh-h-h!" Eva said, her eyes widening. "That's one of the suites, isn't it?"

"I suppose so. I believe another man's traveling with him. Probably the firm pays for it."

"Where's his wife?"

"She died three years ago."

"Oh-h-h! Like him, Sanna?"

"Beginning to."

"Did you say he was an engineer?"

"Well, he spoke of engineering—some place in the Philippines."

"It's a perfect jumping-off place," Eva said thoughtfully, and Susannah laughed. Someone had come over to the table and touched her arm.

"Listen," said Johnny Wardell, seizing the empty chair next to Susannah, squaring it about a little so that his handsome laughing face was close to hers, breaking into the conversation with characteristic impudence. "How about cocktails in Ethel's tonight? She's asked about twenty, and afterward I'm giving a dinner party. It's all gotten up since an hour ago, so don't think you're a fill-in. How about you, Mrs Farjeon? Feel like going on a modest little binge with me? Cocktails seven-thirty, dinner about nine; how about it?"

"Mother's forty-two dollars ahead at bridge, and nothing 'll stop her now," Susannah said amiably, "and I'm dated."

"What! For dinner?"

"Both. Cocktail party and dinner, too."

"Who with?"

"A Mr Carey, who knows people we know in the Philippines," Susannah said, filling in the background of the friendship unscrupulously.

"What's he look like?"

"I'm sure you don't know him. He said he didn't know you. He isn't about very much."

"He sounds fishy," Johnny said suspiciously. "Can't you wriggle out of it?"

"I don't think I can." Susannah was smiling mysteriously as Johnny went away. The quick pressure that she felt at her heart whenever she thought of her meeting with Alexander tonight was all the proof she needed that Johnny's hour was over.

"You came!" Alexander said to her in an odd voice, when she descended to the second-cabin deck that night, and joined him in the secluded little niche beside the rail. And quite simply he put his arms about her and kissed her on the mouth.

"Don't kiss me like that!" she gasped, in a whisper, her arms strong against his arms. He held her tightly.

"How else shall I kiss you!" he said, and Susannah's breath was gone again. "I love you," the man said, his cheek against her hair. "You fragrant, you wonderful thing, I love you."

After a little, still laughing breathlessly and breathing hard, Susannah was leaning against the rail, Alec's arm firm and strong about her, and they were looking down at the wake of the moon that was broken into bright sequins and spangles by the sea, and the lacy outrushing of the foam that spread itself in rich white ruffles on the dark waters.

"Susannah!" the man said, sounding the syllables of her name over and over, as if they held magic for him. And once he said, "Are you surprised?"

"No, because I don't believe it!"

"No," he echoed, with a laugh of rich content, "and I don't believe it, either!"

"This is all like a dream," said Susannah.

"How old are you, Susannah? Your mother said something about your being twenty-four."

"She would!" Susannah laughed indulgently. "I'm twenty-seven," she confessed.

"Does that make thirty-nine seem terribly old?"

"It doesn't make anything that you are seem anything but right," Susannah answered simply, after a moment when her eyes had glinted starshine at him in the gloom.

The ship rose and fell with an unvarying onward rocking motion; the moon went away, and there was darkness on the sea, and still they leaned against the rail, the woman's slender figure lost in the circle of the man's arm. Susannah's head was flung back and rested against his shoulder; he had only to stoop to kiss her eyes.

"Susannah, confess. How many times have you been in love before?"

"I don't know. I'll think it out sometime. But I'm not 'in love' now. I love."

"Do you know that you're a dangerous woman, to say things like that?"

"I hope I am, Alec. And I hope you're in danger."

"I'm in terrible danger. We're going to be married at once, aren't we?"

"Mother says not until I know all about you, and whether you have several wives in the United States, and why you travel under an assumed name."

She could hear from his voice that he was amused.

"Did she say all that? What did you say?"

"That it wouldn't matter, because I love you."

The man was silent for a moment. Then he said in an odd tone:

"You don't mean that. Nobody in the world deserves to have a woman like you say that!"

Susannah's tone was lowered too.

"I'm sorry to say I do mean it, Alec. I've—I've simply *got* it. What all the books and plays are about."

"In ten days?" he asked, for the sheer joy of hearing her answer.

"No. In four. I think it was the fourth night that I came down here that I knew."

"It came to me in a funny sort of way," the man said musingly. "There seemed to be a sort of electricity in everything, all of a sudden. I walked—well, as if I couldn't keep my feet on the ground. I went up to the gym for a workout and found that I was singing. There was the feeling, 'Gosh, life is good!' about everything."

"I know," she said.

"And then, suddenly, 'Why, it's that girl who's making the difference, that girl in the green silk coat, who was down at the rail last night!' And then I couldn't wait for nine o'clock."

"I know."

"I looked your names up on the list. 'Farjeon, Mrs L. L.' and 'Farjeon, Miss Susannah' and they seemed to come to life. Everything's come to life!"

"Is it to be the Philippines, Alec?"

"Would you mind?"

"Mind! Don't you understand English very well? Haven't I been telling you how it is with me?"

"Aha!" he said, on a note of triumph, and she felt the arm about her tighten.

"The only thing is—Mother."

"She'd visit us, of course."

"Could she?"

"Could she? You're talking of taking me straight into Paradise, and you ask if I'd mind having your mother with us occasionally."

"My marrying happily would be the greatest happiness in the world to her. After all, I'm all she has, except the very grand aunt in New York, both of whose daughters have married well. Aunt Nona always patronizes Mother."

"What's Aunt Nona's name?"

"Madame Fernando di Mendoza. My grandfather was a navy captain, and both his daughters married in China. Aunt Nona married an undersecretary at the Spanish Consulate—afterward he inherited a good deal of money. He died years ago. The girls used to be Tita and Drina when they were little, but now they're married they're Lola and Anita."

"I've met Madame di Mendoza. Apartment on Park Avenue."

"You haven't!"

"Yep. Somebody took me there once. Both daughters very dark."

"But pretty."

"Beauties. It seems to run in the family. But that's enough of *them*. Susannah, how do you account for the fact that we've met this way, just in the very hour that you'd broken your engagement, that we've found each other?"

"Fate," Susannah said, her eyes wells of light.

"And you wouldn't mind living on a mountain, in a wooden house, and having your meals with the section managers and their wives?"

"Is it like that in Baguio, Alec?"

"Well, we'd have our own place, of course. And if you wanted to keep house it could be managed."

"It doesn't matter," she said dreamily.

CHAPTER V

IT WAS VERY LATE when they went upstairs. The decks were dark and quiet; the orchestra had long been silent; a poker game was going on in the bar, the men looking absorbed and disheveled as they reached for drinks and sandwiches without moving their eyes from their cards, and in the lounge four nervous women were still playing bridge. Sleepy stewards patted back yawns and stirred to alert attention whenever there was any prospect of concluding the sessions.

"Lord, I hate to have to say 'good night', Susannah. This hour—a time like tonight—doesn't come twice in a lifetime!"

"If we don't," she reminded him, smiling with dewy eyes that were a little dazzled by lights after the dark, "we won't be able to meet at noon tomorrow on the boat deck."

"It's ten thousand years!" Alec said.

"Good night, then."

"I love you," he said in a whisper.

She looked at him quickly; tears were suddenly in her eyes. She did not speak.

"And I love the green coat. Silk?"

"Quilted taffeta. I won it. I won a bet from a man named Dicky Davis, and he had to buy me anything I wanted from the 'Sea-Captain's Shop.' And this was it."

"Why, you gold digger!"

"Oh, shameless!"

Their hands clung together. They were in the dim wide hallway at the top of the stairs now.

"Susannah, do you know that you are one of the most beautiful women in the world?"

"I've been told so."

"By Wardell?" he asked. "By Johnny Wardell?"

"Who's he?" Susannah demanded innocently, and they parted with laughter.

It was magic the next morning to mount to the boat deck and see him standing at the rail, looking off at the hot wide shining roadway of the sea. Their hands and eyes met; Susannah wheeled about, her shoulder brushing his shoulder as they fell into step.

"That was heaven last night," Alec said.

"Did you think so?" the girl asked, with an oblique glance.

"Didn't you?"

"It was heaven for me," she said seriously. There was freshness in the salt air this morning; there was enough breeze to rattle an occasional rope, to stir the russet soft hair against Susannah's forehead. "Mother's gone social," she said. "Her bridge gang is having a farewell luncheon today—twelve of them."

"Farewell?"

"Well, Honolulu tomorrow."

"So it is! I'd forgotten."

"Tomorrow they all swarm to the hotel, play cards, swim, lunch, play cards, dine, and play cards!" Susannah said, laughing. "Honolulu's an old story to Mother; she isn't a sightseer."

"Then you and I have a plan for tomorrow," Alec said, suddenly keen. "Are you sport enough to get up at six? We dock somewhere around five—there 'll be boats out. You and I'll go off to a plantation I know about, and have lunch, and swim—I'll get a radio off right now——"

"Whose plantation?" Not that she cared.

"Friends. But they're in the States, I believe. However, there 'll be someone there. I'll get a car——"

"Don't waste money on me, Alec. You don't have to. I'd be quite as happy wandering along Berritannia Street in the hot sunlight, eating pineapple off a stick."

"I'm going to waste all the money I have on you from now on," the man said.

"Then I'll be the one to save it against our old age."

"You'll never be old, you glorious and radiant person!"

"Bathing suits tomorrow, eh? And a coat? Will I need a coat?" Her eyes danced. "It 'll be fun!" she said.

"I think there are suits out there. It's a big place, managed by this friend of mine; he and his wife live there. But I think she went home to have a baby, and he went along. Anyway, they weren't there a month ago. However, the old housekeeper 'll be there, and she'll look out for you."

Two mornings later, when, in the opalescent summer sweetness of dawn they were sailing away from the enchanted island, she found Johnny Wardell next to her at the rail. Susannah's eyes were dreamy with happiness; her shoulders were wreathed with fragrant rings of blossom, with delicate blue flowers that were combined with the rich heavy cream of the ginger bloom, thick ropes of royal orange, fruity petals of pink and white, purple and gold.

"Before we pass Diamond Head we must throw them all into the sea, Johnny," she reminded him.

"Where were you all day yesterday, Sue? We lunched at the hotel, looking for you; we wanted you to go out to the D'Arblays'."

"We went off on a plantation picnic," Susannah said abstractedly.

"Fun?" There was a note of jealousy in Johnny's voice.

"Oh, fun!" Her tone was faint, vague; she was speaking rather to herself than to him.

"Friends of your mother? Who'd you lunch with? Old friends?"

"No, they weren't there. The people who manage this place, I mean. But the servants served us lunch in the lanai, and we swam, and rode out to look at the sugar cane, and swam again. There was a Victrola, and we had supper on the beach——" Susannah stopped short.

"I thought your mother was playing bridge at the hotel?"

"She was."

"Oh," said Johnny.

Thousands of strands of colored paper were roping the ship to the shore now, but the gangplanks were up, and on the double-decked pier a long line of men and women in white were waving her farewell. On the upper balcony of the dock the band was playing valiantly; as its strains dwindled almost to silence, a handsome square native woman stood forward; her magnificent voice floated across the widening lane of the waters.

Through the bright sunshine silver rain was slanting; the leis had served their purpose now and fell in rings of vivid color on the sea; negotiating the narrow channel the great Augusta tasted once more the waters of the wide ocean, and the haunting scent of the ginger flower died away in the freshening salty airs.

"You like that fellow, don't you?"

"What did you say, Johnny?" Susannah brought her eyes reluctantly from the last glimpse of the headland standing boldly forth in rain and shine, and the black volcanic mass of the island behind it.

"I said you like your friend Carey."

"Oh," said Susannah dreamily, "more than that!"

"You mean—— But, my Lord, you only met him at Kobe . . ."

She did not hear. Alec had come up on her other side; Johnny saw the russet head turn, heard the glad voice.

"Alec, you missed the singing!"

"I had to send some cables off by the tender." Their heads were close together now. Johnny wandered away. After- ward he was on the boat deck and saw Susannah and "Carey" in chairs close together, talking so busily that they did not notice him. Susannah was in blue, crisp and thin; a wide-brimmed hat of blue straw shaded her face. Johnny noted that one of the man's hands lay over hers on the arm of her chair.

"Susannah Farjeon's giving this Carey a run," he told Ethel.

"Ha! Playing him against you," Ethel opined carelessly.

"Maybe." Johnny laughed not quite spontaneously. "He's in one of the suites," he said.

"Three of them in there. Jorgensen and Unger are the other two. They're all engineers; they've been in the Phil- ippines," Ethel, who always knew everything about every- body, said animatedly, almost jealously. "I was talking to Jorgensen last night. They only went out a month ago; he's got a wife in Brooklyn."

"Who? Carey?"

"Nope. Jorgensen."

"Gosh, she looked beautiful today," Johnny said. "She gets sort of pale when it's hot, and her eyes look black."

"Darling," said Ethel, "let's wander toward the bar. It's after one. The blond German has winked at me every time he's walked by, and I'm getting a little fed up on him."

"Maybe he'd like me to mash his face in," Johnny said dutifully.

He did not see Susannah except in flying glimpses again. When the Queen Augusta duly docked several days later in the foggy city, Johnny was conscious rather of watching for Susannah as the customs routine went its slow way, but she had evidently been whisked away. Her new friend monopolized her; well, that was all right, if she wanted to marry an engineer from Manila.

He and Ethel went to Burlingame and stayed with friends; they would presently drive to Santa Barbara, or they might fly to Tahoe; their engagement would be announced just before their marriage in November. Ethel wanted the ceremony to be in a New York church, the reception in her mother's house. These must wait for winter; nobody was married in the city in summer.

They had been in Burlingame three days when Johnny called her attention to a social note in the San Francisco paper:

> "Mrs Lynn Farjeon and Miss Susannah Farjeon, who have been the guests of Captain and Mrs Otis Randall at the Presidio, will leave tomorrow for New York City, where they are to spend the autumn with Mrs Farjeon's sister, Madame Fernando di Mendoza."

"You can't quite get her out of your head, can you, Johnny?" Ethel said.

"Don't be more of a fool than is natural," Johnny answered, with several kisses.

CHAPTER VI

Susannah and eva had a drawing room to themselves; Alec had arranged for it the day before they left, before flying to Gary. On some pretext he had asked to see Eva's reservations, and when he had returned them they had been changed. The train room was sweet with flowers when they took possession of it; there were candy and books.

"Delusions of popularity!" Susannah said, flushed and happy as she saw them. She tore open a letter written on the stationery of the Hotel Saint Francis, smiled as she read it.

It was night when they left the Oakland Mole; both berths were smoothly made with fresh fat pillows and smoothly stretched sheets. Their bags were set side by side on the narrow upholstered seat; Susannah began the processes of cold-creaming and brushing with the new dreamy smile in her eyes.

"Alec is extravagant," she said thoughtfully.

"Perhaps too much so," Eva observed pessimistically.

"Oh, Mother, why do you say that?"

"I distrust these men who do things too well," Eva said, with an air of wisdom.

Susannah was looking at herself in a mirror, brushing her

soft russet hair this way and that. To herself it seemed that her ivory skin had never seemed so transparent, her eyes so liquidly bright.

"I'm getting handsome," she said.

"You think you're in love with that man." Eva was comfortably established against the pillows now, with her reading light turned on. She gave her daughter a suspicious glance.

"Think!" said Susannah, with a laugh.

"While you're thinking I wish you'd think what it means to bury yourself in a place like the Philippines. Manila! Carrie Peyton lived there for seven years; she said it was stagnation."

"This isn't even Manila, Mother. It's a mine or oil wells or factories or something up in the mountains."

"Ha! And how do you know he hasn't got a wife there?"

"I don't, darling."

"Well, you'd better find out before you get yourself engaged to him."

"As a matter of fact Alec was married about four years ago. He's got a little boy of three."

"Where's the wife?"

"Dead. He showed me her picture. She was a Miss Eliza Livingston, very pretty and delicate looking."

"Sanna, are you engaged to him?"

"No."

"Are you going to be?"

"No." But Susannah's tone had changed to one of tenderness and apology. She tossed back her mane, sat down on the edge of the lower berth and laid her hand on her mother's hand. "I'll tell you why, darling," she said. "We're not engaged because I wouldn't be. But we're going to be married next month. We arranged it all yesterday afternoon in San Francisco, just before he left."

Eva lay looking at her daughter.

"Well, you'll ruin your life!" she said at last in a whisper.
Susannah laughed.

"Mother, you're wonderful."

"Don't say that!" Eva said, in sudden sharpness. "You're
going to jump into a crazy marriage with a person you
don't know at all, and you laugh at me when I'm shocked.
He may be a murderer!"

"Darling, I'm not laughing at you. But after all I'm
twenty-seven. If I can't choose for myself now I'm feeble-
minded."

"I think you *are* feeble-minded! What is the idea of this
indecent rush? Your aunt—Sanna, I don't want you to say
one word about this to your aunt! She hates—she *loathes*
—this sort of—of escapade. An engineer from the Philippines, forty years old, and with a little boy to care for?
Is it your idea to go back with him to Manila, may I ask?"
Eva sputtered, trembling and breathing hard.

"Or Honduras, if he's a murderer, or Flatbush or Har-
bin or Napa, California!" Susannah said, almost in a song.
Eva began to cry.

"I had such p-p-plans for you!" she sobbed. "This
probably will be some sort of scandal, and then where 'll you
be! *Nobody* likes that sort of thing! I was so happy about
your marrying Johnny, money and position and everything
—big place in Easthampton—sister married to that copper
or pipe or iron man or whatever he is——"

"Ah, don't cry, Mother. If I'd seen Alec first I wouldn't
have looked at Johnny or fifty Johnnies! I never was in love
with him; he was in love with me, and it was Shanghai, and
a June moon! That's why I was going to marry him. Don't
feel badly, darling. It's so glorious to care for anyone the
way I care for Alec. It's so glorious not to care if he's poor
or unsuccessful or anything else, not to care if he beats me or
runs off with the company's money or anything. I've been

walking on air for two wonderful weeks, Mother; I'm possessed!"

"I don't know what's got into you," Eva observed, drying her eyes, sniffing, and watching her daughter darkly. "I don't know what you're going to tell your aunt!"

"I'm to tell her nothing. Our plan is that we don't say one word to anyone until—let's see, this is Monday, we get to New York Friday, don't we? Well, on Sunday afternoon Alec is to walk into Aunt Nona's usual Sunday tea at just five o'clock, and we're to announce it."

"He won't come," Eva predicted simply.

"Well, in that case I save my face!" But Susannah was humming as she went on with her preparations for sleep.

"I wish you hadn't done it!" Eva's voice was milder now; she spoke musingly. "Lou Beck says I'm too much afraid of Nona," she presently said. "Perhaps I am. After all, Nona's never done anything for us."

"Except criticize."

"I think Lou 'd be tickled to death if I'd go up and stay with her in Newport. After you're married—that is, *if* you're married!"

"I'm as good as married now, Mother. Wedded but not a wife, that's me."

"You're actually crazy about him, aren't you?" Eva asked curiously. "But I don't like the hurry, and I don't like his traveling under a wrong name," she persisted, her tone growing plaintive again.

"He went to the Philippines on a very important mission for his firm, Mother. If his name had appeared in it, everyone would have known. His whole name is Alexander Carey Hazeltyne; he just dropped the Hazeltyne. He and Jorgensen and Unger had to keep the whole thing quiet until after this Gary trip."

"Those weren't their names, either, I suppose?"

"Yes, they were. But Hilary Unger told me that it was

Alec who was really putting the deal through. As for our announcing our plans for getting married, don't you see how it would have hurt him with the higher-ups to turn it all into a honeymoon?"

"Well, I hope he turns up on Sunday, that's all. I don't know what you'll do if he doesn't," Eva said, reopening her book.

"Take my throat into Aunt Nona's guest bathroom and cut it," Susannah answered cheerfully, climbing into the upper berth.

"Don't speak of Nona's. I never feel at home there," Eva said nervously, her thoughts diverted. "She was wild with me when I came home. She said that traveling with any man, even when he was old and sick as old Horace Palmer, caused a scandal. She said no money was worth it!"

"At the same time not offering you any money?"

"Well, no, Nona doesn't, you know. But she'll be furious if anything else goes wrong——"

"Nothing will, Mother," Susannah said, after a while.

"I don't know how you're so sure of that!"

The girl, safe in her high eyrie, smiled confidently, was silent, hoping for silence, and after awhile had the satisfaction of hearing her mother's deep breathing in sleep.

But as the hours went by and were days, and the days brought her and her mother steadily toward the big, formidable city that she had not seen for almost two years, had never known very well, Susannah felt her courage, felt her assurance wane a little. In Alec's presence it was impossible to feel the slightest doubt, but Alec was not with them on the train, and Alec seemed to have nothing to do with Aunt Nona's Park Avenue apartment.

It was a very large apartment on a top floor in a ten-story building. The entrance hall alone was sixty feet long and fifteen wide, paneled in severely chaste colonial fashion, and hung with a few family portraits. The drawing room had a terrace outside its long windows, and all the city lay below the terrace, a very Bagdad of cloud by day and of fire by night.

Susannah's cousin Lola Pope, with Jere and little Jere, were staying with Aunt Nona, so Susannah and her mother were relegated to a secondary guest room, very nice but very small. Their trunks were quite a problem, but Susannah's innocent suggestion that they be allowed to stand in the great hall for a while met with no encouragement from her aunt, and into every other inch of the luxurious apartment something was fitted with a suitability that indicated that it was intended to remain there.

The great tasseled Spanish chairs in the dining room had each a place against the dark carved paneling of the wall; pleasant bowls of glass fruit, lamps that had once been heavy old glass apothecary jars, candlesticks, paintings, rugs, deep davenports, braziers, cushioned prie-dieus and wooden statues of the Blessed Virgin, vestments and tapestries, plates and trays in copper and pewter and silver and glass all had their exact places. A professional decorator had arranged the Di Mendoza house; it could not be improved.

Aunt Nona's two large rooms faced the southwest and had a balcony of their own. Her dressing table was littered with tortoise shell mounted in heavy gold; her carved blackwood bed had once belonged to the Empress Eugénie. It was smothered in transparent embroidered linen and shellpink silk; the carpet was pale pink; the windows curtseyed in billows of handkerchief embroideries and pink brocade. Mantel, tables, shelves, bureau were filled with photographs in heavy crystal, gold, filigree and cloisonné frames. Aunt Nona had met every President and opera singer and celebrity in the world in the last thirty years, and had most of their photographs. Movie queens and real queens vied with each other in inscribing large pictures of themselves to Aunt Nona; dictators scribbled in their respective languages;

maharajahs and Chinese potentates forgot national difficulties and beamed at each other across Aunt Nona's po-
mades and brushes.

Aunt Nona was heavy, florid, important. She dressed
richly and fussily and wore many magnificent jewels on
stout little hands. An abiding sense of her own tremendous
position in life kept her from doing anything with her time
that might distract her from it. Consequently she went on
committees and was much introduced at luncheons; she entertained at dinners when the subject of general conversation was often herself and her distinguished and extraordinary career; she kept to the society of those friends who
never entirely recovered from an attitude of surprise and
admiration at her splendor. Day in and day out servants,
children, tradespeople, beneficiaries, intimates sounded the
one note to her; she moved among them with a sort of regal
dignity, proudly good, proudly charitable, hospitable, gracious, as befitted one of the world's anointed.

Her daughters were small brown women, merry, jealous,
worldly, extravagantly happy or unhappy, loving or hating,
with scarcely a moment and rarely a motive for change of
mood. Each had married a handsome young broker, each
had a child; their mother provided each with a large income. To Eva Farjeon, always hovering uneasily as an out-
sider on the brink of society's enchanted stream, frequently
embarrassed for money, Nona's position was sometimes a
hard thing to contemplate.

The sisters kissed each other when they met, and Nona
showed Eva the great silver bowl that the patients in the
hospital had sent her. She had been chairman of the board
for twenty-five years; it had been quite their own idea to
send her this tribute. The chauffeur sent in a message; no,
she did not need the car again until eight this evening. A
respectful young woman appeared: would Madame di Mendoza look at the flowers and see if she liked them that

way? Other flowers arrived; a maid displayed them in a long box. Ah, beautiful; and put the card on my desk, Berthe. The secretary came downstairs, and was quite impressive to hear Aunt Nona jabber to him in Spanish. After all, she was not Spanish; her husband had been a Toledan. Lola's baby was brought in, a pale little boy with straight gold hair; Lola spoke French to the nurse.

It was all just a little overpowering to the country cousins who were tired and grimy from the train; appreciative, affectionate, but badly in need of baths and change. There would be a dinner tonight; a theater party afterward. Eva and Susannah hastened to say that they need not be included. Susannah began to feel the nervous strain of the last few days; she wanted to be alone, to think.

"Don't count us in on the theater, Aunt Nona. Or send us to any show. We've not seen anything for so long that it 'll all seem good. You mustn't let us upset you!"

"You don't upset me in the least, my dear. Filmore and Silva attend to everything. My life is always like this! I've a nice man for you tonight. As for Eva and me, we'll sit in the back of the box and gossip. But I've Dalton Drew for you—delightful fellow. I wanted Alec Hazeltyne, but he's not in town. He's been away for months; I had Filmore call his office."

"Who did you say?"

"Hazeltyne, very old friend of mine. I've not seen him for years, really, but Lola met him last spring, delightful man! His wife died several years ago—Livingston, she was."

"He was on the boat, coming from China," Susannah said. Eva stood still, as one turned to stone. They had all been moving toward the drawing-room door, the travelers on their way to their room. Madame di Mendoza paused, with an alert look.

"Meet him?"

"Yes, if it's the same man."

"Very good looking, tall, lightish, with dark eyes?"

"All of that!" said Susannah, laughing.

"You know who he is?"

"An engineer, isn't he?"

"Alec Hazeltyne!"

"Well, he said he was." Susannah pressed her foot against her mother's foot, and Eva shut her lips as one from whom nothing could be drawn under torture.

"Well, he may be. But he's everything else, of course. You knew he was very rich?"

"Is he?"

"He's one of the most popular men in New York," Aunt Nona said. "He has a magnificent apartment over on the river. He inherited all the Hazeltyne mining interests, and he's made a couple of fortunes since in Wall Street. I'm delighted," said Aunt Nona, with the first approving look Susannah had won from her, "—delighted that you know him. How well do you know him? Would he come in to my tea tomorrow afternoon, do you think? They said at his office he gets home tomorrow."

"He would not," said Lola. "You can't bag him. Gertrude Altmann knows him. He never goes anywhere."

"As a matter of fact I asked him to call tomorrow; I forgot about the Sunday teas," Susannah said. Her aunt eyed her speculatively.

"He'll come?"

"Well, I think so."

"Why didn't you tell me you'd met Alec Hazeltyne?" Madame di Mendoza asked Eva. Eva sent her daughter a fluttered glance.

"Well, we didn't know—he seemed so quiet—he never said——" she stammered happily. In her faded eyes was the light of sunrise.

"Oh, Susannah," she whispered with all a girl's excitement

when they were safely alone in their own room, "do you suppose it's true? Do you suppose he'll come?"

"He'll come," Susannah said. "But as for its being true, I almost hope it isn't. My little house in the Philippines— Alec all to myself . . ."

She had gone to the window; she was looking down at the gray blur of the city; lights were beginning to prick through the hot afternoon haze; the sky above the river and the prison island was flushed with glory.

Sunday was a strange, unreal day. A dreaming autumn haze lay over the city; no leaf stirred on the red-and-gold trees in the Park. Eva was tired and nervous and excited almost to the point of sickness. She elected to stay in bed, and Susannah brought her her breakfast on a tray at ten o'clock.

Lola's baby was not well, and a trim young doctor was having breakfast when she went back to the dining room. Lola was moodily sipping coffee, muttering, "Damn that damn nurse!" from time to time. The doctor said that these autumn days were bad days for colds. Lola's husband— handsome, dull young Jere Pope—would say, "Oh, shut up, darling, the kid's all right!" from time to time, without taking his eyes from the sporting pages.

Aunt Nona came in, magnificent in dark blue broadcloth generously cut about her wide hips, a blue-and-silver fox fur, white gloves. She was going to High Mass. Susannah made a hasty toilet and accompanied her. Through the long service she listened to a sermon without hearing a word of it, listened to a shrill sweet soprano singing the "Credo" and a deep bass rumbling on the "Agnus Dei" and was not conscious that there was music at all. Afterward she let Aunt Nona go off without her and walked through the leisurely Sunday streets, and to the bank of the sluggish river, and through crowded quarters where men in shirt sleeves were tending babies and smoking pipes. And it was all like a dream.

Luncheon was informal at Aunt Nona's. Between the late breakfast and the inevitable Sunday tea nobody felt much interest in it. Two young men came in, and Aunt Nona sat watching them eat. Susannah had some cold turkey and an artichoke. She was beginning to be possessed by an unbearable excitement now and scarcely knew what she ate. She lay down for an hour or two, trying to read. It was no use, and she put the book aside and lay dreaming, her eyes on space.

At half past four she went downstairs. Her aunt, enthroned on a high Spanish chair with a carved back, smiled at her approvingly. A scattering of guests was already there. Susannah must take the tea table until naughty Anita appeared. Cocktails would positively not be served until six at least. Susannah found plenty to do, and presently was talking with some man—a navy officer—about China. He had been at Hong Kong. Not Shanghai, no. But he knew Bernardine and the McBains, of course.

Lola and Anita came up, giggling over some secret of their own. Anita, looking more like a mischievous gipsy than ever in a wide red hat, put aside her gloves, assuming her duties at the tea table with a loud cry: "It's broiling, out. 1 walked with the baby and Nursey, like a fool! I'm dripping."

"Sh-h-h!" said her mother from the throne. "She's so bad," she said lovingly. Eva came in, still looking drawn and tired; she passed Susannah on her way to a chair. "Is he here?" she breathed, without moving her lips.

"No," said Susannah. "This is Captain Hardy, Mother, who knows your friend McDermott in Hong Kong. Sit here, Captain. Want a fresh cup? Are you going to have anything, Mother?"

"Just colored hot water, Sanna, and one lump."

Sanna drifted to the window. The great tortoise-shell

clock on the mantel said five minutes to five. She concealed herself from the room behind the heavy Fortuny curtains, stood looking out at the world that was clear now in the thin light of sunset. Westering windows flashed flame, but down in the canyons of the streets lights were already piercing the opal gloom.

"Mr Hazeltyne," announced José. The clock struck five hoarse notes. Susannah parted the curtains and turned back to the room in time to see the tall, broad-shouldered man come quickly in. She stood still, unable to move.

"Mr Hazeltyne!" her aunt said, pleased. She left the throne to greet him; they were laughing and talking together for a moment.

Then he saw Susannah and came quickly toward her, and took her hands with that light in his eyes that she never had seen in any other man's eyes. And immediately the room swam into a zone of magic; it was all glorious: the lamps José had just lighted, the scent of delicate tea and of women's perfumes and furs, the clink of spoons and murmur of voices. The great luxurious room was suddenly the one living place in the world, and she, Susannah Farjeon, the most fortunate woman. With Alec's hard hand gripping hers she would not have exchanged places with any woman alive.

She took him over to her mother, and to the tea table, and introduced him to Anita and Lola. Both cousins flashed their white Spanish teeth at him; Lola said that he must remember her; he had come to her debutante party at the Sherry-Netherland. Alec's pleasant smile was ready in reply; of course he remembered her! Susannah lost the thread of their conversation for thinking how unlike any other smile in the world his was; keen and quick and brief, and always with a look straight into the eyes of the person at whom he was smiling.

But then everything about him was extraordinary; his mere presence transformed the room. Everyone wanted to speak to him; everyone liked him. Almost immediately he had one quick aside for Susannah.

"You're dining with me, of course?"

"Am I?"

"I'll call for you at seven."

Then she had to resign him for a little while, but he came back to her, and they stepped out into the autumn darkness of the high terrace, and Alec, in the shelter of a row of potted trees, put his arm about her and tipped her face up to his. The enchantment was about her like a rising tide now, and nothing else mattered except Alec. She was happily, vaguely conscious, a little later, that most of the tea guests had gone and that Alec had kissed Mother, and Aunt Nona had kissed Alec; and that there was a good deal of laughing and kissing going on. Then he was gone, and Lola, with little Jere in her lap, and Anita were sitting on her bed with Aunt Nona, majestic in the small guest room's one comfortable chair, and everyone excited and congratulatory. Eva was enjoying every second of this to the full; she had been waiting a long time for such an hour of triumph and pride, but to Susannah it was all rather unimportant. What was important was that Alec was coming for her at seven.

"You've not met his mother, then, Susannah?"

"I beg pardon, Aunt Nona? . . . No, I've never met her. I gather," said Susannah, smiling, and inspecting her bunched fingernails with narrowed eyes, "that she's rather —impressive."

"She's very handsome," Madame di Mendoza said. "Tall, with white hair. And he's got a child, hasn't he? Didn't the Livingston girl have a child?"

"Phil, yes. Three years old, or nearly. When Alec's mother gets back from Europe next week I'm to meet them both."

"Susannah, aren't you excited?" animated little Lola demanded. "I should think you'd be out of your senses!"

"I think I am," Susannah answered seriously.

But if it was madness it was a sweet sort of madness, after all, to make herself lovely in the old brown-and-silver evening dress that had seen three years' hard wear and yet somehow held shape and smartness, to catch up the brown wrap and descend to find Alec waiting, to feel that earthquaky ecstasy at her heart as he turned from the drawing-room fire to come toward her.

Other persons were standing about. They did not seem to matter. She and Alec left them behind, and in the big car he put his arms about her and kissed her, and they were very happy. They went to his apartment, a penthouse high up above the world, and Susannah explored it, peeping into the kitchen where dinner for two was being cooked, stepping out to the terrace into the glorious black world of the stars. She put her coat on Alec's bed and arranged her hair at his mirror, and they sat down together on the great leather couch before the fire, and it was all enchantment.

There was an Irish cook in the kitchen, Delia, her sister Agnes her helper. Then there was Frost, who answered the bells and waited on the table, and Phillips who drove the car. And in the bedroom was 'Liza, middle-aged and colored, beaming at the lovely young lady who was going to marry Mr Hazeltyne. Everything ran smoothly, the little meal they two shared was perfection, and afterward it was heaven to go back to the fire again, and turn the lights low, and lock fingers, and murmur on and on into the night as if there were no end to the things they had to say to each other. Life was suddenly right, was what she wanted it to be. Susannah felt that all the uncertainties and disappointments of the years were well worth while, that they might add savor and meaning to this hour.

CHAPTER VII

THE DAYS RACED TOGETHER. Susannah bought new frocks; enchanting frocks that did not come in dozens or even pairs, but that were designed for just one wearer, and she that wearer! An evening velvet of dark electric blue with cartridges of ermine trimming it; a transparent silvery lace from Paris embroidered in coral and pearl from the thin frill at the throat to the end of the fluffy train; a wrinkled moire with puffed sleeves and rolled cordings; gold brocade with black fur; blue and silver brocade; striped brown and gray chiffon velvet with sables outlining the low neck and the hem of the spreading skirts. Susannah grew dizzy, trying them all on, trying to remember them; she took a rather deeper satisfaction in two or three plain suits, straight and slim and tailored, and in the afternoon dresses that were untrimmed except for a touch of lace or embroidery at throat and wrists.

Big boxes rustling with tissue papers came home; little square hatboxes; new trunks, new linens, presents. Mary O'Shaughnessy came and made lists. Aunt Nona argued at the telephone; Eva discussed details of cake and announcements; the young married cousins were eternally about, afraid of missing one detail of the wedding, but Susannah was hardly conscious of them. She came and went joyously, hardly hearing what they said to her, thinking only that time was going by, that it was only weeks—days—hours before she must get into the smartest suit of all and the knowing little green blouse and the hat with the line of green against its ultrasmart blackness, and link the royal new sables about her shoulders, and pull on the new white gloves, and give herself to Alec forever.

The day arrived, and somehow she was dressing, with Lola and Anita and Eva all helping, and nice Margot Fielding, and the little Mrs Pomeroy, who was always underfoot, all up in her room helping her. She and Eva had been moved into the spacious guest room now. Susannah reflected that perhaps it was just as well to have distractions and interruptions on such a day; it kept one from too serious thought.

She heard Alec's voice outside, Alec's laugh, and her heart stood still. There were to be only a score of friends at the little ceremony in Aunt Nona's drawing room; when Susannah went out they were all there.

Captain Fletcher, who had been like a brother to her father, had come up from Washington to give the bride away; they all stood about very informally, and Alec at once took Susannah's fingers and held them in his own throughout the service. Afterward he kissed Susannah and tipped her hat, and Anita straightened it, and there was much laughter.

Susannah, without letting go of Eva, who was crying, gave her third kiss to the aunt who had given her her wedding. Then she went up to the formidable tall figure of her mother-in-law standing aloof, magnificent in curled white hair and a tremendous hat.

"I suppose I am to kiss the bride," said Florence Hazeltyne. Susannah, Alec beside her, laughed good-humoredly.

"If you like."

Their cheeks touched.

"Here," said the older Mrs Hazeltyne majestically, "is your boy."

Susannah knelt down before little Phil, a delicate-looking three-year-old who drew away from her kiss and her arms. "He doesn't know me!" she said. The child had turned swiftly from her to his father.

"Are you goin' to stay here now?" he demanded of the man. "Am I goin' to stay with you and Frost and 'Liza?"

"After a while, Phil," Alec said, carried away from Su· sannah on a tide of congratulations, managing to get back to her again. They did not have very much time; there was a toast, somebody told Susannah to eat a sandwich, but after holding it in her fingers for a while she put it down somewhere, and was suddenly being kissed good-by, and hurried away with Alec's fingers under her elbow.

"Ah-h-h!" Alec said, when they were in the car. His arm was locked about her again, and Susannah took off the new hat and laid her head on his shoulder. The autumn miles began to flash past the windows, the city dropped away; they were out among red leaves and farmhouses, orchards that were stripped of leaves, villages lying prim and quiet under the blazing gold of great trees.

"Alec, have you ever thought it's strange that people are getting married all the time, and going off together——"

"You mean that it can't mean to them what it does to us?"

"Yes. You hear of them getting married, and it doesn't seem anything so thrilling. And then you think of this—you and I going off together, always to be together . . ."

Her voice died away; her eyes smiled into his.

"It *is* a miracle," Alec said soberly.

"I wish we were already married ten years, Alec!"

His eyes narrowed into laughter.

"You're not afraid of me?" he said.

"No, it's not that. It's just—perhaps what I'm afraid of is that we won't always love each other as we do now. All this —these weeks have been so wonderful, every time you telephoned, every time we went anywhere, no matter what we did. Just going into shops with you, Alec, and watching you, or just seeing you order a meal. It seems as if I couldn't watch you enough——

"I'm a fool to feel like that; you think I'm a fool," she began again in a changed tone, after a little silence. Her laughing eyes were wet, and there were tears in his eyes as he looked at her.

"I don't think you're a fool," he said very low, his fingers tightly holding her own.

"How does a woman keep a man loving her forever?"

"Ah, you'll have to teach *me* how to hold *you*, Sanna. But I hope and I believe," Alec said, "that when we have been ten years married you and I'll like to remember today —the day you gave yourself to me—and say to each other that we're happier with every year."

"I believe it might be that way," she said in a whisper.

Country roads and barns and trees went by; it was almost twilight when they stopped at an old colonial mansion that had been turned into an inn. Light flooded from the doorway; there was the scent of old-fashioned New England cleanness, the sight of New England beauty and order in the wide warm hallway. A smiling woman in a big apron showed them the way upstairs to an immense front room looking out into maples, with spotless linen and a fat patchwork quilt on a broad four-poster, rag rugs on a polished floor, old chairs of walnut and fruitwood, a highboy, a dresser, glass candlesticks and softly lighted old china lamps. The floor sloped slightly downward to the big bathroom; the paneled old doors wore strange, long iron hinges; dotted swiss flounced the bed and was crossed at the windows. Phillips brought up the bags, and Susannah, going through every motion with the easy accuracy of a drilled actress, and trying to make herself feel that this was only a play, got herself into a Chinese coat of thin persimmon-colored satin banded with royal embroidery in gold and rose and black and blue, brushed her russet mop, washed her face with great handfuls of soapy water, and put on the simple silk Lola had decided was traveler's wear. Triumph-antly fresh she faced him, the round embroidery collar set-ting off her white throat, her wrists looking fine and blue-veined in the big King Charles cuffs.

"Shall we go down, Mr Hazeltyne?"

Alec caught her into his arms.

"Ah, Sanna, isn't this fun! You and I alone up here in this funny old place. I like it. Let's stay here!"

She put her warm soft hand into his, and they descended to find a narrow old parlor with a great fire roaring behind sparkling brass dogs, and a table set for two sending a shadow from it across the shining boards of the floor. Miss Matty brought them their dinner, Miss Prue appearing, only when they had almost finished, with coffee.

"We closed for the season on the first; it's gittin' real cold," explained Miss Prue. "But when Sister got your wire nothing 'd do but what we let ye come. Your mother an' the little boy was here earlier in the summer, an' we remember you folks from our first year here. On'y seems like Mis' Hazeltyne has fleshed up some."

"You're confusing me with the first Mrs Hazeltyne," Susannah said simply. "Didn't you know that the little boy's mother died three years ago? We were only married today."

"You did that beautifully, Sanna. You set it all straight and saved the poor old thing infinite embarrassment," Alec said later, when they were up in their room again. "I do remember coming here with Betty, only it was summer, and a lot of us were squeezed into top rooms somewhere."

"It's so nice and so quiet and so much ours," Susannah

said, her young firm skin emerging fresh and velvety from a treatment of cold cream. "Let's stay, tomorrow anyway. Quebec can wait! Let's have a house like this some day, Alec, all by ourselves, with just a few friends coming down now and then, and books and fires. I'll raise roses and you can have dogs, and we'll tramp about, and cut down trees and really—really *live,* have time to breathe and to be alone together!"

She stood up, gesturing with her hairbrush, and he put his arms about her and smiled down at her fragrance and youngness and beauty.

"Realize that we're alone together now?" he asked.

"Still wondering why you ever came to love me!" she said, smiling back.

"I wish," he said, "that I didn't love you quite so much!"

"Does it always have to die out, do you suppose? A man and a woman liking each other less and less and less until it's all gone?" Susannah asked wistfully, the beauty of her flawless face very close to his own, her hands spread on his shoulders, his own hands gripping hers.

"I don't know, sweetheart," Alec said. "Perhaps you'll tire of your old man some day."

"Ah," she said, with a little desperate laugh. "If I only *could!* If I only needn't care quite so much!"

"I'm going to keep you always loving me like that, Sanna."

"That won't be the trouble," she told him, looking up into his eyes, the brown velvet shadows of her own eyes lighted with gold; "it's how I'm to hold *you.* You're so much more important a person than I thought, Alec. Your friends—the women are all so beautiful, and the men are so rich; you all chatter about things I don't know anything about; you've been so many places and met so many people! I could have gone with you to Manila and kept house for you—we'd have been happy there. But here, sometimes, I get a little scared."

"Brides have a right to be scared," he said, looking down at her unsmilingly. But his eyes were shining.

"Ah, it isn't that. This is where I want to be, Alec; these are the arms I want around me on my wedding night! But I want our marriage," Susannah pursued it, in a puzzled, hesitant tone, "to be one of the—the *always* marriages."

"You're talking sheer nonsense," he said. "As long as there is breath in my body there 'll be only you for me."

Her glittering hair had tumbled to her shoulders; in the soft lamplight the face raised to his was almost a child's face in its innocence of widened eyes and fresh young mouth.

"Then are we just—lucky?" she asked. "To have found each other, and to have everything else, too?"

"Perhaps we are," he said. "But, having found each other, how little the other things count, Sanna!"

"Ah, yes," she said eagerly, "that's just it. They don't count at all, not with any woman, when the man she's dreamed about—the man that she never thought she'd meet —tells her that he loves her!"

And for a moment of silence only their eyes spoke.

"I want you always to love me like that, Sanna. I want you to be the happiest woman in the world!" Alec said, putting his face down against hers, gathering her to him.

"As long as you love me, nothing can stop *that!*" she said.

CHAPTER VIII

THE JOY OF IT, the pride of it, the utter deep happiness of it went on and on; there seemed to be no end to the new delights. For a few exquisite weeks Alec and Susannah were all by themselves, traveling northward in the big car in the autumn glory of red leaves and crystal air, with Phillips to carry their bags into the big hotels. They stayed at lodges where great fires blazed, and over whose low roofs pine branches met; they stayed in the lofty upper rooms of an enormous hotel château, and looked out over cities and rivers as they shared their breakfast in a sunshiny window. Alec bought his wife furs; old silver spoons with Queen Anne's coat of arms upon them; Revolutionary firedogs and fine soft blankets striped in tan and blue. Every day had its gifts, and every hour was an hour of fresh enchantment. To do anything with Alec was to be thrilled and entertained and excited, was to perceive over the simplest pleasures—the waiting hour before dinner, a casual walk, the buying of stamps or newspapers or oranges—a patina of glory.

They came back to New York on a November day of leaden skies and fine snow; Susannah found her new domain in perfect order awaiting her, flowers everywhere, telegrams stacked on Alec's desk, late wedding gifts piled in their boxes in her bed-room. It was great fun to unpack with 'Liza's expert help, to establish herself, handkerchiefs and writing paper, books and slippers, her father's framed photograph, the baby picture of herself and her mother, in this magnificent place.

At intervals, as they settled themselves, Alec and Susannah would step out into the freedom of their spacious roof. Snow was packing itself softly among the dried leaves of the potted shrubs; the oleanders and rhododendrons were neatly cased in straw and burlap. There were two oblongs of dead brown lawn high up here above the city; they were intersected by neat paths of tile. At the ends of the paths, up against the brick parapet, were benches of Roman marble. A tiled arch protected the dry fountain where a stone boy, lean and awkward and sweet, held a turtle high over his head.

"That's the original," Alec said.

"How do you know an original from a copy, Alec?"

"Only by the bill, darling."

They dined with his mother on their second night at home; after that the dinner invitations poured in thick and fast, and it was only a matter of choosing. Alec went downtown to Wall Street at about ten o'clock every morning; Susannah usually had some reason for telephoning him before noon. On the day when he first lunched at the Engineers' Club she felt quite lost; her mother and Aunt Nona joined her, at short notice, and it was pleasant enough to have Frost serve them so beautifully to so luxurious a meal, but she felt oddly lopsided without Alec's forceful presence, his definite voice, his inspiring interest in everything that interested her.

"You've got one of the most beautiful apartments in the city, Susannah," Aunt Nona said. "I hope you appreciate that you're an extremely lucky girl."

"I hope I do! But I no sooner get caught up appreciating one thing," Susannah said, "than another comes along."

"A box at the opera, *imagine!*" Eva said complacently.

"Alec's a director, so we have to have one, but most operas bore him!" Susannah confessed cheerfully. "However, Margot Fielding and I are going to do *The Ring* on all the February Thursdays, and we're having early dinner and going to *Rosenkavalier,* all of us, on the tenth. And then—maybe Europe!" she finished with a wide-eyed look.

"Susannah Farjeon!" her mother said.

"Alec may have to go over to London for a meeting—doesn't it sound wonderful? London! Look, Mother, these are the Italian napkins I told you about; aren't they gorgeous? From the Blake Hutchinsons, whoever *they* are."

"You'd be away over Christmas?" Eva asked ruefully.

"Well, otherwise Christmas presents its problems, darling. I'd like, of course, to be with you and Aunt Nona and the girls. But if you go with Mrs Poett to Santa Barbara you're out of it, and there's Alec's quite impossible mother, who naturally would expect us to be there. And that really wouldn't *do.*"

"Is she so awful, Sanna?"

"No, she's not awful at all. But she's pompous and affected—or perhaps I mean artificial. Anyway, she makes life terribly trying."

"Where's the little boy?"

"Phil? He's in a special baby school up beyond Nyack. He has his nurse with him—it's really an old-fashioned big home, with about a dozen small kids in it. Alec and I went over there on Sunday and took him marshmallows and a scooter; he was very cute. We had to rush back for the Pearson breakfast . . ."

They were always in a hurry. It seemed to be the natural condition with everyone who lived in their world of excitements and good times. They were hurrying away from the perfumed chatter of some tea to jump into dinner clothes and fly to an early dinner; they were eating with one eye on the clock—an opening tonight, and nobody must be late!

It was only late at night that the time could be stretched at all, and Alec and Susannah went on from party to party after the theater or opera or dinner in the only leisure they knew. Often it was two o'clock, sometimes three or four, when they got to bed; Susannah could sleep late if she liked in the morning, but she hated to awaken to find that Alec had dressed and slipped away hours earlier, and usually got up when he did, even if afterward she tried for a midmorning nap.

On the big steamer they had four short days of the old happy routine, only it was winter now; no more white frocks and awnings on deck, no hot moonlight to silhouette the ropes and spars against the sky. But buttoned into her smart new topcoat, and with her cheeks glowing, Susannah shared Alec's morning constitutional on the boat deck; they bet on the ship's pool, played bridge, lost dollars on the horse races and won them back at tombola, and went up in the little elevator to the palms and warmth and lights and soft music on the high top deck for all their meals. Late meals, and usually hilarious, for of course there were friends of Alec's on board, men as smartly tailored and groomed as he, who talked his talk of the stock market, of yachts, of golf and fights, tennis championships and tarpon shooting, and of the luck, bad and good, of their acquaintances. They talked of places in London and Paris and Budapest where extraordinary dishes and wines were to be had; there was no such thing as a good meal in Italy, but there was a place in Barcelona where one of the men had had the best fish, with the best sauce, he had ever tasted in his life.

All these men admired Susannah instantly and wholeheartedly. When she came into the bar at seven or at noon it was inevitable that their tributes to her beauty should be forthcoming; settling herself and her fragrant ruffles or velvets, a smile in her red-brown eyes under the silky waves of the red-brown hair, Susannah would have a feeling that she could pity every other woman in the world. But it was Alec, splendid in dinner clothes, with the look she loved i.1 his gray eyes and the fine hand ready to steady her into her chair, who made it all perfect, who made it indeed significant at all.

London meant to her what London means to all English-speaking, English-reading folk upon first acquaintance. She could not drink deep enough of the atmosphere of the old city; the very names of the streets fascinated her, the sight of the storied old river sliding by the hotel windows, the sound of foghorns and Bow bell. More dinners and more theaters choked her calendar; the three weeks fled by like a dream; they were on their way to Southampton, in a yellow fog; the idle pleasant ship's days were over, and she and Alec had a second homecoming to more flowers, more telegrams. Everyone was going to Florida now, and Alec and Sanna would try to get down there, too, for a brief time, anyway. Perhaps for the club opening—perhaps for the big Lownesdale party . . .

There were fittings for spring clothes, and Susannah had her portrait painted, a very simple study of a russet-headed slender woman with a creamy skin hardly distinguishable from the creamy folds of an old-fashioned gown, but so beautiful that it was the discussed picture of the year, and when Susannah went to the Spring Exhibition she always found a group before it. Aunt Nona took friends to see it: Eva almost permanently occupied a seat on the upholstered leather bench just opposite it, and watched it and the people who looked at it all day long. It was a Gainsborough, said the critics; it had the delicate quality of a Fragonard, the flesh tints of a Rubens.

"You've made me famous, Mrs Hazeltyne," said young Ross St Hubert, who had painted it.

"Well, and I think you've made me famous, too!" Susannah told him. To Alec she said that she felt like royalty.

"Everybody being nice to me, always the best seats and the finest clothes and the nicest food," Susannah summarized it. "We go everywhere we want to, we do everything we like, and everyone praises us for it!"

"And why not, Beautiful?"

"Well——" Her little drawl, her little laugh of childish enjoyment and triumph. "No reason at all why not! Only, can it go on this way forever?"

"Why not?" He worshiped her; that was the real secret of these days of complete joy. His eyes lighted when his beautiful wife entered some great hotel restaurant and came toward him between the potted palms and the mirrors to the sound of hidden music. When, talking to guests, Susannah sent her glance toward him across their box at the opera, she was apt to find his look upon her, adoring, keen, humorous. At such moments there would linger about his fine mouth a little smile, significant and tender, as if he asked her to share with him the thought of some secret that was infinitely precious.

"Alec, did you think Mrs Chandler beautiful tonight?" she asked one night.

"Nini Chandler? Was she? In that tomato-soupy sort of dress?"

"Yes. You were talking to her after dinner."

"Was I? Why, look here! Is this shrew of mine jealous?"

"Jealous! Devoured by it."

"Sanna, shame on you."

"I know. But when you talk to anyone that way—laughing, I mean, enjoying what you're saying, it just goes through me—like knives."

"I'm not to enjoy anything, eh? God knows there isn't much in most of their dinners to enjoy!"

Her cheek was against his; she had come to sit on the arm of his big leather chair; now he gripped her with a firm arm.

"I'm not jealous of Nini," she said, with a faint accent on the last word.

"Who are you jealous of, then?" Sanna was still in the beautiful gown she had worn to the dinner and the opera; Alec kissed her bare arm.

"Nobody. Of time, Alec."

"Time?"

"It's running by so fast. Do you realize we've been married six months—going on seven months? Isn't that frightful?"

"Too quick!" he agreed. "But we've had a lot of fun, Sanna. Europe, Palm Beach, Nassau. Things will quiet down next month, everybody 'll be out of town, and we can take it a little easier."

"Not if we go to the Bancrofts' camp in Canada, Alec, and the Arnheims' in Newport. Not if we go on that cruise with the Ides!"

"Oh well, that 'll all be later. If Mother takes her usual place in Easthampton we can go down there and vegetate."

"Vegetating in Easthampton in July!" Sanna said, with a rueful laugh. "Isn't there ever any stop to it, any evening when we can just have a fire here, and sit down, and talk?"

"We'll fix it for next week," he always said.

CHAPTER IX

SUSANNAH HAD BEEN almost a year a wife before she realized, finally and for all time, that Alec did not like domestic peace, did not indeed know anything about it. His life had always been much too exciting for that. He had always been free enough, and rich enough, to cast about in his mind for whatever amusement seemed most tempting and indulge in it in the smartest possible way; the entire world had been his playground.

Her predecessor, the delicate Betty Livingston, had been a member of a family so prominent and wealthy that every luxury and distinction in life had been quite calmly taken for granted by them. Cousins and uncles had been statesmen and judges; cousins and aunts had married titled foreigners or had ruled their respective social groups in American circles. Everybody had had governesses and years in Europe, riding horses, presentations at the Court of St James's, opera boxes and suites de luxe; great dressmakers had designed the women's clothes; great painters had made them immortal on canvas.

Betty's four years of married life had been four years of constant motion. To Santa Barbara, to France, to the South Carolina place, to Mexico and Alaska, Betty's restless fancy had taken her. She had been eternally afraid of missing something somewhere, of being outstripped by somebody in her race for pleasure.

"You aren't to let me die!" she had said feverishly to the great doctor who had chartered a plane to come from New York City to her bedside in Hollywood. "That's why I sent for you—why else should I wire for you! I've my costume for the Durbar Ball, and besides, there's the baby. My grandmother's dead and Mother's dead—there's no one to look out for him, and he's named for my grandfather the Judge, after all, and he'll be rich . . ."

She had presently cried in despair and rebellion for a whole day. Nothing in her life had made it easy for Betty to die; her last word, her last look for Alec had been reproachful.

"You could have done something about this, you know. There are other doctors—there are serums and things . . ."

Had Alec loved her, had he really mourned her? Susannah sometimes asked herself. She thought not. He talked of her as if she had been a willful child; perhaps she had never been anything else. He seemed to feel seriously the hurt that her disposition of their son's fortune had given him; Betty had chosen her own executors, her husband not among them; little Phil's money had lately depreciated materially in a depreciating world market. Alec was not consulted.

Contemplating the glimpses that she had of this situation, Susannah could honestly tell herself that it was through her that Alec had had the greatest, perhaps the only, happiness of his life. She knew that even while she accompanied him on the mad round of social engagements that was his life, she was softening him, bringing him nearer to a realer and more simple attitude. Driving northward to the Bancrofts' Canadian camp on a heavenly autumn day they shared a picnic lunch beside the road together, and Alec made her happy by saying: "Why don't we do this oftener, we two?"

And there was another occasion, an evening this time, when they dined alone, for almost the first time since their honeymoon.

"Why did I ask Dud and Bill to come over and play bridge?" he said then. "This is kind of fun, just ourselves alone."

But still the old feelings and habits persisted, and when she spoke of a free evening he would say promptly: "Ah, we ought to have the Chamberlains, then. And I'll tell you who's in town, Otto Hoffman. See if you can catch him at the Ambassador. And how about the Princes, Sanna? Don't we owe them a party? I'll tell you what, we'll have a table later at the Bagdad and dance."

For their first anniversary she suggested that they go back for one night to the New England inn that had been the scene of their first married joy. Alec agreed to this enthusiastically, and Frost was asked duly to make arrangements. But when, muffled in furs, and feeling for the first time a little cramped and heavy, Sanna was helped by her husband's hand from the car to the ground, at the doorway, it was to find a surprise party of magnificent proportions awaiting her.

The entire big place was lighted. Thirty of the Hazeltynes' closest friends were grouped in the big warm hallways, laughing and radiant, cheers and good wishes and toasts were the order of the day and of the night, and their echoes did not quite die away until late in the next afternoon when Susannah was safely back in her own apartment, and her doctor was assuring her and Alec that a little dancing and excitement were the best things in the world for herself and the baby, too.

"Well, I hear that your celebration just about cost you your son!" said her mother-in-law, coming to call upon her with two dozen red roses on the following day. Susannah, resting blessedly in pillows, only laughed.

"Alec's idea of a quiet little celebration," she said good-humoredly.

"Alec lost his first wife," Florence Hazeltyne said.

"You get away with the strangest remarks," Susannah observed.

Oddly enough, she and the bitter, brilliant, jealous older woman did not dislike each other. Whatever pangs Alec's mother had to endure in the contemplation of this radiantly happy and triumphant younger woman, her beauty and her successes, were actuated by the hunger of a strong and still vital sense of youth in her dissatisfied heart. There was no personal feeling against Susannah. Florence Hazeltyne had once been beautiful, powerful, admired; she was alone and old and unimportant now, and she had no philosophy, no faith to help her bear the inevitable cruelties of life.

Susannah suspected this; all her self-control had been needed in the beginning of her relationship with her husband's mother to endure the slights, the sarcasms and innuendoes to which Florence Hazeltyne had treated her. But they had been shallow, almost childish exhibitions of spite after all; it had been almost funny to see the haughty transparent effort the older woman had made to annoy and baffle her.

Fortified by Alec's loyalty to her, and impressed by his own generous attitude toward his unreasonable mother, Susannah had weathered the first dangerous crises by laughing at them; shaking her head in complete pity and understanding when malicious messages were repeated to her; assuring Alec that if his mother wanted him to herself for an evening it was no more than his duty to go to her.

"Listen, darling," Alec had said on this occasion, "she proposes a dinner party, women there as well as men, and you left out."

"A-h-h?" But Susannah's tone had still been all temperance and indulgence. "Of course you mustn't let her do, that; it would hurt her more than me," she had said. "But you talk her out of it, nicely, now mind! Let her think that she herself made the decision."

And after a few of these experiences it had been like a sort of play to assume an always dutiful, almost an affectionate attitude toward her mother-in-law. Susannah had formed the habit of going in to see her in the late afternoon, and spending with her a part of that bad time of day when she felt lonely and sad, and would sit grieving in the dusk over the joys, the power, the youth that were gone forever.

A magnificent reader and actress herself, she presently coached Susannah for her part in certain private theatricals, and Susannah was generous in her acknowledgment of help. Taking her curtain calls, she bowed to Alec's mother, sitting beside him in the front row of seats on a wide lawn at Oyster Bay, and directed some of the applause to her.

"I'd still love you if you hated my mother as Betty did," Alec said to her. "But, my God, how men like to have their women friendly!"

So that Sanna had fresh reason for daughterly good behavior and, when the old lady and she were together, treated her with a sort of bold affectionate easiness that, although she would have died before giving Susannah the satisfaction of knowing it, delighted Florence Hazeltyne deep down in her contrary heart.

Susannah had to give up a Miami visit in the second January of her marriage, and in February had ruefully to let Alec go to England without her.

"I'd do a lot more than that for my son," she told him philosophically, when she was down at the boat with him on sailing night.

"Oh, it's to be a son, is it?"

"That's the present arrangement. I love poor little Phil," Sanna said, "but I wish mine was your first baby. You've had all the excitement before."

"Is it so exciting?"

"Oh, Alec, the most thrilling thing in the world! Perhaps not for you, but for me it's simply a *miracle!* And d'you know," Susannah continued, "I hope when this little fellow gets a good start we can have little Phil back with us. He's getting much too big for that nursery-school stuff."

"He'll be big enough for boarding school in a couple of years; they take 'em at six. City's no place for kids," his father said, after a moment's thought. "And yet I don't like having him at Rhinecliff, either."

"I don't feel—quite happy about him," Susannah began doubtfully. "He seemed sort of friendly and wistful and—I don't know!—*little,* at Christmas. Maybe this year we can have him for the long vacation."

"He's an odd, shy little chap," Alec mused. And in another moment the distractions of sailing had absorbed him; he was to be gone only four weeks, but they seemed a long time to Susannah, inspecting his cabin, chattering with the crowd of friends who were seeing him off, steeling her heart to the strangeness of twenty-nine days without Alec.

The Margetts and the handsome Mrs Archibald were sailing. They seized upon Alec with rapture. "We'll take care of him and see that he gets back in great shape!" they told Susannah.

"I'd rather he'd come back battered and hungry and shabby," she said. "I hate him to be able to get along without me!"

She was laughing as she waved him good-by; she planned to welcome him home with laughter. Even when her ordeal was suddenly upon her, a month too soon, and she had to face a night of strange pain without him, she meant to greet him gaily.

"I don't know whether we've got a little girl or a baby monkey!" she meant to say, lying on her heaped pillows, dressed in the filmiest of silks and laces.

But when he actually did enter her hospital room, concerned and eager, she forgot everything except that she loved him, and that she had needed him in hours of loneliness and danger, and stretching out her arms to him she burst into tears.

Instantly Alec had her tight and safe in his arms; he was laughing, but with tears in his own eyes; his hard cheek was firm against her own, his voice was like wine filling her veins.

"You beautiful, you've had a hard time!"

"No, not a bit. Except the scare." Susannah's wet eyes were smiling. "But she—Evelina, was so sick, poor little mouse!" she faltered. "It was all so queer without you!"

"Everything all right now." He presently inspected the small, dark, mussed-looking scrap that was Evelina. The baby wore a mop of fine black hair; her skin was dark as an octoroon's. She had weighed only a short three pounds at birth; there was a slight heart condition. "She'll come out all right," Alec said.

"She's all right now!" Susannah's heart was tied to the child in a fierce pain of love and loyalty. Betty, his anemic, hysterical, cocktail-drinking, night-club-frequenting first wife, she reflected, could have a sturdy little son like Phil. Her child was a delicate little thing from the very beginning. Life was queer.

After her hospital fortnight life went back to its old grooves. Only they were not grooves; they were race tracks. She and Alec went for a week to the Singletons' in Bermuda; Susannah's heart trembled at leaving her child, but there was a wire from Evelina's nurse every day, and the baby went on nicely in her mother's absence. In June they went to California for a few amazing weeks; then they were all down at Easthampton: little Phil and his nurse, Evelina and hers, Phillips, Frost, Agnes, Delia, 'Liza.

Susannah played bridge late at night, went on yachting

trips, danced, planned picnics, drove about with Alec to weddings and all-day parties at Oyster Bay and Sands Point,
went to Forest Hills for the tennis. They flew in Dud Fielding's plane to the Bancrofts' in Canada for ten days of
camping; they visited the Ides at Shippan Point.

"Some day I'm going to have an awning put up over that
bit of lawn, and have tea out there," she said idly one morning at breakfast. Alec laughed.

"D'you realize that we've got just two more week ends
here?"

She looked at him aghast.

"Two! We hardly seem moved in!"

"Yep. Phil and Nursey go back on the twentieth, and if
we're going abroad again in September we'll have to get the
baby settled in town. We're getting around to our second
anniversary."

"Oh, dear, how it runs away!" It was too perfect; she
could not hold it. Life, happy or sad, did not stand still. Less
than two years ago she had not even known that such a
person as Alec Hazeltyne existed. Now they seemed always—from the very beginning of things—to have been
man and wife, to have belonged together in this miracle of
pride and possession. She seemed to herself never to have
had any other existence. She looked at him in complete
satisfaction and adoration; her husband, at home here in the
shaded glass breakfast room over the blue sea, with flick-
ering light from the water coming in through the jalousies
and trembling over his lazily stretched figure in its white
linen, his fine hand, his absorbed face.

"There's something I want you to do for me," he said.

"Anything," Susannah said amiably, but with a glance
that showed that his rather constrained tone surprised her.

"I want you to be nice to Merle Sargent," he said.

A fine pain, like the touch of a frozen pin point, pierced
Susannah's heart, and her world shook. She did not know

why; it was all instinct, a mere pang of vague blind fear. It was everything and nothing, gone almost as soon as it came.

"The—the Russian girl in your office?"

"In Hutchinson's office. No, she's not Russian—her mother was a Russian countess, but her father was English. I wondered—you'd be awfully decent if you would, Sue —I wondered if you'd ask her down here for her vacation— just a week. Next week. Otherwise, poor kid, she'll have to spend it in a boarding house in Lexington Avenue."

"Down here!" Here, in her house with him and with her and their child, this strangely mannered, strangely beautiful girl of eighteen, who was so definitely not one of themselves? Susannah was smiling pleasantly at him over a very earthquake of spirit.

"If you like," she said. And for her the light had gone out of the summer sunshine and away from the garden and the blue sea. Alec came around the table and kissed her.

"I'm going over to get some tennis with Bob," he said. "I'm two pounds overweight. You're a darling," he added, too carelessly. "I'll telephone Hutchinson's office today; she may not be able to come, but it's a nice gesture, anyway. She won't bother you much; she seems a quiet little thing. See you at lunch!"

He was gone. Susannah sat where he had left her; sat very still, staring unseeing into space for a long, long time.

❧ CHAPTER X ❧

LIFE WENT ON, brilliant and successful and amusing; months went by, and Susannah's tiny Evelina could be exhibited at teatime, her little French frocks hardly a span in length from the ribbon sash at her armpits to her bare knees, her gold curls brushed up into a glory about her small, mysteriously smiling little face. Nursey took care of her, Dr Jardine inspected her chart every week. Phillips drove the big cars with especial care when the precious baby was his passenger. Little Phil was at home for a few days' interval between the closing of school and the opening of camp and was shyly sweet with his baby sister.

Susannah could always go into the nursery to see Evelina; nobody could stop her. But Nursey and Milly, who helped Nursey, never needed her. If Evelina had a cold or was croupy a trained nurse was instantly in possession; otherwise the processes of bathing, naps, bottles, the meals of prune pulp and cereal, the details of sterilizing bottles and airing cribs, sending away masses of damp, tumbled baby linens, accepting back ironed armloads of fresh, sweet clothes, were all managed serenely without assistance or interference from Susannah.

Evelina had her supper at five, after which she lay gurgling until the quick sponge bath an hour later, after which again she was zippered into the monogrammed linens of her crib, stuck her thumb in her mouth, hummed like a bee, drowsed off, had her thumb firmly but gently removed, stirred, settled down again and was asleep. Sometimes Susannah came in to finish up feeding the prunes, sometimes she came later and saw Evelina tearful and alarmed in her tub and Nursey ready with the big warm towel. Sometimes on Nursey's day out she made a special point of being free in the late afternoon to help Milly. But on these occasions Milly was ultraofficious; eager to show that she was quite equal to managing Evelina all by herself.

Susannah rather stood in awe of Nursey, but she liked breathless little Milly, and she liked Milly's adoration of the baby, as contrasted to Nursey's rather superior attitude. Nursey had taken care of the Ridley baby and the Hunter twins and referred to them constantly to Evelina's disadvantage.

But, whatever happened, Susannah's visits to the nursery were unsatisfying. Adoring her baby, longing to be constantly with her, yet she seemed to have no choice. She could not assume the entire charge of the child herself without sacrificing her morning hours with Alec and all her late-afternoon engagements. Babies of Evelina's age were safest in the care of nurses. Alec expected Susannah to meet him at teas and cocktail parties, to be free to talk to him when they got home.

The constant presence of Merle Sargent in the group was a reminder to Susannah that if ever she were going to fail Alec, it must not be now. Alec considered himself the discoverer of the demure little Russian-English girl who, hardly out of childhood and strangely unsophisticated, was yet so sure of her charm. Merle asked nothing, claimed nothing, got everything. It was becoming rather the fashion to do something nice for Alec Hazeltyne's little Russian girl, who played the violin so divinely and was so grateful for everything.

Merle had come down to Easthampton to spend the ten days of her vacation with Alec and Susannah. She talked very little, but what she did say was with the pleasantly clear English accent. She loved the water, and in the smart blue bathing suit that was Susannah's gift to her she spent contented idle mornings and afternoons; sometimes at odd hours they heard her practicing her violin, but she was rather shy about playing.

To please Alec, Susannah loaned her an evening gown, a furred opera wrap. Merle's slim body was lovely in them, her dark skin a smooth olive, her hair smoldering Russian gold, her mouth extraordinary in its mobility, its moments of ugliness, its times of strange passionate beauty.

When at last they persuaded her to play for themselves and some friends one evening, they saw a strange change in her. The child had become woman, a woman of dangerous mixed bloods. Sometimes, her cheek against the dark polished wood of the violin, she moved like a panther and was the soul of Russia, dark and mysterious; sometimes, glowing and swaying like a flower on a wind-blown stem, she was as fresh and young and innocent as an English daisy.

Everyone watched, and everyone asked Susannah how she liked Alec's latest ugly duckling.

"She's really a darling when you know her," Susannah said.

But she wished, even as early in the affair as this, she wished with all her heart that Merle Sargent were safely out of the picture, or that she never had entered it; married to anyone, gone anywhere, just out of Susannah's scheme forever. Merle was pretty and she was fascinating, but there were plenty of pretty and fascinating persons in the world without her. There were girls much better looking and violin players much more gifted.

Merle was "Alec's little Russian" now. Women telephoned Susannah and asked how they could get hold of her for the charity benefit or the dull dinner. Susannah would sometimes hang up the receiver and sit stupidly at the telephone, wondering how all this had come to pass. Her life had been cloudless a few months ago. Cloudless? It had moved in a burst of trembling, exquisite, perfumed April sunshine. Now this annoying little shadow was always there. She would not have admitted it; perhaps she did not appreciate it herself, but in these days she thought more often of Merle than of anyone else in the world; Merle was more in her mind than even Alec or Evelina.

A maddening chance was accountable for all this, and that made it seem somehow even more unnecessary! Alec had met Merle on his return trip from England at a time when he was alone; Susannah at home awaiting Evelina's birth. He had given Merle the job in Hutchinson's office upon what seemed to Susannah a preposterous pretext that her knowledge of languages would make her useful. He had asked his grim old battle ax of a private secretary, Mrs Wix, to find her a safe and comfortable boarding house. He had loaned her a trifling hundred dollars, since repaid. And of course the child was disproportionately grateful!

So that through all the glory of her little successes Merle did not forget Alec, to whom she owed them. She had a pretty way of coming to him with the tale of her triumphs, of asking his advice. She kept her job, even though she might have gone in for an endless series of house visits. No, that thirty-five dollars a week was precious to Merle, the first money she ever had earned, and she would not surrender it.

Susannah felt, when the summer was over, and a second quick trip to Europe for Alec and herself was over, and when they were settled again in the city apartment, that there was no day that did not bring her some unbearable proof of the rising of Merle's star. She could go nowhere without hearing Merle's name; Merle had written a little sketch about New York, and one of the magazines was going to publish it. Merle had been away for the week end with the Hardistys, the Pennrhyns, the Morrises, the Days. Merle had snubbed Littleton Ten Eyck. Merle was perhaps going to be offered a part by Paulheim, in his new big Broadway review.

Merle could have had all these things, could have had them multiplied a thousand times without disturbing Susannah. Other women had flashed like comets across the world in which she lived now, had made successes in the drama or in letters, had achieved brilliant marriages; it was a glittering and successful arena, this one in which she found herself. It was only inasmuch as Merle attracted Alec that Susannah considered her at all. To hear that her Russian-English rival had made the richest marriage in the world, was moving from triumph to triumph, would have been good news to her, if only Alec had not cared, if only that door to miserable suspicion and uneasiness might have been closed forever!

But Alec did care, of course. No twisting, no writhing away from under the teeth of the harrow could save Susannah from that knowledge. Everything confirmed it. She could ignore, discard, depreciate nine pieces of evidence; the tenth was always there to present itself as incontrovertible, not to be ignored, not to be depreciated or denied.

"He had lunch at the club after the golf on Sunday," she would think, following his calendar from day to day, from hour to hour. "I know he did, for Jim Jessup said he'd played eighteen holes with Alec." And for a few hours perhaps there would be in her heart one little chamber in which there was peace. "Jim, you and Alec surely didn't play after lunch on Sunday! After eighteen holes in the morning you must both have been dead," she would hazard, with a great air of casualness when next she saw Jim. And there would be blackness again.

"Don't you remember, Sanna? Alec and you had a date; he had to get home by one," the unsuspecting Jim would answer. "He didn't lunch at the club."

"Oh, of course he didn't!" Susannah would take the sickness of her spirit elsewhere, the phrases, "He met her and they had lunch together . . . he met her and they had lunch together . . ." hammering in her brain until she feared that quite involuntarily she might some day cry them aloud.

"Let's see . . . what time did he come home Sunday . . . he lied to me about it . . . what time was it . . . we had to go to the Southerland thing . . ."

And then quietly, reasonably, but with her heart still beating madly:

"He came in at about four and said that they'd lunched late at the club, and had gotten to playing 'Signal.' And I'll see her at Dot's tonight, and she'll have that sable evening coat on: 'Some old skins of my mother's.' I'll say, 'How are you, dear?' and she'll have something to say about winter days in the office . . ."

Meanwhile the winter season flashed its many-faceted glories upon the richest and most scintillating circle in the world. There were play and opera openings, with England's and America's first interpreters, singers, clowns, playwrights in evidence, crowds packing the sidewalks outside the theaters, mounted police clinking and wheeling on the sidewalks in the lighted city night. There were picture exhibitions and symphony concerts, dinners and dances; every night had its after-show party in some enormous studio or drawing room, and Susannah's and Alec's names were first on every list. They went where they liked, and what Alec liked was always the cream of the cream.

He took great interest in Susannah's appearance, and her

succession of beautiful gowns was so swift that she sometimes hardly remembered herself what had hung in her wardrobe, what was there now, what was coming home next week.
Other women exclaimed in envious approval as they met her
at luncheons and teas.

"Now, Sanna, listen. Where did you get it!"

"Janetta."

"Well, where did *she* get it! It's simply adorable. It's the
cunningest thing I ever saw in my life."

She became accustomed to a chorus of approval for her
clothes. It was not her doing, this distinctive beauty in dress
that marked her as one of the smart city's smartest women.
It was Janetta and Steinhart and Carolynne and Hacker;
it was Hattie Cadogan and the Maison Labouchère. It was
Bond Street and Regent Street and the Avenue de la Paix.
Susannah grew weary of the brocades and the lawns, the
delicate undersleeves like masses of foam about her wrists,
the "Little Women" hats demure with curled feathers, the
beaded mantle that her great-grandmother might have worn,
but upon which all the fashion hawks swooped as the later-
than-latest thing.

One day she met Alec at the Ritz for luncheon. She was
late in arriving and was ushered at once by the headwaiter
to Mr Hazeltyne's table. She had supposed herself lunching alone with Alec; not that it mattered. One lunch would
not make or break the relationship between them either way.
Finding that he had two guests, she smiled an easy welcome.

"Hello, Merle. How do you do, Mr Paulheim? Did we
meet before? I think we have; was it at Alice's music afternoon? Wasn't it? Anyway, we've managed it now, and we'll
make up for lost time."

She slid into her seat. Alec was radiant. Susannah had
never looked more lovely; music was playing, good food was
in immediate prospect, and Merle was in the company. He
pressed Susannah's foot significantly with his own.

"I was lunching with Sam here," he said, "and I thought it might be a good idea to pick up this young lady at the office and let them get acquainted."

"Girls are of course entirely disinterested when they try to meet you, Mr Paulheim," Merle said demurely, determinedly bright.

But this was going too fast for the impresario, who turned to Susannah as he said uneasily:

"I don't see much of the girls myself. It's all done through Lew Brice's office."

Susannah, sensing the chill, rushed tactfully into the conversation.

"I can imagine that you're the busiest man in New York," she said, in a sympathetic undertone. "I read that interview on Sunday; it tired me even to read it."

Sam Paulheim looked at her gratefully.

"I made that feller," he said. "He's one of the smartest boys in the newspaper game today. But I don't see much of the girls."

"There's one very darling little girl you see something of," Susannah reminded him smilingly. "She was in a box with her mother at the *Peter Pan* opening. Adorable little thing."

"That was Sylvia. I have a boy, too—by my first wife," Sam Paulheim said.

"Well, the little girl and her mother made a beautiful picture," Susannah pursued cordially.

"My wife has got a beautiful nature. She's got one of the most beautiful natures I ever saw."

"She looks it. I was in the next box with Mrs Fielding and her children. I wished afterward that I'd introduced myself to Mrs Paulheim."

"You could walk right into a play yourself the way you looked when you came into this room," Sam said, waxing gallant.

"First time I've worn it," Susannah told him apprecia-
tively. "So I'm very glad you like it."

"It's simply divine," Merle said, somewhat subdued, and
edging herself cautiously back into the conversation. "And
the hat is the most stunning—I mean it is *absolutely* the
most stunning thing I ever saw."

Susannah loosened sables over the plain lines of the brown
velvet suit; the curled cock feathers of her hat touched the
great burst of brown-and-cream orchids on her shoulder.
The dining room and the encircling low balconies were filled
with luncheon groups now; some of the loveliest women
in the world were here today, but she was the most beautiful woman in the room, and she knew it. Only somehow it
all seemed rather flat.

"Is Mr St Hubert going to paint you in that outfit,
Sanna?" Merle asked.

"I don't know. I'd prefer something simpler myself. I'm
to go to the studio this afternoon and talk to him while he
paints Senator Miller, and I suppose we'll decide. He's
never been quite satisfied with the portrait he did two years
ago, and he wants to try again."

"It's the best portrait he ever painted," Alec said.

"It made him," Merle, who knew nothing about it, agreed
enthusiastically.

Susannah shrugged. The conversation veered, drifted
about through other topics without her being keenly conscious of anything that was said. She was thinking only of
Merle; Merle in the plain blue suit she wore so beautifully,
the black cloth coat with the tiger-skin collar, the small
tiger-skin turban that set off so dramatically the tipped oriental eyes, the dark clear skin, the Russian gold hair. The
suit had been made for Mary West; Mary, suddenly obliged
to go into mourning for Arthur's father, had given it and
several other handsome garments to Merle. They had all

only served to make Mary look dumpier and homelier than ever; they became Merle royally.

"You wouldn't care to see a preview of the new Hegermann picture, Mrs Hazeltyne?"

"I'm so sorry, Mr Paulheim—" What was Alec murmuring to Merle—what was Alec murmuring to Merle?—"but I'm taking some friends to the symphony."

They all stood up; waiters handed purses, held coats, dragged chairs back. The music went on playing, the atmosphere was still that enchanted air of fragrance and luxury, laughter and beauty that it had been two years ago, when Susannah Farjeon, engaged to marry Alexander Hazeltyne, had first come here for luncheon. But it held no glamor now; Susannah felt heavyhearted and helpless, stupid, near to tears.

"Are you going my way, Alec?"

"My dear, I'm not. I've got to look in at the office. I'll take you along, Merle; I have to see Hutchinson a minute. You're going to be at St Hubert's when, Sanna? Five?"

"About five, I should think." She spoke steadily; she could not smile; the muscles of her throat ached.

"I'll try to drop in and come home with you. What are we doing tonight?"

"Flagg. And opera. *Butterfly.*"

"Oh hell," Alec said simply. "Well, come on, Merle!"

He and Merle turned away; the party was out in cold, snowy Madison Avenue now, and the starter was holding Mrs Hazeltyne's car. She got into it, nodding good-by to Sam Paulheim. As Phillips turned the car, she passed Alec and Merle, waiting on the corner for the traffic light; they did not see her. Alec had one gloved hand under Merle's elbow; the girl was looking up and he looking down, Merle exaggeratedly earnest, Alec with that little half-smile Susannah knew so well tugging at his handsome mouth. The smile of the admiring, humoring, conquering male. There wasn't any mistaking it! There wasn't any mistaking it!

The wretchedness of knowing that she had lost him burned in Susannah's heart like an acid; she could say nothing about it that afternoon when Alec came into the warmth and pleasantness of Ross St Hubert's studio. A dozen of his friends were there, artists, musicians, bohemians generally; there were cocktails; Susannah and Alec loitered until the last possible moment and then took three other persons uptown with them in their car. No chance for a word alone, and no chance before the early opera dinner, for which they dressed rapidly in their separate dressing rooms. Susannah came home before Alec did from the after-opera party and was established comfortably in bed and reading when he came in at one o'clock.

He looked extraordinarily handsome in his full evening dress, she thought, with his hair somewhat untidy and his mood good-natured and mellowed after a good evening. But then Alec was always handsome.

"Sneaked out on me, did you?"

"Well, you'd just started another rubber, and I knew that if I went Kathryn could get to bed."

"Pretty good music. I mean what's-his-name, the little Frenchman."

"André. Yes."

She was answering him guardedly, only waiting her moment to strike. The resentment that had been burning in her heart ever since luncheon had long ago formed itself into the words she meant to use. Susannah lay comfortably in her pale rose-colored pillows and soft satin comforters; her reading lamp sent a rosy glow over her serious face and the hanging superb braids of bronze hair. The ivory satin of her nightgown was no softer in color and texture than her skin.

Alex proceeded unsuspectingly with his preparations for

bed. He went to and fro in the dimly lighted place, sometimes yawning a little and sometimes humming.

"Think opera's worth while?" he presently asked.

"Sometimes." Should she begin now? "Alec," she intended to say quietly and firmly, "you hurt me very much when you asked me especially to lunch alone with you, on my birthday, as it happens—not that that matters—and then ask Sam Paulheim and Merle Sargent to come, too. It isn't that I don't like Merle, and that I'm not perfectly willing to lunch with your men friends, but I simply want to ask you how *you* would feel if I took a great fancy to some attractive young British-Russian *man* and asked him to come along on our parties—included him in everything we did——" "What did you say?" she interrupted her thought to say aloud, suddenly realizing that he had asked her some question, and had paused in the center of the room expecting an answer.

"I asked you if Lynn told you about Barb and Lippy."

"No," Susannah said, startled out of her determination to be brief and unfriendly. "What is it?"

"Splitting."

"Not getting a divorce?" Susannah asked, shocked.

"Yep. She found out about him and that little blonde—remember? The girl he had at the theater that night, when she was in Europe. We saw them."

"But, Alec, with those two little girls! I think that's awful."

"Why should she care?" Alec demanded, sitting down as he took off his shoes. "Why should she *care* what he does?"

"Well, but, Alec," Susannah argued, but in a much less firm tone than she had intended to take a few minutes earlier. "If he actually did—if he actually *was* unfaithful to her, don't you think she had a right to resent it?"

"Not in that case, I don't."

"You mean on account of Freddie?"

"Well, of course. I was best man for Lippincott when he was married to Barbara Watts," Alec said. "I've known them both since I was a kid. She never has had any sense!"

"Yes, but, Alec, she never went as far with Freddie—I *know* it, I know it from the way she talks! Barb wouldn't —she'd go pretty far—but nothing serious. Honestly."

"That's the way women work it out—that everything's all right as long as they don't actually jump over the traces," Alec observed, returning from the bathroom in pajamas and getting into his own bed. "My Lord, I'm tired!" he interpolated with a yawn. "They can hurt a man, make a fool of him, get everyone talking," he went on, "but just so long as they stop short of the final thing they're not to be blamed, and they can kick him out if *he* goes too far. Lippy has had an affair with this little Ada—Ida, whatever her name is—everyone knows that! But Barb never knew about it until it was practically all over. He never flaunted his affair in her face the way she did hers with Freddie. He never played with it and gloried in it the way she did! Why, I remember, down there at Alan's once—you were there, and she came down to the dock and said that she was going into town in Freddie's yacht—remember?"

"Yes, I know. But, after all—that's Barb. She was proud of having gotten Freddie away from Marlys. She was just showing off. It seems perfectly terrible to me to have those people break up. Those nice little girls and all——"

"You can bet it seems terrible to *me*," Alec said, jerking covers about and shoving pillows away preparatory to sleep. "And some day I hope women will get it through their heads that it's just as rotten to pretend to be doing a thing —to want to do it and not have the nerve—as to do it!"

Distracted from her original intention, Susannah lay musing in the soft pink circle of the night light. And as she mused, a certain mood of satisfaction, a certain sense of well-being, took possession of her. Men and women must

not be too critical of each other; marriage did not trans-
form them into angels. Hers was an exceptionally distinguished position; she must not hold Alec to any line of conduct as a mill girl might jealously hold her man. Everyone
in Alec's circle flirted, there was far too much freedom, it
was considered smart—almost necessary—to be playing with
some little love affair on the side. She must stop thinking
about Merle.

Alec, just going off, roused up.

"Oh, the Len Grants wanted us for Sunday. It was rather
a satisfaction to say that I couldn't possibly go."

Instantly her jealousy was burning at white heat again.
He had an engagement with Merle, of course! In a rather
constrained voice Susannah said:

"What are you doing on Sunday?"

"Why, aren't all of us going to Palm Beach on Saturday?" he demanded, sleepily surprised.

"Oh, of course we are!" Susannah was trying to laugh
at herself and her fears as she went to sleep.

❧ CHAPTER XI ❧

Just a month later the sittings to Ross St Hubert began. Susannah had recently attended a bal masqué in a costume copied from Holbein's beautiful portrait of Christina, Duchess of Milan. The severely plain lines had been so flattering to Susannah's splendid height and regular features that it had been decided between herself, Alec and the painter that the new portrait should be fashioned after the old one.

The straight velvet underdress was of violet velvet so pale in tone as to be hardly darker than orchid; the heavy rich upper garment, also of velvet, was of plum color, furred in sable; odd wisps and feathers of Susannah's bronze hair crept out to curve themselves against the sober black velvet cap. She wore no jewels; her flawless hands, like those of the dignified little duchess, were clasped upon a fine lace handkerchief.

Standing on the model's platform in Ross's big studio, Susannah dreamed endless dreams and remembered one by one the events of her crowded thirty months of married life. When one day the painter said curiously, "What are you thinking about, Mrs Hazeltyne, when your eyes go blank that way?" she could answer with a laugh, "Everything. I've not had time to think like this for years."

The bright panorama was only a panorama, that was the trouble. Under its undeniable joys and excitements, the pattern of flattery, travel, the opera, visits, dinners and swims, the tennis and dancing and theater, the opera box and the Tiffany pearls, there was a strange emptiness, a feeling that somehow reality was escaping her, that the business of being amused was altogether too successful. Life wasn't, after all, only amusement—or was it? Was one supposed to be fortunate in finding it only a matter of hurrying into delightful new clothes, racing to new places, meeting new people, helping oneself to chicken aspic, shaking one's head at the terrapin, consulting with 'Liza about Friday's dinner, sending flowers to the Dinsmore funeral, the Spottiswood wedding, the Frawley baby, the poor Tina Morris still in the hospital?

All these things were pleasant, of course, and to be young and nice looking and popular was more than pleasant. But somehow one never had time to stop and savor the taste of life as the stream of it flowed by. It would be good to find some quiet inlet where the waters were still enough for reflection, where one might sense the joy of the moment, rather than plan breathlessly for a dozen mingled treats in the future.

The two or three weeks immediately following Evelina's birth should have been a peaceful time. But between her own two nurses and the baby's nurses, scores of boxes of flowers to admire and acknowledge, and a daily stream of callers, Susannah had found that this time flew by like a dream with all the rest. The trip to Europe had been only a succession of social events—on the boat, in London, in Paris; back on the boat again there had been always cocktails, men and women in evening dress, bridge and dancing, brief walks about the deck constantly interrupted by greetings, by stewards with bouillon or tea, by encounters with friends old and new.

Palm Beach had of course been the same thing, accentuated and underlined as everything was in Palm Beach. Soft warm air, waving palms, white-clad women drifting by the smart little shops, luncheons under club awnings, afternoons at the green tables, hours on the sands gossiping and watching, and then the inevitable dressing for dinner and getting into a motorcar to go somewhere—anywhere—to meet other folk who had duly dressed for dinner, too. Great admiration among all the women for each other's clothes, murmurs of troubles and divorces and mistakes and indiscreet asides, music somewhere, and trays of canapés again . . .

"Why couldn't there be some little place where Alec and the baby and I could be alone together?" Susannah mused. "Nothing normal can live in this sort of atmosphere— nothing normal *does* live. These men and women aren't really married; they don't depend on each other, need each other. The children haven't any real home life, any real parents. Divorce has split up most of their homes, and even the others have no home associations. Boarding schools and summer camps, tutors taking them to the Junior Symphonies and the Academy of Natural History, tickets for every movie or show that seems educational or suitable for children—that's not the right way to bring them up."

And she thought with an ache in her heart of the tiny Evelina. Well, she really was only a lump of sweet little unconscious baby flesh now; Nursey and Milly could do all and more for her than her mother could do. It would be a ridiculous affectation for Susannah to assume full charge of her, exhaust herself giving the baby baths and bottles, sit beside her while she slept.

But the months were moving fast—far too fast for those fortunate few in the troubled big world who could spend all their time in being amused. In a short while Evelina would be talking, walking, forming her microscopic first impressions of life. How could Susannah contrive then to be with her more constantly, and to draw Alec into the picture, too, win him to hours of domestic quietness and har-

mony beside the study fire, with his wife relaxed in the big
chair opposite him and his small daughter triumphant on
his knee? How wonderful it would be if they could keep one
day free in every week, lunch alone, take Evelina without Nursey for an afternoon drive, perhaps go up to the
Pomfret School to see little Phil, come back to a late-
afternoon idyll over the baby's going to bed, and then dine
alone together and see a picture or a play quietly and be
early at home for a long, restful night.

It sounded so simple! It would be, she knew, almost impossible to accomplish. The demands upon Alec and herself
could easily have filled three times the luncheon, dinner,
evening hours at their disposal. Twice a month they must
dine with his mother; sometimes Susannah accompanied
Nursey and Evelina on the baby's weekly calls upon her
grandmother. There were engagements they really wanted
to keep; interesting personages were always in the city and
always being entertained. There were theater openings that
would be discussed for weeks; there were flattering invitations from diplomatic headquarters in Washington; there
were debutante dances so magnificent in details of entertainment and decoration that they were spectacles not to be
missed; there were inevitable funerals and weddings; for
Alec there was his office, with the usual conferences and
emergencies, and, for Susannah, dress fittings, beauty-
parlor engagements, women's lunches. In early June she
must go several times to Easthampton to look at houses; in
late June she and Alec might run across to Europe to see
something of the season in London, buy him a new wardrobe in Regent Street, take in a play, and get herself a coat.

"I'll be sorry when these sittings are over, Ross," she
said one day. The painter stepped back from his canvas and
regarded it and his sitter with narrowed eyes.

"I will be, I know," he said simply.

"It's restful, standing here, and it gives me a chance to

think," Susannah pursued, not without a queer little twinge of wonder as to what his tone meant.

"You can sit down if you like. I'm working on the dress."

She sat down, her eyes wandering idly about the careful carelessness of the studio; the candlesticks and the potteries, the tapestries and the plaster casts. Spring sunlight was barred away from the skylights; canvases were banked against the walls.

"These," Ross St Hubert said lightly, "have been the happiest days of my life, I think."

He worked away attentively, not looking at her, smudged something with his thumb. Susannah, choosing to assume that there could be no possible significance in this remark, did not change her expression, but continued her idle study of the room.

"For which remark," Ross presently added in the same light tone, "I apologize. It was not intentional. As we say in chess, *'C'est simplement que j'adoube.'* "

Her senses just a little fluttered, Susannah said:

"How does it happen you speak such easy French, Ross? Whether it's good or not I don't know. But it sounds so easy."

"I did all my model work with Rochette. I was four years in Paris."

"That must be a wonderful experience."

"It's a wonderful time," the painter said, scowling faintly as he went on with his work. "To be young and working hard and in Paris! The old boys all tell you it isn't what it used to be. But it seemed pretty good to us!"

They talked idly of Paris; what they liked and what they did not like, and of the places they knew; the Dome and La Rue's and the Tour D'Argent. Ross had never been to the Crillon or the Ritz; Susannah knew very little of the Left Bank, but there was plenty to say. It was growing dusk in the studio, and Susannah said that Alec was coming to get her, and Ross said that that was good because he wanted to talk about a party.

"What sort of a party?"

"Cocktails. Music. Everything. To celebrate the finish of the picture."

Susannah got down from the dais and began to walk about the room in her magnificent robes; Ross studied his canvas through a hand glass held close to one eye. The bell rang; someone always came up at this time; perhaps it was Alec.

"Yes, my lady," Ross said, laying on a bit of paint with the thin blade of his palette knife, drawing back to see the effect, "it has been that way since you first walked into the studio. I don't defend it. It seems that I can't quite end these sessions without letting you know it. There's just one person in my world now. There's just one standard of beauty and fineness and charm. Funny, isn't it? Very, very, very funny," he murmured, apparently absorbed in his work. "Very funny indeed."

Alec came in with Nini Chandler and Connie Ide. He said that he was hagridden, that they had met him early in the afternoon and made him buy them things. They all looked at the picture, and the women said that it was the divinest thing that Ross had ever done.

"Yes, it's good," Alec said, "it's swell, Ross. Stand there a minute, Sanna, with your jaw squared a little more. I don't know—maybe that jaw line—— But it's awfully good. It 'll make you famous, Sanna; three hundred years from now someone 'll be trying to buy the St Hubert portrait of Mrs Alexander Hazeltyne."

"My grandchildren will have it, Alec! D'you suppose you could get them to part with Grandma's picture?"

Some men came in, and there were the usual drinks and crackers; it was all very safe and flattering and happy in the romantic studio setting. Alec settled himself on a hassock at Susannah's knee; just the touch of his shoulder against her, the nearness of his smooth head, the sound of his voice was happiness for her. Ross went about waiting on his guests; once his eye met Sanna's steadily, and she felt her color rising in the instant before he turned away.

He was a handsome man, Ross St Hubert, in a Mephistophelian sort of way. He had a thin aquiline face, dark skin, very black eyes that tipped up at the corners a little, heavy black hair. Over his red thin mouth was a line of mustache; he was tall and thin and dressed carelessly and picturesquely, as became his calling. Women all loved Ross St Hubert; he did everything that flattered and charmed them in the most flattering and charming ways. He bent his head over their hands at meeting and parting; he wrote enchanting notes; he played the piano; he painted; best of all, he talked dangerously and significantly to them, as one who perfectly understood their weaknesses and their desires.

It was arranged tonight that the tea for a private showing of the portrait should take place in just a week, and Susannah went home happily with Alec, flattered that the much-courted painter had chosen to do a little courting in his turn, and as always exquisitely content when she had her husband to herself. Afterward she remembered the gracious softness of the spring city in the lingering light; there were flowers for sale in curb carts, and the flowers blooming on the straw hats of the girls who, loitering home in the warm dusk, were in no hurry to go into stuffy apartments everywhere and leave this glory of the blooming year outside.

A hundred carefully picked persons came to the tea. Among them, Merle. She said in her simple innocent way that Ross had asked her to come and play and that she had been perfectly delighted to get "an engagement." Susannah, knowing who was paying for the portrait, had no difficulty in deciding from just what source Ross had derived the idea.

Merle wore a plain shabby little frock of olive-green brocade; her head was bare except for a strange Russian crown
of gold and glassy stones, green, red, purple, yellow, that
winked in the light as her dark-gold hair moved against
the violin. She and her music were a great success, and she
stood, after she had played, in the full stream of praise and
laughter that flowed about her at the big piano, looking like
a happy little girl. Susannah somehow felt foolish in her
heavy furred velvets; she went up with the rest.

"Beautiful, Merle," she said. Merle's strange oriental eyes
flashed at her gravely.

"I owe it all to you and Alec," she said quickly.

It was on this day, when her heart was sufficiently heavy
with the increasing sense of her own helplessness and a
wretched conviction of the other woman's charm, that that
moment arrived that struck a definite death knell to Susannah's happiness. Happy she would be again in this world,
but never with the old freshness and confidence that had
been hers since those days on the Queen Augusta, when she
and Alec had leaned on the rail and watched the dark night
waters flowing by, and the ship's white wake mingling with
them, and had first found each other.

The circumstance was in itself trifling. Only a few words,
but they were words she was not intended to hear, and their
significance was unmistakable.

It was when the tea was over, and the spring sunshine was
dying away from the grimy big city and the lofty studio,
and when the hilarious men guests and the women in their
smart frocks and Easter hats were beginning to drift away
by twos and threes that Susannah, standing in the little
passage between the studio and Ross's own quarters, and
half listening to something Rosa Arnheim in the bedroom
was saying over the distribution of coats and bags, heard
Merle's voice, quick and quiet, somewhere out of sight. She
might have been in the little studio ingle behind the model's

dais, or she might have been on the piano bench half hidden by easels and canvases; wherever she was, Alec was close to her, for his answering voice was as quiet as her own.

"If you're taking Sanna home, look out for my gloves in the car," Merle said; "like a fool I left them there."

"I will, dear. I'll remember," Alec said.

That was all. But the simple words left Susannah stunned, and she went home in a dream of pain and bewilderment. There were other persons in the car with Alec and herself; she was hardly conscious who they were or what they said to her or she to them, if indeed she spoke to them at all. She felt physically sick; the solid earth was shaken beneath her.

From that day on she watched and pondered. No use raging, reproaching Alec, giving way to futile tears. This was a problem, not a mere grievance; she would gain nothing by lessening her own charm for her husband; that would be only to augment the other woman's charm.

Merle had left the office and moved herself from the English boarding house where she had first lived to an attractive little apartment in an old brownstone dwelling near Washington Square. Its high-ceiled narrow rooms and deep window casings spoke of a long-gone era, but there was a roomy spacious living room with white paneled walls and a coal fire, and three floors down was a long strip of back garden into which Merle could escape whenever she liked for a breath of air. Susannah and Alec went down to see her shortly after she had moved in; the sparseness of her furnishings and her satisfaction in them were in themselves charming. There was something very natural and appealing in the contrast between the handsome old samovar, the valuable violin and the splendid table linens, and the china and glassware that had come from the five-and-ten store. She was getting real money for private engagements now, she told them elatedly; she was being asked to play for club luncheons and private dinners. And while Sam Paulheim had not been immediately encouraging, he had asked her to come and play for him again.

What was there in this girl that so fascinated Alec? Susannah wondered, watching every movement of Merle's as she went about admiring and interested. What *was* it that made every word of Merle's important to Alec, bound him to her every gesture and intonation, blotted out the rest of the world for him? There was no answer; there never would be an answer. The mystery that draws one human being toward another must remain a mystery to the end.

Outwardly the life of the Alexander Hazeltynes flowed on with its wonted brilliance. Susannah and Alec loitered over their late breakfasts in their own breakfast room with the summer sun shut away by jalousies, or in the Newport house, or on ocean liners, yachts, in the country places of friends. Little Evelina, tottering on small unsteady feet encased in diminutive buckskin pumps, or tinier than ever in a span-length bathing suit, continued in Nursey's jealous charge, with occasional affectionate intervals for Mother. Tennis, golf, prize fights, opera and theater, bridge hands and divorces were discussed by the women, idling on the sands or on awninged porches.

And all the time, under this glittering upper current flowed the deeper one of Alec's infatuation for a gold-headed, oriental-eyed girl who played the violin. Everyone knew of it now; he was with Merle almost every day. He did not want to accept an invitation that took him away from her, and when she went into the Berkshires to a quiet little camp for a month, Alec was constantly there.

At home he treated his wife with the friendliest courtesy imaginable. He read her excerpts from the news at breakfast, discussed his plans for the day and hers, took an approving look at his daughter, demure among blocks and woolly animals in her white-and-pink-and-blue pen, and was gone. Sometimes he said briefly: "I won't be home for dinner, dear"; sometimes the message came later through his secretary and Susannah's butler. Mr Hazeltyne was sorry, but he would not be able to get home for dinner, and sent his love.

Occasionally he even quoted Merle to Susannah, or spoke of her. She was a "funny, ambitious little thing." He had never in his life seen anything like the gratitude and appreciation she showed for his first helping interest; why, the girl wouldn't buy herself a hat without his approval.

"She's in love with you, Alec," his mother had said once sharply, hearing something of this. Alec had only laughed unalarmedly.

"Well, if she is it won't hurt her! She's nineteen; she's got to be in love with somebody. Your son is forty-one."

The insufferable thing was that Susannah had to go on, her head held high, her eyes sealed to what they could not help but see, her ears deaf to whispered pity and whispered sympathy alike. In marriage it was always in the power of one partner so to hurt—so to shame—the other; it must be borne, that was all.

Her own mother, fluttering back from California to admire the wonderful grandchild, fluttering ecstatically to Europe, and thence to China—"where all my old friends are, really, Sanna"—could be no help. Eva Farjeon did not want to hear that anything was wrong with Susannah's life; her return to the Orient was planned for the principal purpose of boasting to the old crowd of Susannah's success, her happiness, her incessant triumphs. She never spared Aunt Nona a detail of it.

Alec's mother, brooding over her poetry books, asking old friends to rich luncheons, retailing the embittered adventures of her life with spicy relish, was an equally unsuitable confidante. Susannah even suspected her of a sort of enjoyment in the mischances of other women. "Well, if she couldn't hold him——" she would say, with a warped old mouth twisted into a smile, and the silk and lace of her narrowed old shoulders raised in a shrug.

Aunt Nona had moved to distant Pasadena to spend her remaining years in the sunshine; Lola's and Anita's lives ran in quieter currents and different from Susannah's. They had never achieved her social heights; St Hubert had never painted their portraits; their names were not included in the list of boxholders on Monday nights at the opera.

But Susannah did have a close friend in lovely and gentle Margot Fielding, to whose old-fashioned comfortable home in West End Avenue she went for the quietest and realest hours she ever knew. Margot was older than Susannah; her two girls were seven and nine years old. But there was a boy of Evelina's age, and as Evelina grew into enchanting babyhood, Susannah sometimes took her out to spend an afternoon at Margot's house.

"Margot, mind hearing about my troubles?" Susannah said one day, when the two babies were asleep and their mothers were talking beside an autumn fire.

"Sorry to hear that you have any, Sue," Margot said, with a glance up from her knitting. "It's Alec, of course," she said.

"How did you know?"

"I don't know, Sue," the other woman said honestly. "I've just—heard. I knew something was worrying you, and I supposed it was that. Is it the little violin girl?"

"Merle Sargent. Yes."

"Isn't she Russian?"

"Her mother was a Russian countess, but she died when Merle was only a baby. Her father was English."

"How serious is it?"

"Alec's affair with her? He says, or he implies, that it's just big-brotherly protection and advice. He says that she's absolutely straight."

"Well," Margot said, knitting away busily, "perhaps that's true."

"Meanwhile I have no husband," Susannah said dryly and stopped, her voice thickening.

"He's never home? You were together at the Allens' the other night."

"Oh yes; he's home most of the time. Always at night. Kind and affectionate; never an ugly word. We go to occasional dinners, we go to parties. If she's there he doesn't make me conspicuous by neglect. But we're both dead—dead—*dead*," Susannah said, suddenly breaking and finishing on a desperate note.

"H'm," Margot mused. "It happens that way sometimes," she reminded the other woman briefly. "Do you quarrel?"

"Oh no; Alec won't quarrel. If I say anything bitter he just walks away. He doesn't feel that he's doing anything wrong. He has just discovered this wonderful girl and given her a helping hand, and she's grateful."

"She's in love with him, of course."

"Obsessed. He's her god."

"How much does he see her?"

"Constantly. All the time. She played with a symphony in Montreal last month; Alec was there to hear her. He told me that business would take him up there—as a matter of fact he has a branch office in the town."

"But you don't think she's his mistress?" Margot asked thoughtfully.

"I'm sure not. I don't think that would satisfy Merle," Susannah said, her lip curling, her eyes narrowed.

"Then it won't stop there," Margot said. "Has he asked you for a divorce?"

The room began to sway in slow circles for Susannah; she gripped her hands dizzily on the arms of her chair. It was all nightmare: the pleasantness of autumn sunshine at the windows, the little sucking noise of the coal fire behind the polished steel rods of the grate, Margot's pleasant full figure and bent brown head over her knitting.

"No," she whispered. *He daren't!* she meant to add, but the words would not come.

"I think you have to face it," Margot said, looking up with her kind face a mask of sympathy and distress. "Dudley's always been like a father-confessor to Alec, you know. Dud came home last night worried to death about it all. He thinks that's what is in Alec's mind. You've got to think, Sue, if his infatuation for this girl really is as bad as it seems, just what you're going to do."

❧ CHAPTER XII ❧

"SANNA," ALEC SAID. He folded his newspaper, cleared his throat, looked at her across the breakfast table.

Susannah's heart stood still with instant instinctive fear. She faced him soberly, shadows in her brown eyes.

"Alec." She said it quietly, expectantly. She knew what he was going to say. But if she had steeled herself to listen, she could see that he had steeled himself also to speak. No attitude on her part would stop him now.

"This is the thing," he said. "Do we want to go on this. way?"

"This way?" Susannah swallowed with a dry throat.

"What do you feel about it?" he asked.

She looked down, too shaken to answer. The bright colors of her plate swam together; the water in her crystal goblet sparkled like a diamond. There was a great square diamond flashing back at it on the trembling hand with which she laid down her spoon.

"I mean, neither one of us is happy this way," Alec argued.

"No," Susannah said, very low, her throat hurting her, "neither one of us is happy this way."

"Well, what about it?" he said.

"You mean—what, Alec?"

He came over to her side of the table and sat down near her, squaring a chair about so that he could face her. Outside of the high penthouse windows a gray heavy sky lowered over the city. Susannah could hear the rush of the elevated trains far below, and the sound of whistles on the cold, slow-moving river. Agnes came in with hot coffee, went away again.

"I'm as sorry about this as I can be," Alec began in his kind, anxious voice. "You know that, Sanna. It's going to be rough on you—not as rough," he added, in the inevitable self-defence, "as it would have been when things were different. But I know how you're going to hate it."

"How do you mean 'when things were different,' Alec?" Susannah spoke lifelessly, her heavy shadowed eyes upon him.

"Just that," he answered simply. "The truth is this, Sanna. Why don't we face it? I want," he went on seriously and steadily, his face reddening a little, but his eyes fixed on hers without flinching, "—I want to marry Merle. We've come to love each other. We're neither one of us happy about it. It's a wretched situation. But I suppose it isn't the first time it's happened. This half-and-half gets us nowhere. It's making me completely miserable, and it's killing her."

A sudden wild fury shook Susannah like the grip of giant fingers. She felt a sensation of actual vertigo; she felt her mouth suddenly water and her limbs suddenly weak. She got up and walked to the window and stood looking out at the bleak, unfriendly winter day. Alec followed her and stood beside her.

"This isn't a sudden impulse," he said. "It isn't a thing I wanted to happen. As far as you're concerned my feelings haven't changed; they never will change. I'll always feel for you the deepest—the *sincerest*——"

"Oh, please!" she said, suffocating. There was a moment of silence.

"Look here, Sanna," Alec suddenly began again, in that tone of affectionate comradeship that had gone straight to her heart at the very beginning of their acquaintanceship, "what *am* I to do about it? This way—the way we've been going on for weeks—isn't fair to anyone. It's a sort of half-life; not one thing nor the other. You're unhappy, I can see that; anyone could see that! I'm unhappy, feeling that I'm failing you and not one bit closer to her, and of course—— But I'm not bringing Merle into it, because she naturally hasn't any rights in your eyes. But she's heartbroken, of course. She feels that she's your friend, that you were kind to her——"

He stopped on an eloquent note of appeal; Susannah's back, turned toward him, did not move a muscle, her head was held high.

"I'm not going to waste words telling you that I think you have lost your mind," she finally said icily. "But you must be crazy to talk to me this way. Are you seriously proposing that I step down and give my place to a Russian girl of nineteen who happened to be on the steamer crossing with you last year? I love you too much," Susannah faltered, suddenly breaking, "to let you make such a *fool* of yourself!"

"I'm sorry you feel that way about it," Alec said stiffly in the silence.

She turned about and faced him and put a hand on his shoulder.

"Ah, Alec, it can't be you and me talking to each other this way! What's gone wrong, dear? How have I failed you? You and I loved each other once, such a little time back! What's the matter now?"

He went to the table and sat down and put his head into his hands, his elbows among the scattered plates and glasses.

"I don't know," he said in a whisper. "I don't know. I only know that I can't help it, Sanna. It's the only thing I ever met in my life that I couldn't lick! When I'm with her, then it seems so easy. It seems so easy to keep it friendship, to like her and help her and let it go at that. When I'm away from her, I'm sick; I'm thinking of nothing else, wondering what she's doing, wanting her—wanting her——"

He finished on a mere breath. He did not look up. It was as if he spoke to himself.

"But that won't last, Alec," Susannah pleaded eagerly, sitting near him, her fingertips touching his arm. "Think what it means, dear. To your mother—Evelina—myself, everyone! This is only a passing thing; it can't be permanent. Couldn't we go away—anywhere—Europe or California or China again—*anywhere!* You can't break up everything for an impulse—an emotion——"

He raised his head and looked at her with wretched eyes.

"Sanna," he demanded simply, "what *else* can I do?"

"Ah, well," she said, confidence rushing back like a great freshening tide into her heart. "You can't do *that!* Because I love you, Alec, and for my sake, and the baby's sake, and your mother's sake you're going to stay with the wife who loves you. You're going to be fair to Evelina and me, and yourself, too. This would hurt me so, Alec, and our little girl, too, and you most of all! Darling, try to see that side of it."

Was he listening as the eager low flow of her words went on? She could not tell. His handsome haggard face was strangely set as he looked off into space, his eyes narrowed, a faint frown on his forehead.

"I don't know why you love me, Sanna," he said presently, in a despairing tone. "I don't know why I get this way about a girl who could easily be my daughter! I know—I know exactly how it looks—an old fool taken in by a pretty face! I don't defend myself, God help me! But I've been *crazy* seeing you the way you've been for weeks, listening to her —knowing that it was up to me to do anything if anything is going to be done. I tell you I've been crazy!"

He put his head back into his hands again, gripping it so that she could see the muscles of his fingers whiten. Susannah sat silent, finding nothing to say.

"Crazy!" Alec said again in a whisper. "Well!" he added, in a different tone, "I'm late now. Cutter's here from Washington and was to be in the office at ten."

She walked with him to the door, dismissed Frost with a nod, and held his big coat for him.

"I will never let you go, Alec," she said seriously.

"Why you want to hold onto an ass like me——" he answered, with a broken little angry laugh.

"Ah, well, that's my business."

He turned suddenly, shamefacedly, in the little hallway, after she had pressed the bell for the elevator.

"Kiss me, Sanna."

And with the kiss for the first time she broke into tears and went back blindly to her bedroom when he had gone, crying bitterly.

The day went on. Susannah went in to see Evelina in her bath, to take the big towel from the polite and patient Nursey and dry the firm little wriggling body herself, to hurry away to the first of the morning's engagements. Her program included a stop at the beauty parlor at eleven, a hospital call at noon, luncheon at the club with Elinor Jessup and ten other exquisitely dressed and groomed and perfumed women, and a pleasant nine-blocks walk with Marjorie Hunter afterward to the gallery, to take another look at the portrait. It was decorated now with two prize ribbons: the Paul Stein portrait prize, the Peabody International Medal. And it was to be sent to Boston for further competition.

Ross was there looking at it, and when Marjorie rushed away to meet a friend at the Penn Station, Susannah and the artist strolled down the Avenue together in the glum cold shadows of afternoon and looked at the brilliant windows and the cars twinkling and slipping on the frozen dirty remnants of last week's snow. The sky, far down toward the Washington Arch, turned cold opal at five o'clock; Susannah declined tea at Pierre's; she wanted to get home to see Evelina to bed, and at six some people were coming in.

"You can loiter about for a cocktail if you like, Ross."

"No, thanks. I've got to get home and dress. Any chance of your coming up to Boston to see what we have to beat, Sanna?"

"Not much. I'd love to, but it does bite out such a big slice of one's day. Five hours there and five hours back. I had a card. After Christmas, is it?"

"January. They're making quite an occasion of the opening. Evening reception, mayor and all that. My sister's coming all the way from Washington for it and will stay overnight at the Bellevue."

"Mrs Ames. Is she? When are you going, Ross?"

"I'm going to fly up the day of the opening."

"Ah." They walked on in silence. "It 'd be fun," Susannah said.

"Here's your doorway. No, I'm not going up. Sanna," Ross said, his dark, handsome, sinister face very earnest as he held her hands in good-by. "There's something I want to say to you, and I don't know whether it 'll make you mad or not. It's this: if the time ever comes when you would feel happier to know that there's someone in the world who worships you—I sound like a kid, but I'm not a kid, and I *worship* you. I don't ask anything and I don't expect anything; it isn't that. It's just that there are times in our lives when we need—we need to think well of ourselves— we need to know that we're loved, that we make the whole scheme better for someone. I'm saying this rottenly, but that's what you mean to me. That's what you'll always mean. And now good night, my dear."

Before she could speak, if indeed she could have found anything to say, he was gone. Susannah stood looking after

him as he went away. Then she turned slowly and entered
the elevator.

"Colder, Mason."

"Yes, madam. Yes, madam, it is colder. It is almost like
snow tonight, madam."

"More snow!"

Susannah went into her room and got into a loose, comfortable dress. 'Liza knocked discreetly before coming in,
delivered the not unexpected message.

"Mr Hazeltyne telephoned, Mrs Hazeltyne, and he will
not be here for dinner. He said that he knew you would
have your bridge game without him, and that he would be
in at about ten o'clock. He was suddenly called to Philadelphia."

"Thank you, 'Liza." The Philadelphia fiction was not for
Susannah's benefit, of course. Alec had long ago stopped
that farce with her. That was what she was to tell Miriam
and Bob Arnheim and Peter Eckles when they came in for
an informal dinner with her tonight. That was what Alec
would plead when he got home fresh and friendly at eleven.

"I'm horribly sorry," he would say. "Hello, Miriam, Bob.
Awfully sorry not to be here, Mr Eckles, but something
came up at about four in the office, and I was able to catch
my man in Philadelphia and rush down there to have a talk
with him. Hello, darling."

And immediately, with that confidence and friendliness
and charm that were his peculiar assets, Alec would be the
center of the group, playing a few sensational bridge hands,
challenging Bob to three games of backgammon, winning
the strange new Englishman just as inevitably as he always
won anyone he cared to win. Remembering Merle's sad, shy
sweetness at dinner, glowing from her last words of loving
and despairing "good night," he could do that and yet not
be insincere about it, not be contemptible or false.

Afterward, when the guests were gone, he would say one

or two civil things about lights or weariness or weather or
the friends who had just been with them, and disappear. He
slept in what had once been his study now; there was a bed
there not half as comfortable as his own. When moving,
three weeks earlier, he had made a little ostentatious explanation for the benefit of the servants; he had a heavy cold and
he did not want Mrs Hazeltyne or the baby to get it. But
the trifling cold he had had was long gone, and he did not
come back to his wife's room.

The wretched balancing of scales went on. Susannah suspected from his manner that there were scenes with Merle;
perhaps she reproached him, tried to terminate the fruitless
affair. Sometimes when he came from her he turned toward
Susannah with such a wistful, such a pathetic, effort to
restore the old confidence between them that her heart ached
for him, in spite of its anger and hurt.

But even when that happened she knew from his manner
that the chain that bound him to Merle was not broken. He
would listen nervously for the telephone bell, start up
eagerly. "Was that for me, Frost?"

And if it was for him, he deceived neither himself nor his
wife when he answered it hardily as one man to another:
"Oh, is that you, Hutchinson? Wait a minute, I'll take that
in my study. Windows open in here!" or, "Radio going in
here," or, "Everyone talking in here!" Any excuse would
answer that gave him a chance to say hurriedly and peni-
tently to the woman who held him in so complete a spell,
"So am I. Desperately sorry. . . . No, I didn't mean it. You
were a darling to telephone. . . . Yes. Yes. . . . Yes, you
know I do. . . . Yes."

One cold dark day before Christmas, when she herself was
recovering from a cold brought on by fatigue and worry and
by utter lack of heart in what she was doing, Susannah can-
celed all her engagements and stayed at home on the excuse

that the baby had a cold. It was Nursey's regular afternoon off; Evelina's nap would carry her safely from one until almost three o'clock, and Milly was on hand to make herself useful as an assistant. Susannah, after a delicious hour of play with Evelina, was standing at the drawing-room window looking down into the street, with Evelina in her arms, when Merle Sargent walked into the room.

The two women had not seen each other since late summer, when they had been together on the three-days yachting cruise. It had not been long after that that Alec had made his awkward, ineffectual bid for freedom; since then Susannah had wished neither to see Merle nor to hear her name.

She looked at Merle now with a level measuring gaze that might well have daunted a less confident woman. But Merle had steeled herself to this encounter; she was ready for anything. "She can kick me out, dearest," she had said to Alec at luncheon; "she can have Frost open the door for me. But I've simply got to go see her. Something inside of me—something stronger than I am—is making me go."

"What funny little twist of honesty is that, do you suppose?" he had asked, watching her. "You'll not accomplish anything by it."

"Oh, I know I won't, I know I won't!" Merle's strange eyes had shone upon him darkly. "But I have to go, just the same," she had said.

And now she was here, actually in the stronghold of Susannah's drawing room, nervously putting a hand upon the small Evelina who was in her mother's arms.

"Well, you darling!" Merle said, her eyes all for the child. "How you grow up! And curls! I've not seen the curls before."

Milly, apprised in the mysterious way in which the servants always seem to be aware of what was going on, had appeared in the doorway.

"Take the baby, Milly," said Susannah, "and get her started on her cereal. I'll be there in five minutes."

She turned cold eyes upon Merle, and they walked to the fireplace together. It was just five o'clock, but Susannah made no gesture toward tea; she sat down, and Merle sat down on the wide divan near her and spread out her arms, flattening her palms against the rich, dark red velvet of the upholstery. So posed, she was the incarnation of exotic youth and beauty; she was all in black today, except for a twist of salmon-colored scarf at her throat and the coral balls in her ears. Susannah thought her thinner than she had been, more like a lissom young panther than ever. Lean and young and appealing, Merle tried to smile as she opened the conversation:

"Sanna, I think I'm doing the very hardest thing I ever did in my life!"

Susannah answered unencouragingly, quietly:

"I wonder why, Merle."

"You—you wonder why?" Merle stammered, a little at a loss. This open, undisguised unfriendliness was unexpected. Perhaps she had felt that Susannah would at least keep the surface smooth.

"Because I'm so unhappy," she improvised quickly. "Because I want so terribly not to hurt—not to have any of us hurt—and perhaps to have you understand, Sanna, how—how all this happened."

"All this," Susannah said, without expression.

"Well . . ." Merle began waveringly. And in a rush she added: "You see, Sanna, we're both horribly sorry about this! It isn't what you think—I mean, our just liking each other and being selfish about it, no matter what it costs you! We've tried to break it up—we can't."

"I don't quite see——" Susannah began and stopped. When she spoke again it was in a different tone. "We accomplish nothing by this," she said.

"I came to ask you—I came to ask you," Merle insisted, "if you couldn't possibly see things our way! I know how strange it must sound to you, but, Sanna, it's destroying both of us. And you're not happy! You're not happy. If you were——"

"What on earth," Susannah asked icily, as the other woman paused, "do you expect me to do? I've known for months that you wanted Alec. You don't suppose I'm in any doubt about that? I wouldn't have gone out of my way to talk of it, Merle. But since you've come here to—well, I don't know exactly what to do—I may as well say that I prefer to discuss things that concern us with Alec directly. And really—really," Susannah finished, getting to her feet and moving toward the door, "I haven't anything further to say on the subject."

Merle was up with the quick spring of a panther, between her and the door, holding to Susannah's shoulders with both her young hands.

"Please—please!" she said. "Don't talk that way! Please be honest, Sanna, and help us all! I'm not proud of it—I'm not enjoying it. God knows I've shed more tears in the past few months than in all my life before! But you've got to be generous, Sanna. He says you're the most generous woman in the world. Give him to me! Won't you? Won't you! It's not his money—listen to me, please—*please*—I'd go barefoot with him—I'd go anywhere—any little hole in India or China—where we aren't known—anywhere——"

Susannah shook herself loose and walked from the room. For a few instants the wild rush of words went on; then there was silence. She went slowly down the hall to Evelina's room, sat mechanically handling the baby, her small garments, her gold spoon and bowl. After a while she rang for Frost.

"Did Miss Sargent go, Frost?"

"Yes, Mrs Hazeltyne. I saw her to the elevator."

Susannah brooded, breathing hard. She was completely incapable of thought, she made no attempt to reason. Her emotions swept her consciousness about blindly; now she was rehearsing something that she must say to Alec, now remembering some actual word of Merle's, always fevered, confused, her senses plunging about without order or sequence, her mind one wild confusion. And for a little while she thought that she would die.

❧ CHAPTER XIII ❧

BUT DYING WAS NOT the way out, of course. After a while she was in her room, sitting vaguely at her dressing table; a clock said seven, and 'Liza came in, discreet and light-footed, to say that Mr Hazeltyne had telephoned that he would be late at the office because day after tomorrow would be Christmas, and they were finishing some work.

Day after tomorrow would be Christmas, of course. On a long table specially placed in her room were piled packages ready to wrap with silver papers and dark-blue ribbons. Susannah had decided, in some hour that had held infinitely more energy than she could command now, upon blue and silver for Christmas wrappings. She began to segregate the various gifts: tortoise shell, silver, crystal, silver again. She took them out of delicate papers and sturdy little flannelette bags and clean fine boxes and marked them and tied them and put them back again. Silver cherries decorated Connie's; two little silver deer were tied saucily and tightly to Margot's. The packages looked beautiful when 'Liza began to stack them ready for delivery tomorrow.

"Shall I bring you all those from the closet, Mrs Hazel-tyne?"

"Yes. . . . What is it? I didn't hear you, 'Liza."

"While you're at dinner would you like me to get all the others down?"

"Dinner? Why, what time is it? I'm not dressed."

"Frost announced it about fifteen minutes ago, Mrs Hazeltyne."

"Oh. I'll wash my hands. I thought—I was thinking of something else."

She sat in a stupor over her soup. Tomorrow would be Christmas Eve. It was a bitter dark cold night outside. But high up here in the penthouse there was warmth and tempered light; pink roses sprawled in crystal on the table; pink candles, flanking them in crystal candlesticks, burned bravely. Wind was howling over the roof.

"You don't care for your soup, madam?"

"No, take it away, Frost, thank you." The little oyster dish—whatever it was—bubbled hotly in its silver ramekin. Delicious, for she tasted it and crumpled the slim, crisp hot roll. Salad glistening with oil, Delia's incomparable cold boiled chicken, just enough of everything to be tempting, to make one wonder if it *was* enough. A cool frozen thing in a glass, orange or grapefruit and persimmon and some liqueur, appetizing beyond words. Susannah mussed it with her spoon, smiled an apology at Frost and found her eyes filled with tears. She went quickly back to her package wrapping, and 'Liza followed her there with a small cup of hot coffee.

"Oh, thank you, 'Liza," Susannah said thickly, very busy with pasters and ribbons and tissue papers. Her hands got sticky and black with paste; she stooped at her desk to write "To Evelina's Gran, with Evelina's love and her mother's," and felt her back on fire. She and Alec would have dinner with his mother on Christmas night; an ordeal, but not to be escaped. She would take Evelina to spend Christmas afternoon with her grandmother, and Mrs Hazeltyne senior would explain that she had sent out for the dinner, very much easier and twice as delicious.

At eleven o'clock everything was marked and tied and embellished to the last stage of perfection. 'Liza, loyal and sleepy and admiring, cleared away the scraps and cuttings, and the Christmas gifts stood in a pyramid of glory in the firelight; big ones, little ones, everyone remembered.

Susannah took a hot bath, brushed her hair, opened a window to the sweet piercing night air that cut through the smells of paper and wintergreen gum and crushed peppermints and spilled perfumes like a knife. She got into bed and steadfastly moved her eyes from line to line of her book; she was wide awake at twelve o'clock, when Alec came quietly in, and called him.

He came at once to her doorway, looking tired and a little surprised, and she spoke to him somewhat confusedly, having not planned beforehand exactly what she meant to say:

"Did you get some dinner?"

"Caskey and this fellow from Cincinnati and I had a steak at Tony's."

She did not believe it, but she could question and he asseverate whatever he chose indefinitely. She patted the side of her bed.

"Alec, come sit here. I want to speak to you."

"Wait until I get rid of my coat. I'll come back. It's beginning to sleet, and I'm all wet."

"Didn't you have your car?" She could see the water glistening on his coat sure enough. That much was true. She lay listening to the rattle of doors and the creaking of dresser drawers in his dressing room, her heart beating hard. He would not see it, but it gave her courage to know that she never had looked any lovelier than she did now in her laces and pillows, the cunningly knotted little satin ribbons of her nightgown, the rosy shadows of her low lamp.

Alec, in pajamas and dressing gown, came back. He did

not sit down on her bed as she had invited him, but on a chair a few feet away.

"Dead," he said simply, as an indication that he was not ready for a long talk. She noticed that he looked pale and tired.

"I know you're dead." Susannah felt the membranes of nose and throat tickle as she began; she steadied herself and managed a smile. "Alec," she said, very simply, "why have you stopped loving me?"

"Why do you talk like that?" he countered, speaking in the same controlled key she had used, but with a note of resentment. They looked at each other for a brief second; then Alec averted his eyes again.

"Because, if it's my fault, surely there's something I can do about it, dear," Susannah said.

She was trembling within. But it was not with fear. It was with a wild triumph that she had gotten as far as this, that she had dared to face him with her questions at last.

"Surely," she said, "it's not fair to let me be as lonely— as bewildered as I've been all day and as I was tonight without giving me some reason for it."

"I wish I knew the reason," he mumbled, looking away.

"We've been so happy together," Susannah pursued, swallowing tears now, blinking and smiling over them. "Surely it isn't all going to end like this? There's no quarrel between us, Alec."

"Oh, God, no, there's no quarrel!"

"Then what *is* it? Why can't I get at it? Why can't we talk it over and see what is the best thing to do?"

"It's not as simple as that," he said after a pause.

"I don't think it's simple. I know how much you—how deeply you care for her, and how she worships you," Susannah presently went on. "She was here today; she told me. I was terrible to her—I couldn't stand it. Whatever— whatever you and I decide, it—it stunned me to have her

walk in here, into my house, where I was playing with Evelina. . . . I don't know what I said to her, really, except
that there was nothing to say, that I didn't want to talk to
her."

Alec sat quiet in his chair, his eyes far away, his locked
fingers dropped between his knees.

"She shouldn't have done that, Alec."

"She's a strange child," he said. "She's only nineteen,
after all, and I suppose there's Russian fire in her. I've just
come from the hospital, Sanna. I've been with her since
eight o'clock. She tried to kill herself."

Susannah could only sit staring at him, paralyzed with
horror. She tried to speak and failed; her mouth was dry,
and she felt ice water on her spine.

"She's all right now. She opened her eyes; she knew me,"
Alec went on. "It was a close call; they made a transfusion
at about half past eight, and they were all ready for another
at ten. But she had rallied so well that Stern didn't think it
was necessary. I just telephoned now while I was undressing,
and she's sleeping quietly. She cut her wrists."

"Tonight!" Susannah heard her own whisper against a
background of night stillness and tapping rain.

"About six, the hall man said. A waiter from the grill
across the street had taken her up a cup of coffee half an
hour earlier, and it just happened that he had to check in
his tray and coffeepot and whatever it was. It's a rule. So
he went up, knocked and thought he heard a kind of sighing
noise."

Alec stopped short, straightening his back against his
chair, putting one hand tightly against his eyes.

"I stopped in there about that time," he presently added,
still in a low tone of reluctance and shock. "We got her to
a hospital, and I got Stern. It was tight going for a few
minutes, but we brought her round, and she opened her eyes
and knew me. . . ."

"She was sunk down under the sheet," Alec continued, as Susannah found nothing to say; "she'd been sick—nauseated, I mean—and she had on the hospital nightgown. They hadn't dared move her to clean her up, and she looked like a child; she looked no more than seven years old when she opened her eyes," he went on, thinking only of what he was saying, with small consciousness of his hearer. "My poor little girl, my poor little girl!"

"Alec," Susannah said, finding voice and anger at once, "she is nothing to you! Can't you see the absurdity—the *ridiculousness* of a man in your position following a young girl—being seen with her continually? I'm sorry for tonight. It's shocking, it's horrible. But balanced women don't do things like that—come to see women in their own homes to ask—to demand them to give up everything they have, and then rush off to cut their wrists. I am here with my child and my name and my home and my position, and she steps in to dramatize—yes, and enjoy dramatizing!—her feeling for you, and then does a thing like this. Why, there would be no civilization—there would be nothing——"

She stopped. The look of gray misery in his face did not change. He was staring haggardly into space; he came back to the moment and the conversation with a deep sigh.

"Alec, play fair with me," Susannah pleaded. "Put yourself for one moment into my place."

"Oh, I try to. I try to!" he said, almost absent-mindedly. A telephone in his dressing room rang, and he was instantly beside it. "Yes, yes, yes," Susannah heard him say quickly and nervously. And then, in a tone of relief: "Oh, thank you, Miss—Miss—— Thank you very much. You telephoned Doctor Stern? . . . I'll be in the first thing in the morning. . . . Thank you."

He came back, spoke simply:

"Everything fine. She said Merle hadn't stirred, and that the pulse has been gaining very slowly but steadily.

What a miracle transfusion is! My God, what a miracle!
Life—that's what it is—put from one person into another.
Cancel whatever we're doing tomorrow night, will you,
Sanna, and the night afterward, too?"

"The night after is Christmas night, Alec," she said steadily. "We're to be with your mother. I'm taking Evelina to
Margot's Tree tomorrow afternoon, and we are dining here
alone Christmas Eve.

"Ah, well, that doesn't matter, then," Alec said, absorbed
in his own thoughts. "Well!" he murmured, departing toward his own room. "Now perhaps I can sleep. Whew-w! I
feel as if I'd been dragged through a wringer since this
afternoon. Good night."

"Good night," Susannah said, holding herself quiet. For a
long time after he left her she lay without moving, her
lip lightly bitten, her eyes narrowed, her breath coming
shallow and fast.

It was on New Year's Eve that he told her that he was
going away. The days between that time and the night of
Merle's attempted suicide had been dead days for Susannah.
They had passed in a dark dream. She had moved about
among the shadows of her beautiful home, the costly rugs
and lamps and chairs; she had sat at the exquisitely appointed table like a person under an evil spell. There had
been a ghastly Christmas dinner in the senior Mrs Hazeltyne's handsome apartment; on all sides there had been
presents and bells and tinsel and shop windows trimmed
with silver and scarlet; voices had said, "Merry Christmas,
Sanna!" and she had heard her own voice echoing, "Merry
Christmas!" But none of it had been real.

Alec had all but lived at the hospital where Merle was
slowly coming back to life. He had appeared at his mother's
table for Christmas dinner in a mood of abstraction too
deep to be broken, had roused himself for a few perfunctory

monosyllables, had left early in the evening with a muttered explanation of headache; he had said he felt "rotten."

On the following morning Susannah, hearing him moving about in his dressing room at eight o'clock, had called him into her room. She had been completely dressed; she had turned about from her desk when he came in and had asked him to sit down for a few minutes.

And then, as well as she could remember and follow the course of the imaginary conversation she had been having with him for despairing days and days, she had talked to him. Quietly at first; then the force of her own eloquence, the strength of her case had finally stirred her to bitter feeling and to tears; shaken with the most violent grief she had ever known, she had reminded him of their love for each other only a few years earlier, of their dependence upon each other, of the little girl who had a right to her father's love as well as her mother's.

He had listened, troubled and pale and reluctant, but not affected. He had been sorry, she could see, but then from the beginning he had been sorry. He had never taken a harsh or rigid position. He had appeared only distressed and quiet, as one forced into inevitable action and hating to cause pain.

"Don't cry, Sanna," he had said more than once in sympathy and impatience. It was as if he blamed her for not bearing better a misfortune which equally affected them all, for not facing more courageously a crisis for which he was no more to blame than she.

And on New Year's Eve, after silent days when the somber winter world wrapped in cold had seemed a fitting setting for the icy misery of her feelings, he had said quietly that he was moving to his club.

"When?" Susannah had asked dully.

"Today," he had said.

She was in Evelina's room late in the afternoon, sitting

beside the spattered high chair in which Evelina was squirming and shouting, when he came to the doorway.

"Sanna," Alec said. Susannah, frightened, yet not believing that the moment had come, not knowing what she believed or what was happening, got quickly to her feet and went out with him into the hallway. "Good-by, my dear," he said quickly and quietly. For one moment his arms were about her, and he kissed her lightly on the hair. "Kiss the baby for me," he added and was gone.

Other things happened in the hour that followed. Connie Ide telephoned to know if Susannah would serve in Florence Haviland's place on the hospital board. The Havilands were going away. Poor Walt Haviland had to live in New Mexico for a year at least. There was a telegram from Marie-Thérèse Randall, proudly signed "Marie-Thérèse Ford," for Marie-Thérèse was at last happily a bride, saying: "Brand-new husband insists on meeting you and Mr Hazeltyne. We will be at Weston: please telephone tomorrow. Love." There was a heap of New Year's telegrams on her desk, the envelopes gaily decorated with bells and red ribbons as seasonal messages: "And may the new year . . . our heartiest and most affectionate . . . and including the small person, of course . . . heaps of love and all our good wishes . . . everything good . . . everything happy . . . everything your heart desires . . . may we take this occasion . . . with many thanks for your share in making our own year so happy . . . with unchanged love—in which all the family joins . . ."

Agnes came in, crying. Delia was "terrible sick" with the pain of the ulcerated tooth that was as lar'rge, according to Agnes, as a little chestnut you'd pick off the ground itself, and Agnes wanted to go with Delia to the clinic. Susannah made the arrangements; 'Liza and Frost could serve a dinner for one woman between them. She was dragging herself about her room at seven o'clock, trying to make up her mind about dressing for the solitary meal, when Ross St Hubert was announced.

They stood in her dimly lighted drawing room a few minutes, talking. Susannah looked at him dazedly, trying to think who he was and what he was talking about. She did not ask him to sit down.

He was going to a charity supper and dance at eight o'clock. Every important writer, actor, critic, playwright in the city would be there. Ross had done their most important poster for them; Susannah had seen the picture of the kid in the hospital bed, and they'd sent him a box. What were she and Alec doing tonight?

"He's with his mother."

"You're not free?" Ross's dark face lighted.

"No, I couldn't. He's coming—he's coming back."

"Ah, no luck!" Ross said. "This is really going to be tops, you know. Everyone there. Bee Phipps is singing, and George and Pete are doing their turn from the *Follies*. You'd love it."

Heat and smoke and loud blaring of trumpets and saxophones, confetti and laughter and men and women jumbling about, bumping into each other. It all sounded childish and far away and vague to a woman wrestling with the bitterest realities of pride and love. Whether she said good night to Ross or not, Susannah did not know; after a while he was gone, and into the awful silence of the house pain crept again and rose about her like a tide.

Every lighted perspective of the beautiful rooms said Alec; Alec was everywhere. She could see his fine hand shaking out his dinner napkin, gathering in the tricks at bridge, tying his white tie at the mirror. She could hear his voice: "Sanna, here's a funny one . . . That your new gown? . . . Listen, darling, do we have to go to the Gracie thing?"

Silence. Silence. After a few days Susannah wondered if

it would drive her melancholy mad. Drawn irresistibly to the telephone, she called Alec's club. Mr Hazeltyne had gone with friends to Nassau. Young Potts at the office cheerfully told her the same story. She telephoned the hospital, disguising her voice from the possible suspicion of the nurse who could not by any chance have known it, and asked for Miss Sargent. Miss Sargent had left the hospital a few hours earlier.

"Now, I'll tell you what you'll have to do, Sanna," Margot Fielding said seriously. "You'll lose your mind, this way. Other women—other wives—have had the same thing to face and have weathered it. It happens. Just go on with your life as best you can. Tell people anything: that Alec's in Europe, or that he's in Florida, or anything. Some of them will know exactly what's going on, everyone 'll talk of it behind your back, but nobody 'll face you down, and in a few months he'll be so sick of the whole thing that he'll creep back. And then you can make up your mind that you're going to forgive him or not going to forgive him."

"Forgive him?" Susannah echoed, her lips trembling, her eyes suddenly brimming with tears. "But I love him! If Alec wanted me I'd *always* forgive him. I've no life outside my life with him. My room seems so empty—invitations seem so dead. I've nothing, except Evelina. I can't talk to her! She's too little, thank God, to know anything about it!"

"But, Sanna," Margot said, "that's exactly where you make your mistake. We can't afford to depend for happiness on anyone else; it always spells trouble. You're thin, you're not sleeping, you look ten years older than you are; you sit in that penthouse day after day, crying, breaking your heart, and there's no *sense* to it! If Alec suddenly did walk back into his own house——"

"Oh, don't!" Susannah said, overwhelmed. "He'll never come back! Happiness like that doesn't come back. Oh, I hate her!" she went on, under her breath. "I *hate* her! A girl of nineteen, coming to a strange country, being treated with hospitality and kindness everywhere—befriended by a man like Alec, who's kind to everyone——"

"Alec is as much to blame as she," Margot said in the pause, with a tonic firmness.

"Oh, I know that. But men are simple, Margot; they believe everything women tell them. He thought—and of course her attempting suicide proved it to him!—that she couldn't live without him."

"How you love him in spite of everything!" Margot commented rather than asked, in a low, musing voice, after a while.

"How can I help it, Margot? Alec's the most wonderful person I ever met in my life. You don't know what it is to miss him, having had it all, having had him to talk to, to go about with!"

Susannah stopped, choked. Presently she dried her eyes and cleared her voice.

"He's given me almost all the happiness I ever had," she went on. "Most women don't have hours of it. I've had months and years! Loving him and having him love me, belonging to him, having his arms about me. That's been—elixir. That's been heaven, Margot, and he can't—he can't seem any less to me just because a Russian—a Russian *cat*——"

"Yes—get mad—call her names!" Margot put in, laughing. Susannah laughed ruefully, too.

"You think I ought to buck up, Margot, and wear clothes, and go places?"

"I do. It's the only way. I suppose she's with him in Nassau," Margot surmised, with uplifted brows. Susannah winced.

"I don't know."

"Well, whether she is or not, he'll hear about you, sooner

or later. You've got money and looks and friends. Capitalize
on them. That's what Alec admired first—not stringy hair
and a red nose and reproaches."

"It's never been that," Susannah said with dignity.

"Well, you told me you cried so those last days that you
couldn't talk. Pull yourself together, Sanna. Be seen places.
Talk to the men Alec knows, so that they'll wonder what on
earth was the matter with him. That's the way to fight it.
He doesn't want a divorce any more than I do. He just
doesn't want to fail Merle because, in that lovely English
voice of hers and with those Russian eyes, she's flattering
him within an inch of his life."

"Dorothy's party, do you think?"

"Certainly go to Dorothy's party, and have your photograph taken with what's-his-name, the fascinating Captain
Eckles. Treat Alec's performance as the—the whim of a
crazy man!" Margot said, snipping off a strand of blue baby
wool definitely, and holding a small square blanket up for
final inspection. "Lord, I wish they stayed little like this!"
she murmured.

"Ross wants me to go to Boston for the big picture show.
It's a loan exhibition for some charity, and the Dexter
Medal. His sister's going up from Washington; I could stay
at the hotel with her."

"Well, why not? It 'd be thrilling to be there, wandering
about with everyone identifying you. How are they going?
Flying?"

"I believe Ross is. I don't know how his sister is going."

"Well, go. It 'll shake you up. Got clothes?"

"Oh, I've always got clothes!"

"I haven't," Margot said. "It isn't that I don't buy
them," she added thoughtfully, "but I simply never seem
to have them. If it's Miami, I've got splendid things for
winter sports. If its St Moritz, I've got nothing but shade
hats and linen suits. In Paris in winter I seem to have

trunks full of organdies, and right this minute I have to go pour for a tea at the Italian Consulate, and I'm reduced to hostess dresses and evening gowns. When we were first married I'd have one dress and wear it to everything, but now . . ."

Susannah was listening with an abstracted half-smile.

"Margot, Ross is making violent love to me. Does that matter?"

"Doesn't he make violent love to everyone?" Margot asked practically.

"Well, exactly," Susannah said. "But I think—probably —to only one woman at a time," she added moderately.

"Oh, that of course!" Margot conceded with a little laugh. "But he is one of the fascinating persons of all time," she added. And after a moment she asked, "What do you call 'violent love,' Sanna?"

"The sort of thing he does," Sanna answered indifferently. "Flowers—compliments—the usual thing."

"Do you like him, Sanna?"

"Oh, very much! You have to like him."

"Like someone—something—anything!" Margot advised her fervently. "Keep going, having your hair done, being seen places! Don't slump. The worst of us women is, when anything goes wrong, we slump. Don't have anyone tell Alec that Susannah never does anything but sit around and cry."

"You're good for me, Margot," Susannah said, gathering her wraps for departure. She stopped to kiss her friend good-by and went out to her car. It was half past three o'clock on a burgeoning wild day that held in its freshness of winds and height of cool blue sky an untimely hint of spring. Phillips set her down at the wide steps of the big Museum. Susannah dismissed him; she would walk home presently.

She went up the steps and through the turnstile at the

doorway and into the great, softly warmed spaces of wide stairways and arches; sauntered up the stairs, drifted into one room in a long chain of rooms where canvases of Romney, Constable, Lawrence, Reynolds hung in dignified beauty upon expertly lighted gray walls.

He was there; he was waiting. Their hands touched, and their eyes smiled at each other. They went on together, stopping before this canvas and that, Susannah amused at the detail of a Guardi, Ross studying the bold brushwork of a Sargent.

"You couldn't come on with me at five to a brawl at Valetto's?"

"Never at five. I've let Nursey go, and I'm always at home then for Evelina's bath and supper."

"Let Nursey go? Why?"

"Bossy. We never really liked each other. This way works beautifully."

"Have you decided about Boston?"

"I think so. It would only mean one night, wouldn't it?—the two o'clock train on Monday, getting there at about seven for dinner, and the—say ten o'clock train back on Tuesday. I'd only be away from the baby one night."

"That's all. Or you could fly. I'm going up—I've got to, day after tomorrow. I'll make reservations for you at the hotel."

"Your sister's coming up from Washington?"

"Lavinia, yes. But she's going to fly, make one trip of it, and have her New York visit on the way back. Why not come, Susannah? As well do that as anything else. We'll take a good walk Tuesday morning, get on the noon train—all three of us—and lunch on the train. It 'll be fun."

Susannah sighed, her face very serious as she walked on past the old canvases. Nothing was very much fun.

"Where's the picture now, Ross?"

"It went up last week. It's probably hung."

Well, it was one of the things one did. Went in beautiful evening regalia to galleries, met dignitaries, talked art to the little group of art patrons who had arranged the loan exhibition. She and the artist and his pretty little blonde sister would walk about among the crowd and be pointed out . . .

"I'll truly make up my mind tonight, Ross. I'll telephone you in the morning, positively."

"I couldn't come up tonight and have a bite of dinner with you and find out how you feel about it then?"

"We're having a foursome dinner and bridge at Jean's."

"Have a headache instead."

She laughed wearily. A faint incessant headache, a strain from too many tears, was always with her now.

"I can't. But I'll telephone you."

He walked home with her; saw her into her own elevator. When she had left him he took a telegram from his pocket.

"Regret to inform you loan exhibition opening postponed one week," the telegram said. "Death of mayor's wife causes change of date. Arrangements otherwise as scheduled for one week from original date. Kindest regards."

It was signed by the chairman of the Boston Committee for the Loan Exhibition. Ross looked thoughtful as he re-read it. Afterward he tore it to small fragments and dropped them into a convenient rubbish can in the street. As he turned toward his next stopping place in Valetto's studio he began to whistle softly.

CHAPTER XIV

BOSTON LOOKED DARK and forbidding in the blackness of a winter night. Snow was piled up in the streets; a bitter wind blew across the snow. Susannah, wearied and flushed from four and a half hours in the Boston train, looked about the station confusedly. Ross was there; he came forward, smiling in relief, and took possession of her and her bag.

"You! Shouldn't you be at the gallery, fighting about something?" Susannah said, hurried along by him through the churning confusion of the big station, helped into a taxicab, and smiling from the richness of her heavy furs at her companion.

"I couldn't have you arrive and run all this yourself," he said. He had registered for her at the big hotel; they went upstairs at once, and Susannah took possession of a luxurious room, as she had taken possession of so many luxurious rooms in London, in Paris, in Miami, everywhere.

Pink lights and pink satin comforter, rosy rugs and rosy garlanded curtains. The black night was shut away now, and everything was cozy and snug. In her big bathroom the towels were pale pink and the soap pink; Susannah took her time about changing her clothes; the reception was not until nine o'clock, and they certainly did not want to be the first persons to arrive at it.

"Is your sister here?" she said, coming out to join him in the sitting room of the suite half an hour later, at her loveliest in peacock-green brocade. Ross was superintending the arrangement of a little supper table by an open coal fire. "Oh, this is delightful!" Susannah went on. "Let's take it very easy, and be late at the party!"

"Let's!" he agreed, with a flash of white teeth in his dark face.

She took a velvet chair by the fire and commented approvingly upon the hotel.

"I've never been here before, and I think this is lovely."

"I've ordered practically nothing. Oyster stews and salad and cheese."

"It's a night of all nights for oyster stews. There seems to be so much more winter than we need this year. I'm so horribly tired of cold, and too hot places, and going from them out into *cold* again," Susannah complained. "Where's your sister?"

"I don't know. She hasn't sent me any word. Exactly like Lavinia; she never lets anyone know what she's doing. But she'll be here," Ross said easily. The waiter put the oyster stews on the table and disappeared. "The truth is, Sanna," Ross went on, when they were alone, "the mayor's wife died on Friday, and they've put off the show."

"Oh? For how long? You might have told me before I got myself into evening clothes."

"Week from tonight."

"Oh, dear! When 'd you know, Ross?"

"Only today."

"Stupid!" Susannah said. "Perhaps Lavinia saw something about it in some paper. I saw the newspaper notice of the funeral, or something," she added, busy with her oysters. "But it never occurred to me that it would change the plan. Well, that means going back—with the trip for nothing——"

"Don't say 'for nothing'! *This* is something," the man said mildly.

"Oyster stew is certainly something. I never tasted anything more delicious! But just the same it's maddening to have come all this way, and then have the thing put off."

"One of the dear ladies who was buzzing around the galleries yesterday told me that it would give them more time to sell tickets," Ross said. Susannah's eyes came to his suspiciously.

"Ross, you knew yesterday!"

"No, no, no, that was today."

"Well," she said, with no further comment, "it's eight o'clock. And I think the Symphony is here. We might slip in, a little late, since we're both dressed."

"Let's sit and talk instead," he begged.

Her level smile broke over him good-naturedly.

"Let's not. This illicit little dinner is quite excitement enough for us."

"Ah, but, Sanna, it's such fun to be here together, just you and I, in a strange city, with the wind howling and a storm coming along! Why should we barge out into the bleak unfriendly airs of Boston? Let's sit and talk."

"Let's get a newspaper and find out if the Symphony is here. And after it you'll take me to the train."

"The train?" he asked in dismay.

"Certainly, you idiot. Do you think I want to spend the night and fill tomorrow morning somehow and not get home until five, if there's nothing to keep me here?"

"Why isn't this fun enough to keep you here?" Ross asked reproachfully.

"This is very nice. Only I'm sorry I didn't know in time to spare myself the trip," Susannah said inflexibly but mildly, "and I've got to get started back tonight."

"Sanna, what a Puritan you are!"

"I'm such a Puritan," she said, laughing yet annoyed,

"that the puritanical aspect of all this never occurred to me for one instant. I'm a married woman with a child, and I can go where I please without getting any thrill from the naughtiness of the escapade. If I wanted to, I'd go to Paris with you or any other man and let the gossips say what they liked and think what they liked! But I came up here to see the Loan Exhibition, and as there isn't any, I'm going home. You're an extremely charming person, Ross," Susannah added lightly, crossing behind his chair on the way to the telephone, "but I wouldn't come all this way just for an oyster stew with you. We can have one at my house any time you like!"

She called the porter's desk, asked about trains. There was a train at ten-twenty, a midnight train. The midnight train, then. A drawing room for New York. And have the lower made up.

"Now, what about the Symphony?" she asked, coming back to the table. The waiter was taking away plates and substituting the salad course.

"Get me the newspaper from the table in that room," Ross said to the man, indicating the door opposite that of Susannah's bedroom. Her eyes went to his again.

"Is that your room?"

Ross did not answer until they were alone again.

"Why not, if we are so sure of ourselves?" he asked. "I thought Lavinia was coming when I engaged the suite. I thought you two would be in there and I'd be in here. I'm sorry if you don't like it."

"I don't like it at all," Susannah said simply. "It seems to me rather—elementary. It puts me in a silly position, Ross, racing up here to look at my own picture, and finding that even that excuse has been taken away from whatever brought me here!"

"I suppose I was a fool to think that you might like a little break like this, Sanna; the fire and the dinner and you and I here, and nobody the wiser. I'm not," Ross said in dignified resentment, "—I'm not so elementary as to suppose that it would go any further than that. Our dinner and an hour or two of talk, and then good night. And breakfast in the morning, and perhaps an hour at one of the old bookstores. You and I had a marvelous hour at an old bookstore down on Astor Place the other day. There are bookstores here——"

"I know there are," Susannah responded crisply, as he paused. "And there's a Symphony concert, I believe, and there's a train at eleven. It's made up at eleven, at least, and I'm going to be on it. So!"

"I can see nothing of a concert," Ross said sulkily, rustling pages. "I don't see why you can't be friendly. We've been meeting each other, looking at pictures and having walks, all week. Now you quite suddenly have gone *mean*."

"If there isn't a concert there's a movie," Susannah said, sitting down beside him and holding onto the other side of the newspaper. "Yes, there's a picture that I want to see, and there's the Broadway company in *Hollywood Next Stop*. Have you seen it?"

"No," he said. He threw aside the paper and put his arm about her. "Be nice to me," he said. "If you were living at this hotel you might ask me to dinner and sit and talk books for a while—literature or charities or art or whatever you like."

"That would be different. I don't feel conversational," Susannah said definitely. "I'm going in now to change and pack. I'll be out in fifteen minutes, and we can take my bag to the station, and have the taxi man check it."

"Why won't you stay here and go down with me tomorrow? Why do you have to join with every other dear good decent woman in the world in thinking there's something wrong because a man and a woman happen to stay at the same hotel? Be a sport, Sanna. Lavinia may get here any minute; really she may. And you know me well enough to know that the minute you say you want to turn in I'll walk into that room there and lock the door."

"Of course I know it. You're the one whose mind evidently runs along the usual lines, Ross. It's simply that I don't want to stay, that I wouldn't have come if I'd known that the exhibition had been postponed, and that I'll be much happier getting home for Evelina's breakfast tomorrow!"

Briskly and composedly she returned to her room, dressed and packed, and came out to Ross looking quite her sophisticated best in her trim hat, heavy furs, white gloves. A bellboy was summoned, her bag went downstairs; she and Ross followed it. Susannah affected to enjoy the movie immensely, despite the sulphurous silence of the man beside her; he left her at her train at twenty minutes before twelve.

"I hope you're not angry at me?" he said wretchedly, in the station. Her eyes met his unsmilingly.

"I think I am," she said measuredly. And when she was alone, the metal door of her drawing room locked, her reading light turned on, and herself comfortable in the smoothness of the wide bed, she looked off her magazine thoughtfully for a moment and repeated the phrase aloud: "Yes, Mr St Hubert, I think I am. I think that was rather a—rather a low thing to do. I think it is exit for you from now on."

He came to see her two days later and was dismissed. Even before Susannah could tell him that their friendship was at an end he knew it, and begged her not to send him away, to forgive him what was at worst a stupid thing to have done.

"It isn't a case of forgiveness, Ross. It's a case of my drifting into something that my heart isn't in at all. I don't blame you; I blame myself. It *was* rather thrilling to meet you at the galleries and walk and have tea. The old bookstore was fun. But I've let Nursey go now, and I'm busy.

And the Boston experience made me realize suddenly that—well, that my heart simply isn't in it at all."

"But I can come to see you?"

"After a while. I'm worried now, Ross," Susannah said honestly, going to the door with him. "I'm not in the mood for engagements."

"I know what you're worried about, of course."

"Well——" she said forlornly. He stooped and kissed her hand quickly and went away, and Susannah went back into the empty house.

CHAPTER XV

THE ENDLESS DAYS WENT BY; Susannah felt so wearied by unavailing thought that they all merged into one, and there was no morning, no afternoon, no time. The endless nights wheeled in blackness and cold over the city; snow fell white and pure in a gracious, unwrinkled mantle, became grimed and spotted and heaped into harsh banks hardly more manageable than so much coal, was shoveled away. And before the spades had stopped clinking, a fresh delicate fluttering of white filmed the sidewalks again.

Evelina was zipped snugly into eiderdown-lined garments of dark blue, her cap was firmly tied, her small fat hands were engineered into tiny gloves, and she and Milly went every afternoon into the Park with a bucket, a spade, and two green tin molds with elephants stenciled upon them. They returned rosy and exhausted two hours later, and Susannah welcomed her daughter with hungry kisses, and began the happy process of getting her out of her clothes, into her warm bath, into a great soft warmed towel, into her mother's arms.

After that there were cereal and rusk and applesauce and sometimes a small section of molasses taffy measured out as carefully and conscientiously by Susannah and Milly as if

Evelina were not going to smear at least half of it on her face. Then Evelina had to be superficially sponged again as to visible portions of her person, and became highly entertaining in the warm, well-lighted nursery, in a desperate effort to postpone her bedtime. She dashed about, beaming through chair backs and under lamp shades, in effusive "peekaboos"; she whispered "pitty!" to her mother's rings; and plastered soft little meaningless kisses on her mother's cheeks.

In bed at last, she beat upon her blankets resentfully, accompanying the exercise with a gradually diminishing grumbling and scolding that presently died away into complete silence. Susannah usually sent Milly out to her supper and loitered in the nursery until the performance was over. Then came the loneliest, the hardest hour of her day; the hour that had always brought Alec home.

She would go into her bedroom and stand at the window staring aimlessly down at the lights of the city, pricking through the lengthening dusk of March and April; she would mechanically brush her hair, perhaps change her gown for dinner; she had no spirit left to go out even to the simplest of social gatherings. Theater and opera had lost their charm; voices and questions hurt her; she shrank away from curious eyes.

Now and then she went to dine with Alec's mother. The two women did not discuss him. The older Mrs Hazeltyne might ask if Susannah had had any word from him; Susannah's answer was always a brief negative. There was no real congeniality between them, but Susannah clung to anything that was a tie with Alec, and in the atmosphere of his mother's old-fashioned elegant rooms she felt safe; she did not have to do any pretending and explaining. Sometimes she took Evelina to see her grandmother in the afternoons; once the older woman expressed some anxiety about Alec's son—something had gone wrong at school and little Phil was unhappy—and Susannah took the long trip to Pomfret to see him. But the boys were on a tramp, it appeared; they had started early on the day of her visit and would not be back until night, and Susannah returned to town with no news of the child, except that he was physically well and that his teachers were inclined to think his complaining letter had been written in a passing mood of discontent.

On a certain April morning when fresh winds were ballooning galleons of cloud against a blue sky, and crocuses and tulips were beginning to go about town in rickety horse-dragged carts, a certain young lawyer called upon Susannah. He was representing Mr Hazeltyne, he explained, in the matter of the divorce.

Susannah listened to him with what stunned endurance she could muster until she understood that Alec was asking her to go to Reno and set him free. Then she coldly requested him to leave the house.

"I cannot discuss this at all. I think that's all we have to say to each other."

"You mean that you refuse, Mrs Hazeltyne?"

"I mean that I absolutely refuse."

"And if my client went to Reno himself, or applied for a divorce through the French courts?"

"Then I would fight it."

"Mrs Hazeltyne, you appreciate that these are very delicate matters, and that it is as—as trying for us lawyers sometimes as for our clients," Mr Baker said pleasantly. "Do you mind telling me why you refuse? Mr Hazeltyne, before he left for Europe, placed this matter in our hands. It would simplify things very much if you would be kind enough to tell me just what your position is."

"I don't consider that it in any way concerns you," Susannah said, trembling.

"Only in a professional way, of course."

"Then you might tell your—your client that for the sake

of my child, my position, for his own sake, I will not consider a divorce, now or at any time!"

"He is prepared to make you a very generous arrangement, Mrs Hazeltyne."

"I have asked you to consider this interview as ended," Susannah said over her shoulder, from the window.

"I don't mean only in the matter of alimony," the lawyer hastened to say, on an apologetic note. "I mean as far as the child is concerned. Mr Hazeltyne proposes to leave the little girl entirely in your hands."

"If you don't mind——" Susannah said, in a tense voice.

"Exactly. Mr Hazeltyne," Franklin Baker pursued lightly yet determinedly, "will probably not return until the fall. But we are in touch with him. He is reluctant, I know, to be the one to ask for this divorce. That's very natural. He wishes to protect you. He made a point of our not annoying you in any way. At the same time, since this has been put into our hands, I would like to ask you one question, if I may. Am I correct in believing that you went to Boston on the nineteenth of January and remained there for the night in the company of Ross St Hubert, the portrait painter?"

Susannah walked swiftly from the room and through the adjoining dining room to the pantry. Frost was there cleaning silver in the company of the admiring Agnes.

"Mr Baker is leaving, Frost. Will you see him to the elevator?"

She went back to her own room. The taste of the late interview was like an actual acid poison in her mouth. Susannah jerked her head, trying to be rid of it, but her whole being was shaken, and her breath came shallow and quick. It was as if spirit as well as body trembled at the indignity, the insult that this pleasant-voiced stranger had been empowered to come and offer her.

After a luncheon in which she merely played with the food that seemed to be made of plaster of Paris and chalk, she dressed herself for the street and walked rapidly, feverishly, to Margot Fielding's house. Margot had her own heavy anxieties now, for Jane, seven years old, had acquired an infected ear, and the doctors were allowing Jane another twenty-four hours of fever and pain before deciding upon surgery. Margot looked tired, and her face was drawn with anxiety, but her patient was asleep, and she could spare Susannah an hour's talk.

"It doesn't sound like Alec!" Susannah finished, her color faded to ash, her eyes haggard, when she had finished her story.

"It isn't Alec. He simply discussed divorce with this lawyer, and the rest is the lawyer's own idea. Those are the methods they use," Margot said. She cocked her head toward the sickroom, listening.

"Margot, your heart's in there with Janey. My troubles can wait."

"No, no, Sanna. It's good for me to think about something else. No," Margot said, resuming the subject closest to Susannah's heart, "all divorces are like that, more or less. It's a cold, grisly business. It oughtn't to be allowed!"

"But if there weren't divorce," Susannah reasoned, "then Alec would be tied to a woman of whom he's tired, and I'd have to go on pretending that we loved each other."

"And a good thing, too," Margot persisted stoutly. "You can't keep people loving each other at honeymoon heat. But you *can* preserve the decencies! And that's exactly what Alexander Hazeltyne isn't doing, and I must say I'm disgusted with him, and Dud is, too. Alec's first wife, Betty Livingston, was having affairs all over the place—Alec would have brained her eventually if a merciful Providence hadn't taken her off in the nick of time. She was a complete little fool! Then he gets a woman like you, Sanna, a woman *everyone's* in love with, and he must needs run after a little Russian—*puppet*, like Merle!"

"Margot, you're so comforting! What will I do?"

"I've been thinking it over for days. I'd simply go away," Margot said.

"I know; you said so on Sunday. Dud said to go to California to Mother. She's been there with Aunt Nona for six weeks, and they seem to be getting along serenely enough. But I can't do that! They think of me as at the very peak of happiness and success, and God knows I was!" Susannah said, tears suddenly flooding her eyes. "I can't go out there and be just one more divorced woman with a— with a grievance, and an alimony, and a child! It's for his sake as well as mine that I *won't,*" she finished, in a lower, stubborn tone that was perhaps partly to convince herself.

"I don't think you should," Margot said promptly.

"Don't?" Susannah echoed, encouraged. But immediately she looked away into space again. "I don't know what to do," she said.

"I think he'd marry Merle instantly, if he could," Margot said. The words touched the other woman like flames.

"You do think so?" she asked, in a sick voice.

"Oh yes. And when I think of any sane man marrying that—that superficial little transparent——" Margot hesitated over several nouns, finally chose a mild one. "That *person,*" she said. "That complacent little self-centered egotist! Well, there's no use discussing her. It's you I'm interested in. I agree with you, I think it would be a mistake to go to California. There's a regular colony of divorced women there, comparing incomes and playing bridge. You'd hate it! No, you go somewhere else."

"Easthampton," Susannah suggested, with a little twist to her lips.

"Heavens, no! Not there. Listen, Sanna," Margot said reflectively. "What about your little place up in Connecticut —or is it over the Massachusetts border? Didn't Alec buy you a little farm up there a year or two ago?"

Susannah's face suddenly brightened: Margot, watching her, thought that she had not seen it so interested—so like the old Sanna—for many weeks.

"At Pemberton!" Susannah said. "My farm, I'd forgotten it! But it's an adorable place—it's wonderful. And alone, and quiet——" She interrupted herself, her face clouding. "But then he would think that I'd go there, he might remember it?" she submitted, on a questioning note.

"Well, if he did, Sanna?"

"Yes, of course." Susannah laughed ruefully. "If he only would!" she said honestly. And then, with irrepressible optimism: "He might, you know, Margot. If the baby and I were there, and it was summer, and he drove up just to see how we were getting along—he must feel *something* for us—he must still *like* us——"

Her throat closed and her eyes filled.

"Is it modernized, Sanna? Is it fit to live in?"

"I don't know. I don't know anything about it, really, except that the outside is perfectly enchanting. Colonial, with chimneys, and tremendous trees, and with an old stone wall half propping the house and half holding the garden. We bought it——" Her voice dropped, softened. "Ah, that was a happy day," she said, under her breath. "We were driving through, on our way up to the Rogers' camp, and we stopped to have a tire changed, and we saw this farm. It had a big sign on it, and Alec and the Pinckneys and I walked about it, and I simply went mad over it. Well, it seemed that Alec walked over to the little real-estate office before the tire was finished, and about a month later, one night at dinner, he handed me a long envelope with a deed in it, and said, 'There's your summer home!' That was before Evelina was born, almost two years ago, and I've never seen it since. We could go there, couldn't we? We could go there. Nobody 'd know, and nobody 'd care where we were. It wouldn't be *too* primitive, and I could fix it by degrees." Her face grew thoughtful. "It doesn't solve anything—it's running away, really?" she said, again on a musing note.

"He who fights and runs away may live to fight another day," Margot quoted bracingly.

"Yes, and this is a fight," Susannah conceded. Her narrowed eyes were fixed on space; she spoke dreamily. "For the first time in my life I have to fight," she said. "I have to do something that will interest him, that might hold him. This might be it."

❧ CHAPTER XVI ❧

IT WAS NOT, as she had said, a solution, but the thought of escape from the problems and humiliations of the present situation was a bracing one, and Susannah walked home from Margot's with a quickened pulse, with a mind diverted from the wearisome track of despondency in which it had struggled so long.

She stopped in to spend a few minutes with Alec's mother. The old woman, encased in her luxurious setting of rugs and cushions, attentive servants, delicate meals, flowers and soft lights, was often lonesome and depressed at the best of times; Susannah knew that she was anxious and apprehensive just now about Alec's domestic affairs.

Coming in to the close, scented atmosphere from the fresh air of the street had always had the effect of checking Susannah's spirits: it had that effect today. There was a sort of elegant deadness here; a thick clothy richness to everything that definitely subdued her. Old Mrs Hazeltyne's magnificent friends had made her endless magnificent presents in the course of the long years; they were all about her, onyx and crystal lamps, silver trays and frames and vases, books in tooled leather. There was nothing in her entire apartment that was not expensive and heavy.

Her dress today was expensive and heavy, too; real lace

tumbled in frills over her discolored, lame old hands; her fingers were crusted with gems that sparkled as she poured tea into gold-flowered cups that stood in gold holders.

Susannah stretched her young length in a winged leather chair, sighed, setting aside her handbag and gloves. She and the older woman talked sympathetically enough, but at first a little guardedly, each one afraid to stir the deeps of her feelings, to embarrass herself or her companion with an unexpected show of emotion.

But presently, after she had drained her first cup, looking keenly across it now and then at her daughter-in-law, Alec's mother asked quietly but abruptly:

"He's with her all the time, eh?"

"I suppose so," Susannah answered, also quietly, but with a sudden narrowing of her eyes and tightening of her mouth. "Of course I don't know anything about what Alec's doing, or where he is, now," she added lightly. "He isn't at home, you know."

"He went to Nassau, he made a flying trip to London," his mother said. "He slept here two nights a few weeks ago—I couldn't get anything out of him. Now I believe he's gone to San Francisco. He's reorganizing the agencies out there."

"I had to telephone the office about a very urgent cable from England," Susannah said. "They said he had gone West."

"Reno, perhaps," his mother suggested. Susannah raised darkened eyes.

"He can't, unless I consent," she said quickly.

"I thought they could."

"Not without the other party's consent. He's asked for it, and I've refused it."

"You told me." His mother's voice dropped, and there was a silence. "He's crazy," the other woman said simply, then. After a moment she added: "He wants to bring that woman here."

Susannah felt a stabbing pain in her very vitals. She leaned back, weak and sick, her voice dragging thick in her throat.

"Merle?"

"Whatever her name is. Yes, Merle."

"What did you say?"

"What could I say? I'm a civilized woman, after all. I'd give her a cup of tea, I suppose, and remark that at last we were having some real spring." Old Mrs Hazeltyne's voice, under its sharp, scornful bitterness, held a hint of hard resignation. "We live in today," she said.

Susannah spoke after a long silence, during which she had stared blindly into the coal fire that was half asleep behind old-fashioned polished steel rods.

"I hang onto him, I follow him and coax him. I cry about it and pray about it," she said in a low, thoughtful tone, as if she spoke to herself. "I keep repeating that he's crazy—that he'll come to his senses. But perhaps I'm all wrong. Perhaps we're all crazy—all blinding ourselves deliberately to things that are perfectly plain—perfectly obvious. He's tired of me, and whatever I do only makes him more tired of me—more anxious not to see me, not to be drawn into scenes! My God," Susannah murmured, getting to her feet now, gathering up her furs, "how hard it is to believe that anyone's stopped loving us! Such glorious love—an ocean of it—there whenever I wanted it—turning life magic. And now, not even liking—not even toleration——"

She was talking to herself, her voice hardly more than a whisper, her eyes brimming with tears as she linked her sables, tucked her bag high under her arm, busied herself with the pearl buttons of her white gloves. The other woman watched her without speaking.

There was a stir behind them. Old Mrs Hazeltyne looked up from the tea table; Susannah wheeled about. Alec and Merle had entered the room and had come toward them.

It was his mother's voice, speaking to Alec, that broke the moment of stunned silence that enveloped all four.

"Well, sir," she said. "When did you get back?"

Handsome, groomed, serious, Alec bent over his mother's chair to set a kiss where her artificial silver curls met the cosmetic smoothness of her forehead.

"Flew," he said briefly. "I left Chicago at nine and had lunch here."

"Sanna, I'm so glad to see you," Merle said, in a timid, friendly voice. Merle wore a gray silk dress with Russian embroidery in rich colors at the smocked neck and wrists, her gray hat had corresponding touches of color in cross stitch, her suède shoes were gray. She did not look smart, she was never smart, but there was a gypsy picturesqueness about her, with her blackened eyelids and gold hair, and the great soft new chinchilla coat that enveloped her would have made her conspicuous anywhere, without any additional detail. Alec was introducing her to his mother; Susannah, occupied only with the need to escape, could hear Merle's pleasant clipped British accents on the murmured phrases, ". . . always wanted to know Alec's mother because he just thinks you're the most wonderful woman in the world" and ". . . you'll have to like me because I like him so much!" as she walked, in a whirlwind of emotions, to the doorway and through the softly lighted foyer and pressed the elevator bell.

Alec was suddenly beside her; ringing the bell again; not protesting her going, but not unsympathetic, either.

"Sorry for this, Sanna," he said. "I wouldn't have barged in——"

A silence. The elevator arrow shot from floor to floor; third, eighth, tenth at last! The heavy doors rattled open.

"Evelina all right?" Alec said. Susannah made no answer; she did not raise her eyes to his.

"All right," she said quickly, impatiently to the boy. He closed the doors reluctantly; it was over. She was out in the sweet languid air of the late spring afternoon, out in the hurrying streets again. Her face burned, her heart hammered, her thoughts were in wild, angry confusion. What sort of a world was it, when a woman's husband, the father of her child, could so encounter her, could so hurt her?

"Or perhaps I'm the fool," Susannah told herself, walking fast and blindly, not knowing where she was going. "Perhaps Alec is the smart one. Love for a few months, a year or two, and then the slate washed clean, and another love! Children? What do they matter? When they're old enough they'll have love affairs of their own, and until then nothing counts. Nothing counts except men meeting women, and wanting them, and beginning to shift their whole lives about so that they can have them."

Alec had seemed quite himself, his happy and occupied self. It was incredible to his wife that while her own life was being rocked by earthquake he could be so simply contented, so groomed, so naturally affectionate with his mother, so proud of Merle. He had carried off an insufferable situation with his own maddening qualities of politeness and consideration, his kindly air of sparing everyone embarrassment.

It was not to be borne! Susannah walked into her own house, went to the nursery, talked quickly, feverishly to 'Liza. She liked 'Liza the best of the maids, and 'Liza adored the baby.

"'Liza, I am thinking of going into the country. You lived in Vermont when you were little, you won't mind it?"

"If it was France or California or one of those places, it 'd be different, wouldn't it?" 'Liza submitted, interested at once.

"This is Connecticut."

"Oh, I'd like it," 'Liza said, her face brightening.

Just a week later they made the change. Susannah moved as hurriedly as she could through the final stages of packing, of dispersing the household staff. She never wanted to see the apartment again, that luxurious place where she had been so happy! She wanted never to see Frost or Phillips or the big car or Agnes or Delia or Milly—kind as they all were, sorry as they all were!—again. She felt that she could not breathe until she was away from it all, off into the clean bare country, alone with her heartaches and her child. 'Liza would help her drive if she got tired; no one else was with them when at last all the leather bags and the boxes were packed in the back of the car and she and 'Liza and the baby started on their long drive.

It was a heavenly spring day after rains; the countryside was basking in green beauty; every dooryard in the little towns and suburbs through which they passed was a bouquet of fragrance and color. 'Liza commented favorably on the landscape; she had been born and bred in country somewhat like this. Susannah breathed deep of it; Evelina, sprawled in 'Liza's lap, asleep, seemed to breathe deeper, too. The baby's face was flushed to exquisite apricot; her dampened curls were plastered on the delicate velvet of her white temples.

"There might be peace here," Susannah thought.

They reached the little farm late in the afternoon, when the languor of the untimely heat of the day was lying on the fields of buttercups and on the hard-budded branches of the great trees. 'Liza carried bags and boxes into the house with the help of the Trimler boy. Laverne was installed, grim, capable and cleaner than a willow whip in the kitchen.

"Them men are goin' to git this place a mass of mud, Mis' Hazeltyne," observed Laverne. "Well, you look like you'd had a real good nap!" she added, approving of the dewy-eyed and red-cheeked Evelina, sitting on 'Liza's lap in a kitchen chair. "I made up beds like your letter said," added Laverne, "and I got milk from Swineburgs' until we git a caow, and

I've redded up some. The place ain't anything like clean yet, but it takes time, these places that hev been shut up for years. You'll have to take one day off my month, Mis' Hazeltyne, for I went t' my aunt Kate Trimler's funeral last Tuesday—she went off very sudden, an' nothin 'd do for Al but I'd go over there an' run things. Now you'll want to see upstairs, an' I've got the stoves goin' . . ."

Laverne Trimler talked all the time, but so did 'Liza, on the slightest encouragement, and Susannah decided that they could meet each other on equal terms. She went about with Laverne through the primitive roomy place, finding the old-fashioned comfort of lamps and airtight stoves everywhere; the halls were like iceboxes, but her own blankets and sheets were warm and comfortable on the beds, and a filling New England supper including honey, biscuits, ham, hard-boiled eggs, tea, apple pie, doughnuts, cheese and crabapple jelly was waiting for her when she was ready for it.

First the little jars of artichoke paste and prune had to be opened and warmed for Evelina, and the rich country cream stirred into the milk for her gold cup. The child was drowsily deep in her small bed when Susannah descended for her own supper. She ate it thoughtfully, silently, alone, but somehow there was peace in her heart.

After dinner she walked out into the dooryard in early spring dusk. The air was chill; bare branches clicked high above her head, were still again. The sweetness of the country night, the peace of it, flowed about her like an anesthetic.

The farmhouse stood back from the road by perhaps a hundred feet, on a little rise that was reinforced by a rock wall, deep embedded in moss and grasses. Back of it a home orchard and paddocks rose up against a long slope of hill; the tumble-down old buildings and the straggling fences were made beautiful tonight by the lingering darkness that was mingled with early moonlight. Grass was springing up everywhere, and although the great elms above the gracious line of the low roof were still bare, willows along the creek were spouting up like fountains of green, and Susannah, in the exquisite stillness, could hear the shouting of boys a quarter of a mile away in the village, and the peeping of frogs somewhere along the weedy creek where the cresses were already crowding together on their jointed stems.

Nearer was the pleasant domestic warmth of the kitchen, with the occasional clatter of a pan and the girls' voices that showed that 'Liza was helping Laverne in good country fashion and that they were making friends. Susannah walked down a crooked, deep little lane to her own gate and leaned upon it, looking down the road.

A man and a woman walked briskly by in the gloom; not country folk, for their voices sounded cultured, and the woman's laugh was unmistakably that of a gentlewoman. They saw Susannah, and their greeting came to her, a man's and a woman's tones together:

"Good evening! Did you get moved in?"

"Oh, very comfortably, thanks!" she called back, liking the flavor of the little neighborly gesture.

"That's good!" They went on into the darkness, and Susannah went back into the house with her heart oddly warmed. She asked Laverne a little later who the two could be.

"That's Terry Duquesne an' his sister Mis' Lambert—she was Anne Duquesne," Laverne answered readily, brushing crumbs into the old black-mouthed fireplace in the dining room. "She's got two children, Jerd and Nancy; they ain't but about ten an' eight, I sh'd guess."

"Widowed?"

"I don't know what possesses Albert Lambert. No, he ain't dead. He was round here a few months ago, when my cousin Lizzie Trimler washed for them. I never heard he was dead, an' I don't know," Laverne added frankly, pausing to rub her chin and look dubiously into the fire, "as I ever heard he was more 'n half alive, Albert. He was kinder "sleep on his feet most of the time. She wan't young when she married him, Anne wan't. She was always kind of bookish and quiet, an' after old Doctor Duquesne died she kep' house for Terry for some little time. However, 'bout 'leven years ago Albert Lambert come back here with his doctor's certificate—Anne was a good bit oldern 'n he was, and som'p'n went wrong. I don't know what 'twas, but he didn't ever practice much; he jest lived on Anne's money, I guess, an' after a while he kinder drifted away. He's in Massachusetts somewheres."

Susannah was wearied, glad to take her glass-bowled lamp at half past eight and go stiffly through the icy hallway up to bed. An airtight stove in her room was roaring away hospitably when she went up, and Evelina, exquisitely asleep in her crib, was so warm in her pink blankets that her mother loosened them about the little shoulders and opened a window with a jerk and a creek to let in the fresh icy knife of the air.

She attempted no reading tonight; her preparations for bed were of the briefest. 'Liza came up and asked if she might leave open the doorway between their two rooms; everything was so still that 'Liza was a little scared, and Laverne had gone home. Susannah agreed, secretly not sorry for 'Liza's nearness, and lights were out in the "old Huntress place" at nine o'clock.

Susannah had not for weeks been sleeping well. Tonight she slept as soundly as Evelina did and awakened with real spring sunshine in the room, to find Evelina, who had been quietly carried off by 'Liza at seven o'clock, returned and sociable, seated astride her mother. There had to be another fire in the stove, for a chill still lingered in the sunny air, but when Susannah went out a little later with 'Liza and Evelina to see what the old farm looked like, there was real warmth in the sun, and the world was brimming with beauty and scent.

There were woody old lilacs on the place; there were roses and grapevines. Only hard leafless branches now, but close inspection showed the buds packed at the tips of the twigs; the early flowers, dogwoods and laurel, broom and fruit blossoms, were already beginning to flower.

For ten years the farm had stood untenanted. The silver barns, the old fences, the sheds and stables were empty and neglected. But Susannah found charm in them all. She and 'Liza and the baby penetrated on into the woods back of the house, mounted the path around the little hill, looked down upon gracious valleys beyond gracious valleys with cows in pastures, farm chimneys smoking, and horses dragging plows through the dark loam.

"Oh, this is a lovely place to be!" she said, going back happily to Laverne's good luncheon, stretching herself out on her bed when Evelina went to sleep, with her steamer plaid over her feet and a good book for company. To read now; one mustn't think.

She kept herself busy. It was easy to keep herself busy as the spring came like a flood tide to the weather-beaten old houses under the new green of the maples, and the village turned itself inside out in house cleaning.

The Trimlers did everything for her. Whatever she needed done could be done and indeed was promptly and efficiently done by a Trimler. They cleaned the garden and put the barn in order; they bought the chickens and found a good, reliable, quiet dog; they built odds and ends of brick bulkhead, fixed the draft in the dining-room fireplace, raked, built bonfires, dragged furniture up and down stairs, brought milk, and carried away Evelina's linen to be laundered. Aged Trimler uncles toiled mysteriously among the farm buildings; a Trimler mother, crisp and friendly at fifty, came over to call with rhubarb pies and a handful of sweet peas.

Susannah gardened vigorously, with Evelina sweet and distracting beside her. She had bookcases built in the old parlor, had the wood paneling of halls and stairways painted cream color, moved things into the hall, moved them back into the room. She gathered flowers and filled the vases with them; wrote her mother cheerful long letters about the adorable old place she and Evelina had found for the summer "while Alec is away"; she read books she had been intending for years to read.

The plumber Trimler installed a bathroom for her. A small bedroom was sacrificed to it, and somehow it never looked like a bathroom; it was the wrong shape; it was too big, and it had two large, ordinary windows. But it was a great comfort, and she felt on the road to being clean again when at last the muddy waters sputtered into the tub that still wore its factory label.

She sent 'Liza away for a four-days vacation and assumed entire charge of Evelina, an exhausting responsibility. And she received a charming call from her neighbors: Anne Lambert and Terry Duquesne. It all helped to fill the time There was so much time to be lived through, somehow!

❧ CHAPTER XVII ❧

ONE JUNE AFTERNOON she went to return the Duquesnes' call. She had seen them several times. Anne's children always cut across the corner of her orchard on their way home from school and were friendly little creatures, getting her name quite readily, and affectionate with Evelina. Terry had stopped in more than once with her letters when he was going home from the village, or called to her on his way down to know if she wanted anything from the store.

Both he and his sister were tall persons with carroty red thick hair, blue eyes, and long features powdered with freckles. They adored each other and Anne's children and were apparently the happiest mortals in the world. Boston had been their home during the winters of childhood. The old place in which they lived now had been their grandfather's house, and his grandfather's before him; it dated back earlier than the Revolution and was filled with enough beautiful old Americana to make it a real museum. Except that Anne never would let anything be merely ornamental; she stuck daisies into old Spode teapots and used Chippendale chairs for garden lunches with complete carelessness.

They were strangely alike, the two, but what was rather brusque in Anne—her deep voice, abrupt movements, crisp

174

comments—was somehow charming in Terry. Susannah liked them both. In their cultural interests, their literary tastes, their simple philosophy of field and kitchen, she presently came to believe them to be almost the wisest man and woman she ever had known.

Three or four times a year they went to Boston for a week or two. They had kinspeople there, took with them the correct clothes, and transformed themselves for that time into the sophisticated folk they really were. But when they got back to Pemberton's peace and beauty, the clean sweet air, their own books and beds, fireplaces and garden, their paeans of gratitude and delight echoed about the house for days. The smell of wood fires, the oaks and maples, the roses outside the dining-room window, the peace of it, the silence, the freedom, the independence—these were their grateful themes when they came home again.

Jerd and Nancy were attractive children; the girl homely but sweet, with gold bands in her big mouth and brown freckles meeting on the bridge of her aristocratic nose; the Loy was blond and lovely and lazy and a little spoiled. Susannah knew at once that he was like the father who never was mentioned.

The old Duquesne house had been built in 1736 at the top of Postroad Hill; a wooden fence skirted the garden, and elms and maples had been set out around the building and on the drive. The village straggling away down the hill was not very different today from what it had been when Washington had ridden through it in buff and blue with mud-splashed saddlebags; but the Duquesne trees had towered skywards, and the garden was a jungle in which moss roses and creepers strangled the old pickets that had once protected them.

Susannah, coming to make her first visit, could see at a glance that the front door was never used. It stood in a sort of tent of lack wooden millwork and was flanked by pointed-topped mullioned windows neatly shuttered on the hot July day. A path led around the house, and she followed it, passing a chintz-curtained bay window so embedded in shrubs that it seemed as if the room it lighted must be lower than the garden level.

At the back were the obvious interests of the whole family. Susannah found the brother and sister there and discovered later that when they were at home they were almost always there. Terry had a typewriter on a long table in the arbor; scattered papers were all about; Anne had a sewing basket. There was a fascinating lawn beneath trees; there were chairs, children's wagons and coasters and toys of all sorts; ladders upon which Terry mounted to prune roses or mend roof shingles, pans into which Anne shelled peas. And there were the pea vines themselves, a tangle of tomatoes, peach trees, long rows of berry bushes, and a distant perspective of sheds where eggs were gathered and paddocks where cows waited to be milked.

They were not only nice people, Anne and Terry, she thought, they were essentially fine. Susannah never had been in the sort of atmosphere they spread about them, and she blossomed in it. There was a sincerity, a simplicity, an honest deep enjoyment of life in their point of view, their ways and pleasures and occupations, which fascinated her and drew her close to them. She had not been two months at Pemberton before she came to feel herself privileged in knowing them at all.

There had been writers in the family; one recognized poet; there had been a portrait painter in England. Upon their walls hung some of his fine, delicate work, a study of their mother as a child, with the hanging straight masses of hair, the scalloped collar of the mid-Victorian era; a portrait of their English great-grandfather, magnificent in flowing whiskers, dreamy of eyes. Books were their daily bread; Susannah was bewildered by the easy scope and variety of their reading, by the readiness with which their long, clever hands could snatch any book from the worn lines of books on their shelves, the swiftness with which their eyes could find whatever passage was needed to clinch a point or illustrate some phase of the talk. Terry was a writer; he had an occasional essay printed in the *Atlantic* and had a small list of slim books to his credit.

When they were at home both dressed rather shabbily. The man wore loose old linens in summer, corduroys and a disreputable thick old leather coat in winter. Anne was eternally comfortable in short skirts, flat heels, loose smocks that changed with the seasons from dark blue chambray to dark blue velvet, but that were always the same in cut.

Sometimes there was company at the Duquesne house, but not often. A certain Sir Noel and Lady Baxter came once and stayed for a week; there were Endicotts from Amherst who were old friends; there were one or two others who occasionally came and went. Anne kept up a vigorous correspondence with someone called "Laura" in Montreal, and someone called "Polly" in Rio. And yet when it was all added together there was so little distraction in their lives that Susannah thought of them as hermits, buried in their sunny back garden, gathering their fruit, lopping branches from blackberry and currant bushes, exclaiming over the rescue of an abandoned kitten in the woods or the establishment of a bird's nest above the kitchen doorway.

They lived, she told them after weeks of friendly study of their lives, like children. Everything interested them, and every day was too short a day. Sometimes she found them cooking busily in the kitchen, or Anne would consult her brother about a salad as if life depended upon it. At other times they would stuff a cut of cheese and a roll into their jacket pockets and be off for an all-day tramp that might not be ended until the moon was shining.

There was an outdoor grill where Anne preserved berries and peaches and crabapples. There were magazines from which they read political or literary essays aloud. There were endless puzzles. Terry solved them, invented new ones. He was never far from a sharp pencil and the little cardboard to which clippings of some start were strapped. And they had the eternal living interest of the children. Whether Terry or their mother loved Nan and Jerd the more, it was hard to say. To both, the young creatures were a lasting delight.

Susannah's whole world changed slowly during that summer. For the first time in her life she seemed to meet herself, to look fairly at this person who was Susannah Farjeon Hazeltyne, to consider what she was and what she might make herself. New vistas opened before her eyes; she began to visualize dimly the responsibility that lies within each human heart; the responsibility of making itself better, raising itself. As the beautiful summer country days went by, the mornings sweet with dew and fragrance and bird songs, the long, happy hours filled with a child's duties of weeding, washing hands, resting, walking over to Grandma Trimler's for the milk, a child's content and confidence blossomed again in her heart. It was good just to be alive, to eat and drink, to put Evelina into the green cart and drag her over to the Duquesnes', to sit in their back garden and watch Terry mending a fishing rod for Jerd, Nan struggling with the typewriting of rules for the new camping club she intended to form among the girls of her gang, Anne feeding an injured baby squirrel with an eye dropper.

The jumbled events of the past few years straightened themselves out into a processional that moved in order before Susannah's eyes. They had been strange years. A few months ago she would have said that they had been utterly happy. Now she was not so sure. Now they seemed to have been happy only with a fool's joy; the surface joy of hurrying and competing; the material joy of food and clothes and ease. Magnificent dinners at which nobody was hungry; glorious operas to which nobody listened; trips on great ocean liners during which no one either spoke of or looked at the sea. It had not been real living; those had not been real friendships or contacts; small wonder that when it had all begun to totter like a pasteboard moving-picture set she had not known any way of saving it.

Sobered and much alone, and yet strangely not unhappy in the new life she had found out for herself, Susannah pondered on these things. All through the long summer days and in the moon-washed summer nights she struggled on with the slow, hard process of finding her own soul, and peace came to her, and the taste of her simple hours was sweeter to her than anything she had ever known.

She thought continually of Alec. It seemed a dream that this definite and masterful man had entered her life, and that she had shared his brilliant scheme for a little while, and that she had loved him with all her heart, that they had traveled, laughed, rejoiced together, and that the fair little rosy Evelina was his child. So complete was the metamorphosis of her soul and mind that the old Susannah seemed a person she could not understand, a person who bought hats and walked in the smartest of tweeds on steamer decks, a person who wore emeralds to first nights at the opera.

All that was over now, and left of the exciting play was only its score—her love for the man who had introduced her to it, her need of him. He would be changed when they met again; she knew herself already changed almost beyond recognition. But he would come back, and she would hear his voice, and this time they would know that it was forever.

Just what Anne Lambert's tragedy—or tragicomedy— was, Susannah could only guess. Anne sometimes alluded to something that had gone all wrong in her life with a sort of amused philosophy, but that attitude did not deceive Susannah into thinking that she would speak easily about it. Albert Lambert was alive. He had passed his doctor's examinations in medicine fifteen years earlier, but he had never practiced as a doctor. And Terry had watched his sister's affair, her surrender to this country lad's wooing, with consternation and amaze. So much Susannah knew. No details were vouchsafed her, but once Anne said to her lightly: "Don't be bitter, Sue. It's a lesson I had to learn, not to be bitter. One may have been a fool, but there's no foolishness like being bitter."

"How much do you know about me?" Susannah asked her on this occasion. She had been spending the afternoon with Anne; they had taken the children up into the woods for an hour.

"More than you think, perhaps. I know you've been badly treated. But you have plenty; you have the old Huntress place; you have Evelina; you have looks. That puts the sum total 'way above the average."

"We don't seem to go by averages, do we? They don't seem to matter."

"No," Anne agreed, smiling ruefully. "They don't seem to matter." Neither woman spoke of her own affairs again.

Susannah walked home alone in early autumn dusk. The day had been warm, but at six o'clock there was a softening coolness in the air; long shadows stretched across the country road; the delicate earlier flowers were gone, but goldenrod and Michaelmas daisies burned in blue and yellow along the edges of the fields, and in Susannah's garden were sunflowers and cosmos, dahlias and hollyhocks, and the inexhaustible marigolds. There was a wide peace and quiet over the world in the resting time of the year; the Trimler cows were filing in toward the shed; an early whippoorwill filled the dusk with his plaintive note.

Evelina and 'Liza were in the side garden. The baby was rushing about in that excess of sportiveness that affects small children and small animals at the close of day. She concealed herself behind shrubs, leaped out at the obligingly amazed 'Liza with screams of triumph, disappeared again. Susannah smiled at the picture; the two figures were part of a bigger picture, and she found it good. Back of 'Liza and Evelina was the farmhouse, sprawling and low-roofed and gracious under its big trees; smoke was going up from the wide old brick chimney into the fading colors of the sky; crows flew homeward with loud caws that seemed to emphasize rather than disturb the composite quiet and homely comfort of the scene.

'Liza, with Evelina dragging to and fro in staggering half-circles the hand that held her, came up to Susannah with an anxious and significant expression.

"There was a telephone message for you, Mrs Hazeltyne. I called the Duquesnes', but you'd left. It's Mr Hazeltyne. He's driving up. He's on his way here now."

♣ CHAPTER XVIII ♣

ONE END OF THE LONG TABLE in the dining room was set for two. Susannah lighted four candles in silver candlesticks that had come with her from China and set them on it. The evening was warm, and candlelight was not so hot as lamplight. She went up and down stairs, looked a dozen times at Evelina, asleep in her crib, stooped to look at herself in her dresser mirror. She was trembling with a wild fear that had happiness in it; this hour had long been awaited; she was not completely unready for it now that it had come. Alec! She had not seen him; she had not heard from him in six long months that seemed as many years. But at last he had come back!

"He phoned from Morristown," 'Liza had said. "So he can't be here much before half past seven."

"No, and we'll have to allow for his not knowing just where the house is." Susannah went restlessly into the kitchen, smiled at Laverne absently with brilliant eyes, stepped out into the warm early moonrise, and paced the brick path of the side yard between the shabby berry bushes and the drying flowers. The air was warm and soft and scented by hay fields and apples and distant brush fires; there was no mistaking this for a summer night: everything spoke of harvest. Winter would be coming as soon as the red leaves had burned themselves away along the low hills against the thinned blue of the skies, winter with pumpkins and snow, and mittens for Evelina, and early dark in the low-ceiled kitchen.

She heard a deep-throated motor throbbing through the dark. Her heart plunged. That was Alec's car; it was coming steadily nearer and nearer; its great eyes were sending fans of light up the narrow lane and flashing on the trunks of the guardian oaks and maples. Susannah walked down the drive and was standing by the garden gate when it stopped.

Phillips was driving. Alec got quickly out. Susannah heard his voice again. The quick, clean, unforgotten voice!

"Get your supper, Phillips, and come back about ten."

Then he turned to her, put his arms about her shoulders, touched her cheek with a light kiss. And Susannah forgot everything except that she loved him and clung to him, her eyes drowned, her breath short, her whole body limp against him.

"Hello, dear," he said, steadying her. "Well——" he added, in a touched voice that he tried to make amused. "Hel*lo!* It's good to see you again, Sanna."

"It's so good to have you here!" she said, regaining her composure, somewhat shamed by his own. "Come in, Alec. You've not had your supper?"

"Supper?" The old notes of surprise. "What time is it?"

"Dinner," she corrected it, managing a shaken laugh. "It's only a little after seven. But we're country people here!"

He looked about the dining room approvingly. The candles were burning bravely; Laverne, all suspicious interest, immediately entered with a tureen of soup.

"My Lord, I haven't seen one of those things for years!" Alec commented, sitting down with an air of heartiness. Susannah introduced Laverne, and he spoke to her pleasantly. The meal began.

"Sanna, you look in the pink," he said.

"I'm wonderfully well. The country agrees with me."

"I thought you might have gone to California."

"No; Mother's gone back to China now. I think she's going to marry her faithful Captain Sweet. She came on here and had a month with Evelina and me, but she hates the hot weather."

"It doesn't seem to have hurt you."

"I like it. Are you just back, Alec?"

"About ten days ago. I drifted around over there—went up to Scotland, went to Budapest. I saw some of the gang at Antibes."

"You've seen your mother?"

"Oh yes; I'm staying there."

"How is she?"

"Fine."

All this for Laverne's benefit, and for the benefit of 'Liza, who was loitering in the kitchen to help Laverne. Susannah was too much excited to eat, but Alec had his usual good appetite and complained that the food was only too good.

"We haven't done much here," Susannah presently explained, nervously filling silences, leading the way to the parlor. "We've done some painting outside, and I've put a bathroom in. There was an old bathroom downstairs beyond the kitchen—the girls use that; but Evelina and I are very luxurious. You were too late to see her. Would you like to take a peep at her?"

"She's walking now, of course?"

"Oh, running. And saying everything. She's completely adorable. It's rather stuffy in here," Susannah said, in the parlor doorway. "Suppose we go out and sit on the steps?"

Alec produced a pipe.

"I ate too much dinner," he complained, as she had heard him complain a hundred times. "I'd put on a pound a day with what's-her-name—Lafayette—cooking for me."

"Sh-h! They hear voices sometimes." Susannah sat with

her back against the railing of the steps, looked up at the stars. A sudden desolate sense of helplessness and failure enveloped her. At the dinner table, in the soft candlelight, with his handsome, keen, interested face opposite her, she had deluded herself for a few minutes with the hope that everything was all right again, that it was only for her to forgive him. Their being together again had seemed the solution; the separation had been a time of conscious nervous strain; Susannah had never received a letter or a telegram without a wild sudden hope that it might be from Alec; she had planned their reunion a thousand times, in a hundred different ways.

But now that they were actually in each other's presence again there was a certain flatness, there was a sense of anticlimax about the situation that daunted her. She could not cope with it. There was neither on his part the honestly penitent and pleading attitude that she had expected nor on hers the softness and pliability. She felt hurt and antagonistic; it was almost as if Alec's coming were an interruption that spoiled her dream of Alec.

Pushing her shoulders hard against the porch rail, as she sat just the width of the old wooden steps away from him, locking her fingers tightly together in her lap, she felt angry and baffled. Hot tears pricked her eyes. Alec smoked for a few minutes in silence; Susannah would not speak. Through a blink of her wet lashes that sent arrows and sparkles of gold across the blackness of the country night she saw the red blur that was the Duquesnes' lighted parlor, beyond the dark trees at the curve of the hill, and below it other village lights under the overhanging trees.

There were delicious scents abroad in the darkness, autumn scents of apples and yarrow and meadow thyme. A bird was complaining somewhere in a low bush; a little protestant flutter and chatter and rustle of leaves. Then there was silence until the liquid sweet call of the whippoorwill sounded far away in the woods, and an owl hooted near by, and then far away. Susannah's windmill creaked, with a splash of water.

"Get on your nerves?" Alec asked abruptly, putting his pipe in his pocket.

"No," Susannah answered, starting up from revery, clearing her throat. "Not that," she added simply.

"You look as if it agreed with you. I never saw you looking any better," Alec said.

"I love it."

"What? This place?" he asked, in genuine surprise. "I should think it would bore you to death."

"No. It doesn't." There was a silence again, and again it was Alec who abruptly ended it.

"Well!" he said. "I don't know that I could stand it."

She knew that he was trying to edge a deeper note into the talk and did not know how to accomplish it. He got to his feet, a tall bulk in the gloom, and walked away a few irresolute paces, and stood with his back toward her, staring off into the dark.

"Alec, what *is* it?" she ventured, in the wife's tone, all sympathy, patience, affection, trying to reach him, trying to break him down. His answer came so low that she could hardly hear it; he did not turn.

"I don't know. I wish to God I did! I don't know."

"Come here and sit down," she commanded. For a moment he did not obey her, but continued to stand facing away from her, his hands in his pockets, his head fallen slightly forward, the strengthening moonlight shining on his smooth hair as light falls on water or on metal.

Then he came back and sat on the step below her, his body twisted about so that his knee was almost touching hers, his eyes shining just below her own.

"I'm terribly sorry about this," he said, with a little visible effort. "Why d'you think I came up here, Sanna?"

"Perhaps," she began steadily, but she felt her throat thicken as she spoke, "you wanted to see me?"

He brushed this aside with a restless little unhappy laugh, and she felt how false her words had been and felt the color rising in her cheeks in the covering dark.

"I suppose I hoped," she said, not quite steadily, "that you had come home." And as he merely averted his eyes, slightly turning his head, by way of answer, and did not speak, she went on eagerly: "Alec, it isn't right—it isn't dignified—for you and me to act in this way! I know there ought to be apologies and explanations and forgiveness. But we can afford to skip all that! All this time that I've been up here alone, thinking about it, it's been coming to me more and more clearly that it isn't for us to go in for long scenes—going back over it all—rehashing it. I don't want that. I'm a human being, and human values—being your wife, having had your child—those are the real things— those matter. Up here, with the trees and the woods and the being alone, I've seen it—I've felt it—so clearly——"

She stopped, appealing for an answer, waiting for him to show that she had reached him, touched him. But in a silence, when he had shrugged his shoulders restlessly, cleared his throat, he only said in a gruff, uncomfortable voice: "You've always been a sport, Sanna."

"That's not being a sport," she said after a moment, chilled.

"Well," he said, turning back to her, making himself speak, "what am I to say?"

"But we don't seem to be talking to each other—reaching each other!" Susannah murmured, in quiet despair. She made a little outflung gesture of her hands.

"You make me feel that this is all my doing," the man said.

She saw her advantage, rushed into it.

"Alec, is it mine!"

"No, I suppose it's—just fate," he answered, as readily as she.

"You mean the fate of loving a person, and then—stopping loving that person?" Susannah asked, unflinching.

"Well——" he agreed, a little huskily.

"And I hoped," she said steadily, "that you had come home."

"I've no right," the man answered after a second, "to ask to come home. I've behaved badly. I know it."

"Unfortunately," Susannah said in a low tone, her voice not quite steady, "it doesn't matter."

There was a silence during which she looked at his silhouette bulked on the steps, the face turned away into the darkness.

"I don't deserve that, Sanna."

"I've wanted you, Alec," she said briefly.

"When a woman wants a man," she recommenced, as he did not speak, "there doesn't seem to be any use discussing who was right and who was wrong."

"Neither one of us is wrong!" he said impatiently. "It's just—this way!"

"Well——" she said on a weary note, and again there was a little silence between them.

"I feel for you," Alec said then steadily, "what I have always felt for you, the deepest affection I ever will know for any woman. It isn't that."

"What is it, then?" Susannah asked, her heart lead.

"I don't know," Alec answered. After a long while he began again: "I came here to ask you to forgive me, and to ask you to do me a favor."

She knew now that any hopes that she might have had of happiness were dead. They had merely slept through all her despair. She had been fool enough to dream of his tears and his kisses, his apologies, his pleading for forgiveness, and that he would find his answer in her arms. That was all

over now. This was Alec sitting near her in the dusky moonlight, stabbing her last hope with his words.

"I want to be free, Sanna," Alec said, very low. He had
knocked the ashes from his pipe and put it into his pocket;
his arms were folded on his chest now; he had almost completely turned his back upon her.

Tears rushed into her voice and choked her, although she
did her best to control them.

"How can you say that? When were you ever anything
but free, Alec?" she faltered. Her voice sounded high, weak,
feminine to her. She interrupted herself and was still.

"Well, you know what I mean," he said again.

"You want to marry her." There was no question in the
words.

"No, not necessarily. I want to be free."

"There is no freedom for people who love each other, who
have a child, who have established a home," she began. The
futility of the argument, the weakness of the words overwhelmed her.

"Can't you see my side of it, Sanna?"

He was seated on the upper step, she one step below him.
Now she turned and moved a little nearer, so that her upturned face was near his as he bent forward, and in the starlight he could see the glisten of tears on her cheeks.

"You think I have no pride," she said. "You think I'm
trying to hold you to the shell of a love that is dead. It isn't
that, Alec! It's that I love you—you made me love you, and
I can't stop! You ask me to see your side—her side. I do; I
try to! But what of mine? I'm so—so horribly lonesome,"
Susannah said, her eyes brimming and her lip trembling
afresh. "I can't live without love. No woman can. I play
with Evelina; I dig in the garden and take walks and read,
and through it all I'm talking with you—you're back again,
at the breakfast table, in my room, kissing me, needing
me——"

She drew away from him, sobbing, burying her face in her hands.

He did not speak for a long while, and when he did his voice came low and thick:

"Don't, Sanna. Please, please don't. You don't know what you make me feel like.

"I'm not a fool," he presently went on, in a quiet voice. "I know the kind of woman you are; I know what it is to have a woman like you care for a man like me. I think of you—I think of those first years of ours together! I don't understand myself what's happened to me! I've not got an old friend in the world, Sanna, who hasn't written to me—talked to me . . ."

Susannah dried her eyes, straightened her body against the weatherworn old rail that was sending a pattern across the shallow steps in the strengthening moonlight. The moon, enormous and mellow, was coming up above the Fassetts' barn, was sending streams of milky glory through the Fassetts' oaks.

"Then what's the matter, Alec?" she asked.

"Things—things end," he said briefly, reluctantly.

"Real things don't."

"No, real things don't. Real things don't," he muttered, and there was a note of desperation in his voice. "But this—this is real, too," he went on. "What she feels—what she suffers—it isn't anything I wanted, God knows—it isn't my choosing——"

Susannah was silent for a full long minute, while the moonlight turned the grapevine pattern to black lace on the garden path, and stars swam in the wide-flung arc of the Milky Way. A wandering breeze brought them again the smell of dew on dust, of apples and drying meadow sage and yarrow. The owl cried from the wood, a little dry sound like a hinge creaking.

"Where is Merle now?"

❧ CHAPTER XIX ❧

THAT NIGHT and during the following nights there were frosts almost as deep as snow. The leaves blazed and, when the sun was setting, the maples turned to turrets of fire at all the crossroads, and every shabby little farm flew banners of scarlet and gold and clear transparent pink.

Susannah moved through the hours like a woman in a play. She did not cry, she made no complaint, she was not even conscious of suffering; she was stunned. Sometimes when she was with Terry and Anne she looked at them thoughtfully, if they spoke to her directly; she seemed to have to gather her senses together to reply.

"I think it's the husband. He was here, you know," Anne said to her brother. "I think it's another woman."

Terry, scraping dried mud from a gaiter, did not look up.

"You gather that she loves him, then, in spite of it?" he asked.

"Ha!" said Anne, mysteriously.

"And what——" His lean long hand was busy with the short stick. "What does 'Ha!' mean?" he asked.

" 'Ha!' means yes."

"I see." His tone was so strange that Anne looked at her

brother sharply; his face was turned away, but his ears were red.

"Does it matter?" she asked simply.

"I'm afraid," Terry answered mildly, tossing the stick away into the garden, straightening up to his tall length, and still not looking at her, "that it matters more than anything else in the world."

He went away without a backward glance, and Anne sat stupidly staring after him.

Laverne found a charity case for Susannah; Susannah duly went to the Pensey's wretched, collapsing shack with food—eggs and potatoes and bread and beans. She saw the stringy children peering like famished wolves from behind their stringy mother's back in the weather-beaten doorway, she saw the shiftless father dragging about under the unpruned old woody apple trees indifferently gathering the windfalls. She measured Helene Pensey against herself, with the blue wool dress in mind.

Later she told Anne about them.

"The Penseys!" Anne said, in her hoarse deep voice. "Oh, dear, are they back! We got them all equipped and shipped them all to Texas last winter. Of course one has to help them, Sue; children must eat. But I declare that Roy and Helene and Sonia are just as bad as their parents are!"

"I sent them groceries."

"That's really all one ought to do."

"It was something to do," Susannah said, not very steadily.

Anne gave her a shrewd glance.

"Bad as all that?"

"Pretty bad."

"What happened? I heard that your husband had been here."

"Only the end of everything," Susannah said briefly, after a moment.

"Can't patch it up?" Anne asked, wiping paste with a

damp rag from the snapshots she had just put into a big black album.

"No-o. It's not that sort of thing. No quarrel."

"What then?"

Susannah could not answer. She looked at the fire.

She and Anne were alone in the Duquesnes' sitting room; the room whose leaded windows she had seen from the outside, jutting into the garden, when she had first come to call. She had thought then it must be a low room; she had since found it to be one of those old parlors that seem to hold the atmosphere, the culture and hospitality and comfort of a long-gone day. Soft electricity lighted the room on winter nights, but the lamps themselves were of old-fashioned brown glass, with crystal pendants; the horsehair-and-walnut furniture spoke only of old New England; the hearthrug was dark brown with a tobacco-brown Newfoundland dog embroidered upon it in colonial wools; there was a beaded fire screen, and a black tin coal hod with a bunch of ribbon-tied roses stenciled upon it. Children's books were on the lower shelves of the cases that lined the room; on one of the upper shelves Terry had his precious collection of his hundred favorites. He and Susannah and Anne often wrangled about them.

This afternoon rain was falling, and a low whining wind was bringing down the last of the leaves. Susannah, in rubber cap and coat, had been driven by the restless misery within her to a long walk; she had ended at Anne's fireside. She was watching the clock now, with Evelina's bedtime in mind.

"The way I work out your particular complication, Sue," Anne presently said, pasting away expertly as she spoke, "is that you still love your husband, and he still—he has other plans."

"Right!" Susannah said, still shakily, but smiling.

"Another woman?"

"A girl," Susannah answered bitterly. "An English-Russian girl twenty-one years old."

"That can't last."

"It's lasted now for almost three years—for two years and a half, anyway. It began just about the time Evelina was born."

Anne looked at her speculatively.

"Strange," she said thoughtfully.

"It's happened before," Susannah said.

"I know. Of course it has. But the strange thing is," Anne went on, "that anyone looking at you—your mother, say, or someone else close to you—wouldn't think of a man as ever *stopping* loving you, once he began, Sue."

"Well, that's comforting," Susannah said, with a rueful little laugh.

"And yet your life will go this way," Anne resumed, "and some homely, lumpy, dull woman will get a man who thinks she's a miracle for twenty-five or thirty years, adores her, takes her about, buys her things, and talks everyone to death about her!"

Susannah laughed again.

"These last weeks—since Alec was here—have been the hardest in my life," she said. "I don't know exactly what I hoped would happen; I don't know that I thought it out very clearly. But it was always Alec coming back and saying the things I imagined he might say—explaining—telling me he was sorry——

"Every thought I had was of that. Every thought all this long summer since Evelina and I came down here has been that," she added in a silence.

"I know," Anne said briefly. In the pause rain whipped against the low, leaded windows, and a gust of wind brushed wet shrubbery branches with a sweeping sound against the roof.

"I'd my own problem," Anne went on, in a lighter tone,

rising to take her photograph book and set it under some heavy volumes for pressing. "There was an Englishman when I was twenty-two."

She came back to attack with a poker the coal fire, in its round iron grate, smashed a lump or two, started it burning more brightly. In the outside world there was still wet and rainy autumn dusk, but the parlor that was sunken almost into the garden was quite dark. She lighted a light, took a low seat opposite Susannah, looked into the little red and blue flames.

"Terry and I were in London," she said. "My father took us; our mother was dead. *His* interest was only in old books and men in museums who knew something of polar records, but Terry and I—well, everyone ought to have a season in London at twenty-two! We didn't know many people, but they were the right ones. Terry 'd just come in for my grandmother's money; we had to be twenty-five to get it, and he was just twenty-five. He fell in love; I fell in love; it was all intoxication and glory. My man was much too important to break up his life for me—he'd a wife and a son—he held a position, holds it now, for that matter, that made that sort of thing out of the question. So he got himself transferred to China, and Terry brought me home."

"What went wrong with Terry's affair?"

"Nothing for a while. She was perfectly exquisite, a dancer. When we first saw her she was in a white-and-silver ballet—there must have been fifty girls in it, but Diana was the most radiantly beautiful of them all. She had about five minutes of solo dancing, and in those five minutes Terry's affair was settled. We went—he and I—every time she danced. It was like a drug with him; he couldn't keep away from the theater when Diana was dancing, and eventually he met her.

"After that," Anne went on, with a smile and a sigh, "Terry went frankly mad. He walked the Embankment, nights. He couldn't pass her hotel without changing color. He wouldn't do anything more with me, he was so afraid that Diana might telephone. She was a gentle little thing, and she hardly spoke at all. She didn't have to speak. She said everything when she danced. It was love-making, it was passion, it was fever, it was everything!

"The day her engagement ended—it had been a success beyond anything imaginable—she and Terry were quietly married and slipped off to Palermo. It was May; everything down there was flowers and blue sea and moonlight and nightingales. They had three weeks of it, and then they wired me to join them and come slowly home in a friend's yacht as far as Naples, then Paris, Vienna, Copenhagen. Diana had to dance again in June in Copenhagen."

"I never knew Terry had been married!"

"I got Dad's permission and started off at once. Lucky I did, too," Anne said thoughtfully, still staring into the fire. "It had happened only a few hours before I reached the villa. Diana's husband had discovered her, and written her, and Diana had swum straight out into the Mediterranean, poor little thing—poor little beautiful thing!"

"Her husband!"

"Yes, she had a Polish husband. But she loved Terry so that she took those weeks—those few perfect weeks——

"She must have known all along how it was going to end. And on those mornings—he wrote me about them—when the dawn came up over the water and Maria brought their coffee and rolls to the piazza, and in the evenings when they wandered about together, she must have been planning it. They had their perfect time, but it didn't last long."

"Terry!" Susannah said in a whisper, changing her whole idea of him as she listened, and for a long minute there was silence in the parlor. The two women stared into the flickering flames that muttered and sucked behind the bars of the grate.

"But then, where did—where did your husband come into it, Anne?"

"He was a Pemberton boy. He'd been away for ten years or so. He came back; he was here one summer," Anne said. "It was very strange. One day he was simply young Bert Lambert, whose father was postmaster, the next day I was telling Terry that I was going to marry him."

"Terry hadn't seen it coming?"

"Seen it coming? I hadn't seen it myself. I was simply married to Bert—I was a married woman—I was making allowances for Bert in my life," Anne said, with an air of honest bewilderment that made Susannah laugh. "My father had died," she went on; "his mother had just died. But that doesn't really explain anything. Bert was going to practice here; we would go on living with Terry; it was all accomplished before anyone knew that we were even engaged. From the beginning I acted as if I were being obliged to take step after step. I wasn't, of course. No one in the world could have made me do what I didn't want to do. It wasn't even a case of wrecking Bert's life; it wouldn't have wrecked his life. He would probably have accepted his dismissal with complete philosophy and been much happier with someone else!"

She stopped, and Susannah laughed incredulously.

"I don't believe it."

"Something impelled me—forced me," Anne resumed. "Terry wasn't enthusiastic about it; Terry was simply stupefied with surprise at the whole arrangement. Bert is seven years younger than I; he isn't Terry's sort."

"I wonder if something of that—that impelled feeling is what Alec is having now?" Susannah asked, listening absorbedly.

"I was thinking that. Perhaps that's what started me on this," Anne answered, glancing up, glancing away again. "Anyway, I went straight ahead. Looking back, Sue," she diverged, on a note of puzzlement, "it is simply impossible for me to remember what actuated me. From the day of our marriage my life was complicated with difficulties I had never dreamed could exist in the world. Bert was quarrelsome, sensitive, jealous; he wouldn't get up until noon, meals never satisfied him, Terry and I lived in a sort of fever, he ashamed to look me in the eye and I ashamed to look at him!"

"Is it a divorce, Anne?"

"No. Oh no! Albert finally went off to visit a friend, a doctor in Springfield. This man is married and has a noisy, handsome wife who is tremendously admired by both her husband and Bert. He lives with them and has a position on the staff of a factory hospital. He is perfectly content. I know he has affairs—I don't know how far they go—and occasionally he gets into debt, and Terry and I straighten him out. And my Lambert-Duquesne children," Anne finished, with another vigorous onslaught on the fire, "are so much finer, so much more normal and handsome and smart than some of the Duquesne cousins in Boston that there's no sense to it at all!"

"Funny," Susannah murmured, profoundly impressed. "Aren't lives funny? Here we three are in a little New England town, and who'd ever dream that China and London and Palermo were a part of our backgrounds. . . ."

Much later, when she was buttoned into her raincoat and cap again, she said: "Anne, why is it that hearing of other persons' troubles makes one's own seem so much less?"

"Balance," Anne said, peering beyond Susannah through the side door into the darkness to see if the children were returning from their party. "It gives us a sense of proportion. There's nothing so upsetting to one's philosophy as meeting an entirely happy person!"

"All summer I've been thinking of you and Terry as the happiest—the most sensibly happy—persons I've ever known."

"We are happy. But it's quite different when you've fought through hell to get it, Sue."

"Yes, that's true, too. Anne," said Susannah, arresting her in the doorway with a hand on her shoulder. "What do you do when it suffocates you—when you can't believe it—when it seems as if you couldn't go on?"

Anne's lean face, crowned with its heavy braid of red hair, looked down at her seriously. She made no answer.

"Sue, good for you; I hoped you might be here, I'll see you home!" Terry said, looming suddenly up in the wet blackness that was shot with sparkles of rain.

"You will not!" Susannah protested. "Please, Terry; it 'll keep me from coming over to see Anne, if every time you think you have to . . ."

She was finishing her protest now merely for the sound of it, for long before this Terry had grasped her by the elbow, braced her with an arm about her, and was rushing her through the dark and wet. Shrubs brushed against them; the cold sweet rain was in their faces.

"Step lively now, gal," said Terry. "No shillyshallying. Whew—what a night! End of the summer this time, Sue. There won't be a leaf anywhere tomorrow!"

They went in at her own side gate and up the dripping drive across which timid shafts of the warm red glow from the kitchen and parlor windows were sending long beams. Everything twinkled and splashed in the light.

"I'm not going to ask you to come in, Terry. It would only mean that you'd have to get out into it again."

"No, I'll dash back and get a shower. See you tomorrow some time!"

She was in the warm bright kitchen, standing dripping on one of Laverne's immaculate rag rugs.

"I left my coat on the porch, Laverne, but I don't know what to do about my shoes."

"Step out of 'em jest where you are, and give 'em to me.

Don't worry one mite about the rug; I was goin' to wash it, anyway," Laverne said. "Look what you're gettin' for supper. Ma made it. I run over there this afternoon—she thought I's crazy—Ma don't ever stir out of the house in wet weather . . ."

Susannah went on through the ordered peace and warmth of the rooms. The halls were like iceboxes, but Evelina, rollicking about her mother's room, was safe in the softened pleasantness of air heated by a roaring wood stove; lamps were lighted, the crib turned down, and 'Liza and 'Liza's twin sister Bernice were playing with the baby.

Bathed and dry and comfortable in house clothes and low-heeled slippers, Susannah sent the girls downstairs for their supper and monopolized Evelina for the last sweet hour of her day. She sat facing the fire. Evelina, occupied with a silver powder box that had a chain to it, and, turning the little French trinket about and about in soft fat little hands, was momentarily quiet in her arms. There was a dreaming silence, while Susannah, fallen to musing, looked into distances far beyond the homely farmhouse bedroom, the stained old walls, the deep-silled, many-paned square windows. She remembered China, and herself an eager girl with a mane of hanging hair, exploring the dust-white lanes of old Peking, entering the courtyards that lacquer and carved stone made so sheltered, so romantic, so beautiful. Again she saw lights shining across the narrow enclosed gardens and through the moongates; color living in old lanterns, old tapestries, mellowed old bits of flowered porcelain. How her eager young heart had seized upon it, what long letters she had written home of the thrill of the old world that to her had been so new!

She remembered girlhood changing into womanhood in that atmosphere of sophisticated diplomatic life: balls, receptions, races, set against the background of the primitive peasant world that swirled about it like a river about a pleasure boat. She remembered Pat Lilienthal, amusing, rich, handsome, devoted, and the Pao-Machang races, and Pat's little Siberian pony, Terrafirma, winning the cup. Susannah had had a pink linen coat that year and a pink linen hat; she had had pink linen shoes made by that little Japanese shoe-maker in Shanghai who merely fingered one's foot with his quick brown hands and sent home the perfectly fitting shoes that same afternoon with never another trial.

Her heart contracted, remembering that her father had been with her in those happy days, remembering how every-one had loved "Lucky" Farjeon, what sunshine and security had seemed to be wherever Dad was.

"Not for Evelina!" she thought, her eyes suddenly filling as she looked down at the baby, now sprawled deeply and luxuriously asleep in her lap.

Her musings went idly on to later days, shrinking away from those that had followed her father's death, drifting along with the years when she and her mother had wandered, had visited Aunt Nona as grateful and appreciative poor relations, had gone back to China, always so glad to be in-cluded in this embassy dinner or that legation tea, always playing the careful, tactful game that must end some day or another with a good marriage for Susannah.

Then there had been Johnny Wardell. She couldn't visu-alize him at all now. Johnny Wardell and Ethel Mallock seemed as far in the past as little-girl schooldays before Daddy had been sent to China, and the chums and teachers, the loves and hates of childhood. Everything real that she had ever known had come afterward: the dark deck of the second cabin and the bulk of a man's big figure leaning against the rail in the night shadows; speckles of light flick-ering on the white lacy wake, faint strains of orchestra com-ing from somewhere upstairs. Her husband . . .

Her heart yearned toward Alec with a fierce, possessive hunger. She longed, with a force that was like an ache of physical need, for just one more hour with him, one more talk, one more explanation. The man who had sat with her on the porch steps a few weeks ago, wretchedly but stubbornly telling her that their love was over, that another woman possessed the love, the comradeship and kindness that Susannah had had for a few happy years, never seemed really to be Alec. Do what she would to bolster her pride and her dignity, Susannah could only long for him to come back and to give her a chance to say that she forgave him.

"No one else seems *real*," she said to Anne one day.

"I know," Anne said.

"In my own mind I'm always arguing, explaining. It's always coming all right again. And then I realize that it—it just isn't coming right again."

"Oh, don't I know, Sue!"

"Marriage ought not have to meet that situation," Anne Lambert presently said musingly. Terry was in Morristown for the day, and she had come over, after her own children's supper, to have dinner with Susannah. They sat by the dining-room fire, for the room was the warmest in the house on a heavy, chill late-autumn evening, and Anne had protested that she must go home early; no use lighting the parlor fire for her.

But the evening was no longer young, and still Anne sat musing in her chair, her knitting neglected in her lap, and still Susannah twisted about, rested her elbows in one of the arms of the high-backed old ingle seat, and cupped her chin in her palms, and stared into the fire. And still the two talked on and on.

"But how can we ever outlaw the other person? People are free . . ." Anne's voice trailed off into uncertainties; she hesitated for a moment. "Either there is marriage or there isn't," she began again. "*Is* there such a thing as marriage? I mean is there an ideal we work for? But why can it be so easily destroyed?" Anne pursued. "Our relations with our mothers and fathers and children and friends are definite enough, and they're almost all pleasurable. We delight in them. I love to have the children with me; I used to love my father—love to be with him. It never occurred to me that anyone else would ever cut me out with my father, or draw the children away from me. My friendship with you, or with any other man or woman, is pure gain; no worry in it; we love to see each other; it's all serene enough. But why, then, is almost every marriage a strain on the man or the woman—why is it that half of them, more than half of them, go on the rocks?"

"One wonders what would happen if there simply wasn't divorce—on any terms, for any cause."

"Well, it was like that for centuries, and I suppose they— did other things. Had mistresses, streets of red lights——"

"Queer! Queer if anyone could show you, Anne, when you were quite young, what life was going to be like."

"I know it. The happiness of those old first days in London, Sue, when Terry and I were doing everything, loving everything, meeting everyone! We never thought of ourselves as back in New England with our fingers burned."

"Perhaps all youth has a glamorous, happy time, a time when life seems too sweet to be real. I remember Peking and the races, when we all seemed so young and gay. Here's Terry!"

The two women roused themselves and smiled as Terry came in, cold and red-fingered, to loosen his muffler at the fire and stand smiling back at them.

"Get talked out, gals?"

"Perish the thought," said Anne. "Take off something. Sit down!"

"No, you're coming home. Susannah's eyes look as if they'd been punched in."

"They do not," said Susannah. Their glances met.

"Terry, you were nice to stop in for me," said Anne. "Get seeds and rakes and everything?"

"Everything. I couldn't possibly have gone by Susannah's light." He looked at her pleasantly as he said it, a smile on the freckled, intelligent thin face under the red mat of hair, and Susannah smiled back.

"I wonder if you two realize what this place would be without you?" she asked.

"We think you enhance it for us, too," Anne answered neatly.

"No, but it is great luck—finding one's own sort in a little, buried place like this."

"It's great luck finding your own sort anywhere," Terry said, throwing his cigarette into the fire, forcefully drawing Anne to her feet, turning her about, and starting her in the direction of the door.

"Come on, my gal, you can moralize tomorrow! I'm all in," he said. "Good night, Sue! Come to lunch tomorrow; I got Anne some curry, and she'll be mad to try it out on us."

"We've no bananas," said Anne.

"We've bananas and peanuts, too. I got 'em."

"Oh, really, Terry, you have your points!" Susannah heard Anne say, as brother and sister stepped out into the black darkness. She was smiling as she went upstairs.

She and Evelina had their Thanksgiving dinner at the Duquesnes'. There were sixteen at table; cousins had come from everywhere; the big house was filled with cot beds and mismatched chairs. It was like turning the pages of American history back a long way, she told Terry, as he plunged his sharp knife into the first of three turkeys, and she waited at attention with the gravy ladle.

"Hold steady!" she said.

"That's the gal, Sue!" he approved.

"Uncle Terry," asked a red-headed girl of ten, on his other side, "Mrs Hazeltyne isn't any relation to us, is she?"

Terry straightened a limp damp sliver of white meat carefully on a plate.

"She is not," he said.

"But if she married you, Uncle Terry, she would be, wouldn't she? Mar'gret said she wouldn't be," a slightly older boy said argumentatively.

"Oh, then she would be. Only I'd have to kill her husband," Terry said, continuing his serving. "No dressing on this one, Sue," he added: "that's Pete's."

"Oh——?" the boy said, slightly baffled. The little girl laughed in great satisfaction, as one who has scored, and Terry said in a comfortably conversational tone to Susannah:

"At that, I might consider it!"

"Oh, you're only too kind!" Susannah said.

At Christmastime, in a fine powdering of blinding snow, she took the baby down to spend Christmas Day with her grandmother. Little Phil was there, rather subdued with a heavy cold. Alec's mother chose to ignore the subject of his defection entirely, and Susannah found it rather a strain to keep the conversation natural under the circumstances. But she duly accompanied the older woman to church in the morning, exchanged presents ceremonially before dinner, admired the tree that a florist had trimmed and set up for the children, and sat after the too heavy dinner listening to carols on the radio, and talking intermittently on neutral subjects.

It was heaven the next day to escape from the hot, overfurnished rooms, the dull hours and formal meals, to the clean, sweet whiteness of the country, to the homely pleasant smells and warmth and order of her own home. Susannah and Evelina reached the farm late. She and the child had their supper of milk and toast together, and Susannah got in between her smooth, chilly sheets and reached with icy feet for the blessed heat of hot-water bags almost as soon as the child was in bed.

"Blizzard," she said happily, reaching for her book. "How good to be all snug and warm in a blizzard! We'll go over to Anne's tomorrow and help cook Sunday lunch, and the next day and the next and the next nothing awful will happen—and there 'll be no engagements—just snow, and old rooms with fires and books in them, and friendliness and peace!"

And then suddenly: "I wonder—I wonder if at the end of all this there might be peace? I mean being sure of myself—sure that Alec—that any man must find me attractive, must think of me the way men think of Anne, cultured and gentle and clever and good? I wonder if it's taken me thirty years to find the right road after all?"

There was no answer. The mysterious silence of a winter night brooded in the spacious old-fashioned chamber and was accentuated and underlined by the faint chirp of some chair or bit of wainscoting contracting in the cold, the click of an icy branch outside the window. Shadows lay rich upon shadows in the high ceiling corners; snow embroidered the crossbars of the window panes. Susannah looked about at it all, and smiled, and went to sleep smiling, as if she had found one answer at least to the perplexities of life.

❦ CHAPTER XX ❦

THE SNOWS WERE HEAVY and lasted long, but the old farm-house had been built to weather snows, and there were always snugness and warmth under the high sweep of its whitened roof. Susannah and Evelina made a business of getting dressed in overshoes and heavy coats and caps every morning, and floundered in to the village a quarter of a mile away, and went on to the Duquesnes'. Or they stayed in their own yard, and Nan and Jerd and Anne and sometimes Terry joined them, and they dug and scrambled in the soft, white, inexhaustible stuff, their faces hot and red, their mittened fingers wet, their hair curling up damply against the enveloping caps and tied shoulder shawls.

'Liza carried off armfuls of wet garments; Laverne smiled grimly as she announced meals; the entire Duquesne group might stay if it would—Laverne never failed with her quick biscuit, her chicken pies, her baked pumpkin and preserved blackberry roll.

The Duquesnes went to Boston for the holidays; Susannah welcomed them back a few days later, and they all had dinner together at her house on New Year's Eve. Snow was falling again in the silent night. At midnight Susannah, Terry and Anne went to the porch door and opened it wide

to chill, sweet air, to look into the fluttered white and blackness of the night and listen to the clamor from the old
steeples.

"I feel as if I had learned more in this year than in all
the years that went before it," Susannah said. "I don't
mean that it's been a happy business. I'm not sorry to see the
old year go."

She turned her head to look over her shoulder at Anne,
supposedly standing close beside her. But Anne was not
there; it was Terry whose face was close to her own. He
was smiling naturally enough, but there was no mistaking
the expression of self-consciousness and confusion on his
face; for a moment he did not speak, and Susannah could
not. Then they both laughed a little, and Susannah turned
back to look out into the steadily falling soft, light curtain
of flakes that the hallway's light captured in a white shaft.

"Not such a bad year," Terry said presently, in an unsteady voice.

Susannah did not choose to answer.

"There's something beautiful about America," she began
instead, after a moment. "There's nothing in the world more
beautiful than these little New England towns in a New
Year's snow."

"It's the first New Year Anne and I have had in Pemberton in—oh, fifteen years perhaps," Terry said unguardedly.

Her head came about again suddenly, her surprised eyes
challenged his.

"Oh, you didn't come back on my account? Oh, you did!"

"No, no, no, we didn't! Honestly."

"I just about half believe you," Susannah said, still suspicious. "We'll get pneumonia in this doorway, Terry, but I
hate to shut it out—the pink lights on the snow and the
bells."

"I think—if you once get used to it, gear yourself to it,"
Terry said, "there's nothing quite so filling as this sort of

thing. We got home at about two o'clock today, and I went out and chopped wood for two hours straight. Jerd was out there with me, and a couple of the men; the barn smelled good, old Gracie came out and began to putter around for eggs; it began to snow again outside the big open barn door. I don't know, I felt tremendously content, all of a sudden; I didn't want to change places with anyone, or be anywhere else, if you know what I mean."

"I do know what you mean. I think I'm—what was your word?—I think I'm geared to it, too, or getting geared to it. It's the essentials of living," Susannah expressed it, "reduced to their simplest and their—their nicest proportions. It's Jersey cream and thick soft blankets and maple trees and brooks——"

"You can look out into snow and talk of maple trees and brooks," Terry murmured, as she paused. But she knew from his tone that he hardly knew what he was saying. His face was close to her shoulder; he was not touching her, but it was as if his whole tall lean body were stooped and curved to enfold her.

"Sue," he added, "I want to ask you something. Does it get any easier?"

He had never hinted to her before that he knew that she had a personal problem. Susannah looked him gravely in the eyes.

"Not much. I—I—Evelina and I—you see, we love him," she answered, her voice suddenly faltering, and tears thickening in her throat. And she went past him and back to the drowsy heat of the parlor. Anne was wrapping herself up to depart.

"Sue, let's each make a wish for the New Year?"

"Well——" Susannah agreed, her tone still a little thick, but her eyes very bright. "But not out loud?" she added in alarm.

"Oh, goodness, no!"

"All right, here goes for all our wishes. We ought to join hands, I think."

With her warmly red-brown hair and flawless skin she was very lovely in the cream chiffon velvet that left her smooth shoulders bare. She extended vital, quick hands, and brother and sister joined their hands to hers, and there was a moment's silence, when their laughing eyes moved from face to face and their lips were tightly closed as if to hold their secrets safe.

The little ritual left them somehow feeling closer friends than before, and Anne quite simply and for the first time kissed Susannah, and Susannah turned from that kiss for a second to Terry's arms and the brief touch of his lips on her hair.

"My wish was that I'll never make a break like that again, Sue," he said, when Anne had preceded him through the outer doorway.

"That," she said smiling, "is a good wish."

"I'm sorry!" he said. The door closed, and they were gone. Susannah extinguished lamps, carried a candle upstairs. Her room was warm; shadows flickered in darkness; beyond the black mirrors of the windows snowflakes were slipping and crawling. Evelina lay asleep in the glorious abandonment of babyhood, dark gold curls moist on her forehead, small legs and arms sprawled starfish fashion under the snugly secured coverings. In the candlelight her upturned face wore the flush of a new-ripened peach; the small blossom of her mouth was half open. Susannah stood staring at her for a long time.

Then she lighted her reading lamp and set about the business of going to bed, a brief affair tonight, for it was late, and the bathroom was icy cold.

Before she got into bed she took the lawyer's letter from her desk and, when she was comfortable on her pillows, read it again, and still again. Mr Hazeltyne wished to express his appreciation of Mrs Hazeltyne's generous action in the matter of consenting to the divorce, and to ask her if the following arrangements would be entirely satisfactory to her.

First, at present the entire custody of the daughter Evelina Hazeltyne. When the child had reached a suitable age, her father hoped that Mrs Hazeltyne would not object to an occasional visit to him.

Second, at stated intervals, preferably quarterly . . .

Susannah let the paper fall and lay staring into space. The pain at her heart was like a physical thing. Alec was "Mr Hazeltyne" again; Alec was thanking her through a Reno lawyer for her generous action in freeing him, in separating their lives forever!

She tried to forget it all, to read. The lines of her book were meaningless. There was nothing for it now but sleep; she could always sleep, and in sleep there was peace. The book was placed on her bedside table, and Susannah put out her light and turned on her face. Heavenly drowsiness at once enveloped her; she was comfortably tired, and it was almost one o'clock on New Year's morning. Tomorrow would be just one more happy day of warmth and light and many small affairs indoors, and fresh, sweet, bracing snowiness without. She and Evelina were to lunch with Anne and Terry . . .

Terry. Her thoughts stopped with his name, and it was with a little comforted sense of his kindness and nearness and liking for her that she went to sleep.

They saw each other every day, he and she and Anne, and shared a hundred interests. Terry read to the two women what he had been writing; he organized long walks; they went to village meetings and sat in brightly lighted, hot schoolrooms to discuss the new bridge or the school board with the butcher and the blacksmith and the school superintendent; they went to village concerts and plays.

Susannah found families to help, through the good offices of Mrs Lonny Mitchell, who always began by wringing her heart with the stories of the suffering, and usually ended by condemning them bitterly as worthless impostors.

"Are you taking charge of those Gibberts?" Mrs Mitchell would demand. "All right, my dear, it's a wonderful thing to have someone here who really will do something with our Charity Committee. But if that lanky complaining man doesn't get something to do, and that dreadful ailing woman doesn't forget her kidney trouble and clean that place up, I don't think they deserve anything!"

Mrs Mitchell, the doctor's wife, was president of the woman's club. She had four fine sons, two of whom were doctors, and all of whom had babies and wives and homes and character. Susannah respected Mrs Mitchell very much, and for nothing more than for the old doctor's tender devotion to his wife, his admiration for her, his toddling back in his greatcoat and red muffler to the lunch table to kiss her good-by. She wondered sometimes what element existed in certain marriages, that they could endure so beautifully.

"They're stupid," said Anne, when Susannah spoke of it. "That's the answer."

"Anne, you don't think so!"

"I do. I think people have to be rather simple to think each other wonderful, and to hear the same jokes, and express the same opinions for fifty years. I've always noticed that the persons who had golden weddings looked rather dull," said Anne.

Susannah laughed.

"You don't think so, Terry?"

"I don't know," he said. "No, I don't think so. But I do think that a whole half-century of marriage would indicate two persons with—well, with wonderful dispositions. No particular fire, no restlessness, no temperaments. Temperamental people couldn't do it."

"It's a wonderful thing to see," Susannah said soberly. "It's sweet to see how Mrs Mitchell's face lights up when the old doctor calls for her after directors' meeting."

Terry Duquesne had been working his way along the bookcases of the room, pulling books out here and there, glancing into them, carrying them to other parts of the shelves. Susannah and Anne had been playing cribbage; they had pushed the table aside upon deciding to ask Nelly Filmer if they might have tea. It was not a daily custom, but this day was bleak and windy, and the three had walked to Brown's Mill and back after lunch and were hungry and warm and tired.

"What are you doing, Terry?" Susannah said. She came to the bookcase and studied the volumes in helpless bewilderment. "How do you ever know what you have and what you haven't?" she demanded. For although this big low room was library as well as parlor and lined with high plain shelves, there was not a room in the Duquesne house that did not have its rows and rows of books; there were books in the slope-roofed old attic and books in the cellar; the bedrooms boasted lines of them; the entrance hall was crowded by two big cases; and even in the dining room there were books.

"Oh, this is easy," said Terry. "The others get mixed, but I never have any trouble with these. It's the novels and the strays that drive you mad, books like *A Hundred American Short Stories* and *Herbaceous Borders,* and *Menus for All Seasons* and *Chaucer Illustrated.*"

"Large illustrated books are the destruction of the American home," Anne declared. "Someone's always sending us books of Burne-Jones or the old English hunting songs with color plates. We look at them on Christmas Day, then they go flat there on the floor, in that corner of the case, and there they stay. *American Masterpieces, Modern Colonial*

Homes, Rip Van Winkle two feet square, and *Historic Inns!* Why do they *do* it?"

"What are all these shabby, horribly dull-looking ones, Terry?"

"Those are about the best books I've got. I've been twenty years getting those together. That's thrilling reading, Sue. That's all polar stuff."

"Polar? Br-r-r! It sounds cold."

"It is. Kane—now, that's one of the thrilling stories of all time. And Hayes—he was with Kane, and broke away, and managed to get back again, across a frozen sea. And McClintock and Melville—you'd go wild over these, Sue."

"The Worst Journey in the World," she read. "Why does anyone want to call his book that?"

"That's a modern; that's one of the best. You've got your hand on Shackleton, there, and that's Nansen next to him. And André—let me show you some of the photographs that lay up there in the snows for thirty years waiting to be found."

"And these are all mutiny?"

"Those are all the Sepoy Rebellion, yes. And here—these three cases, these are all crimes. These are just general biographies, but there—behind you—those are all biographies of men and women of letters, those are good. Carlyle and Boswell and Walt Whitman and Gorky and Mrs Gaskell's Brontës."

"Where do you *get* them all, Terry?"

"Oh, catalogs and old bookstores; it's a kind of a fad."

"You are a man of fads. It's Kerry cows, or it's bulbs, or it's essays on the origin of slang, or it's playing chess games by postcard with some poor old bookworm in Minorca!"

"Fads are good," Terry said mildly, his long, thin hand, upon which a fine down of red showed against the light, still shifting and moving books.

"Fads are good. I think," Susannah said, "that I am going to become a countrywoman, with fads. I think—since you can't live seven ways at once—that I like country living."

Terry spoke lightly, levelly. Yet it was as if electricity were flashing between them.

"That's good."

"What seven ways at once? Come have some tea, Sue," Anne said, from the fireside.

"Well," she said, still loitering with Terry at the book-case, "there's the Shanghai life, races and dinners and freaks and celebrities coming along, and everyone entertaining for them. And talk about chits and mafoos and the Bund—that's one world. And then of course there's the New York world as I knew it when I was a poor relation visiting Aunt Nona, years ago. Making appointments for her at the beauty parlors and taking her to movies she wanted to see and ar-ranging dinner parties. Admiring Lola's clothes and Anita's clothes and being tactful when Mother said the wrong thing——"

"Lots of women are doing that sort of thing in New York," Anne said, handing the smoking cup. "Every rich woman has to have a few of them—nieces or secretaries or impecunious friends."

"There must be thousands of types of living in just one big city," Susannah presently went on, sitting back in her big chair, her cup in her hands. "Little successes and little failures, and love affairs everywhere—everyone thinking that his life is the typical one, the important one! Men and women jammed into three rooms—two rooms—noise, dirt, fights, poverty, ignorance——"

She stopped, smiling and shaking her head, and Anne said in the pause:

"Most of them would pity us this afternoon, Sue, shut up here in a village ten feet under snow, and with one movie a week!"

"That's a consolation," Susannah conceded, sipping her tea, looking into the fire dreamily. "And then there's the top life in New York, I suppose the top life in all the world," she added. "I mean the opera-box life, the limousines and the reserved tables, the dressmakers designing one costume after another, the jewelers rearranging stones into new patterns, music everywhere, food everywhere, lights and service everywhere. And everybody being amusing, saying the smart thing or quoting it, writing plays or being in plays or buying plays, setting the pace for the whole world's amusement, making one sport popular this year and another next year—never stopping—never anywhere long—just back from Miami and off for Hollywood, just back from Hollywood and taking a house in Antibes——"

"It makes me ache to think of it," Anne said, as she paused.

"I don't know," Susannah mused, "I don't know that it's a very happy sort of life. It's exciting. And it's exciting to feel that so many outsiders would like to try it. But I can't think of anyone we knew, Alec and I, who was very happy."

The coal fire was a mass of glowing red glass now; in the low-ceiled book-lined room, with its leaded bay window thrust out into the snow-laden shrubs of the garden, the pleasant scent of tea and toast was beginning to spread. Terry sat silent in his deep low leather chair, his long legs stretched before him, his teacup balanced carefully in his thin, nervous big hands. The women talked idly, with pauses between their words.

"Not for me," Terry presently said, reverting to the previous topic. "I like an occasional look at New York or at London; now and then there's a Symphony or a dancer or a picture show that one can't afford to miss. But the competition, the excitement, the mistakes of that sort of thing aren't paid up by what you get out of it."

"Terry, have you been brooding over that all this time?" Anne asked, amused.

"Trying to see Sue in it, I suppose. I've never tried it myself."

Susannah gave no sign of feeling. She continued to smile dreamily over her teacup. But deep within her she felt a sudden thrill. This man's most casual word was beginning to have power to excite her. His nearness, as her neighbor, lent interest to her life.

It was not only that she had come to have the same effect on him. She knew that was the case. It was something heart-warming and heart-comforting, to think about; that this man, with his books and his essays and his garden and his strange knowledge of men and affairs, found her dear, was, troubled and happy and confused and content when she was by.

They went to Boston, he and she and Anne, in the wet, wild close of March, and Susannah stayed with their cousins in an old house wedged in between great new apartment houses, and dined on old plates with thin old silver knives and forks, and looked at old samplers and chairs and finely darned beautiful linen, and liked it all. Evelina and 'Liza liked it all, too. Evelina came down with her nurse to tea for a few minutes every afternoon, and leaned against her mother's shoulder, and ran with little shy rushes and stamps of small slippers on the old carpets, and glanced like living sunshine on the square angled stairs and in the somber spring shadows of the Park.

There were one or two shows worth seeing; there were galleries. Susannah remembered the long-ago days when she had come to Boston to see Ross St Hubert's portrait of herself in one of them. They seemed to belong to another life. She reveled in books—new books and old—sending home package after package to Pemberton, and looking forward, even during the excitements of winter Boston, to the hour when she should be unpacking them in the home parlor, remembering their forgotten titles, anticipating the moment of opening this one and that.

She bought kitchenware for Laverne; pots checked cheerfully in red and white, Spanish baking dishes, tablecloths from Perugia in thick cross-stitch. She found an old fruitwood sewing table with flaps and took Anne to see it.

"But you never sew, Sue."

"I know. But I'm in love with it."

"Then get it," Terry said firmly, when consulted. "That's what makes us all different—liking things."

"My parlor," lamented Susannah, "will be piled to the ceiling with loot when I get home!"

But she loved the thought of it; her books coming home to her library, under the mellow slant of her own roof.

May broke over the world again, in a wash of green and warmth and sweetness; fruit blossoms fluttered down upon Evelina's flushed little face as she waded in grass and dandelions; there were laurel and dogwood in the frail green of the woods again; maples were crimson at their branches' tips. Susannah opened her windows wide, at night, to the sound of swelling soft winds, the rushing of released creek waters, out in the dark.

She pushed a wide straw hat from her forehead and wiped her wet face with her sleeve. Straightening an aching back, in the sunny flood of May morning light, she smiled at Terry.

"Where's Evelina?"

"'Liza just bagged her and took her in for her nap."

"And Anne?"

"Some woman came to the fence to talk to her, and she went up the lane."

They were alone in the trembling sweetness of the garden. Terry threw an armful of damp fresh cuttings on a smoldering handful of fire. He came close to her, and she looked up at him, smiling and lovely, the rich damp hair pushed back from her brow, her lashes wide apart, like a surprised child's lashes, the firm lift of her young breasts showing under her thin cotton shirt.

"Sue——" the man began, and stopped. He saw the color come up into her already flushed face; her eyes lowered a little, as if apprehensive. "Anne told me you're free," he stumbled on, his lean, freckled, intelligent face, under the untidy red hair, as self-conscious as her own.

"Yes," she answered in a whisper, not moving her steady look. "It's a divorce, now. And they're—they're married."

Terry, returning the look, was silent for a full minute, while the fragrance and stillness of the garden enveloped them like an enchantment. Presently he said suddenly, in a boy's embarrassed voice:

"We've come to know each other pretty well, haven't we?"

"Yes——" she said in a whisper, pain in her eyes.

"Is there ever going to be a time when I can say it, Sue?"

"Not now," she murmured, under her breath, like a person speaking out of a dream.

"But some time?"

Suddenly he saw her lips press together and an odd constriction change her face; her eyes darkened; her breath came quick and shallow on a sharp little sigh. He had never seen her cry before; as she turned from him and half walked, half ran toward the house, he saw that she was crying.

❧ CHAPTER XXI ❧

ON A CERTAIN HOT, spring afternoon the blow fell without warning, and the world for Susannah went black again.

There had been rains, but now the sun was shining warmly. Evelina, businesslike in denim working shorts and brief sweater, had been all morning long digging rapturously in a small tributary of the creek under the orchard trees, plastering mud against streaming mud, spattering herself from head to foot.

At noon, taking her in for a bath, Susannah found the sweet little muddy girl sleepy, and somewhat surprisedly had seen her settle down for a nap before lunch.

Lunching herself, she commented upon it to Laverne.

"A mite tuckered out," was Laverne's diagnosis, as she set the smoking asparagus and the cold chicken and the fresh cherry tart upon the table. There was no formal service in Susannah's house in these days. "She's goin' to be as hungry as a hunter when she wakes up."

But Evelina, drowsy and sweet and wanting very much to be held in Mother's arms, was not hungry at all when her long nap was ended. She said her legs hurt and that her face felt fuzzy. Susannah sent 'Liza to the telephone, and within twenty minutes Anne was there, and with Anne young

Dr Trine, who had recently come to Pemberton to be Dr Mitchell's assistant.

As one in a dream of terror too fearful to be real, Susannah looked from face to face, as Anne, the doctor and 'Liza examined the fretful baby. Evelina was still in her mother's lap. 'Liza took the small shirt off gently, mussing the rich, bright curls. Anne told Evelina about the bad, bad pussy. George Trine knelt close beside his little patient, stethoscope in hand.

Then there was an interval when Anne stayed with Susannah in the darkened bedroom, and Evelina dozed fitfully, and fretted, and dozed again.

"But what could it be, Anne? At noon today she was shouting in the orchard, digging in the creek."

"I don't know. They go into things like a flash and come out of them again."

"But she's never been ill."

"I know. He said that; Trine said that—that she had a magnificent constitution. That 'll help."

"Help! But you don't think she's so sick, Anne?"

"No, I honestly don't."

"Have Jerd or Nan ever had anything like this?"

"Oh, of course. That is—yes, they've had everything. Jerd was shivering in pneumonia one day when I was trying to urge him to go out and get warmed up with a snow fight! Oh yes, they all do it."

"Pneumonia!"

"This isn't pneumonia," Anne said definitely.

"Well, what then?"

"He's gone to Morristown as fast as he could go. We'll know as soon as he gets back. It's four o'clock. He'll be here by seven."

"She may be completely normal by six," Susannah said, looking down at the flushed little face against her arm.

"You have these scares. They're nothing to the children,

but, Lord, what we go through!" Anne murmured. "Want a pillow there, Sue?"

Time went by. The women talked abstractedly. Evelina awakened and demanded water. Laverne brought up a bowl of finely chipped ice.

"I thought you were going to George's, Laverne?"

"I thought I stay round an' see what the doc said. Not that that young feller seems to know much," Laverne said in her disconsolate tone.

It was half past five when Terry came upstairs and into the sickroom unannounced. Somehow the grave smile on his face frightened Susannah even before he spoke.

"Well, how's the sick girl?"

"She's been asleep. She seems quieter now." Susannah spoke in burning anxiety. Evelina had opened her eyes; they looked heavily without interest at Terry, sank shut again.

"Trine just telephoned from Morristown; he's at the hospital, Sue. He thinks we'd better get this young lady over there tonight. He's going to wait."

The shadow of coming agony blackened the room for Susannah. Somehow she got to her feet, put the child gently on the bed, turned to Terry a colorless face. She spoke quietly:

"Right away, Terry. 'Liza, pack me a nightgown and slippers—whatever I'll need. Should we have an ambulance, Terry?"

"Nope. Just roll her up snugly and take her crib mattress on the back seat. He suggested that. Do you want 'Liza to go?"

"I don't know." Susannah stood in the middle of the room, looking vaguely about. "I can't think. What did he say—what did he think——" she muttered, staring with suddenly haggard eyes into Terry's face.

"I don't think they know anything about it, Sue. He

simply said that the child might be sicker than we had thought and that, since there are no hospital conveniences here——"

"They depend so on that hospital stuff," Anne said, as Terry paused. Susannah had put her hands on his shoulders.

"He didn't say anything more? He didn't say—he didn't say——"

"On my honor, no! That was all he said. That time was important, and did we have a comfortable car, and to be sure to bundle her up well, and that he would wait."

Susannah turned drearily away.

"Then that's what we must do," she said in a broken whisper. "My little girl—Uncle Terry's going to carry you downstairs for Mother. Mother's right here. . . . Thank you, 'Liza. Mr Duquesne will bring you over tomorrow, if we need you. . . . Thanks, Laverne."

"We may all be home tomorrow," Anne said cheerfully. Her brother, accepting from Susannah the rolled blanket that was Evelina, touched her foot with his foot.

The nightmare journey began. Susannah sat on the edge of the rear seat, close to the mattress where Evelina was bundled. Anne, in the front, was turned about with her arm hooked over the leather upholstered back, so that she could see and talk with Susannah. Terry drove swiftly and steadily, without speaking.

All about them was spread the glory of the slow-moving spring dusk. The untimely warmth of the day still lingered on the old farms and on the fields through which they went; orchard bloom was pearly in twilight. Children and dogs and gossiping women were astir in the villages. The snow was gone; the winter was gone; there was greenness and life in the world again.

But ice was pressing against Susannah's heart. She seemed to herself never to have lived, never to have felt anything in

life before, never before to have gotten the true values of
April and the new green of trees, the significance of homes,
with smoke rising from their chimneys, the village lanes
with children straggling home reluctantly to supper. It was
all set now in blinding and piercing light. It seemed to have
new dimensions, new meaning. Her frightened spirit was
sick to get back to the old simpler values again, to life that
was safe and comfortable and lived on other terms than
those of shaken terror.

Only yesterday, only today she had been able to say carelessly: "Put on her pink dress . . . What wakened my bad
baby? . . . I'll bring Evelina . . ."

Now everything that concerned the child had moved into
another zone. The little name hurt Susannah when she
thought of it; the shadow that lay over the child had engulfed the past and the future with the dreadful present.
Desperately she looked at the moving scene about her, de-
termined not to think—just not to think.

The new, strange crystal light was penetrating the hospital, too. A keenness of perception almost deafening made
the voices of doctors and nurses sound loud and harsh. The
tragedy of glimpses of the children's ward with small forms
restless in narrow high beds was almost more than Susannah
could bear.

She steadied herself determinedly. No use breaking down.
Mothers were always breaking down in hospitals, and nobody liked them any the better for it. It would not help Evelina for her to break down. Everything was being done;
they were doing all they could.

They had a room and nurses in readiness. Dr Trine, his
young homely face serious, said that he had taken the liberty
of telephoning New York to ask Dr Richard Richards to
come up. "We've often had Doctor Richards here," the chief
nurse remarked at this point pleasantly. Susannah seized
upon the words.

"You have? Even at this hour?"

"Hours don't mean much to doctors," George Trine reminded her.

"No, I suppose not. We forget that."

Evelina had fallen off into a deep sleep; a nurse was sitting beside her. Dr Trine was having supper somewhere. There was a little breathing spell.

Anne, Terry and Susannah whispered in the hall.

"I'm taking Anne home, Sue. I'll be back."

"Oh, what for, Terry? You needn't come back."

"Well, I may not. You're staying here?"

"Oh yes. Did Trine say anything to you, Terry?"

"Not a thing."

"Perhaps I was too frightened. Now that things are quieter and there's nothing to do but wait, it doesn't seem so bad. But it seemed to spring on me like a tiger—Evelina, and fever, and hospital, and ambulances! I haven't breathed since that moment when you came upstairs into my room this afternoon."

"We'll know more about it when Richards gets here," Anne said, kissing Susannah good night. "What do you want 'Liza to bring over in the morning?"

It began to sound normal and ordinary. Of course it was fearful—fearful—to have darling little limp Evelina hot and drowsy in a high hospital bed, but one must not think only of that side of it. One must keep repeating, "Loads of children go to hospitals. Richards is the best man they have. She may be thin and convalescent for weeks; it won't matter. 'Liza and Anne and Laverne and I'll take care of her— she'll get better . . ."

Susannah had a clean, pleasant room, not too suggestive of an institution. A smiling nurse brought her a tray at about eight o'clock. Jelly and an orange salad with chopped nuts on it and broiled chicken. A roll, ice water, a china pot of tea. All so nice. All so nice.

"I wasn't hungry, but the tea was delicious," she apologized when she met the nurse in the hall. They could not keep her away from Evelina's door. She sensed that they did not quite like to have her lingering there. But they were all very polite.

Dr Richards had been in the hospital an hour before she saw him. That seemed funny, when she was the person most concerned. But Susannah was too sick with nervous chill to be critical. She smiled at him feebly and appealingly when he came into Evelina's room. He was perhaps sixty, businesslike and pleasant but brief.

"We have a very sick little girl here," he said.

The nurse touched Susannah's elbow.

"Wouldn't you rather wait outside?" she asked. Susannah obediently went out into the hall and to a window. She looked down at an ambulance arriving. That patient went into the Maternity Wing, and Susannah thought with a pinched heart of the day when Evelina was born. The darling —the little dark spotty darling she had been . . .

At ten, surprisingly, blessedly, Terry was back. 'Liza had sent her wrapper and her old soft velvet slippers. Susannah took Terry into her room and unpacked them and looked into a small square of mirror at a colorless face and disordered hair.

"Richards is here," she said.

"So the nurse said. Did you meet him?"

"Yes. He was here quite awhile first, it seems, talking to Trine and another doctor. He seemed to know everything about the case."

"Like him?"

"Did I? I didn't think—yes, I do like him. Terry, will they operate? I can't bear it if they decide to operate."

"I don't think they will."

"You were so good to come back."

"I wanted to. After the doctors finish you'll go to bed, won't you, and get some sleep?"

"I don't feel sleepy. . . . D'you mind if we go back to the hall, Terry? I keep thinking they may come out, and I don't want to miss them. I don't feel sleepy at all, just terribly excited and strained, and so afraid that we aren't doing something we ought to do."

"You needn't be afraid of that, Sue. They'll do everything. You caught it only a few hours after she was taken sick. You didn't miss a minute."

"No—no. That's something, isn't it?" They were in the hall now. The mysterious stirring that is a hospital night was all about them. The air was thick with disinfectants. Nurses quietly came and went. Doors opened and shut. The white-clad elevator boy murmured to an orderly. A stretcher came through from the surgery, something very limp and still wrapped in sheets upon it. A man and a woman in outdoor clothes followed it in tense silence.

"She's fine. She's coming out of it already. She stood it wonderfully," an elderly nurse, one of her bony big hands guiding the stretcher, said to them encouragingly. Susannah looked swiftly into their faces. Ah, good news was a wonderful thing! She felt her eyelids sting. She would have good news, too, if she could just bear this waiting for it— she would have good news, too . . .

Floor windows were opened upon the soft warm night at the end of the hall. Susannah and Terry stepped out onto the fire escape and looked down upon the roofs and tree-tops of the town and its lighted windows; groups were sitting on steps in darkness that was broken only by the occasional red dot of a cigarette tip; scraps of laughter and talk floated up. Figures came out to waiting cars; there was the chugging of motors; lights flashed against the tree trunks and garden fences, and wheeled, and were gone.

"One gets through these hours," said Susannah.

"One gets through everything. I remember times . . ." A long silence.

"Suppose they'd throw me out if I lighted my pipe out here?"

"Not out here." Another silence. Susannah leaned on the balcony rail. "She said she'd let me talk to the doctor," she said. "Terry, why does this sort of thing happen?"

"I don't know, my dear. It does seem aimless."

She glanced up at the bulk of the hospital behind and above them. Dimly lighted windows rose in tiers against the early stars.

"One doesn't often think of hospitals," Susannah mused. "One doesn't often think of people suffering."

"No, and yet you so horribly want sympathy when you are suffering."

"Did you, Terry?" she asked, rather low. For she had never spoken to him of the long-ago tragedy in his life.

"I wanted to die."

"I know."

The nurse called her, and she followed the white stiff uniform along the corridor quickly, saying only to Terry, "Ah, I'm scared!"

He saw her again some forty minutes later. The doctor had gone then; Susannah was talking to the head nurse. She came toward Terry in the corridor, and he saw that she was deathly white, with her reddish brown hair swept off her forehead and her eyes dark. But she was completely self-controlled, and when she spoke her voice was steady and her words quick:

"It's bad, it's very bad, Terry. Richards is gone. He says we won't know just how serious it is for—well, perhaps days. He says there's no telling—nobody knows where it comes from, nobody can tell anything about it. She's quiet now, and I'm going to get some sleep and be with her when she wakes up in the morning. Doctor Richards says our one great hope is that we caught it so quickly."

"No treatment?"

"Oh yes, they gave her a spinal treatment right away. He says not to hope——" Susannah's tired eyes met the man's eyes with the shadow of a smile. "But of course I hope," she said, swallowing a little on the words, but speaking as if their full meaning had not reached her. Or rather as if her conception of their meaning had swept far beyond their ordinary value.

"Not to hope," Terry echoed slowly. "My God!"

"We mustn't think of that," Susannah said steadily. "We'll go on beyond this—this will be only a bad dream——"

"Richards comes tomorrow?"

"Oh yes. Early. He has two other cases almost exactly like hers. Poor mothers!" Susannah said. She rested her hand for a moment on Terry's shoulder; her whole body swayed toward him wearily. "You're so comforting," she said.

His arm tightened about her; he brushed her uncovered hair with his cheek.

"Buck up, dear," he said.

"Oh, I'll be all right!" said Susannah gallantly.

"I'll be here in case you need me. Messenger service. Perhaps you ought to telephone her grandmother."

"I will, tomorrow. It 'll be tomorrow *sometime*," Susannah murmured in weary courage, as she walked with him to the elevator. "It seems to have been night so long!"

"You get to bed," he said, for good night.

But somehow she dared not go to bed; dared not be alone with her racking anxiety; dared not stretch herself flat, a prey to the terrors of thought. Susannah undressed, got into warm, heavy silk pajamas and wrapper, and wandered the silent, brightly lighted hospital halls, now exchanging a few words with a nurse, now glancing into a clean little white diet kitchen where coffee was being brewed in the strange night hours, or where two uniformed girls were laughing and whispering together.

❧ CHAPTER XXII ❧

Evelina had been moved now and was in strict quarantine. Her mother was not permitted to go into her room. Susannah stayed at the hospital for four days and four nights. She saw the baby only once again, at the end.

Afterward she was very quiet, obediently taking Anne's suggestions, following Terry's advice with a quick pathetic eagerness and gratitude. She herself was incapable of thought. Hours passed and things happened. The days went by; everyone was kind. The Duquesnes took her home with them, but even on that very first afternoon she said that she would rather go to her own house, and walked up the lane and through the gate at the top of the meadow, and so away under the new green leaves of the towering trees, and out of their sight.

Walked into a world of whose existence she never had dreamed before: a world at whose very gateway she felt herself stripped of everything that life had given her. She had no philosophy for this; she had no understanding of it. All values were gone—books, garden, friendship were but words. She could not live; she could not breathe the suffocating element that surrounded her, and she knew that she would not die. She was not conscious of needing Alec, al-

233

though in one or two of the hospital hours her heart had cried out to him in a very bitterness of need.

Silently, her wide, shadow-ringed eyes tearless, Susannah put away all the things that had been her child's. 'Liza's black face was swollen with weeping. Laverne's voice trembled as she added a "dear" to her answers when Susannah spoke to her. But Evelina's mother did not break.

In those first summer mornings of silence and loneliness in the old farmhouse Susannah worked, stopped to stare for long periods into space, set desperately to work again. In the empty afternoons she wrote one or two long letters, answered a shoal of sympathetic cards.

And through these hours she felt the black tide creeping upon her, felt it rising black and heavy and sinister to her knees, to her hips, to her heart. The day came when she could struggle no longer. The day came when she went upstairs slowly, like a woman lamed, one hand pressed tightly against her heart, and lay down on her bed, her wide-opened eyes on the ceiling, and let the waters engulf her, cover her, drown hearing and sight and feeling in one great blackness.

Day followed day, night followed night, and Susannah kept her mind, and as much as she could her hands, busy. She had talked in the beginning of going away. But she did not want to go away, and after a month or two she thought of it no more. The early summer enveloped New England's low hills and scattered farms in a glory of richness and fruition; warm rainstorms swept over the world in rumblings of thunder and blue-white flashes of electricity; the hot sunshine came back, and Susannah, transplanting tender little wallflower slips, weeding about the young rosebushes, felt her face grow flushed and wet under her wide old untrimmed shade hat of straw.

If she did not walk over to Anne's house in the afternoon, Anne came to her. Terry was in and out two or three times a day; the hours began to drag heavily when two or three of them had passed without some sign of him. Susannah, more beautiful than ever in the new thinness and gravity, would show him an ailing, forlorn old dog, taken in from desperate searchings of the summer roads where some master had purposely deserted him. She talked of chickens and of pruning the heavy blue-green branches of the apple trees, too heavily bent with fruit.

The two older Penseys and the Gibbert girls came to her two or three times a week. She and Laverne taught them cooking, housewifery; they had ice cream afterward and sewed on new cotton gowns. They were dull girls, bent upon making their homely bodies pretty with oily curls and too white powder, but they came regularly, and she hoped that they learned something. She read to blind old Ma Pettit, in the village; or rather she held an open book and listened while Ma gossiped of old village tragedies—so many tragedies, even when Ma had been a light stepping girl of fourteen, crying because Lawrence and Robby and Willy were off to the war. None of 'em to come back. No, sir, their names was onto that column down by Town Hall.

But Lizzie had married Robby's cousin Sam that 'd been too young to go. And if Lizzie's own boy Bob hadn't gotten killed of the dysentery in Manila twenty-eight years later! Wasn't that luck for you? And *his* boy—for Bob had married six weeks before he went away in '98—had died of flu in Camp Dix six weeks before the Armistice.

"I guess the Parmenteer fam'ly has done what it could for the nation," Ma Pettit would finish up in grim satisfaction.

Susannah wrote a few random thoughts about war and showed them to Terry. It was only a few weeks later that Terry asked her if they might be made into pamphlet form, hundreds of thousands to be distributed wherever men and women could read English.

"Who wants to do it, Terry?"

"The organization. One of the great peace organizations."

"But *why?*"

"Because of something you felt when you wrote it, Sue. Something that made me cry, and Anne cry—she couldn't finish reading it. Just those few words about lost children——"

"Please——" she said in a whisper.

"It's something to have done, Sue. To have helped bring the time a little nearer when there won't be any more wars."

"Ah, if one could, Terry! Sometimes in the nights it all comes over me, the empty rooms—the rooms from which the boys have gone away—their names, their young, strong, eager names just lines cut into marble——"

She could not go on. The tears came up in a flood, choking and blinding her, and she stumbled away from him, her slender figure swaying like a young willow in the wind. Terry did not follow. It was good for her to cry. There had been a time when she could not cry.

He lent her books. She plunged deep into the written lives of scores of other men and women who had lived and suffered and gone their way into the shadows. She read of boys, little boys of twelve and fourteen, who had drummed the ranks in through the broken walls and the hot gunfire of Cawnpore and Lucknow, their lifeblood running from their own little breasts as they drummed. She read of mothers who had held their children's hands when the cobbled streets of Paris were rough beneath the wheels of the tumbrels in which they rode, and the red smell of the guillotine was hot in the air. She read of that President's wife who had moved into the White House only a few days after the last of her three children had been laid in the wet spring earth. She read of slums—Chinese, Turkish, English; of haggard mothers quarreling in slimy streets for the crusts that meant life for their young.

"The thing to do is to eat very little, Terry," she said, "and read Shakespeare and poets and the four Evangelists, and lessen human suffering as much as you can and sleep. That's all there is."

"That's all there is."

"Wouldn't it be wonderful if we could make Pemberton the one place where there weren't suffering and poverty and misery?"

"Have to change the people, too, Sue. It can't all be done from the top."

"No, I know. One can do so little!"

"Not you. You're showing us all the way."

"Oh, *I!*" There were impatience, amusement, protest in the monosyllables. "I'm nothing," she said, in a whisper. "I thought once I was something. Susannah Farjeon, who danced and gossiped and knew the horses in the races and the players in the hai-allai court! Oh my God—how long ago!"

On the little visits he paid her every day he rarely stayed more than a few minutes. Often he came merely to bring a book and lingered only long enough to speak of it. Sometimes he showed her a new solitaire, or left with her the first fruits of his kitchen garden: two big smooth tomatoes, a basket of great red currants, a rough-powdered, flannel-skinned quince.

"Quinces and currants have gone out, Sue. Why don't people eat them any more?" he asked her.

"I was wondering when Anne and I looked at them ripening the other day. Too many other good fruits always in season, perhaps. We've rather lost the old feeling of things being in season, I think, with grapefruit at Christmas and strawberries in February."

"Dad used to talk of oranges at Christmastime as a once-a-year treat when he was a boy."

"We ought to try to capture that old American feeling, in some of your essays, Terry, and make a book of it. Mrs

Prentice commenting on the convenience of having a rubber end on her lead pencil, and what ice was going to do to syllabubs and pandowdies!"

"Did she?"

"Oh yes. And girls scalloping sacques—how frightful they must have been!—and putting circles of brandied paper on jelly glasses. And Susan Morgan—one of the darlings of them all—making her special soldier a shirt of dark blue piped with red."

"Let's begin on notes, Sue?"

"Let's. Even if we don't do it for years." She bought a handsome account book that afternoon and showed it to him with a schoolgirl's satisfaction in being businesslike. And though later in the evening he found her crying, a blur of spread dimity skirts and bent head in the summer evening shadows of the terrace, somehow he knew that a faint flicker of interest in life had stirred in her again.

He sat down beside her and gathered her into his arms, and she did not protest or draw away, but buried her head on his shoulder and for a while let the tears have their way.

Afterward she drew back, very busy with her handkerchief, both hands to her face, and presently a ray of moonshine showed her wet lashes and the glint of a smile in her eyes.

"Finish your article about the Mexican lady—what was her name?"

"Calderón. Yes, roughly speaking. But it was such a perfect night—and Anne was sleepy——"

"Is it so late?"

"It's ten. Not so late. But it tempted me to take a walk——"

"And if it had been windy or raining pitchforks or snowy or thundering, you would have come just the same," Susannah said on a note of delicate, grateful irony.

"I would indeed."

"I'm glad. I—needed something tonight."

"Me perhaps?" Terry's voice was a little hoarse in the darkness. He spoke very low.

"Someone. It's so good to have hands—voices—human sounds—someone who cares," she said a little thickly. She felt the grip of his hands tighten on her own, but he said nothing more. They walked after a while to the slope of the hill behind the barns and leaned on the fence and looked off across the meadows swimming in white moonlight and the blots of shadows under the trees and the outlines of the low hills. And still neither spoke.

"Well——" Terry said, after a long silence. Susannah turned, unprotesting, and they went down to the house again.

"Thank you," Susannah said at the porch. "I can sleep now." Instantly he put his arms tightly about her, and she put her head back, and they looked at each other in the dull glow that fell on the path from the hallway. But he did not kiss her, and after a moment he released her, and Susannah went in to the warm, airless emptiness, the haunted shadows and doorways and chairs and tables that were home.

On another moonlight night he and she took the highway and climbed the hill and crossed through a belt of dark woods to come out by the Constable farm and walk home from the other side of the village. And on this night he talked to her a little of the marriage that he had made fifteen years earlier.

"Only it was no marriage," he said. "She was not free. She had told me of this Pole, that she was a little afraid of him. But I thought—in fact she told me—that he was her manager and her cousin. I thought she had tied herself up to him with a contract—if I thought at all. . . .

"I'd watched her dance and bought her pictures for ten days before I met her. Then I asked an actor my father knew, Sir Gerald du Parc, if he knew any way in which it could be managed. 'When d'you want to meet her?' he asked.

We'd been lunching at some club; it was about three o'clock. I said any time—any hour—anywhere—and he said that he'd felt that way about one of our American actresses years before. It made me hot and cold and ashamed and proud all at once," Terry said, with a little laugh. "I went along with him to this big gallery or loft or whatever it was. There were dozens of girls there practicing steps, and a man at the piano. Someone called 'Diana Petrovich!' and she came running with that light step she had—her head twisted up—she was a little thing. . . .

"I asked her—there wasn't a performance that evening—if she'd dine with me and my sister, and she began to shake her curls, 'No,' and then she looked up at me and put her hand out and laughed and said, 'Yes.' I called for her at some hotel, and she came out—so little—in a sort of fluffy blue thing . . ."

He and Susannah walked on in the New England moonlight, and the night air was rich with summer smells of yarrow and ripening pears and the barns of the old farms. Once they passed close to a cow paddock and got a whiff of milky-sweet breath from some great creature breathing close and unseen in the dark.

"After that, Terry?"

"Ah, after that it was all a blur! When she danced I watched her; I almost could not bear the moments before she came on, when I knew she was coming! The music would play a certain theme, and there would be my little girl, so serious and so absorbed, whirling and floating. And then, afterward, supper, when we told each other how much we were in love and planned our marriage.

"My uncle was on a special mission to Paris then. We were married there in his parlor and off that afternoon for Florence—Naples—finally Palermo. She never showed me any hint of shadow then. Sue, what a time it was! But once, when we'd been swimming at Mondello and were lunching on the terrace, she said to me, 'Gigi, if something happens that makes you anxious for me, some day, will you remember that I wanted it that way?' "

They had reached Susannah's dooryard now. She was sitting on the steps where she and Alec had sat less than a year earlier. Terry was standing, looking down at her, his hands thrust into his pockets.

"I thought she was trying to tell me about a baby," he said simply. "I was so proud! I told her that whenever she was ready to tell me the secret I'd be ready to tell her how happy it made me. That was the day, I think, that she planned it. The end, I mean."

"Terry, how did you know? What happened?"

"We were on the terrace, just above the sea. Some Americans my uncle knew had come out to have lunch with us, and Diana 'd been in wild spirits. She used to look like a white swan often when she danced, and she was singing her swan song that day, higher and shriller and sweeter, only I didn't know it. Everyone was enraptured with her. Some other people came—there were about a dozen of us, and we all went swimming. It was a terribly hot, unseasonable sort of day; we'd been in the water that morning, but we were all glad to go back. We went down to the little stone pier; everybody was swimming. She swam beautifully—much better than I did. But she came out of the water rather early and came and kissed me—I was drying off on the steps— and said in my ear: 'I'm a little scared, but you must remember I'm happy!'

"I went on talking with Wilkinson—the bath woman, one of the maids, came down and began to spread the wet suits on the rocks. She said to me, 'Where is the Signora?' and I said, 'Oh, dressed, Maria. She went up long ago!' 'Non ancora,' she kept saying, shaking her head, and one of the girls called to me and said, 'Diana went back into the water. She said she was going to take one more dip!' I stood up

then, and Wilkinson stood up, and we looked off across the
bay. Clouds were beginning to wreathe around the way they
always do in the afternoon there, and we saw her, with her
arms plunging as regularly as pistons, and the shoulder of
her blue bathing suit, and her blue cap. And she was still
swimming away from shore.

"The Wilkinson boy ran to the edge of the water and
dived—he had swimming medals—he went after her like a
rocket. But it was like trying to run from here to—well,
say Pinckneys'. Diana was only a speck; there was more
than a mile between them. I ran up for the launch—the man
wasn't there, and it was chained, but we broke the chain
and were out on the water in her within—oh, perhaps three
minutes.

"But they didn't find her until two days later. By that
time I'd found her husband's letter. He'd written her that
he was coming. Anne had arrived, too, and we came home."

Susannah got to her feet, came close to him.

"Thanks for telling me."

"Shall I tell you something else?"

She looked straight up at him in the silver light and the
black shadows.

"I think I'd trust you to tell me anything, Terry. I think
you'd know what not to tell me."

"Yes," he said, after a moment, "I think I know what
not to tell you. Except perhaps this: that it doesn't hurt so
much now. It doesn't hurt at all, Sue. It's like something
very beautiful that was too sweet to last."

"Thanks," she said again thickly.

"One's richer for having had it, Sue."

"Not always, Terry. One's so—poor!"

The last word was almost inaudible. Immediately she
looked up and spoke in her usual controlled, easy fashion.

"Thanks so much for this grand walk, Terry. See you
tomorrow!"

~ CHAPTER XXIII ~

ONE AIRLESS EVENING IN LATE JULY she was dining alone
in the dining room's candlelight. Susannah had been delayed
at the Flicketts' cabin, where there was a new baby, and had
come home to find Laverne and 'Liza still absent. It was almost seven o'clock on a Thursday. On Thursday nights the
girls were free and usually went to Brown's Mill to the
movie on the six-ten bus. Tonight they had probably taken
it for granted that Susannah would dine with Anne.

Rather pleased than otherwise at the spacious order and
quiet and emptiness of the old house, Susannah had managed
to find herself the sort of supper she liked, had set her place
at the end of the big table and had lighted the candles.

But although she had propped a book up against the pot-
tery salad bowl, and had moved the nearest candle into position to light it, she did not read very steadily. Only an hour
earlier she had had in her hands the pulpy little warm body
of the smallest Flickett. "Leroy" was to be the name, the
mother, sunk in dirty blankets on this hot day in a dirty
room into which no air was admitted, had decided faintly.

There were already nine Flicketts; pale little stringy boys
and girls whose natural advantages of pure country air and
clean country food were more than offset by the horrors of
the Flickett environment and the limitations of the Flickett

ideals. This little boy, like his brothers and sisters, would be ill dressed, ill sheltered from his birth. He would be fed at odd hours from smeared spoons and bowls; his diet would include cheap strong-flavored candy, doughnuts, pork chops, fried potatoes, pie, cucumbers, anything else that he happened to fancy or that his mother happened to have at hand.

Susannah had lifted him to her cheek in the first hour of his life when, through her ministrations, he had been bathed and powdered and clad in decent simple baby clothes. She had pressed her face against the softness and fragrance of him, her whole heart going out to him in love and pity, her mind visualizing his future in one wide sweep; the lights that would dazzle his delicate eyes, the shrill angry voices that would echo in his ears, the sour, infected food that would be put into his exquisite little body.

Tonight she was thinking of him still, wondering what might be even the beginning of a move to save him, to ensure him at least a chance, when, raising her eyes, she saw, standing like a little shadow in the doorway that led into the kitchen, the figure of another boy, a thin, bedraggled little fellow of perhaps seven or eight, who had approached quite unheard and was looking at her timidly.

Frightened for a second, Susannah's instant reaction was of reassurance. She knew this boy.

"Phil!" she said. "My darling! Where have you come from?"

He came slowly forward, and she saw that he was very dusty and looked as if he had been walking a long way. The small, sensitive face was pale under dirt and tear stains.

"I came to see you," he said, in his old-fashioned little way.

"I'm so glad you did! Have you had your supper? It's very late, and of course you have!"

"No," he said, close to the table now and looking at cold chicken and sliced tomatoes eagerly. "I've not had my supper." He put out his hand and took a piece of chicken and ate it quickly. Susannah was speechless with shock. He couldn't—Alec's child couldn't be hungry!

"Who's with you, Phil? How did you get here, darling?" As she spoke she had pushed up a chair, put a buttered bun into his hand, reached for a glass from the sideboard and filled it with milk. "Sit there and eat, anyway," she said, resuming her seat, "and we'll talk later."

"Nobody's with me," he began brightly. And instantly he was overwhelmed, and put his dark, beautiful little head down against his grubby little hands and was weeping.

Susannah pushed her chair back and went about the table and knelt down beside him, putting an arm about him. He twisted himself about; his hot wet face and tumbled hair dug, baby fashion, into her neck; his pipestem arm went about her with a convulsive clutch.

"Tell me about it, Phil." But she held his glass and his bun ready for him as he began his story.

"I guess you wouldn't want a boy in your house who ran away from camp, would you, Sanna? I guess you wouldn't!" he said with trembling lips.

"Camp? But isn't that miles from here?"

"No, it's the new camp. It's up in Bakerlake Grove. And they were mean to me; Sturges and Jones were *both* mean to me," the little boy said, in a fresh burst of reminiscent resentment and grief. "And we saw a sign that said 'Pemberton, seven miles,' and so when they were all reading after lunch I came downstairs and started for here!"

"Not all alone!"

His eyes flooded again. "Yes, all alone."

"And how did you find the house?"

"I asked at the gas station."

"That was smart of you! You poor little fellow!" Susannah said the last words to herself, noticing, as he talked, the baby softness and beauty that still lingered about the white nape of his neck, the innocent upcurve of his eyelashes.

"Sanna, could I stay with you tonight?"

"Tell me more about what the boys did, and what Mr Mason said."

"Mason said . . . and so Jones laughed and said he wasn't a baby, anyhow . . . and Mrs Moore said . . ."

She listened, watching him, her heart wrung. So little and so helpless, and Alec's son, and she had hardly given him two consecutive thoughts in her life. Susannah's heart swelled with a sudden love and pity for him that were agonizing, that loosened the floodgates and made her feel sick and weak with something like an actual vertigo. It was in a voice that was not steady, and with tears brimming her smiling eyes, that she finally said:

"Phil dear, while you're finishing your cookies I'm going to telephone to camp. There's a telephone there?"

"Oh yes, in Captain Mason's cabin. But I don't remember the number," he said anxiously. "Are you goin' to tell 'em 'bout me? Will they come get me?"

She was still kneeling beside him. Her eyes were filled with pain as she asked:

"If they did come and get you, would they punish you?"

"No, they don't punish us little fellers, Sanna. But I don't want to go back tonight on account of Jones. Couldn't you poss'ly let me stay here tonight?" he pleaded.

Susannah put her arm about him now and kissed him for the first time.

"My darling, of course you will stay here tonight. You and I'll make up your bed and see what we can find you for a nightgown. But I must telephone Captain Mason; they must be terribly worried. And I'll tell him that you're going to be with me, now."

"Not stay with you?" he said incredulously.

"As long as you like, Phil."

"Do you mean a week?"

"I mean longer than that, if you want to stay."

"Till the boys go back home after camp?"

"And after that if you like. You can go to school here with a boy I know named Jerd, who's about your size. And you and I'll have picnics, and you can see the puppies out in the barn tomorrow, and you needn't ever think of school or the boys again!"

He had stopped eating; he was looking at her intently.

"Can't they come and get me?" he asked fearfully.

"Not if I say they can't."

"Won't Gramma make 'em?"

"Not if I ask her not to." And Susannah remembered the stately old lady, tears running down her cheeks, her old hands holding Sanna's hands tightly, her voice harsh with emotion as she said: "My dear, why couldn't it have been the other way! Alec's boy has been changed to another school. He's not happy, the poor little fellow; we're nearly distracted trying to find the right place for him! You lose your child, and nobody wants the other one."

This had been said in so black an hour that the words had made no impression. Susannah had not been listening. She had been able to hear only the sound of men's voices, low and considerate, in the adjoining room—the men who were taking away the beautiful waxen little statue that had been Evelina.

But the words came back to her now, and with them the blood seemed to run more lightly, more swiftly than it had run for many weeks in her heart, and she got to her feet with a sense of buoyancy that was almost happiness, the wonderful sense of being able to solve all life's problems for a child and dissolve them into happiness.

He would not let her go to the telephone without him. It touched her that he accompanied her and wedged himself against her while she talked, his breath caught in excitement, his eyes never for one instant leaving hers.

"What did he say, what did he say?" he demanded eagerly when she had finished. "Did you say I had to see a doctor?"

"I said that, Phil," she explained, with a smile that took him into her counsels, "because I *am* going to have Doctor Mitchell see you; but not because you're sick—just because he's a great friend of mine. And I thought if I said 'doctor,' Captain Mason might think you were just ill enough to stay in bed a little while and not be in a hurry to come after you. And now do you know what I think you and I ought to do? We ought to walk over to Jerd's house and borrow some clothes for you. So suppose you wash your face and hands and we'll go right now?"

"Oh, I love to be with you!" Phil said. Susannah did not answer. But during the short walk in the sweet summer night she never let go of his friendly little firm hand.

The hour that followed was one of the good hours. Anne and Terry were reading, Jerd and Nan skirmishing up and down the stairs in their nightgowns, when the visitors arrived. There were a few moments of dazzled smiling and explanations. Then Anne was seriously consulting Phil as to nightwear, and Nan, hanging upon the arm of Susannah's chair, was rapturously interrogating her about the newcomer.

"Is he going to stay? . . . Is his name Phil? . . . Will he play Indians with Jerd and me? . . . Is he going to sleep in the little room where I slept that night?"

Susannah answered her gravely, point by point. But Terry, idle in a chair in the bay-window ingle near by, thought that he had not seen Susannah so animated, so like herself for a long time. And he noted, too, that already her eyes went once or twice to the stairway, as if she hoped Phil and Anne were coming down again.

"Come on, Phil," she said, when he appeared. "You must be a pretty tired boy tonight. Say good night to Nan and Jerd—and Aunt Anne—and Uncle Terry. That's a darling."

Phil again put his hand in hers, and it was still there when she mounted the stairs in the home hallway and showed him the little room in which he was to sleep. He looked up at her trustingly.

"I guess we can keep our doors open, so if we want to talk in the night we can hear each other?" he suggested, and her heart went out afresh to the little fellow who was still baby enough to be frightened in strangeness and dark.

"Yes, let's do that, Phil."

He was businesslike and independent in the matter of undressing, but she hovered about, smoothing sheets and opening windows in case he should need her. She suggested a bath.

"Do I have to?" he asked, sitting on the edge of his bed in bodily wrestle with shoelaces.

"Of course you don't have to!"

"Then I won't." He came across the room in Jerd's faded old pajamas to raise both his arms up to her for a goodnight kiss. Susannah tightened her own arms about him, pressed her hungry cheek against his little shock head. "I'm so glad I got here!" he said sleepily.

"I'm glad you're here!" Susannah said, but not to him.

❧ CHAPTER XXIV ❧

THAT NIGHT SUSANNAH SAT UP until after midnight writing letters. One was addressed to little Phil's grandmother, one went to Alec's lawyer in New York City, a long one to her own mother in Peking. She had written her mother only once in the recent past weeks; a first letter after Evelina's going when she could hardly hold her pen to the paper or see the words she wrote for tears. But she found that she could write tonight and make the letter one not too hard for her mother to read.

Phil awakened her in the night. Her clock's hands stood at twenty minutes to three when she heard his anxious voice close beside her.

"Sanna!"

"My darling!" she said, starting up bewildered, touching a light. Against the shadowy background of the wide room he stood, small and flushed in his little pajamas, looking at her with troubled dark eyes.

"Sanna, I thought maybe they were coming to get me."

"Ah no, they wouldn't do that!" She flung her covers wide. "Get in here, dear, and I'll get you your own pillow."

This arrangement evidently was satisfactory. He settled down upon the pillow, happily conversational.

"I guess I had a bad dream."

"I should think you had! But, Phil," she went into it very seriously, "they'll not come after you. I telephoned them to say that you were going to be my boy for a while, and I've written Dad and Granny that you're here."

"Oh, *did* you?"

"Just now, while you were asleep." Susannah, on her side of the bed, reached her hand toward the light. "Now you've got to go to sleep, it's almost three o'clock," she said.

"Gee, you're kind!" Phil murmured.

It was darkness again.

"Will you go to sleep now, Phil?"

"Well, I was lyin' here, thinkin'."

"Don't lie there and think any more. Go straight to sleep."

"I thought Captain Mason was a big spider."

"That was only a dream. You won't have any more dreams."

"No, I won't have any more dreams now."

He was almost immediately asleep. It was Susannah who lay wakeful, thinking. But the nearness of the little, trusting, deep-breathing creature was strangely soothing, too; after a while she gingerly turned herself into a sleeping position, felt a heavenly drowsiness take possession of her.

He was still deep asleep when she awakened in the summer morning, and saw opal colors shifting on the walls of the old room, and green light filtering through the high elms at the window. Phil was sprawled over two thirds of the bed. Susannah felt quite cramped and stiff from having been gradually pushed into the remaining space.

She got up cautiously, stepping about the room quietly. He was tired out, poor little chap. He had trotted seven miles on his eight-year-old feet, with God knew how many detours and delays!

"We have company," she said to Laverne, in the kitchen.

"Terry Duquesne stay overnight?" Laverne asked with

country directness. Susannah felt her color rising as she laughed.

"A very much younger gentleman—Mr Hazeltyne's little boy—my husband's little boy by his first wife. She died soon after Phil was born, and he's been handed about between schools and nurses ever since."

"Well, 'sakes," Laverne observed. "It 'll be kind of good to have a——" She changed the phrase: "It 'll be nice to have him here," she said.

The big kitchen had windows facing east and west; the sun was at neither now, but the room was full of subdued morning light. Its woodwork was scoured clean, its big stove twinkled in nickel and polished iron, and Laverne, stepping between the shining faucets of the sink and the smoking coffeepot on the electric plate, was like a presiding goddess fittingly attired in crisp percale and a flowing checked apron.

"All I fixed for you, Mis' Hazeltyne, is your fruit and toast."

"Well—we have some cooked cereal, haven't we?" Oh yes, there was cooked cereal still in its big box on the long pantry shelves. Susannah's heart reminded her with a stab why that box was there, and of the little voice that had said, " 'Verne b'ingin' my bowl!" so happily at many a breakfast hour.

But the pain was swiftly gone when Philip's voice behind her made her turn. He was descending the narrow angled flight of the kitchen stairs; he looked deliciously fresh and rested, with water still hanging in drops upon his combed hair, and yesterday's dusty khaki shirt open to show his throat.

"I talked to 'Liza," he said.

"Oh, did you, darling? This is Phil, Laverne."

"Well, say, hello, Phil," Laverne said, pauses between the words.

"She was makin' her bed!" Philip announced. "I heard

her singin' and I went in. And she showed me how to come down."

"You came down the back way."

"It's a sort of nice way for a boy," he said. "D'joo have your breakfas'?"

"No, not yet."

"Come on, then," he said, his friendly hand held out.

"Laverne's put my table out here on the grass, Phil. You ask her for your plate and napkin."

They sat down together, and the sunshine and shade filtered down upon them in blots of mellow shadow and morning brightness. In the beginning Phil was a little anxious for fear that he would be followed and taken back to camp, but Susannah ultimately reassured him. And toward the end of the meal Terry came over with little Nan and Jerd, and Susannah had the satisfaction of watching the children in the swift process of making friends, hearing their shouts and laughter as they drifted further and further away up the shady stretches of the orchard, calling back to them entire sanction when from the brookside the demanded permission to get "maybe sort of a little wet."

"How'd he find you, Sue?" Terry said, helping her with the cutting of overgrown raspberry whips and blackberry vines, while this was going on.

"Desperation, poor little chap. He was at camp seven miles from here, and terribly unhappy. He had a nurse much too long. She was a nice, intelligent woman, and she brought him along fast enough, as far as that went, but quite suddenly Alec's mother dismissed her and packed him off to a boys' school, and then a camp, and he wasn't ready for them."

Susannah paused to look for sympathy in Terry's expression. She had on an old ticking apron that had been hanging in one of the closets of the house when she had moved in. Laverne had laundered it, and it had become her favorite

gardening wear. On the back of her head was a broad-
brimmed straw hat of the farmer type, bound in black tape;
her slender wrists disappeared into big gauntlets.

"D'you know you're very beautiful?" Terry observed. Susannah smiled.

"That's the way to talk!"

Some days before, in the jungle of the side garden, she
had discovered a buried path and a lost gate leading into a
sunken and long-abandoned lane. Completely submerged
now in a wave of berry bushes, these once had provided a
short cut in the exact direction of the Duquesne house; by
clearing them, crossing the road, and taking the little path
back of the Simmonses' barn, the distance between the two
places would be appreciably lessened. Now Susannah and
Terry were beginning an onslaught on the thirty years' ac-
cumulation of garden growths that choked the old way.
Flushed, disheveled, eager, she turned to his always ready
look a smile that he had not seen on her face for weeks.

"Are you going to keep this little gent?"

"Keep him!" she echoed, beginning her hacking and dragging again. "I should always have had him," she said. "I'll
never quite forgive myself that all this time I didn't take
him! His nurse—she really was a friendly nice kind of person, and he adored her; she took him up to Lake George—
she had cousins there, I believe, in the summers—that part
wasn't so bad. But to have let him go off to school——

"Terry, how the mean things we do to children hurt us!
I remember now that when—when we were with his grandmother last Christmas he rather made love to me, he asked
me if I didn't think boarding schools were rather lonesome
places for boys—blind, stupid, cruel brute that I was——"
She stopped on a mirthless laugh.

"Susannah!"

"I know. They sound affected—those words. But I never
saw his little problem at all. Oh, Terry——"

She left the jungle of the berry bushes and walked toward the house and sat down in a wicker chair at the terrace table, one muddy, stiff gauntlet pressed against her eyes, her elbow on the table.

"Sue," he said anxiously, beside her.

"Oh no, I was just thinking," she said in a whisper, as he knelt down so that their faces were close together, "I was just thinking how sweet—how unutterably sweet she was that Christmas Day, rushing about in the firelight, and how much we made of her, and how little of him! He came and stood beside me and dug his little head into my shoulder, and I never saw it."

Breathing shallow and fast, as if she had been running, she looked at him with darkened eyes. Terry spoke tenderly, as if to a child:

"You'll make it up to him now! Don't forget that you were in terrible distress about your divorce, last Christmas, and that he had a father and a grandmother and a devoted nurse——"

She was looking at him thoughtfully. Now with a hand that she bared with a sudden gesture, a hand that felt warm and soft from the glove, she drew a fingertip across his eyebrow.

"You comfort me," she said slowly. "I wonder why God put you just where He did to comfort me, Terry?"

"I don't know," he said in a whisper.

"I'm going to make it up to him, Terry."

"To the little fellow? To Phil?"

"He's going to have the happiest childhood any boy ever had. He's going to have a treetop house and a robber's cave and a cook stove, and all the chains and ropes and hammers and nails in the world, and books, and Jerd here whenever he'll come."

"His camp experience will only make it more wonderful to him, Sue," Terry said, as she paused.

"Oh, I hope so! Oh, Terry, if someone could only do it for every boy. One thinks of all the thousands who want the country, want the woods and the creek——"

"Think, instead, of all the millions who have them, Sue."

"I know," she said, comforted. And then with a sudden change of mood, "Come on! We're just getting under way!"

They went back to battle with the dusty, long, angry tentacles of the vines again, to drag them from their clutch upon stumps and underbrush, to heap them triumphantly upon the wilting pile that blocked the drive.

Phil and Jerd appeared, panting, perspiring, businesslike.

"Kin we have a rake and some kine of a bucket and kin we have a rope off the stable door and kin we take our lunch up there becuz we haven't a gose of a chance to get through with what we gotter do?"

Terry saw Susannah put her arm about the smaller boy, lay her lovely flushed cheek against his, heard the cadences in her voice as she said: "Take anything you want. But be sure you tell Chess. Come back when I call for you and I'll have your lunch ready!"

After that she and her boy were everywhere together; often their hands were linked as they went about; often, in the Duquesnes' parlor in the early autumn evenings they saw him, tired from playing, go to her and climb into her lap while the grown-ups talked. And when he did, Susannah changed her position to accommodate his little dark head, braced him with an arm about him, rested her cheek against his hair.

In September he started off to the Pemberton school between Nan and Jerd. Susannah had her supper at six o'clock now, the better to accommodate his hours. He was an exquisite child, affectionate, sympathetic, eager and understanding; his gaiety kept the house noisy; his small feet stamping on the stairs, his shouts, the sound of his laughter and of his shower bath, his prized "B.B." gun and his bumps

and breakages effectually scattered the long silences. And
when he was in trouble, when he cut his hand, when a bigger
boy wrenched away his velocipede, when he needed Susannah, his wild rush for her, his stammered explanations, his
serious acceptance of her verdict that he must forgive the
bad big boy, that he mustn't be mad at anyone, made him
seem in these times dearer than in any other.

"Is he like him, Sue?" Terry demanded suddenly one
night.

She had given Phil his supper alone on this occasion and
had seen him started, under 'Liza's guidance, toward bed,
before coming over to Anne for dinner. There had been
guests—a rather pedantic professor, his eager, charming
wife who quoted Patmore, and their two big, gawky, clever
boys. Now Anne was driving them to their train, for Terry
had cut his foot, and it was bandaged largely, and Susannah
and Terry were sharing a small coal fire and waiting for
Anne to come back, to discuss the guests.

"Is—is what, Terry?" she asked, looking up.

Terry flushed and laughed, meeting her eyes with an
ashamed smile.

"I don't know why I asked that! I wasn't thinking."

"If Phil was——" Her own color rushed up, and she
smiled too. "You mean like Alec?" she asked in return.
"Were we talking about them?"

"No, we weren't," he admitted. "But I thought——"

There was a silence.

"I'm always thinking about one thing," Terry confessed,
looking into the fire, grinding his long-fingered hands together.

Susannah did not speak.

"And it just occurred to me," he floundered, "it occurred
to me—I spoke really to myself——"

"Oh yes, he's terribly like Alec," Susannah said, after another pause. "His smile—and the way he throws back his

hair. They aren't alike in features exactly, but I see Alec in him all the time. Everything," she added, in a lower tone, as if she spoke to herself, "everything that I loved in Alec."

"Past tense," Terry said, not looking at her.

"Present, too," she said, with a rueful little smile.

"Is it that way, Sue?"

"Oh yes. He isn't the sort one—stops loving." She let the words rest in the air for a few seconds before adding: "But that isn't why I adore my Pips. It's because he came into a great big aching hole in my heart and began to plaster it up with those square little hands of his. And because he is affectionate, and because he needed me, and because he loves me."

"There isn't ever going to be any chance for anyone else, Sue?"

"I'm sorry, Terry." She glanced at him now, and smiled like an apologetic child.

"Nothing to be sorry about. I'd rather—fight with it," he said, keeping his tone carefully casual, "than not have it. I can't go back now, even in my own mind, to the time when you weren't in that house up the road. Every time I go for the mail, or open a window on your side of the house, or see anyone moving in the lane, I think it's you. Or it may be you. There was a woman in a hardware shop in Morristown the other day whose voice was rather like yours; I stood perfectly still until she went away—I couldn't have moved to save my life. I found myself staring into windows of women's hats—women's shoes, thinking, 'She has a blue like that,' or 'She said she wanted some good heavy walking shoes.' "

"You've a genius for friendship—you and Anne both," Susannah said.

"The whole world's ablaze with you," Terry added simply. "Possessed with you. You walk over here with Phil and call: 'Where are you, Anne?' and I'm done for, for fifteen minutes."

Self-possessed, smiling at him in mother fashion, she sat enthroned in her high-backed chair, a gracious slender figure in a dark, thin flowered frock that spread about her like the petals of an inverted rose.

"It's made a great difference to me, your liking me," she said simply. "Don't think I'm not proud of it. Don't think it means nothing to me that I'm liked by a man like you— perhaps the wisest man, in the way he lives and thinks, and the things he does——"

She stopped, but Terry did not speak. Grinding his palms again, he stared into the fire. After a moment Susannah went on:

"Perhaps the wisest man I ever knew," she completed it. "A man who lives as he believes, and sends his money to causes that are great causes, and works in his garden, and loves every day for what it has, and not for what tomorrow has or yesterday had——"

She paused on a bewildered little laugh.

"I'm outlining your philosophy for me, Terry, not for you. You've taught me how to live, you and Anne. To live on in spite of the mistakes and the losses—to live happier, it may be, happier because of them. Sometimes," Susannah ended, her voice thickening, and the eyes that had been fixed on the fire suddenly brimming as she looked up to smile at him—"sometimes for a few minutes, Terry, I catch a glimpse of the—the Kingdom within, and then every red leaf and every scent of brush fires and every sunrise and every slice of Laverne's good homemade bread seems to have light through it!"

"And a little of that," he said, clearing his throat, and speaking with a boy's shamed embarrassment, "—a little of that is because your big brother is across the road?"

"A lot because of that."

"Then you couldn't go so far, Sue, without going further. Without letting me hope that some day it 'll be you and I and Phil always together."

She did not answer, and Anne came in, and presently they were all talking of the Genungs, whether Sally wasn't cleverer than Joe, and if those boys were really so smart that they seemed dumb or were really dumb. Afterward Laverne stopped with her own car for Susannah, and Susannah would let Terry come only as far as the door to say good night. He must take care of that foot! And lunch tomorrow? There was no other moment of sentiment between them.

Yet she went home with an oddly warmed and stirred heart just the same.

CHAPTER XXV

SHAKILY, TREMBLINGLY, her heart took hold of happiness again. There were still hours in her life when the bitter waters of grief engulfed her, and when for a little while she could see no light beyond what, as she told Anne and Terry, was all "blackness and drowning and not being able to breathe."

But between these times, and exceeding them in duration by seven hours—ten hours—sometimes even by days, were times of peace. The shelter she had found for herself in the old farmhouse was the home her heart wanted. She came to realize as the months went by that there is such a home in the background of every woman's dreams, sometimes humble sometimes pretentious, but hers, and that there can be no happiness for any woman until her setting fits her with the same comfort that her shoes must.

Such a setting, for herself, was the farmhouse. She loved every inch of it: the garden that blossomed so royally under her hands, the mellowed old silver barns and fences, the way the hills rose rambling under other farms and orchards all about her, the mighty towers of her dooryard trees and the rise of her steep rooftree beneath them.

Every one of her dozen or more rooms was dear to her. It was impossible to count the rooms exactly for the wide hallway that divided the house crosswise and that caught the morning sun on its eastern windows and the sunset at the other end was used as much as any room, and Laverne's quarters, reached by the little back hallways upstairs and the twisted stairway from the kitchen below, rambled off into the "other kitchen chamber" and the "spinning room" and so went into the "barn chamber" over that particular barn which had been turned into a garage. Also there were the big dormered attic with two dim cluttered rooms partitioned off at one dusty end, and the "sick bay" beyond Susannah's own room, where she had a cushioned steamer chair for winter sun baths, and window shelves lined with potted plants. There was no end to the rooms.

Opposite the parlor, across a narrow entrance hall from which the front stairs steeply ascended, was another big square room that had been long unfurnished except for books and chairs and summer awnings and all the other miscellany that was not in immediate use. Susannah restored the parlor to its ancient estate with a fine rug or two that might have been brought straight from the Orient in an old sailing vessel, with polished fruitwood chairs, samplers and old color prints, prim curtains of scalloped dimity bound in shining green glazed calico, and a wallpaper dimly figured in vales and trees. On the mantel and the whatnot shelves she put whatever she could find of old treasure: a ship in a green glass bottle, a Dresden shepherdess eternally curtseying in a froth of white lace skirts, paperweights in glass that prisoned a thousand Botticelli flowers, bottles of etched blue glass, fire screens in fine point.

But the dining room was the real living room; a long, narrow apartment, somehow its simple old proportions had the indefinable quality of charm. The blackened oak wood of the floors was worn to oily softness and sloped almost imperceptibly to the fireplace at the north end; the chimney mouth was seven feet wide; the firedogs had come from England before America had been America. Bedded in the chimney bricks, back of the blaze was the ancient iron plate that bore a coat of arms, blackened now by thousands of fires, but still providing a tie between the old world and the new.

In this room the rugs were of braided rags; the chairs all of the same period were mismated, the candlesticks on the mantelpiece wore crystal danglers. At the south end two floor windows gave upon the terrace; in summer the table was set here, out under the green leaves. In winter it went to the fireplace end, and it was close to the heartening blaze that Susannah and Philip ate their first Thanksgiving dinner together.

He was broadening now, had put on weight and height, and was no longer the forlorn little figure who had broken in so suddenly upon her solitude on that August night. Noisy, eager, imaginative and vital, Phil had made himself a place not only in her life, but in that of the Duquesne household, and indeed of Pemberton itself, and Susannah found herself eternally amused, proud, concerned, occupied with his interests.

He was the sort of child who leads, and as he grew into the most real happiness, perhaps the very first, his life had ever known, he developed powers that involved the building of Indian camps and tree houses, the digging of caves, the planning of excursions, the organization of clubs. He wanted a printing press and a jig saw for Christmas; he managed a circus in the barn and collected the nucleus of a museum in one of the empty sheds behind the barn.

With all this he had his moods of a thoughtfulness so exquisite, a sensitiveness and sympathetic understanding so far beyond his years that Susannah, her arm about him as he talked earnestly to her, could only wonder whether a son of her own could ever have been closer or more dear. He worshiped her with the wholehearted devotion of a child who has hungered, without knowing that he hungered, for a mother. At movies he must wriggle himself in close beside her; at night she must give him a last kiss and hug before he would sleep, and at meals, no matter how many or how important her guests, she must carry his plate and glass to the place beside hers.

"I guess I can squeeze in here. I guess 'Verne forgot that I b'long here," he would say.

Phil had the lead in the Sixth Grade Christmas play at school, when, straight and serious in mud-spattered buff and blue, he impersonated Washington; and Jerd, gallant in British scarlet, as Howe, warned him that his was a lost cause.

"You are bein' foolush, General," said Jerd. "The rebel col'nies mus' retrac' their boas'."

"Never, wile I am abul to command a man, a horse or an ideel of humin freedim," the father of his country said undauntedly in reply.

Terry, Susannah and Anne went to the school auditorium to see the Christmas festivities and entertainment; indeed for some weeks before the event they had all had much to do with the arrangement of the tree and the gifts. The hall was hot on the bitter cold winter night, and filled with an admiring audience of children who stamped and clapped at intervals while waiting for the curtain to rise, and with flushed and crimped mothers in best silk gowns who percolated about nervously and followed with anxious, silent lips the words their own children had to say.

The Eighth Grade opened the entertainment with a dance of the Zingari. The High School took up the entire second half of it with a Christmas legend, in which pilgrims, peasants, kings and shepherds were pleasingly intermingled, snow fell, red lights shone from a stable door, and a chorus off-stage sang Yuletide anthems. In between these offerings the Sixth and Seventh Grades had their little play, "A Country Is Born," and whether it was because Nan as a heroic colo-

nial wife, Jerd as the British commander, and Philip in the
immemorial first regimentals of the new republic were
their own, or perhaps because the little play really did have
a certain simplicity and truth and power about it, their three
most interested auditors were in tears.

But many another proud parent and friend was in tears
that night, and after the tears came laughter, and singing,
and the distribution of gifts, and the cutting of many a cake,
and the clean, piercing smell of coffee, going about on trays
carried by smiling girls. It was only one typical American
school party among the thousands that were going on all
over the nation that night, but to Susannah it had real feeling. She loved it. She circulated about among the happy folk,
too busy and too much needed to remember what her heart
might have remembered, to sink into the black gulf of pain
whose surface was not yet quite bridged.

There was much bundling up at midnight of sleepy, happy,
talkative children. Christmas Eve was coming in black and
frozen when Terry and Anne and Susannah steered their
excited charges out into the darkness of starlight on snow,
the solemnity of night under bare trees and clicking, snow-
laden branches.

"That's my sleepy boy. I was so proud of you!" Susannah murmured, engineering Phil into a dimly lighted house,
shivering her way upstairs, finding her big room and his
adjoining little one almost too warm from the red-bellied
iron stove, finding a boiling hot-water bag safe among her
sheets. Laverne and 'Liza had of course shared the school
party, but one or the other, or some available Trimler, had
slipped away two or three times during the evening to keep
up the fires. She and Philip could shudder in all the delight
of returning warmness as they undressed, with doors
sociably open and conversation not interrupted until the small
boy crept under his blankets too sleepy even to say good
night or feel her kiss on his forehead as he went off.

❧ CHAPTER XXVI ❧

ONE DARK JANUARY DAY when Phil was at school and snow fluttering down from a leaden sky, Susannah was upstairs in the little boy's room going over his wardrobe and putting his effects in order. Phil had been moved now from the very small bedroom next her own to a big front chamber that Susannah had delighted to furnish with two plain flat beds covered with dark brown-striped blankets, a linoleum floor with a compass and map engrained in it, long bookcases already filling fast with the adventures of Mowgli, Tarzan, Billena of Oz and Nils of Sweden, and plain tobacco-brown curtains at the many-paned square windows that today looked out upon a world all gray and white.

In the airtight stove that was safeguarded by a low grille of iron from the rolling, bounding, leaping and racing of Phil and his associates, a comforting fire had been burning for a long time; the air was soft and warm, and in the darkness of afternoon Susannah had lighted a lamp. In the cone of radiance it shed upon her she was examining a box of odds and ends that had come in Phil's trunk from school two months earlier.

Answering telegrams that had granted her desire to keep the child had immediately come from Alec's lawyer. Susan-

266

nah had been oddly touched at their promptness. She knew
that Alec had been in California, had been back in New
York, had gone abroad with Merle; he might have been anywhere when her appeal to the lawyer had gone. She had
reinforced it with a letter to Alec's mother, who had been
in Canada. She had meanwhile refused to send the child
back to school or camp at least until replies had arrived, as
the school authorities had politely suggested.

Within ten days it had all been settled. "Mr Hazeltyne
is entirely willing to give you charge of his son for a
while," the New York attorney had wired, "wishes to express appreciation of your interest." Alec's mother had been
frankly grateful for this solution of the problem, too. She
had come to Pemberton to see her grandson and Susannah
on a clear, hot, dreaming autumn day, and had approved of
everything at the farm, and especially of the glowing brown,
eager child into whom Phil had grown.

So that that had all been satisfactory. But there had been
details that must be adjusted with more leisure. Captain
Mason had sent Susannah a printed form to augment his
explanation that in case of a child's removal from school or
camp all moneys paid in advance for board and tuition were
forfeit, and Susannah had replied, agreeing fully with this
regulation. Phil's belongings had then been sent from camp
and from school to his grandmother in the city, as another
school regulation decreed that only to the person originally
assuming responsibility for a boy could his possessions be
returned. The older Mrs Hazeltyne having gone at this time
with friends to South America, a long delay ensued, and it
was Christmastime before the outgrown clothing and all the
miscellaneous treasures of his small-boy days had reached
Susannah's hands.

Philip had by this time outgrown toys as well as sweaters
and socks. Susannah had taken great delight in outfitting
him anew. Now she was assorting all the old things with an

eye to the miserable Penseys and the Gibberts, who always had children of all sizes in need of wearing apparel.

In the trunk with them was the child's picture of his mother, framed in chased gold, with Phil's initials and his mother's cut on either side of the frame. Susannah studied the pretty, spoiled little face in the soft lamplight. She had seen this picture before; Alec had it. She had forgotten just what a determined-looking little person Betty Livingston had been; her looks fitted in well with what Alec had said at odd times of her willfulness and her caprices. The boy was like his father, yet Susannah saw something of his mother, too, in the set of his beautiful eyes and the way his heavy dark hair waved away from his forehead.

Broken wrist watches, broken cameras, broken chains and boxes and water pistols and patent pens and pencils—what a mess it was! Susannah discovered a magnificent box of tracks and trains and remembered buying it with Alec only three Christmases past; she found wallets and suitcases and leather toilet appurtenances marked with little Phil's initials in silver and gold. Only a baby, and they had felt their duty done when any expensive gift, "something suitable for a little boy," had been selected and sent!

Letters. There was a little sheaf of letters in one of these leather cases. Susannah's heart contracted when she recognized Alec's office address engraved in the upper left-hand corner of the envelopes. He had dictated his letters to Phil! But what matter? The child had been far too young to appreciate any distinction here.

One handwritten letter from Honolulu. Susannah opened it. Its date was more than six months old. Alec had written:

MY DEAR PHIL:

Your grandmother may have written you that your little sister died very suddenly about a week ago. She cabled me, but I was at sea, and the cable waited here.

Merle and I got here only this morning. This is very sad news, and makes me wish that I were not so far away, for although you only saw the baby occasionally I know from your letter last Christmas that you loved her, and I would like to talk to you about her. Sanna is of course heartbroken, and I wish you would write her a letter saying that you are sorry. When I come home, which will probably be just as soon as I can get my Manila business going, I am going to suggest to her that she build a little wing on the hospital in Morristown in memory of the baby. Don't you think that would be a good way to help other babies not to get the same sickness? This is a very beautiful place, all flowers and beaches, and some day I will bring you here. Much love, my dear boy, from your affectionate,

FATHER.

Susannah crushed the letter against her heart, the full bitterness of loss washing over her in dizzying waves. She felt her head rock with vertigo. For a moment all the forces in her body seemed to be plunging in a sickening confusion, and she shut her eyes and steadied herself with a grip on the arm of her chair.

Then calm came back, and she could look again at the words Alec had written. Far away in the scented silver rain and shine of the semitropical islands he had thought of her; his heart had ached for her as well as for his child. Alec had always been kind, except in that one thing that had carried him away from everything that was characteristic of him, and away from kindness with the rest.

Somehow, as she packed the letters away in a box on a high closet shelf for Phil's reading at some future day, and as she straightened the boyish-looking room and carried the books and boxes to their various destinations, it helped her to know that Alec had been sorry for her. She went downstairs to talk with Laverne in the warm big kitchen and finally settled herself beside the dining-room fire. Presently Phil with a galaxy of boys his own age burst in, red-cheeked, scattering snow in damp clots on the oilcloth of the entry, demanding the attentions of 'Liza and Susannah, much rushing about for towels and slippers, and heavy inroads on chocolate cookies and long glasses of milk.

"Phil Hazeltyne, how did you ever get yourselves so sopping! And where 've you been for an hour? It's almost four."

"The scoutmaster took us on a walk—good ole Bricky!" Phil sputtered, as she flourished a great bath towel about his dripping head and combed his hair. "Gee, we snowballed him!"

"Jerd, should you have done that?" Jerd was the balance wheel of the gang, and all matters of manners and morals were referred to him.

"Oh, sure, he told us to, Aunt Sue!"

"Cooky, Gordon?"

"Thank you, Mis' Hazeltyne," Gordon Crocker said, embarrassed.

"Mom," said Phil, who occasionally substituted the name Jerd had for Anne for the "Sanna" he had always called Susannah, "what can we do?"

"Why, I found all your trains and tracks this afternoon. 'Liza and I opened all the boxes, and that brown box marked 'coats' was full of trains——"

That was all that was needed. They were streaming away from her upstairs before the last syllable was reached. Their shouting went on uninterruptedly for an hour, with occasional outbursts of tooting and whistling. Before six, mothers were telephoning and muffled fathers and small well-bundled figures were disappearing from the red glow of the side doorway into the softly falling curtain of twisting white flakes. The snow was assuming the dignity of a blizzard now, and all children belonged at home.

Susannah telephoned Anne.

"Anne, Jerd home safe? . . . Anne, I'm not coming over because it's so thick; Laverne went up to the barn to speak to Chess, and she said she had to find the fence to get back. . . . No, don't let Terry come for me, because I'm as lame as a tree from that walk this morning, and tired from putting things away this afternoon. Call me around eight tomorrow and we'll conspire for Nan's birthday."

She settled down to a supper of Laverne's cheese whip, bran muffins, damson preserves, with a Phil who apparently had entirely forgotten the hearty midafternoon meal of cookies and milk. They talked of their respective expeditions; Susannah and Terry had walked all the way to Martin's Crossing that morning; Phil had been out with the Scouts that afternoon. And they did Phil's homework.

For his activity of mind and body was of such a sort that merely eating did not fully occupy him. It exhilarated and stimulated him, and Susannah took advantage of that exhilaration and stimulation to discuss his history lesson, point by point, or open his arithmetic beside her plate and go seriously into the matter of Hugh and his oranges that were three quarters of the oranges that Thomas had and seven tenths of George's oranges. Under these circumstances Phil would concentrate. There was nothing formidable or terrifying about this way of getting through, and by the time a hot apple pudding was on the table he was working away cheerfully, bringing down subtrahends and minuends in fine style. Usually he and Jerd worked together for a little while after supper, but Jerd could not come over in the storm, and Phil's work was finished by the time supper was, anyway.

After supper Susannah settled herself in the chintz-frilled big low chair by the fire, and Chess Trimler came in with snowy armfuls of wood, and Laverne carried the dishes away. Phil, in his own chair, was savoring for the fifth time the colored sheets of Sunday's funnies, but when the clatter in the kitchen pantry ceased and the house grew very still, when 'Liza and Laverne had gone upstairs above the kitchen and there was no sound except the little tickling noises the snow made against the windows and the little tickling noises the fire made in answer, he got into Susannah's lap and rested there for a little while, dreaming, with wide-open eyes fixed on the burning logs.

"Sanna, do you think my mother would care if I loved you more than I did her?"

Her cheek went down against his hair.

"I don't think so, Phil. She's in heaven, and they understand everything there."

"She would know I was lonesome," he said. And after a while, "Sanna, do you s'pose anyone there is bein' as kind to your baby as you are bein' to me?"

"I think so."

"Could it be Mother?" he said.

"Perhaps so, Phil. Perhaps because you and I have found each other, she's found my little girl." She could talk to him sometimes of his half-sister; never to anyone else of Evelina.

"Will we always be with each other, Sanna?"

"Always, Phil."

"That's what I want it to be," he said. "I know you're not my mother, and I know I'm not really your boy, but I love you more than Sonny does his mother and more than Gordy Crocker loves *his* mother. An' I tole 'em so, too."

"But nicely."

"Nicely." He was getting very sleepy now, and Susannah was meditating going upstairs herself and getting into bed almost as soon as he, when there was a floundering and laughing and stamping confusion in the passage, and Terry came in with snow on his hair and melting snow on his boots.

"Anne wanted to be sure that everything was all right," he said shamelessly.

"Terry! In this snow!"

"I liked it. I had a lantern, real country fashion. Sue, you are comfortable in here! Hello, Pips."

"Hello, Uncle Terry. Gee, Uncle Terry, Sanna found all my old trains that I never could use at school . . ." Phil leaned against his shoulder, expatiating upon tracks, switches and semaphores, and Terry listened with his fine aristocratic face turned sympathetically to him. Susannah presently summoned the child from the doorway.

"Come on, Phil, 'Liza's upstairs. I'll be up in fifteen minutes. Don't forget *teeth*."

She took her chair again and smiled in the mellow lamplight at Terry.

"Crying, eh?" the man asked.

"I had a bad crying spell this afternoon," she admitted, in a puzzled, unaffected voice. "But I thought I'd powdered it out of sight. Phil didn't notice it, anyway, and he's usually pretty keen."

"What started you off, Sue?"

"Some letters of Alec's, I suppose. Letters to Phil. His room is all finished now, and we moved him in Saturday, and these letters were in some boxes they sent from school. It—it shook me up. One was about—last summer. It doesn't harm me to cry now and then, Terry. I think it makes me feel better, really."

"H'm!" he commented, glancing at her briefly, glancing back at the fire again.

"Would you talk to me about him, Sue?"

She raised shadowed eyes.

"Nothing much to say."

Terry looked at her, as she moved her gaze back to the flaming logs, looked at the fine hand against which the wide, full sleeve lay loosely, the whiteness of her temples against the rich red-brown of her wavy hair, the bronze eyelashes that were lowered on her cheeks. The cut of her gown was low and square in the neck, and he saw the beautiful curve of her breast, and the faded dull pink of the ashes-of-roses gown no softer against the skin than the skin itself.

"He still matters terribly, doesn't he?"

Susannah made no answer, except with a brief glance.

"I've come over tonight," Terry said, after a pause, and not looking at her as he spoke, "to say that I'm not equal to it, Sue, and that I'm going away."

There was a hint of a smile in her look.

"You had to come out in a blizzard to tell me that?"

The tall man, with his red hair, his thin, aristocratically featured face, rather reddened, too, just now, by firelight, his long hands locked, his head slightly dropped forward between his shoulders, and his narrowed eyes fixed on the fire, answered her quickly and forcefully, in brief, separated phrases:

"Exactly. I had to come—out into the blizzard—tonight. I tried to work—to read. It wasn't any use. You were here, across the lane, through the snow—you and this fire, and the lamp, and your voice. I'm not apologizing, or explaining. I had to come and I came."

There was a silence.

"If anyone had told me a year ago that I could possibly come to care for a woman as I've come to care for you, Sue, I would have thought it was funny," Terry presently recommenced. "Why, our group in Boston is full of attractive women, and they've made me a sort of standing—well, what?—joke for years. They've played me against their young men and told me their troubles and treated me generally as if I were the safest and most confirmed proposition in the world. I've felt myself to be!"

"One or two, according to Anne, haven't felt quite that way," Susannah interpolated dryly.

"No, one or two haven't," he admitted, with the same forceful, almost angry brevity of tone and phrase. "There,

was a very handsome smart little widow—her husband had
been my friend—who thought it would be a good arrangement for her and the children to take me on, and there was
a sweet young thing of about eighteen who decided that I
was lonely and that no woman had ever understood me. She's
married now—this Sylvia girl is—and the widow told me
this Christmas that she was running a very successful real-
estate agency, and didn't know whether she would marry a
man who is importuning her to that effect or not. I advised
her to marry."

He sometimes spoke with a unique and characteristic in-
cisiveness of diction. She had told him months earlier that
it was sometimes like listening to someone reading aloud. He
was speaking so now, quietly, indifferently, but with that
easy selection of words that made his speech so pleasant to
hear.

"So I think," he added, after a pause, as if the talk had
gone on in his own mind to further conclusions, "that I'll
get on a Norwegian steamer sometime in March, and go
through the Canal, and then go on from San Francisco. Aus-
tralia, maybe."

"Terry." Her heart sank a little at the thought. "To be
gone how long?"

"As long as I can stay away."

"But since when have you been thinking of this?"

"Oh, for a week. Two weeks maybe."

"Have you ever been to China, Terry?"

"No. I've never been to California, even."

She considered.

"I'm sorry," she said simply.

"Nothing for you to be sorry about. It's just—the way it
is. I can't stand it, and I'll have to try to get over it."

"No gardening this spring," Susannah commented.

"No anything. No anything." He ground his big hands
together. "I realized tonight," he recommenced in a low

tone, "oh, of course I've realized all along, almost from the first time I ever saw you—but I realized tonight that it's stronger than I am. It's obsession—fever—anything you like."

"I wish just liking—tremendous liking, were enough," Susannah commented, after a moment of silence, in an embarrassed voice.

"Ah, Sue, but it is enough!" His fine intellectual face was working with eagerness as he looked up.

"Oh no, Terry, it's not. I'd be a fool," Susannah said, speaking as earnestly as he had, turning toward him her troubled eyes, "not to appreciate what it means when a man like you cares about me. I know what you are, Terry, and I know how happy you'd make your wife. To have Anne and the children, and our farms here, and Boston for holidays— why, nobody'd want a lovelier or safer life than that."

"Don't talk that way," he said, under his breath.

"But, Terry, I mean it."

"But then why won't you risk it? Why won't you believe that that's the safest way—the only way—to happiness? Our liking each other, feeling such a bond of companionship, in books and ideas and the way we like to live and the things we like to do! Why not trust me, Sue? Isn't it just possible that I know you better in this than you do yourself?"

He crossed the rug and knelt down beside her chair and took possession of her hands. Susannah leaned back against the flowered limp flounces of the old chintz; her eyes welled amber lights in the glow of the lamp.

CHAPTER XXVII

So the moment had come? She had known, of course, that it must come. Her thoughts had fluttered about it many times; that this man kneeling beside her in the lamplight and the firelight cared for her, and that he was going to tell her so. She knew as a woman always does know that she was putting sweetness and significance and a forgotten excitement into his life as he was putting companionship and peace into hers. But she had hoped he would not urge the issue so soon!

"Sue, can't you let me hope?" he said.

"Terry—dear," she answered slowly, her look moving over him half smiling, half pitying.

"No, don't be sorry for me, dear, but think—think how simple it all would be. We're always together now. There isn't a day when we don't see each other a dozen times. It would only mean our being a little nearer. . . .

"You seem already to belong to me," he went on eagerly, as she did not speak, but only leaned back, watching him with her thoughtful, sympathetic eyes. "I've watched you now—all these months—in your sorrow—in trouble—with Phil—and every instant of you is exquisite, and every instant I need you. Not until next autumn if you like—not

until you're very sure. But then mightn't there be a chance
for me?"

"You don't know," she said slowly, "no man can ever
know how it makes a woman feel when a man she really—
really loves, Terry, says this to her. It puts one in a—a
strange position. I suppose that not under any other circumstances does any one friend have to say to another, 'I like
you. But not enough!' "

"Not only that side of it," he argued, "not only that, Sue.
There are other considerations, aren't there? You like it
here; you like the way we live. Wouldn't it mean certainty
—being settled, after so much change and moving? And
then," Terry went on, flushing a little, "it might mean children. You love them so. Your own was everything in the
world to you, and you've made Phil a mother such as not a
dozen boys in the world have. That's your natural vocation;
you're not going to let the years go by—and the years go
by—and never have a child in your arms again?"

"Oh—children!" she breathed, mystic lights in her eyes.

"Well, think of it. Other children racing around here—
yours and mine. You and I looking out for them, managing
them. Life couldn't hold very much more than that, Sue."

"No, life couldn't hold any more than that," she repeated
musingly, her eyes far away.

"Then what's keeping you, dear?"

"Oh—weariness, perhaps, Terry," Susannah said, bringing her look back to meet his. "Just—being so tired. Tired,
I mean, of planning for myself—tired of thinking that this
would make me happy and that would make me happy, and
then having the whole house of cards come tumbling down
about me. These last months with Phil I've just been living,
not thinking or planning. And it's a restful way to do it;
it's saved me, I think. I think he saved me."

"Perhaps you saved each other," Terry suggested.

"Perhaps. But I feel secure now, hidden away in this quiet

little place, buried under snow. I feel equal to what I have to do. The minute I step out of it the glare and the heat and the cold winds of the world blow on me again."

"You wouldn't step out of it. You'd step deeper into it."

"Give me time," she said, scarcely above a whisper.

"Sue, you mean that time might bring it about!" He raised her two hands to his lips; she smiled at him without drawing them away.

"I know this," she said quite seriously, when her hands were again in her own possession, and Terry had risen to his feet preparatory to going, "you are the closest and the dearest friend I ever had, or any woman ever had. There's nothing about you that I don't love, as a terribly proud sister might. I love your work, I love our rainy afternoons with books and our walks in the snow. And I've been happier on those hot spring days when we worked in the garden than I thought I ever would be again. And when you say that, you're going away, Terry, I realize suddenly how much you mean to me—how little there is about you that I don't love and don't need—every day—always. And if that be treason or anything else," Susannah finished, laughing with tears in her eyes, "make the most of it!"

"Then I shan't go, Sue?" He was close to her, looking down; he did not touch her.

"No; don't go." She put her hands on his shoulders.

"But, my darling—my dear, do you know what you're saying?"

"I'm not saying it yet, Terry. I'm not saying anything—yet. But I think, in this rebuilding and changing that's been going on in me," Susannah said, "you're playing a part. Why, Terry," she added, affectionately, shyly, "you don't think there's a woman in the world who wouldn't be proud to be your wife? Only—only not yet. I've thought of myself for so long as Alec's. Not that he wanted me! But still— Alec's. Alec and—Evelina, they were my world. Now all that world is gone, the penthouse in New York, the trips to Florida and Newport—Nursey and Frost and Delia—everything. I happened to see in a newspaper the other day," she went on, holding still to his shoulders, but looking away from him and speaking almost dreamily as if she spoke to herself, "something about Doctor Jardine. He was Evelina's doctor. She never was ill, you know, but every month she had to go down and see her doctor. 'Nursey, this is Jardine's day,' I used to say. It brought it all back."

Terry did not speak; he watched her with bright understanding eyes. After a while Susannah said:

"Now I've found—other things to do, other persons to love. My little boy—Anne and the children—and you. But I want to go slowly, to be sure."

He put his arms about her, and she felt them bracing her, holding her close.

"How long do you want?"

"Oh?" He saw the glorious color rush into the ivory of her face. "May?" she asked. "Shall we think about it until May?"

"May third. That's my birthday."

"Mine's the seventh."

"Somewhere in between May third and seventh, then, I'm going to make you a very serious offer, Sue."

"I'm glad you are," she said. And then, detaining him for just one more moment at the door, "Terry," she added, "suppose that it wasn't the old feeling on my part? I mean the silly, the girl's feeling of excitement? Would you still feel that it would be a success without that?"

"Don't you?" he asked instead of answering, looking down at her.

"You'd not be afraid to try?"

"No, Sue. Because I know that I can make you a completely happy woman. I know," Terry went on, "that when I get that Oxford work to do three or four or perhaps ten years from now, and when we take our girls and boys with us to England, you'll have forgotten all this time, Sue. Or you'll remember it only to feel more secure—more happy."

"Oh, I believe it!" she said, laughing shakily.

"Trust me for it."

"I do trust you!"

He went away then; he did not even offer to kiss her good night. But there was a sense of security and rest in her heart that kept her awake for the most peaceful waking dreams that she had ever known. The years ahead of her seemed to have found their pattern at last; she could contemplate them with equanimity.

She saw sunshiny spring orchards stretching through them, fresh soft shadows on fresh grass, fruit blossoms scattering down through fragrant soft air upon the bobbing heads of little children. She saw summers when picnic baskets would be packed, and small forms gotten into bathing suits, when up in the green shade of the woods the creek would babble, and a man's voice would read aloud something written in England a century—three centuries—earlier. She saw herself, a figure maturing into happy motherhood, dressed in thin ruffles and shade hats for summer, velvets like tonight's old velvet to make comfortable her arms as a children's refuge in winter firelight. Laverne and herself putting up jams, summer light shuttered away from the parlor, autumn with the fluttering of golden leaves, and November crisp and hard underfoot and with the first shy caresses of the snow.

"Doctor Duquesne thinks . . . Terry says . . . Ah, that would be fun, Terry! Darlings, Dad and Mother are going to Boston for two whole nights, and will you be very good? Anne, are we to take the whole crowd of them there for Christmas? I'll take . . . who'll you take?"

They were lovely pictures that formed themselves and dissolved and formed again, always with the weathered old

houses and the orchards for a background, and always with
the tall red-headed man with his high-bridged, aquiline nose
and quick, cultured accents for their predominating figure.
Susannah went to sleep still dreaming of them, and when
the morning came there seemed to be a new brightness, a
new satisfaction in the world, because her mind was moving toward something so settled, so dignified, so happy.

No more night clubs and opera boxes, no more big tips
and suites de luxe, no more mad rushing from Palm Beach
to Hollywood, from London to somebody's camp near Lake
Louise. No more Alec, critically inspecting the monograms
on his fine English shirts, scowling at the caviar, leaning
back in his chair to look at the date on the wine. Everything real now, and simple and sincere; children, gardens,
friendships, books. And ah, how blessedly the clear waters
of it seemed to be rising in her very soul! To care for a
garden because it had belonged to one's mother, to care for
books because the hands of one's father had touched them,
to care for one's sister, cousins, aunts, in the old dignified
family way; that was to have the very essence of fine living
under control. Fine—that was the word for everything that
Anne and Terry were and said and did, and how little fineness there had been in the feverish world she had left, the
engagements lapping over on other engagements, the gossip
and the envy! Susannah could remember jealousies almost
murderous in their intensity; she could remember the sneers
with which even intimate friends ridiculed each other. No
one was safe in that set, no one was quite rich or important
enough to be happy for more than a few excited seconds.

This was all different; this quiet big country house with
its steep roof and gracious fanlighted doors had enclosed a
century and a half of dignified living. When Washington's
father had been a baby and stout Queen Anne had reigned
in England, the Duquesne ladies had engineered their hooped
skirts and waved their fans in these old rooms. The delicate

flavor of a beautiful and bygone day still lingered here.

Susannah, snug under her linen sheets and thick blankets, watching the last light of her fire die away in cracks and glows of red about the round little stove, savored it with conscious relish. She was stepping into a sort of life that was distinctly her own; she belonged here. The years would go by like a beautiful dream, with their wonted joys and sorrows, and she would know how to appreciate the one and how to bear the other as became an American gentlewoman of the house of Duquesne.

Betsey Bonestell, whose mother had been Marta Duquesne, was married from Anne's house in Pemberton on a glowing July afternoon. Betsey was a little beauty of twenty-two whose motherless condition only meant that she had a score of mothers and fathers instead of a single pair, for her innumerable uncles and aunts vied with each other in trying to spoil her.

Anne had always been a favorite aunt, and so lovely little Betsey chose Pemberton for her wedding and Uncle Terry's house as the place where the wedding must be. The village inn was engaged as an overflow guest house; Susannah took charge of a troop of children, and the festivities, in the old way, actually lasted for days. Betsey arrived with trunks, her grandmother came, relatives began to stream into town along the summer roads, and eventually Pierce Warren Babcock and his parents and his brothers were there, and the gradually rising crescendo of the dinners and lunches culminated in a garden party and lunch on the day whose evening would see the wedding itself.

All this was absorbing and exciting to Susannah. She loved them all—the New England cousins—and they loved her, and quite speedily it became known among them that the enchanting Mrs Hazeltyne was going to marry Terry. There was no definite announcement, but the women questioned Susannah briefly, with affectionate smiles, and there was more than one welcoming motherly kiss from the older women of the family, and more than one significant cryptic toast at the summer dinner parties.

Terry was radiant. He went about the rooms whistling, humming, embracing any of his womenfolk who happened to be available. He came across the lane to Susannah's house, and they made arrangements for the children, buttered square yards of biscuits, opened jars of jams and peanut butter.

Cots were set up everywhere, and a sort of perpetual meal went on on the terrace under the big trees. Nan and Jerd were staying at Aunt Sue's with the other children; the days were too short for their delights.

The wedding was to be at five o'clock in the afternoon in the little church where Betsey's grandmother had been married just before the boys marched away to the Civil War. The midsummer day had shone through hours of flawless beauty. In the afternoon a mystical sweetness and softness came into the air, and every flower in Anne's garden stood as if fixed in a pool of crystal. Coming back from the church, the bride and groom took their stand on the lawn just outside of the bowed leaded windows of the sunken old parlor, and the streams of well-wishers went by them in the glory that is summer sunset in an old-fashioned garden.

Susannah had been busy all day with details, had gone home at three o'clock under orders to rest, and had instead superintended the wedding preparations of a dozen children —Laverne pressing brief white frocks and shorts in the hot kitchen, 'Liza operating upon wriggling boys with a wet cloth and slippery soap, Susannah catching one pair of flying small shoulders to wield a brush upon tumbled hair, catching at another to tie ribbons or jerk a slip into place.

Just in time they had all been ready and, shepherded by Susannah and Terry, had gone in a body to the church. Susannah's first free breath came an hour later, when congratulations and icy drinks were being exchanged generally, maids were moving about efficiently, and the wedding reception was in full swing. Then she found herself again with Terry moving up with the line to kiss the bride and wish the groom happiness.

"Sue, you are perfectly beautiful," Terry murmured, bent over her as he guided her along the line.

"Do you like it? It's two years old, but it came from Paris." Susannah's eyes were full of laughter and confidence as she looked up at him. She gathered the glitter of the transparent blue-and-silver ruffles away from the grass. Her broad-brimmed, dark blue hat, as she turned away, completely hid her face.

"Shall we do it like this?"

"Oh, Terry, I've hardly gotten used to the idea that we're really going to do it at all. Yes, let's do it like this, only in October when it's cooler," Susannah said, in a sort of confidential rush. "They all know it, don't they?"

"They seem to. Do you mind?"

"No, I think I like them to. I feel as if I belonged to you all."

"You belong to me. All this week," Terry said, "has been like a dream of something that I thought never would come back into my life again. I mean—youngness, feeling that it's good to wake up and good to go to sleep, and that the world is all meadows and trees and lanes, and that every supper out of doors is a party."

"I know," she said, tipping her head back to smile at him.

"Here, we must move along, Sue, we're holding them up!" They went on, and Susannah got the confused fragrant rush of ruffles and soft cheek that is the bride's kiss.

"Do you know what I just whispered to Uncle Terry?" Betsey whispered, dragging her down a little. "I said, 'She's adorable, and you're the luckiest man alive!'"

"Betsey, Betsey, Betsey, and what did he say?"

"He said, 'Thanks, darling.' Oh, Mrs Hazeltyne, is it really true?"

"I think so," Susannah admitted. Terry had joined her again now, and they walked slowly across the lawn together, Terry very smart in his white linens, Susannah trailing the blue-and-silver ruffles, looking up at him from under the big hat.

That night, after the bride and groom had gone, when the children were engaging in wild twilight games, and the grown-ups were clustered on the terrace steps and in the terrace chairs, Susannah and Terry came back from her house and mounted the wide levels together, still murmuring, still with eyes only for each other.

It was nearly eight o'clock. The perfect day had died into a starry dusk. Now, with the western glow still not quite gone, a first milky light from the east was beginning to send long, timid shadows over the garden and the woods; the moon was rising tremendous and close over the shoulder of Trimlers' Hill.

"How about it, you two?" Josiah Bonestell said, from the shadows.

The figures stopped; they heard Susannah's laugh.

"Is everybody out here?" she said. "I can't see anyone."

"Nature's protective coloring for the more helpless animals," Terry explained it.

"Here's a chair, Sue," Matilda Rawlings said. The dim gleam of Susannah's ruffles sank into it, and Terry settled himself on the top step close beside her.

"Are we having sandwiches? Oh, good! I didn't get anything either at lunch or supper," Susannah went on, a little consciously. Josiah, the smartest, youngest, gayest father who ever gave the last of five daughters in marriage, repeated his question:

"How about it, you two?"

"We all know," said Mary Robertson.

"Ah, well—if you all know——" Her voice broke deliciously into laughter again. Terry turned his lean, long bulk in the moonshine and took her hand and laid it against his face. And for a little while everything was laughter and congratulations again.

Late in the evening Terry walked home with Susannah. They were both tired after the long strain of the day and preceding days. They went slowly through the moonlight and the shadows, their hands linked; about them the warm summer night throbbed and thrilled with a thousand beauties.

"This is one of the good hours, Sue."

"All today has seemed to be on a—on a peak, somehow. All today—and yesterday—and all these days since I knew you. You've always known, I think."

"Ah, if I only had!" Terry said, with a brief reminiscent laugh. "There were times last spring—all through the spring—when I used to come out at night and walk up and down the road and watch your windows. I'd tell myself that if it wasn't to be, I could bear it, it wouldn't kill me— that men had died and worms had eaten them, but not for love! But not any more—not any more!"

In the deep elm-tree shadows of her own doorway, he put his arms about her, and she tipped her face up for his kiss; the wide shade hat had fallen to the path now, and the silver-and-blue ruffles were crushed.

"How soon, Sue?" he said. "After all, I've waited for a long time."

She escaped him with a laugh, fled through the dark house and up to the dimly lighted, airy bigness of her bedroom. Her whispered good night: "I think we've all gone wedding crazy!" fluttered after her. A later good night came from her window, when he had turned away and was walking

across the grass. "Good night, Terry! 'Parting is such
sweet sorrow . . .'"

He looked up to see her outlined against the window
frame in a checkered light and shadow, and heard her
laugh again for sheer lightness of heart as he put his hands
in his pockets, turned his back, and walked away.

❧ CHAPTER XXVIII ❧

A FEW WEEKS LATER Susannah wrote to Alec the first letter she had written him since the days when her letters had begun with "My own darling . . ."

This letter began with the brief conventional words that any letter to any stranger might have used:

MY DEAR ALEC:

Perhaps your mother has told you that I am to be married early in October to Doctor Terence Duquesne, a neighbor of mine here in Pemberton, who, with his sister, Mrs Lambert, has been a good friend to me since I arrived. They are the son and daughter of Professor Jerome Duquesne, who wrote all the philosophy books, and their old home here is one of the most charming I have ever entered.

My reason for writing you about it is of course the question of Phil. I want very much to keep him with me. He came to me at a time when I bitterly needed occupation and company, and he has been a delight to me ever since, and to us all. He has grown strong and tall, stands high in his school, and is altogether a most intelligent and affectionate and fine little boy.

When he came to me almost a year ago I was anxious about him, for too much babying by a nurse, and then too sharp a contrast in being entirely on his own at school had made him nervous, shy, fearful and backward. But all that is gone now; he is a leader among the boys here, and develops only too fast to please me, for I would like him to be always small enough to need me. I suppose a mother loves all her children equally, but in different ways. It doesn't occur to me to compare what I feel for him with what I felt for my own beautiful baby, but I believe his own mother could not love him more, or try harder to understand him, or feel that she was more successful in doing so.

Our plan is to be married in October and go to Oxford, where Terry is to do some work for a new book. Anne Lambert and the children—she has a girl and a boy —will join us there in November, and we will stay there until perhaps March. Phil knows of this plan and is wild to share it—in fact it never has occurred to him that he might be left out.

Will you give me the custody of Phil at least for these little-boy years? Your mother, who came down to spend a few days with us last week, is entirely happy in this arrangement. I appreciate your immediate permission to keep him last year; now I am praying and hoping that you will be generous enough to let me feel for a while longer that he is—what he often calls himself—*my* boy.

She signed herself, "Always faithfully yours, Sanna."

Whether Alec was in New York, or loitering somewhere on the Riviera, or where he was she did not know. But the letter would go to his secretary in any case, and then probably to his lawyer, and some time in the six weeks before her marriage there would be an answer. She had no misgivings as to his decision, for the problem of Phil had always been too much for him to solve, and he had long ago relegated it to his mother.

With Anne, and with Terry never very far from their councils, she spent the early autumn days getting her house in order, packing her trunks with the heavy clothing that she and Phil would need for an English winter. She and Terry were to come back to the farmhouse, and Anne and her children were to occupy the old Duquesne homestead for a while at least. Susannah suspected that Terry had a deep sentimental attachment to his grandfather's home, and she knew that the practical, capable Anne would never admit to such a weakness. So it was tacitly understood that eventually Anne would move into Susannah's house, and the Duquesnes once more move, this time only a little way down the road.

But meanwhile there was too much immediate excitement to make these future decisions important. Susannah went to Boston for a few days with her neighbors, wonderful happy days when they prowled through the old city, buying books and presents for the children, who had been left behind, and now and then an odd bit of trousseau. Together the three spent a morning in securing tickets, passports, visas, letters of credit; there was something in the sight of these tickets that made Susannah's heart dance as no prospect of travel had ever stirred it before. The cabin with its little slice of adjoining salon seemed to her wholly fascinating, as she leaned over the big map and watched the agent's pencil tracing out the passages to the dining room and the lounge and all the other advantages of the ship.

For Anne and the children, rooms were reserved for the same ship three weeks later. There was great division of important documents in the hotel rooms that night, and the atrocious passport photographs were admiringly passed from hand to hand.

"We are as silly as children," said Susannah.

"Children aren't silly," Terry assured her. "There's nothing silly in the joy of children. They trust the grown-ups, and we don't."

"Ah, well, our grown-ups fail us now and then."

"Theirs do, too." He was too happy to advance any theory that was not completely satisfying. His arm was always under Susannah's elbow now, as they wandered through the crooked streets and watched the yellow leaves falling slowly and sparsely about the old brick houses and the aged grass of the Common.

"Realize that you have only a couple of weeks more of independence, Sue?" he asked her, on their last day.

"I've never wanted especially to be independent. I wish it were going to be sooner; I'm just that shy and womanly, about the whole thing!" Susannah said shamelessly.

"Ah, Sue!" Terry said, his arms going about her, and their lips together. "I'll be glad, too," he told her later, when they were driving homeward in the sweet thin afternoon sunshine, through a world of red-and-gold color. "I'll be glad when it's all an accepted thing, when we're just 'the Duquesnes,' who were married—oh, nobody exactly knows or cares when. I think of our wedding day, Sue, and of your coming away with me that afternoon, and of Boston that night, and the ship the next day, and it's all going to be like a dream. But not any more so than the autumn days next year, and the year after that, when it begins to get cold, and we have fires, and put the books in order. It's all going to be heaven, every hour of it, every minute of it."

The rounded hills and the little towns that were beginning to shut themselves into winter snugness and tightness under the last red leaves went by them. Susannah watched for signboards; the car obediently turned left, turned right. Anne dozed on the back seat.

"There'll be years like this, Sue, you and I driving about together," the man added, after a silence during which her coated shoulder had touched his. Her smile came about to meet his, and went away, and came back again. "You and I driving along, talking together. I don't ever want anyone else in my life!"

"Nor I in mine. Just like this, coming back from a few days in Boston and knowing that Laverne 'll have supper ready, and Phil be all agog, and my books there, and a fire in the dining room. All that wouldn't have meant very much to me a few years ago; it fills my life to the brim now. To add *you* to it—well, that's simply ostentation!"

"Sue, do you know that the very first time I ever saw you I thought to myself that there are two sorts of women in the world. All the others in one class, and you."

"I know that you say so now, Doctor Duquesne."

"I said so then! Oh, I don't mean that I was in love with you—or if I was I didn't know it. But I said to myself, 'There are women like that, are there? Women who move that way—that quick way that seems to be all one motion— and women who smile at one like that, and women whose voices have those notes in them!' I remember saying to Anne that you seemed to me a remarkable woman."

"And I suppose poor Anne saw the writing on the wall from that moment!"

"I don't know. I know I didn't. It was months later, and we were in your garden on a hot night, when you came out of the house and said, 'Anne, should we do anything about the Peet family?' And quite suddenly I knew. I knew that it was you or nobody for me for all the rest of my life, and that if it couldn't be you my life was over."

"D'you know," Susannah confessed, "it wasn't so long ago that I realized that I was in love? 'Again,' I was going to say, but it wasn't again. I've never felt like this before. With Alec, you know, there was so much excitement. I'd been engaged, and the man had broken it off—I've told you that—and to have this handsome, sophisticated, very de-

termined man want me restored my self-respect, somehow.
It made my mother very happy, too, and of course I was
dazzled into loving him very much indeed before we'd been
married very long. He's a dazzling person. He did everything with tremendous dash and easiness; he could always
get anything, succeed in anything. When he didn't want to
do a thing he was perfectly unfeeling about it—he'd wire a
hostess at the last minute that we weren't coming, or put
off some business talk that really meant something to someone, or might have—so that we could go off for a week end.
I remember when poor Freddy Flint wanted ten of his
friends to buy his yacht, Alec was perfectly cold-blooded
about it. I heard him telephoning Freddy. 'You can't put
this up to all of us,' he said. 'It's your party. You've got to
work it out some way that doesn't ask for fifty thousand
apiece from all your friends. I don't want a yacht, or any
share in a yacht, and neither does Tom nor Alberson nor
Billings.' It made my blood run cold," Susannah ended,
remembering it with a sigh and a smile, "but to Alec it was
a perfectly natural way to act."

"It's a world I don't know anything about," Terry said,
"that world of his. Stock market and yachts and midnight
parties and champagne; I've never had even a bowing
acquaintance with any of them!"

"It's a horrible world, for all that it sounds so fascinating," Susannah assured him. "First nights that are failures,
parties where you sit next the wrong person, this person repeating to you that little bit of scandal and that one repeating
the other. And being tired and bored at tables in smoky
places, with half-naked girls dancing, and saxophones going
full blast. But what I started to say, Terry," she added,
after a minute, "is that all that time seems a part of what
I felt for Alec, a sort of awed admiration that in such a
terrific race—under such competition—he could not only
hold his own, he could be the top of the heap!

"When I began to need you," she went on in a lower tone, as Terry merely glanced at her with his pleasant smile and drove on without speaking, "it was so different. It was friendship first, and then—then help, talk and books and—well, I suppose your philosophy, Terry. I don't think Alec has any philosophy or has ever needed it or ever will. And finally it reached the point when if any hour—not week or day, but hour—went by without my hearing you banging at the side door, or whistling down on the terrace, or arguing with Laverne, I missed you. And then—but this was only a few months ago—it went on to—to disgraceful lengths," Susannah ended. "It went on to the point when the sound of your voice was the only sound in the world I wanted to hear, and when the only meals I wanted to eat were the ones you shared, and when no book or plant or walk or charity case or news in the newspapers or village rumor meant anything until we'd talked about it together."

"Why don't we say these things when I'm where I can put my arms around you, Sue? Do you want me to stop the car?"

"No," she said, laughing. "But I'll probably go completely tongue-tied on my wedding day, and merely be able to articulate 'uh-huh' if you should ask me if I loved you. So I'm saying it all now."

They had reached Pemberton. Twilight had turned to dusk now, but a warm stream of light poured out from Laverne's kitchen across the brick path and the massed shrubs, and Phil was running toward her with open arms as she got out of the car. He escorted her into the house in a jumble of questions and kisses and embraces, and Laverne and 'Liza, scarcely less welcoming, gave her all the news of the town. Less than four days away, and it seemed weeks!

When Terry came over at eight o'clock Phil was in bed. Susannah was seated by an open fire in the parlor with a mass of letters in her lap. The room was so rarely used that Terry looked surprised as he came in.

"All my letters were on my desk here, and 'Liza suggested a fire, and it seemed very comfortable," Susannah explained. "Shut that door, Terry." And then very quietly she added: "There's a letter here from Alec. Read it. I didn't want the girls to hear."

"Something's happened?" he asked quickly, sitting down with a single typewritten sheet in his hands. "He'll not give you Phil?"

"He doesn't speak of Phil, but it isn't that. It's about the divorce," Susannah said. "But read it."

"Sue, don't let this worry you," Terry said quickly, really frightened by her pallor. But his own color had changed.

"Oh, Terry, it frightens me terribly. It can't put things off, can it? It can't mean that there will be delays!"

"No, I don't think so." Terry's eyes moved rapidly over the lines of the letter. "Why didn't they let you know about this?" he said.

"I don't know! You see that he says there that he thought I did know. Read it. I don't think I got the sense of it."

Terry read:

"My dear Sanna:

"I am deeply concerned to realize for the first time that you are not aware that there was a technical flaw in the divorce decree obtained by me in Reno more than a year ago. My lawyer informed me of it when we returned home from a trip around the world in January. This was just at the time of the tragedy of my marriage, when we had both come to see that it was a mistake, and Merle immediately decided to go to England and accept an offer that had been made her by the movies there. As ours had never been a marriage, I could not persuade her to reconsider, and I believe she is there now. My own affairs have been in a bad state and steadily growing worse for some time. Chandler, in an effort to protect our customers, has gotten things into such a mess that my leaving him again for Reno is completely out of the question. We can probably extricate ourselves without serious trouble, but at the moment I am needed here. I am therefore obliged to tell you that you are not free; I regret the inevitable delay and perhaps disappointment that this must, of course, cause you. Naturally I will consent to any arrangement or any steps you decide to take. The whole thing has been trying and difficult for you beyond words, and I am sorry.

"I am writing late at the office, and alone, so please forgive my unfamiliarity with the typewriter. It would seem to me almost imperative for you to come to New York and have a talk with me. Will you wire me any day that is convenient for you?

"Yours always affectionately,
"A.B.H."

Terry finished reading, and he and Susannah looked at each other. Her eyes were fearful.

"What does it mean, Terry?" she whispered.

"It means that we'll have to wait," he said quietly. She saw the muscles spring up on his hands as he crushed the letter in them. "I don't know much about these things. But it looks to me as if it might mean that you still were his wife, Sue," he said.

❧ CHAPTER XXIX ❧

THE STREET CORNERS were strangely familiar, the wide,
clean, rubbery smell of the enormous square office building
in Wall Street seemed as natural as if she had smelled it
only yesterday. Susannah found herself shaken to the very
fibers of her soul as it all came back: her coming down to see
Alec in his office in the early days of their marriage, his
proud, amused smile as he introduced her to some of his associates, the smart club restaurant on the roof in which they
had had luncheon. Merle had worked here; he had seen
her every day in those weeks when first her spell was taking
possession of him; he had brought her up from the office in
his big car on that day when he and Susannah and Paulheim
had lunched together at the Ritz. Now it was all so changed
—everything changed—and Susannah's very nature and
being with all the rest.

She went into the outer office, once again was in the atmosphere of magnificent spaces richly carpeted, paneled
walnut walls, high windows, busy, quiet clerks at clean-
topped desks that looked as if no business in the world ever
were being conducted at them. Alec was waiting. He came
forward, and their hands touched, and immediately he led
her through the familiar hallway and into his own corner

office at the end. Susannah was confusedly and vaguely
aware that they were being watched. Everyone knew, of
course, everyone knew; the only thing to do was walk
through it steadily and quietly. They reached Alec's big
empty sanctum, and she saw the baby picture of Phil on the
wall. Once a great picture of Betty had decorated his desk,
and afterward one of Susannah. There was no woman's
picture there now.

Alec looked a little paler than she remembered him, but
that was perhaps because Terry, by contrast, was so brown.
Susannah could hardly look at him at first; the strange meeting stirred her emotionally far more than she had thought it
would. The sound of his voice was strange in her ears; it
was as if she heard her own voice, or one that had once
been her own, coming back to her. The effect was shattering
to her nerves. She had meant to carry off this interview with
brevity, dignity, self-command. All she could do was sit
trembling in this once familiar place, fitting the setting
in which she had once been so happy to today's mood of
forlornness and insecurity, and wait for him to speak.

"You look so well, Sanna."

"Oh, I am—very well."

"And you've Phil with you? Mother takes the greatest
satisfaction from that, and of course I do, too."

"Phil's—Phil's the joy of my life. It was about Phil
that I wrote you, of course."

They had been talking in low tones while Miss Logan,
one of the office assistants, was in the room. Now she left
with a little smile and bow, and they were alone. Everything was rich and quiet and perfectly in taste: the great
center desk, the matched silvery eucalyptus of the paneled
walls, the few big comfortable chairs in leather, the fittings
in handsome dull silver. She remembered every detail of it,
and remembered, above all, the well-groomed, faultlessly
dressed figure of the man opposite her, his smooth fairish

hair and keen gray eyes, the strong beauty of his fine hands, locked together easily just as they always used to be when he was talking in his office. Recollection too poignant to be borne was stirring her to the very deeps of her being as she began the talk she must have with him.

"Alec, I wired you that I would come in to see you because I don't understand," she said, serious and beautiful as she faced him. "It didn't seem the sort of thing that one can write. Evidently I've missed some letters or papers or something since last spring. What has happened? I had your letter and then the lawyer's letter, and I cannot understand it at all. We are—certainly you and I are divorced?"

She could look at him now; their eyes met.

"That's just it, Sanna. It seems we are not."

"Are not!"

"No. I feel terribly about it," Alec said simply.

"Terribly!" Aghast, she echoed the word. "But—but why aren't we?" she demanded.

"Sanna, do you mean to say that you didn't know?"

"How should I know? I was notified more than a year ago that we were. Since when has it been any different?"

"Of course I supposed someone had told you!" Alec said, in a shocked voice. "That is, I did if I thought of it at all," he added honestly. "It was all a miserable mistake, and my fault. I went to Reno to get a divorce, and stayed there at a ranch outside the city for six weeks. I supposed it was all straight enough. But in that time I went down to San Francisco—flew down, as a matter of fact, and was there for ten days. Nothing was said about it at the time; it didn't seem to have any significance to me. But when we got home this last January there was a letter here from my lawyers to say that that had invalidated the divorce."

"The divorce? But how? But you and Merle were married! It was in the papers!"

"It was Carter's fault—my lawyer's fault. Well, and

mine, too. I didn't want to stay in Reno, I wanted to go down to San Francisco during those six weeks. Carter said that old Judge Hodges was a good egg and that he'd wink at it. I thought those fellows were fixing those things all the time, that it 'd be all right. I got my divorce all right, and Merle and I were married that day." Alec fell silent. "My God, what a fool!" he said presently, under his breath.

Susannah was staring at him in consternation.

"Well, then what?" she whispered.

"Well, then Hanks, the district attorney out there, began some sort of investigation, and Hodges was put off the bench. Every divorce he'd granted—or at least a lot of them —were thrown out. Carter kept my name out of it somehow, and I never knew it until Merle and I got back here last January. There was a letter from him here to say that it was all off."

"But you and Merle had been married!"

"Certainly; in San Francisco, the day I'd gotten my decree."

"The decree that wasn't valid."

"Exactly."

"Nor your marriage to Merle?"

"That, too, of course."

"But what could you do?"

"Nothing, except go back to Reno."

"And what did they do then?"

"I didn't go. As a matter of fact I couldn't go. Ferguson and Chandler had been running things here and had gotten everything into a mess. We'll get out of it—we'll get out of it all right, but it's meant the hardest work I've ever done in my life."

"Did Merle go to Reno?"

"Merle went to England."

"But why to England? Is she getting a divorce there?"

"Ours was no marriage, Sanna."

"Of course not—of course not." Her face was very pale as she began to grasp the situation; her eyes never left his. "But then," she began again, puzzled, "what did you do? Why did she go?"

"From the beginning," Alec said in a low tone, looking away, "that was a great mistake. She was wretchedly unhappy. I—— Not that it matters! That isn't the point now."

He was silent. Susannah sat watching him, without speaking.

"The point now," he presently recommenced, "is your problem. You want to get married? And all this time you've not known—nobody notified you—— It's unbelievable."

"What is the simplest and the shortest way out now?" Susannah asked.

"The shortest and the simplest way? Well,"—he hesitated—"I suppose for you to go to Reno and apply for a divorce."

She shrank back in her chair.

"Ah no, I can't do that!"

"I feel very badly about it," Alec said again.

Susannah sat staring with darkened eyes into space. Presently she spoke:

"You mean it's all to do over again? Just as if it never had been done at all?"

"So they say."

"And you've known this since January, Alec?"

"My lawyer's letter told me about it in January, but it was February before I was finally convinced that it couldn't be fixed up. It's inexcusable that you shouldn't have known, Sanna. It's incredible that it wasn't somebody's business to tell you."

"Did the newspapers have this, Alec?"

"No, they managed that much out there. I blame my lawyer entirely. He says in his letter that he himself was away in Honolulu with his family while I was in Reno, and supposed of course that I knew of that regulation. He thought he could fix it up with Hodges, anyway."

"And Merle simply—went away?"

"Went to England."

"And nobody knows."

"Nobody. But *you* should have known. I'll never forgive myself for not making sure that you knew. I'll never forgive myself for not thinking that it might make a great difference in your plans."

"It does," Susannah said simply, almost absently. "It makes a great difference in my plans. I don't know what to do."

"You were to have been married immediately?"

"A week from next Thursday."

"It was criminal of me," Alec said. "I can't tell you how sorry I am."

"I'm wondering what to do," she said, in a musing tone. "We have our steamship reservations for England next week. Mrs Lambert, Terry's sister, was to follow with the children a few weeks later. Now—now it's all changed."

"Could you both go to Nevada, Sanna, and be married there?"

"No. Terry's to do some research work at Oxford. No, we will simply have to postpone it. But it isn't that."

She fell silent, troubled.

"I wish there were some way I could straighten this out," Alec said. "I'm in up to my neck here. This afternoon I'm seeing a man who thinks he can work us out a solution; I hope to God he can! But nobody knows what a hell we've all been living through, one thing after another cracking— every day worse than the day before——"

He wrenched himself from the topic with an effort, brought his interest back to her.

"I've been down here twelve hours—fourteen hours—a

day on a stretch for the past three months," he said. "It's getting me!"

"Not through the summer, Alec!"

"Right through the summer. Through everything." Again he tried to put his own anxieties behind him. "What will you do, Sanna?" he asked.

"I don't know what I *can* do." She had been thinking about it. Her tone, despite her utmost efforts to control it, wavered desolately. Somehow it all seemed so forlorn and cold, so little to show for the years of one's life, this talk with Alec as if they were complete strangers. She knew him so well, every intonation of his voice, every expression in his fine eyes; she knew indeed what that clean-shaven cheek felt like, pressed against her own; she remembered how her heart had once beaten when those arms had held her!

"I've been rotten through it all," he said simply. "There's nothing to be said about it. I had my chance and I lost it. Perhaps things were always too easy for me, too much money, too many people trying to amuse me. I don't know. I know that if I had another break . . .

"There's another thing, Sanna," he presently added, as she sat looking at him, quite incapable of speech, because of the dryness and thickness that was in her throat. "I thought you were very much opposed to divorce on general principles; arguing with me months ago. My mother said that you were. It mightn't have occurred to me that you'd want the divorce if I didn't. I don't mean—God knows!—for any reason connected with me. I mean that the whole idea wasn't your sort of thing."

Pemberton and the tall, thinning trees, and the smoke of brush fires seemed very far away. Susannah thought of Phil having his supper with Jerd and Nan, sleeping in the Duquesne house, in one of the low-ceiled old rooms from which one stepped up or down, and whose many-paned windows seemed to be sinking yearly nearer and nearer to the garden. Rooms with four-posters in them, and old blue-threaded quilts, rooms in which tree shadows moved on hot summer days across braided rag rugs and polished, yellow brown floors.

It was no use. The intervening months were nothing. She was again the Susannah Hazeltyne who had come downtown in the big car with Phillips to her husband's office, to talk with Alec, laugh with him, have him praise the new hat, the new suit; carry him off for tea or a cocktail party somewhere. Presently they would drive uptown, the car carefully guided through the afternoon traffic, and all the world would be scented with the clean sweetness of autumn, and Alec's cigarette, and the dying gardenias on her shoulder.

Presently, gossiping about the group they had just left, they would be upstairs in their magnificent rooms, idly wishing that they were not obliged to go to Marjorie's, wondering who would be there. 'Liza would have laid out Susannah's dress, the exquisite French gown of silver brocade embroidered in pearls and coral, and with it Susannah's Russian vermilion evening coat, stiff and shining like altar apparel, with the rich doubling of sables at the collar.

"Let's make it early tonight!" Alec would suggest, struggling with collar and tie. And fervently she would echo it: "Oh, let's!" But they would both know that it would not be early.

And perhaps then, when he was still dressing and she herself all ready, she would steal a moment to rush down the hall, perfumed and rustling and splendid in brocade and pearls, and half open the nursery door. If Nursey was there she always came swiftly, noiselessly forward in the subdued light, holding Evelina's mother at the door, answering her soundlessly, briefly, without encouragement. The baby was asleep. Yes, everything was quite all right.

But sometimes Nursey had gone out for dinner, and Milly was on guard in the adjoining room. Then Susannah could go in and stand looking down at the child, feasting her eyes on Evelina's softness and smallness and sweetness; the little face flat in the tiny pillow, the petal-hand holding tight to the embroidered and monogrammed linen sheet, the soft little neck wet under its plastered silken curls.

And as this memory came to her, Susannah felt that she would suffocate, and she got to her feet and went to the window and stood looking blindly down at the dazzle of the city under the autumn sun, the antlike caravans crossing the bridges, the flowing gray waters of the river.

She heard the man move; he came and stood beside her, and in all the world there seemed to be nobody except themselves and their wrecked love and their fast-beating hearts.

"Sanna!" he said. "My God, I cannot bear it! To see you standing here—so beautiful—and to think that once—once we were so happy! Once, when you came here, it was all so happy! We would go upstairs for lunch at the club—do you remember?—and afterward—were you thinking of that?"

Susannah made no answer because she could not speak. There was a moment of silence.

"You must forgive me," Alec said then, in a low tone. "For I'll never forgive myself. I'll never love anyone else—that doesn't matter now, does it? But you must say that you forgive me for it all."

❧ CHAPTER XXX ❧

THERE WAS AN INTERRUPTION. Susannah and Alec both turned from the window, and Susannah went back to her chair. She was very pale, but she spoke smilingly to the secretary who had come in with some papers.

"Hello, Mrs Wix."

"You asked for the Carter file, Mr Hazeltyne?" the secretary said, putting the papers down on the desk. Her face was one broad smile of recognition and surprise. "It's so nice to see you again, Mrs Hazeltyne," she added.

"It's nice to see you," Susannah returned, managing a shadow of a smile.

"Oh yes, the Carter file——" Alec said confusedly. He put his handkerchief—how well Susannah remembered those fine, heavily monogrammed handkerchiefs—back into his breast pocket, came forward and laid a hand on the papers before sitting down. "Yes, thank you," he said. "And this is to sign? Send it by messenger, will you? And tell Miss Logan that if Mr Pope calls it's extremely important for me to talk to him immediately. I'll be in Philadelphia this afternoon—he can get me there through Grogan."

He stooped, scratched his quick signature; it was all as if she had seen it only yesterday. The secretary went out; they were alone again. Alec glanced at the papers; she knew now that he was having almost as difficult a time as she to control himself. When he spoke, it was in a low tone and with his eyes on the papers he was idly moving to and fro.

"Tell me about Phil," he said. "He seems to have outgrown those little-boy nervous fits and bronchial attacks—whatever they were. I get his letters—you're very good to keep him at all. My mother is perfectly delighted with the way he's coming on."

"He's a wonderful boy. Brown as an Indian now."

"You're not sending him back to school?"

"Oh no. He and I—— I couldn't get along without him."

"You've been awfully kind to him, Sanna. I'm terribly grateful to you, and my mother is, too."

"He's done much more for me——" She couldn't go on; she was beginning to cry again. "I appreciate your letting me have him," she added unsteadily, after a moment.

"Letting you! My mother was almost insane over the question of what to do with him. He ran away to you, did he?"

"Thank God he did! I might have missed him, otherwise——" But she was not speaking to Alec or thinking of him. Her eyes were far away.

"He found you when he needed you," Alec said.

"Ah, and how I needed him!" she had barely gotten the words out when the tears came in a bitter flood. Susannah put her elbows on the desk and her face into her shaking hands.

"I know," Alec said quickly. "I know. I was so sorry. I was so terribly sorry, Sanna."

Susannah was beyond all power to answer. She felt sweeping through her being the chill vertigo, the faint, wretched sense of actual sickness that any reference to her child caused her. She could not control her tears. She lost all consciousness of where she was or of what Alec or anyone

else in the world would think of her. Everything for a few
dreadful moments was blackness and despair.

She had been his wife, the lost child had been his child,
the child she loved today was his. Why should all these
agonies of parting have come to them all? Why had she
come back into this atmosphere of shops and clubs and hard
crowded streets, to tear apart in this fashion the wound
that had been healing in her heart?

"I'm sorry," she said, gulping, drying her eyes and blowing her nose, and taking out her little compact to repair the
ravages of tears on her face. "I'm very sorry, Alec."

"Was it anything that could have been avoided, Sanna?"

"You mean Evelina? . . . No, they said that it might
have been wrong from the very start, might have been any
germ, anywhere, at any time. She'd been in the country, you
know; she'd not been exposed to anything that we could
discover. I've—we're putting in their research equipment,"
Susannah said, gaining composure as she went along, "and
some day I may believe that other babies are going to be
glad that my baby lived for more than three perfect little
years——"

And she smiled at him through a sudden uprush of tears
that brimmed her eyes again.

Alec got up suddenly and walked to the window and stood
looking down upon the city.

"Where are you lunching?" he asked abruptly, after a
while.

She hesitated a fraction of a second too long.

"I'll take you to lunch," he decided quickly. "I know a
place where we can be quiet. I remember," he added with a
smile, "how you depend upon food at this time of the day.
Remember the day in Paris?"

"At Fouget's. When your friends were exactly one hour
late, and I'd been posing all morning in a cold studio."

"Fool that I was not to get you some soup!"

The memories of those happy days came back. Susannah seemed to see in a quick flash of vision the Place, with the white marble horses and the fountains dazzling white in the blackness of night, and the wet pavements mirroring a thousand stars. She remembered the shops in the arcades facing the Louvre gardens, and the muted, pathetic honk of the old-fashioned, lumbering taxis, and how good it was to get hungry, sightseeing and museum haunting, in Paris, and to know that somewhere near, anywhere near, the most delicious food in the world was waiting to be eaten.

They went downstairs together, and Phillips drew up to the curb at the exact right minute, as Phillips always did, and Alec, as she got into the big car in which she seemed to have been comfortably seated only yesterday, said, "Edouard's, please."

"Old times," Susannah said, looking out at the thronged, sunny noontime streets, saying anything to break the silence.

"I hate it all," Alec sighed. "God, I get tired of it!" he said. "Chandler and Ferguson between them have fixed things so that we pretty nearly had to put up the shutters."

"Alec! Not Hazeltyne & Bowers?"

"Yep. Oh, we won't go out; we're a long way from that. But it's going to be a tight squeeze for a while."

"But, Alec, with enormous interests like yours?"

"Yes, I know." He was sitting with his head dropped forward; now he ran his hand worriedly over his forehead. "But enormous interests can slide like melting snow," he said. "One minute everyone wants to lend you money, buy up your bonds. The next, money's tight, everyone's scared, securities going down——"

He was silent. Susannah could only study his profile in puzzlement and surprise.

"What d'you think of putting up seventy thousand dollars to secure fourteen?" he asked suddenly.

"Well, I should think it would be terrible," she said.

He did not answer her. He was apparently deep in thought.

"Here we are at Edouard's," he said a moment later. They got out at the door of a narrow restaurant that ran under an old brownstone house. An awning came out to the curb; a bowing French manager met them at the door. The atmosphere inside was that of Paris; worn old velvet padding about the walls, little tables pushed up against it, a display of cold meats and cooked fruits in the center of the dark, long room, a serious, heavily bearded, middle-aged man reading a paper while a deft-fingered waiter busy at a smoking blazer measured brandy into the sauce for *crêpes suzette.*

Alec ordered quickly and familiarly. He and Susannah established themselves at the angle of a corner table, their backs braced comfortably against the wall, the lights so low and so placed that their eyes were in shadow.

"They know how to make you comfortable, the French."

"I used to know this fellow in Paris; he used to be at the Régence. I brought him over here."

"I could see you were welcome."

"I think perhaps I've talked too much of the business and of things," Alec presently said, "because, if it were not that we have customers who actually have to be protected, I would slip out to Nevada, settle the whole thing in six weeks, and get back again. It would delay your plans, of course, but it wouldn't put you to the inconvenience of going West."

"There will be sure to be some publicity about it, won't there?" Susannah asked, wincing.

"Some, I suppose. There's no help for it."

"I hate it," she said, under her breath.

"I know you do. I have made things horribly hard for you, Sanna, from the very beginning. I look at you now," Alec said with a little effort and with heightened color, "and I wonder what sort of insanity—— But of course I was insane. Men get that way sometimes; I've seen others do it. But somehow I never thought I was that sort."

Susannah glanced at him, glanced away without speaking.

Something rich and browned and bubbling hot was put before Susannah. Alec broke her off a crust of the hot toasted bread. She fell upon her food with eagerness; she felt weak and tired and cold after the strain of the morning. Her train had been late; she had foolishly taken a taxi to go to Wall Street instead of going straight down in a subway, and the meeting with Alec had seemed to completely exhaust her in soul and mind and body.

"Tell me about Doctor Duquesne. Does he practice in Pemberton?"

"Oh, no. He's a doctor of philosophy. They live—he and his sister and her children—in their grandfather's old house there. Terry writes essays and expositions and arguments and things, and now he is going on a special commission to England."

"You love him, don't you, Sue?"

"He's the best friend I ever had, I think," she said simply. "He's interesting; he writes about Shakespeare and Marlowe —but it isn't that. It's that he's always been—been tremendously kind to me."

"I see," Alec said, flushing again. He bent his attention to his food.

"We live a wonderful life there, and I suppose it will be much the same sort of thing in England," Susannah said. "I work a lot in the garden; the Duquesnes and I see each other every day; it's all very peaceful and—and filling, somehow. Phil goes to school with the Lambert children; we all have picnics—supper picnics up in the woods——"

"You're thinner," Alec said as she paused, speaking as if he had not been listening to her. "But, Sanna, you are more beautiful than ever, and I didn't think it could be done. He sounds as if he knew how lucky he is, this Terry of yours," he went on more lightly. "I hope you'll be happy! Meanwhile we've got to get this divorce question settled in the easiest way for you."

"What is our status now?" Susannah asked. Her color faded a little. She had dreaded asking it; she had put it off a dozen times. It must be asked now.

"You are my wife," Alec answered briefly.

Her color flooded back. She went on with her luncheon; the hand that held her fork shook palpably.

"It's too bad. There seems to be no end to my upsetting of your life, Sanna."

"No—no," she said thickly. And then with a brief shadow of a smile, "There's Phil."

"You love him so much?"

"Almost as I did—— As much as I could love anyone."

"And you plan to take him to England?"

"He plans—he and the Lambert children have it all planned—to follow me there. But now of course that's out of the question. I must think it all over, talk it all over with Terry. The Duquesnes," Susannah added, speaking as if she merely thought aloud, "aren't the sort of people who like divorces. But there's no help for that now."

"I know how long six weeks sounds," Alec presently offered, with a certain air of timidity and gentleness in his manner that Susannah never had seen in him before. "It's a long time to wait, and it's a stupid arrangement that makes it necessary. But you can't get a divorce here. It's the quickest way, after all. And it's a delightful city."

She was not listening.

"I shall have to let Terry sail without me," she said musingly. "Go West myself, perhaps with Phil—he is wild to travel—and then follow Terry as soon as I can. We can be married in England." Her face brightened a little. "It's a delay, that's all," she said, in the most definitely hopeful tone she had used in all this talk, "but I think it's the only way. You'll have to tell me what to do, who to see, how to manage it."

"It's very simple. Carter lives there; he handled our whole affair."

Susannah was looking at him thoughtfully.

"Then you never were married to Merle, Alec?"

"No."

"And as soon as she knew that yours hadn't been a marriage she wasn't willing to go on with it?"

"It was a deliverance for her," he said without bitterness.

"You decided to separate right away?"

"We had decided long before that."

"It was all a loss from the very beginning," Susannah mused.

"All a loss." He spoke simply, shutting his lips tightly when he had finished speaking.

"I wonder why it had to be that way——" But again she was not speaking to him; her eyes were fixed on space.

"If happiness has come out of it for you," Alec began, "I'm glad. There's that much gain, anyway. In a few weeks or months you'll be out of all this. And then some day, perhaps, you'll forgive me, Sanna."

They were sitting in a corner angle; she had only to raise her eyes to meet his. He saw in them an infinitely weary, infinitely kind half-smile.

"That doesn't matter now, does it?"

"It matters terribly to me," he said.

"I don't think I ever thought, Alec, of forgiving you or not forgiving you," Susannah said mildly; "that didn't seem to be the question at all. Whatever you felt for her, you couldn't seem to do anything except what you did do. It wasn't unkindness to me, or kindness or anything, really. I wasn't in it. Even when I felt so badly—even when I cried so much—I realized that."

He put his elbows on the table and his face in his hands for a few seconds, and she heard him whisper: "You cried!"

When he took his hands away his face looked tired and drawn.

"It seems to me now like something I couldn't have done, Sanna. I've tried a thousand times to explain it; there's no explanation of it. Everything seemed so smooth and easy in those days, one did things for no better reason than—well, than that one wanted to do them. It's all so different now."

"Our lives would be much easier," Susannah said, when the man had served the salad and gone away again, "if we always saw things in the same light—if they always had the same values. But they change so—or else one changes oneself . . ."

Her voice died away vaguely, and neither one spoke for a little while.

"I may not see you after this," she began, ending the silence suddenly, "and I want to thank you again for Phil. I think he thinks of me as his mother; I know that we are absolutely sympathetic with each other, perhaps more so than many a mother and son. I don't expect you to leave him always with me, but I know that it would break both our hearts to part for very long. He connects me," Susannah went on, looking at him with her level, honest gaze, "with the end of a time that was hard for him, the end of loneliness and of feeling that he didn't belong anywhere. He has his own room now, his own place, and he likes it. I don't think schools can ever give them that. If you could let things go as they are, at least until he's much bigger, I'd be so grateful."

"You don't think that there's anything I *wouldn't* do if you asked me?" Alec answered, a little gruffly. "After what you've been through—after the way I have failed you, then to have you ask for Phil as a favor! It breaks me up, somehow. Why, you're the only person in the world who's ever stood by the kid, who's ever given him a decent break at all. He's yours, Sanna, as long as in the goodness of your heart you'll let him be. I'd no more move him than if I'd never had a child at all."

"Then I think," she said, acknowledging this with only that same steady, serious look into his eyes, "that I'll take him with me to Nevada. I can carry him on in his lessons for a few weeks, and in Oxford we're going to put them all into school. Terry may be there for four or five months. He doesn't know exactly where he'll find the material he wants, or how long it 'll take him to collect it."

"You think he's very fine, don't you, Sanna?"

"What makes you think I think so? Do I betray myself?" Susannah said, sudden warmth in her heart at the thought of England—far-away England, where no one would be curious about her and her affairs—and of some old house deep in a garden with gables and ivy, and rooks streaming home through high elms, and Terry and Anne, herself and the children having supper there in a dining room with windows looking into a college close. The peacefulness of it, the privacy of it!

Alec was paying the bill, and they walked out together into an afternoon that had suddenly become chilly and filmed with mist. He suggested walking for a little while. Susannah reminded him that he had a three-o'clock train to remember. But now it was only two. They could walk for half an hour without missing it.

In the somber autumn afternoon the Avenue buzzed with life and beauty; the toyshops, the picture shops, the shops with beautiful oriental jars in the window, the candy stores —all vied with each other in carefully calculated attractions. Susannah looked into the windows of her smart little stocking shop of a few years ago; the same nice girls or others exactly like them were behind the counters. She and Alec went into a big bookshop and loitered along the tables, and

Alec tried to find something, rather pathetically and ineptly tried to find something that would interest her. She remembered Terry in the Boston bookshops, his fine thin, rather high-colored face intent, his glasses on his aristocratic nose, his murmur ecstatic. Terry always knew just what tables and shelves held what he wanted, and rarely moved more than a few feet in the course of an hour, always lamenting that he had to go away before he had seen "anything."

Alec drifted along, commenting on the biography of a famous dancer he had seen many times, calling Susannah's attention to the revelations of a certain actress, dramatically entitled *Three Husbands and Me*.

"Remember her, Sanna?"

"Oh, very well. She used to be with Kate Lancaster all the time."

"That's the one. And of course the second husband was Freddy Porter."

"That's so! Horrible picture of her."

"That's Ross St Hubert's portrait of her."

"So it is."

He walked with her to the door of her hotel, and they went inside and stood talking for a minute or two before she went upstairs.

"I'm telephoning Carter tonight. I wired him from the office this morning that I'd call him at eight. That's five o'clock for him. He'll give me the whole thing in three minutes. You'll be in town for a day or two?"

"I don't know. It will depend a good deal, I suppose, upon what I have to do. I thought I would see your mother tomorrow morning and give her the report on Phil, and then, if I must go to Reno, go home and talk the whole thing over with Terry."

Again she made a little frowning face of distaste.

"It's all so horrible," she said under her breath.

"I know it is."

"But no help for it. Only—if I'd known, I might have gone West quietly this summer. However, it's too late for that now."

Alec looked at her for a second or two, apologetic and troubled, before he said on a tone of forced briskness: "Well! I'll telephone you about half past eight tonight. I'll have to cut my Philadelphia meeting. And one last thing, Sanna," he added hesitatingly.

She looked up at him expectantly. There were windows of cathedral glass and palms and soft lights in the quiet corner of the hotel foyer where they were talking. Susannah stood slender and tall and serious against the background they made. In the early afternoon there was a stir of coming and going all about, subdued voices in meeting, laughter, perfume shaken from the garments of beautifully dressed women. In the distance, somewhere out of sight, music was playing.

"I wanted to say that I think you've been magnificent through everything," Alec said quickly, with a boy's manner of haste and awkwardness that were entirely unlike him. "What I think naturally doesn't matter to you. But I do think that. I'd never forgotten you, but I'd forgotten how quietly—how magnificently—you do things. That's all, except that I'm terribly sorry for everything. Good-by."

"Good-by," she said, her heart suddenly wrung. She wanted to add something to it, perhaps to put her arms out to him and say, "Ah, it's all too bad, isn't it!" But instinctively she fought the impulse, crushed it down, and before it could rise again he had turned away; he was gone.

She went up to a hotel room that was cheerful in the dull afternoon light. Someone had lighted a pink lamp near the window; below the window the city was romantic in the transforming autumn mist that beautified even chimney tops and water tanks, turned the bridges to gray rainbows of steel that faded away into the fog, and made the first pricking of office lights a firmament of tiny stars.

Her furs and her hat thrown on the bed, Susannah pushed her hair back from her forehead and stood for a minute in the middle of the room, pressing her palms tightly against her temples. For the first time in her life she had the feeling that she was going out of her mind.

CHAPTER XXXI

ALEC. ALEC. ALEC. The sound of his voice, the touch of his hand, his presence again. The old love was like a vise that held her heart tight in its grip; she tried to writhe away from it; it was no use. The world was ringing and thrilling with him; from the first instant when he had walked forward in the office, with the concerned, kindly, half-smiling look she had always loved to see on his face, something that she had thought dead, something that she had tried to forget, had arisen strong and unforgotten and living, and she was in its power now.

Not even in the old first days on the Queen Augusta had her heart responded to him with the rush of feeling that she was experiencing in this strange hour when she seemed to be torn, body and soul and mind, between the claims of the two worlds: one the old world, and the other the new that she had discovered, had created with pain and tears and loneliness for herself. In the new life waited Terry with his long hands and his haunting voice and the aristocratic scholarly fineness that made Shakespeare and Homer and Keats, Vermeer and Lippo Lippi, Bach and Mozart much more a part of his daily scheme than the radio and theater and movie sensations of the day.

And in the old life was Alec, the man she had loved in those days that had been the most radiant she had ever known, the man whose sophisticated half-smile, whose easy ordering of a luncheon in a French restaurant, whose masterful command of everything the world held that was privileged—friendships with the famous and the rich, trips, yachts, country houses, riding horses, tailor and groom, valet and secretaries—had made him in manner and speech what he was, one of the princes of the earth.

There was nothing ostentatious or assertive about what Alec said and did; he had no need of such props. He need only be himself to stand above and apart from the common run of men. Susannah tried in her racked heart to make him seem unimportant, to belittle him. There was no reasoning about the situation; it was all far beyond reasoning. She had passed into the zone of pure feeling; she was feverish, almost delirious, with excitement. For a long hour, for another hour, she sat at her window in the hotel room and looked out into the mists of the autumn afternoon and let her spirit be carried to and fro on wild tides of feeling.

Afterward she made herself go out and walk; but it was the old world in which she walked, and she had not forgotten it. The matinée crowd was flooding the Avenue now; in the shops there were groups of beautifully furred, well-groomed women. They were all talking about the things she once had known: the smart magazines and shows, the new hats and frocks, the opening of the theatrical season. Candy stores sent out waves of vanilla-scented, chocolate-scented sweetness; the eyes of a half-million cars sent fans of light through the dusk. Green lights, red lights, newsboys, shabby little women slipping into the Cathedral's big swinging doors, green omnibuses with tired women looking out peaceful and triumphant from window seats; it was all unchanged. Shopgirls were going home chattering; moving-picture houses were twinkling in snakes of green and blue lights.

Her New England garden, her little boy wrestling with fractions, 'Liza turning down the beds in peaceful airy upstairs bedrooms, Laverne laconic as she retailed the day's news—these things might never have been. She belonged here, here, wherever he was; they two could not be in the world and apart. Fiercely, breathlessly, Susannah wrestled with the feelings that possessed her; their power grew stronger rather than weaker in spite of her.

She went in to see Alec's mother. He might be there. He wouldn't be there, but he might be. Mrs Hazeltyne was alone.

The two women had an hour's talk. Susannah would not have tea, and the older Mrs Hazeltyne had been forbidden sweets and stimulants and everything else she liked by her doctor. But she always loved to see Susannah and hear about Phil, and if Susannah's heart felt a certain blankness and impatience, a certain wild hunger to be doing something —anything—to get in touch with Alec again, to know where he was, to hear his voice, she did not betray it. She walked home at six o'clock, thinking only that in another two hours or a little more he must telephone her. And perhaps he would say something in reference to the matter that involved them both that would mean that tomorrow she might see him again.

There was no sense to this. There was no sense to it! She paced the floor. She had selected a book to bring with her to the city from her long parlor shelves of books; she tried to read it now. She tried to think of the quiet morning hour when she had said to 'Liza, "I have to go to the city sooner or later, and it might as well be today."

Terry had come over to see her off.

"I'll have to see Alec sometime about this, Terry," she had said, on the station platform, "and I may as well get it off my mind. I hope I'll come back to tell you that everything is all right for our sailing a week from Friday, but I'm afraid not. In any case, we'll have to talk it over, and I've been fretting and lying awake over it long enough."

And in that quiet autumn morning hour with Terry in his old cords and worn brown sweater storing her suitcase in the rack above her head and promising her that all her commissions should be remembered—supper for the cats, and Phil's change of shoes if he got his feet wet playing around where the men were digging the new water mains —and while he was writing the name and address of her hotel carefully into his notebook, and the red leaves of October were softly falling, falling through crystal air, somehow she had lost that old world. It was hard to remember little Pemberton now, the main street flanked with trees, the bland old courthouse staring out from a wreath of red leaves, the dreaming silences of summer days when heat lay like a green thick blanket on the town, the snowy purity of winter, when the squashes were in and the wood piled, when in old-fashioned homes apples still scented the black darkness of cellars, and every chimney sent up its stream of pale gray wood smoke into the whiteness of the sky.

The Duquesnes' sunken, long, low-ceiled parlor came before her mind's eyes: the leaded bow window that pushed itself into the thick shrubbery of the garden, the flicker of firelight on the backs of books, Anne darning, rather silent, Terry stretched in his deep chair with a book in his hands, herself between them, thinking dreamily of what Terry was reading, of what was in the house for lunch and supper tomorrow, of the brackish taste the water had had lately and what had caused it, and of a thousand other homely, happy things that had nothing to do with a hotel room a hundred miles away, and lonely dusk in the city, and a man's voice echoing—echoing—echoing in her ears.

She had her supper upstairs, tried again to read, returned again to the window and stood looking out at the city that was now all blackness of shadow and glittering of diamond lights against the dark. Eight o'clock struck, and half past eight, and it seemed to her that the telephone never would ring. But it did ring, and feeling weak and afraid she went to answer it. It was Alec's voice that spoke.

"Sanna, I'm downstairs," he said. "May I come up?"

"May you——" She had to swallow with a dry throat. She stammered, hardly knowing what she said. Out of the greatest city of them all and the night and her feeling that he was completely lost to her, he was suddenly near her again, and for a moment she could think of nothing else. "I'll come down," she said confusedly. "I'll be right down."

Conscious only of the fact that she was going to see him, she somehow put her hair in order, picked up her purse and her key, went through the halls to the elevator, was stepping out into the passage downstairs, looking inquiringly about. He was there; he came forward; their hands and eyes met.

There was a quiet alcove off the main foyer that was furnished with a few comfortable chairs and two writing desks. It was deserted tonight and only dimly lighted. Alec and Susannah could talk there undisturbed. She took a round-backed green velvet chair, and he drew another close to it, and they began at once a discussion of his talk with Carter in Reno an hour earlier.

"But you were to go to Philadelphia tonight, Alec?" she presently diverged to say.

"I wired Hurlbert that I'd be down on the midnight train."

"You stayed on my account?"

"And on my own. I didn't want to telephone all Carter said."

"But the sum of it is that he thinks I should go West?"

"That one of us must go. Sanna, I would if I could."

"Well, then," she said, reflecting, "I think Phil and I must start West immediately. The sooner begun the sooner finished. Terry will have to go to England alone; we'll follow as soon as we can. Perhaps Anne will go with him now, or perhaps she'll wait and she and I will go together. It's a wretched thing to have to face, but there's no help for it. I'll go home tomorrow and have a talk with them—this is Monday. I should think that we might leave for Nevada on Friday night. I'll take 'Liza."

"Want to wait until Friday? I'll get you your tickets. I'll route you straight through to San Francisco in case of anyone recognizing you or hearing about it; it's better. And I'll have one of our trucks meet you at the station here and move your trunks."

"The trunks get to the city at four; there's only one afternoon train from Pemberton. I'll take Phil up to see your mother."

"And will you and he dine with me? Your train doesn't leave until midnight." He made a note in a notebook. "I'll have them make up your drawing room."

"I'll let you know, Alec, about Friday."

"What time does your train go tomorrow?"

"At ten."

"Then you'd be breakfasting about nine?"

"But aren't you going to Philadelphia?"

"I can go later."

They stood up; the talk was ended. Alec, taking her hand, looking down upon her, spoke suddenly.

"Why don't you hate me, Sue? Why don't you make it easier for me by reproaching me, by making me feel how I've failed you!"

She could only look up at him, speechless, trying to falter out the only words that came to her, "I don't know." He put his arm about her, and the familiar kiss, the kiss for which she had hungered through so many heavy days and wakeful nights, was on her lips, and her whole being seemed absorbed, enveloped in his own.

Two or three times he whispered, "My God!" She heard

nothing more. Then he was gone, and she was alone. Quickly, affrightedly, as if fearing that he might come back, and knowing that she could not see him again, she went through a rear hallway and across a corner of the deserted dining room, and so to another elevator and upstairs. But the touch of him kept her senses whirling. Her heart pounded; she felt faint.

Again in her room she locked the door, made herself go mechanically through the movements of undressing and preparing for bed. The excitement did not abate. She did not want to go to bed; she walked the floor instead, pacing lightly to and fro with the step of some lissom jungle animal. Now and then she spoke in a whisper.

"Oh, my goodness, what am I going to do! Oh, my goodness, what am I going to do!"

❦ CHAPTER XXXII ❧

THERE WAS NO SLEEP for her that night. Her thoughts would not let her sleep. They would have breakfast together; she would see him again. He would take her to the train, and perhaps—standing there in the great arcades—he would kiss her again. A man could kiss a woman unashamed there; a thousand men would be doing the same thing. Her very soul seemed to melt within her at the thought; she was floating —flying—there was no earth anywhere, and no sanity, and no reason.

Lying in bed, she could not sleep. She relived over and over again that moment when so simply, so quietly, so much with his old air of being carried quite out of himself, and yet sure of himself, too, he had put his arms about her and kissed her. And she finally went off to sleep remembering the four words he had used at luncheon and that had been running like an undercurrent to every thought she had had since:

"You are my wife."

He joined her at the door of the dining room the next morning, and they had breakfast together. She noticed that he ordered what she liked without any reference to her: late sweet blackberries, the hot milk she had learned to drink with her first cups of coffee in Peking so many years ago, dry, thin brown toast. When they were eating he said:

"It occurred to me after I left you last night—and by the way, I walked the streets until almost four—that there is one thing I'd like you to understand. It's this: there never has been anyone like you in my life; there never will be. I'll love you until I die. I've always loved you, but I didn't know it.

"It mightn't be now, Sanna," he went on very simply, as Susannah did not speak, "it might be years from now that you'll need me—might need me. I'll be ready then. I'll want you and love you all the rest of my life."

"I'll love you until I die. . . . I'll love you until I die." . . . The words repeated themselves over and over again as she sat in the hot chair car, staring absently at the autumn fields flashing by, and the little villages and suburban homes with their roofs and brick walks so new and their trees mere whips set in dark earth. . . . "I'll love you until I die."

Whenever they came back to her a warm sense of happiness, of being important, came over her. She could not sense them, savor their meaning enough. It was strange to meet Terry at the Pemberton station, Terry so completely unchanged, and think of the crisis of emotion she had experienced since he had brought her to the train only twenty-four hours earlier. Terry had his old overcoat on, for a wild wind was blowing, shutters and doors were slamming in the little town, and red and gold leaves whirling about in the streets. Susannah smiled as she got into a mud-spattered old car. The sweet, soft country air touched her hot cheeks and jaded temples with an infinitely soothing caress. Just the smell of mud and leaves and stubbled fields was delicious; the little headache that had been hovering about for the last hour immediately took flight and was gone. She rested her shoulder against Terry's comforting shoulder as they drove home;

they went to the Duquesne house and found Anne and the children waiting. Phil and Nan and Jerd had had their luncheon; they raced off to school. Terry, Anne and Susannah sat long over a late and leisurely meal and talked over some of the phases of the changed plan: what Anne would do, how soon she and Susannah might follow Terry. Afterward Susannah and Terry walked to her house, and sat beside her parlor fire, and went on with the talk.

"Can't you get some rest before dinner, Sue? You look tired. It took it out of you, didn't it?"

"I'll go to bed early. I feel horribly—restless, somehow," Susannah said. "You see, the probability is that 'Liza and Phil and I will start for Nevada on Friday."

"Friday, good heavens!" Terry ejaculated. "How can you ever get ready?"

Alec had said, "Want to wait until Friday?" Alec would probably have been on a plane this very afternoon. The contrast between the pace at which the two men lived was in Susannah's mind as she explained:

"I want to have it over with. I didn't want to say too much before Anne, for she loathes all this as much as I do. I hate it! It would have seemed quite different, somehow, before I met you. Before we dreamed our dream of books and garden and Oxford," Susannah said. "Now, there's a sort of cold-bloodedness about it, a sort of calculatedness——"

Terry glanced up at her over his pipe. He did not speak.

"Funny how people change, Terry. Not that I've ever had anything but a feeling of shrinking—of fear, really—about divorce. It was Alec who managed it all—or I thought he did. Now it seems that I'm the one who has to face the music, go out there, be identified, refuse to talk to reporters and all the rest of it!"

"I can't see, Sue," Terry said presently, "that there's any other way out. We'll just have to alter our plans to meet the situation. It's not of your making or mine. I'll go to England alone; Anne and the children will wait for you here; you'll join them in six weeks—seven weeks, it 'll have to be, and we'll be married in England." He smiled across at her encouragingly. "It's not our original plan," he said. "But I think I knew from the beginning that there had to be some hitch somewhere. I'm only too grateful that it isn't more serious. I've been walking on thin ice, Sue, the thin ice of happiness that is so great, my dear, that it's about half *scare!* I say to myself, 'It can't be that she's going to be my *wife,* going to live here with me and share everything I do! It can't be that some day I might say, "My son, my daughter, our children!" Those things are for other men, not for me.'

"Why, Sue," Terry went on in his lazy, pleasant voice as she merely looked at him with troubled eyes, without speaking, "I was happy enough as it was. I was happy before you ever came here; life's always been a tremendously happy and absorbing thing to me. I never dreamed of more. I never dreamed of companionship and understanding and laughter—— Do you realize that we two are always laughing? I never thought of *love*. I never thought there 'd be someone pouring my coffee and smiling at me across the breakfast table, going with me to England or Norway or wherever it is I have to go from time to time. Those places are fascinating enough without the—the glory," he said, almost reverently, and not looking at her now, "of having someone like you along! Husband and wife, Sue. They're words that don't mean anything to one for years and years —half one's lifetime. And then suddenly they leap into being, and they seem—sacred, and one's almost afraid to pronounce them."

Susannah left her chair, came suddenly to him and was on her knees, her eyes close to his eyes, her two hands on his free hand as it lay on the arm of his chair.

"Terry," she said, "I wish we might have gone through with our plan! I wish that we were safely—safely married, and to sail a week from Friday for England. This—this change frightens me so. I feel as if I hadn't any right to all the peace and happiness and dignity that we planned. It *will* go through this way, won't it, in spite of the delay?"

He laid aside his pipe, put both his hands over hers.

"Why, what scares you, Sue?" he said gently.

"Everything, Terry. I'm tired, perhaps, and blue and superstitious. But you can't think—you can't think how strange it is for a woman to be talking to the man she married only a few years ago, talking to him just as if they were casual acquaintances! It goes so deep with a woman, Terry. I want these next two months to be *over*—I want to be Mrs Terence Duquesne, living in Oxford. I want our first anniversary and our fifth and our tenth and all this behind me!"

"We can afford to give a few weeks as a hostage to fortune, Sue. They'll melt into the past fast enough. Now, about Friday. Want me to telegraph the agent in Boston tonight and tell him to make reservations for you?"

"Oh! Oh!" she stammered, a little confused. "Well, you see, Alec said he would do that."

"You'll go from New York?"

"I didn't think of doing anything else. I thought—I thought I'd take Phil to say good-by to his grandmother. We get to town about four, and the train doesn't leave until midnight."

"You'd dine with her?"

"Well—I suppose so."

"But isn't there danger that he might be there? Or do you think he'll probably take great care to keep out of your way? He feels badly about his responsibility for all this, I suppose?"

"Alec? Yes, of course he does. He feels terribly."

"He wouldn't be at his mother's, then? I'll tell you, Sue," Terry said, thinking it out; "why not let me drive you all into town late on Friday, and have 'Liza take the boy to his grandmother's and meet us at the train? We can have a little supper somewhere, and I'll see you off. Then I'll come back here and pack for my own trip, and we'll meet in England when all these preliminaries are settled, in October?"

She looked straight at him, a half-smile of appreciation and consideration on her face. But she was not thinking of him. In her mind she was writing a telegram to Alec: "Terry is coming with me to the train on Friday evening. Thanks and good-by."

That meant she would not see Alec again. "You are my wife. . . . I'll love you all my life!" she heard him say. But she would not see him again, perhaps ever. She would not meet him, eager little interested Phil at her side, on Friday. They would not go together to his mother's house; Alec would not presently take her off for dinner. Of course not. What a fool she had been to let her imagination take this particular course.

But the fact remained that she *had* let it do so. The fact remained that a hundred times since Alec had seen her to the train this morning she had thought in anticipation of Friday, thought of herself, smart in traveling clothes, outwardly serious and businesslike over tickets and last arrangements, but inwardly thrilling to the thought that this man loved her, that once he had possessed her, body and soul and mind, and that he had put his arms about her, had said, "You are my wife . . . I'll love you all the rest of my life. . . ."

It was all a strange delusion; she must put it from her as a delusion. Her life was severed from Alec Hazeltyne's life; she might never see him again. She must indeed wish and desire never to see him again; she, the wife of Dr Duquesne of Pemberton, raising a group of eager, intelligent children, gardening, managing the charity committee of the woman's club.

"Let's do it that way then, Terry," she said. But she went back to her chair almost dizzy with a conflict of emotions, not knowing what she wanted or what she felt, only conscious that somewhere within her there was a sense of utter blankness, of unbearable emotion, pain, relief, disappointment, in the thought that she would not see Alec again.

CHAPTER XXXIII

THURSDAY WAS FOR HER a day of such nervous excitement that by noontime she was completely exhausted and lay flat on her bed for an hour before luncheon, closing her eyes, pretending to rest, but inwardly so keyed to a frantic expectation of some message, some telegram or telephone communication, from Alec that she was almost beside herself.

But why—why? She asked herself the question in contempt, in honest wonder and bewilderment. How could she analyze, much less estimate, the significance of the agitation that had taken possession of her from the very first moment of meeting Alec? Did it mean anything at all, would it last, could it be conquered by any act of will on her part? These questions and a hundred others poured through her mind; fever burned in her cheeks. She felt physically as well as morally and mentally incapable of leaving for the West without some word from Alec, without hearing his voice again, and the hours went by and the hours went by and he made no sign.

She had sent him a night letter on Wednesday night, saying that Phil would be with his grandmother on Friday afternoon, that Terry was driving her in to town and would see her to the train. Would Alec please leave the tickets with his mother where 'Liza would get them? And many thanks for taking charge of the trunks; 'Liza would be on the lookout for the truck when the Pemberton train reached New York on Friday afternoon, and the driver could go to Mrs Hazeltyne's for the tickets and bring the checks back there. She had not even said good-by or included any message of affection; she had simply signed the message "Susannah." And all that night and all the next day its phrases rang in her mind, and she tried to imagine Alec reading them, tried to estimate what they would mean to him, wondered if they would strike him with the chill and the disappointment they seemed to her to convey. He was not needed; another man was taking care of her; she had gone out of his life.

At intervals she tried to think comfortingly of Terry. So kind, so clever, so carelessly fine and unself-conscious in his worn old clothes, with his aristocratic fine hand running along the bookshelves to find a particular book, with the cadences of his aristocratic voice sounding on passages from Browning and Wordsworth and Pater and Hume. There was no good book in the world about which Terry did not know; his mind was a very storehouse of culture and knowledge and wisdom. The life any woman would live with him would be a life of intelligent, balanced happiness; happiness on the old-fashioned terms of soul development, mind development, patriotism and high ideals and home security. Filling vases, digging in the sweet damp earth to move limp little seedlings to and fro in the spring garden, playing Beethoven duets with Anne at the piano—Susannah's father had once been proud of her piano prowess—cutting sandwiches for boys and girls, this would be her life under dreaming old elms in still green Junes, or in winters when cold winds whined about the dormered roof. And she would love that life; she wanted it.

No Wall Street; no fierce, hot competition for success; no first-night parties with the rouged, excited star of the new

play the center of the group; no yachts and house parties
and cocktails and autumn costumes designed especially for
Susannah Hazeltyne! All that was over. Anne and Terry
were not rich as Alec counted wealth, but they spent only a
part of their income on themselves; they needed much less
than they had. Terry liked faded old shirts, worn old cords,
far better than new ones; his only extravagance lay in the
occasional expenditure of a few pounds or a few dollars for
some old book. "This is wickedness, gals!" he would say,
with a great indrawn breath of relish when his pipe was
lighted, himself in his own chair, and the book at last in his
long hands. "Kids somewhere could have eaten for a month
on this."

But the numbers of checks that he sent for the benefit of
"kids somewhere" took her breath away. Anne had told her
of it. Anne had her children's future to consider. Terry, she
said, never considered anything except that a very little
money sometimes could save a quite disproportionate amount
of pain.

"I ought to do it myself," he said. "I ought to be in a
slum somewhere, doing it myself. But we aren't all mission-
ary saints. I feel the gosh-dernedest fool talking to people!
My alibi is that what I write may help someone, somehow."

Thus Terry. She had never known anyone like him.
Terry's wife might well feel not only love for him, appreciation of his extraordinary mental ability, but admiration. And
to admire one's husband—did any woman want more than
that? What a wonderful thing, to feel that the man of the
family as he went about his everyday work, writing and
tramping, chopping wood and gathering apples, smoking his
evening pipe by the fire or helping a child with home lessons,
was admirable, was good, was a rock of stability and goodness in a troubled world!

As Terry's wife one would feel that. There would never
be anything ugly or small about him; he was as loftily above

that sort of human weakness as a star. He would take marriage and love reverently, not as something exciting and desired today and cast off tomorrow; he would always be grateful to the woman who united her life to his own.

And yet . . . and yet . . . Susannah lay upon her bed in the autumn stillness of the Thursday morning, half-packed trunks all about her, 'Liza and Laverne going about the house in all the excitement that the sudden preparation for a journey entails, and waited—waited—waited for the telephone to ring. Waited to hear Alec's voice saying anything —anything—when it did ring.

She ate a distracted lunch with Phil and Terry. Afterward Terry suggested a last walk. The Indian summer day was as warm as August, with a thin crystal brilliance in the air and leaves thick and sweet underfoot.

Susannah said that she was all for a walk, and they wandered up the lanes and across the fields and doubled back through the strip of her own woods to where the spring started, talking, their hands linked, the silences, the unfinished phrases of complete understanding, between them. And all the time she wondered if Alec was telephoning now—now— this minute.

Terry got her home in time for an hour or two of rest before dinner. She assured him she would positively take a hot bath and lie down after very little more packing. When he was gone she found 'Liza. Had anyone telephoned? No one.

A bicycle bell tingled in the lane half an hour later when she had finished dividing Phil's clothes into what he might keep and what was to be thrown away. Her heart leaped; she went to a window. No, the boy had gone by. He was going on up to Rountrees', Maybe Rachel Rountree Scraggs had had her baby a little early . . .

"That looked like Jeff Trimler takin' a telegram up to Rountrees'," 'Liza said, packing busily.

"Yes, I saw him." The Trimler boy knew Susannah's house, of course. He would not have gone by if the telegram had been for her. Jeff Trimler was not one of the brighter members of the family, but he certainly knew the Hazeltyne place from the Rountrees', especially with his cousin Laverne working there!

Susannah's face burned, and her hands were cold; she felt her mouth dry, and more than once went to the bathroom and held her hand under the cold-water tap until it ran very cold and drank long drinks of icy spring water. Alec's arms about her . . . the familiar scent of him . . . cigarettes and fine tweeds and firm brown cheek . . .

The telephone at last. She flew to it. It was Terry.

"Look here, Sue, you liar! I thought you were to lie down."

"I was just going to."

"Listen, dear. There was a telegram here when I got back."

"For me!"

"No, for Anne and me. My uncle—my father's favorite brother—was hurt in Boston yesterday. It only says 'street accident very serious,' but that means the end. The old man used to walk a lot, and I suppose he got thinking of his everlasting geology theories——"

"Uncle Frank Wilbur? I remember him."

"Of course you do! I wasn't sure you'd identify him among so many. He's badly hurt, and Kate—remember the daughter with four boys in medical school? Kate wants me to come right away——"

Oh, she despised herself—she despised herself—but a wild dizziness of escape was upon her. Not joy—God forbid!—not love, for she loved and admired and needed this man who was speaking with all of her, mind and soul as much as body.

But something, something in her cried out in a very frenzy of relief. Now—now she might see Alec! Now they would have one more talk, and after that she would neither see him again nor want to see him again.

Her voice had the proper note of regret and protest and sympathy:

"Oh, Terry! Does that mean you have to go to Boston?"

"Right away. I have to. He's always loved me like a son —he lost his only son, you know—and young Frank and I were chums. That means you've got to come over here to supper, Sue. And it *might* mean that I'd have to be here in America for a couple of months at least if I'm executor. But you come over, anyway."

"I'll be there at half past six." She hung up the receiver; her mind was one confusion. Susannah began to feel that she could not stand these alterations of violent feelings of changes and indecisions and surging emotions. They were exhausting her.

"Now, now, *now* what to do?" she thought, turning to her last packing with feverish energy. Terry could not take her to New York, but on the other hand she could not volunteer the news of the change to Alec. She put Alec out of her mind for a few minutes, lay down on her bed and shut her eyes, and listened with what concentration she could muster to 'Liza and Phil discussing the impending trip.

"We go over the Catskills, I should think," said 'Liza.

"Ho!" scoffed Phil. "We go over the Rockies, don't we, Sanna?"

"We certainly do."

"Were you asleep, Sanna?"

"No, darling, I just had my eyes closed."

"You'd think they'd slide off them, the trains," 'Liza mused. "Will he want this, Mrs Hazeltyne? He can't get into it."

"How many nights in the train, Sanna?"

"Four altogether."

"Oo, goody!" said Phil. "No more school. Boy!"

"It 'll be something new for you and me," 'Liza said. "Your mother's made the trip many a time."

"Have you, Sanna?"

"Oh yes. When I was about four, and my father was sent to Cheyenne. Then we went to San Francisco on the way to China, when I was about fourteen. After that we all came home together, and after my father's death my mother and I went West again. And then my mother and I went back to Shanghai."

But this wasn't true, she thought, trying to keep her mind in a safe channel, trying not to let it wander into dangerously exciting courses. It hadn't really been this woman who was lying here on her bed who had done all that, who had been that eager child with a mane of reddish gold hair so many years ago.

"Oh, look, Daddy; oh, look, Daddy!" she had said a hundred times, a thousand times, hanging on his arm as they walked through Yokohama's narrow streets, staring about with eyes that couldn't take it all in fast enough when they went down into the labyrinth of Old Shanghai. He and she had loved it all, had stolen many walks while her mother played bridge or sat at tea with army friends. He had bought her a rug one day in Peking; bought it for a few dollars, but how she had loved it for many years! Pale brown fur one side, pale brown "tribute silk" the other. She had had it on her bed, one of her treasures, from that day until the day she had married Alec. Then it hadn't seemed right. It hadn't seemed to fit into the frail peach and pale powder-blue silks of her magnificent bedroom. It was stored somewhere now. She hadn't thought of it for years.

" 'Liza, did you ever see a fur rug, lined with Chinese silk?"

"I think it's one of the things we put into boxes when we came here. Maybe it's up attic, Mrs Hazeltyne."

"I'll look for it some day."

"Did you want me to look for it? Did you want it on this trip?"

"I wish you would, 'Liza. I believe I do. It's not important." But suddenly it was very important, like her father's hand holding her own, his approval going with her. Suddenly Susannah felt that she could not go on another hour without it. Her father! She needed him now! She needed someone who would always love her, always think that she did right, always stand between her and the cold winds of the world. "I could call Mrs Hazeltyne; he might be there," she thought. "What could I say if I called him? Weakness! He'd know it was weakness. Plenty of women have made up excuses for calling Alec."

"And I have got to *stop* this," she added in her own mind, getting up, running a hot bath, wandering about with brushes and creams. "This is nonsense. It's *possession*. I'll not give in to it. You know this kind of thing doesn't last," she added to herself sternly. "Everyone with any sense knows it! You've lost all your bearings, you're just being silly. Terry —Terry—Terry . . ."

She clung to his name as a sort of talisman. And through all her thoughts still ran the burning hunger to hear the telephone ring, to hear the tingling bell of the bicycle that meant that a telegram was at the door.

The night went by without sleep. Terry had departed immediately after supper for Boston. Susannah and Anne, left alone, had chatted absently for a while, neither woman thinking very much of what she said. Toward half past nine o'clock, when she had twice hinted that she must be on her way, Susannah had suddenly blurted out the question:

"Anne, you never were divorced?"

"Oh no," said Anne, looking up, surprised. Smooth-skinned and with smooth red hair swept off her rather pale full face and massed in a knot on her neck, she was the picture of young matronly placidity as she sat working busily at a strip of tapestry in a round frame.

"Why not?"

"Oh—several things. No object in it, for one. And then —Albert's always been very fond of the children. He comes home—well, you know how often. Every four or five months. There's no rule about it. He's happier where he is, and I'm happier here."

"You never tried to join him, to live there with him, in Springfield I mean?"

"No."

It was quietly said, after thought. It was as if Anne asked herself if she would like that, decided in the negative.

"Have you any—scruples about divorce, Anne?"

"I don't think so. No. My cousin Harriet Slocumb is divorced. You met her. I've always been devoted to her. I don't think it made any difference. I'm sure it didn't."

"She didn't remarry?"

"Oh no."

Susannah was silent. After a while she said that she must go home, and Anne came with her to the door, and they stood there together for a moment before Susannah went out under the autumn stars.

"You're not nervous, walking down the lane alone?"

"Oh no," Susannah said. "When you're unhappy, Anne, things don't frighten you."

"I know how it is," Anne said. "I'm so sorry you're unhappy!"

"It's just this transition time, I think. It's just—— I suppose I'm doing right, Anne?"

"I think you are. I know you are, Sue. Time will make all of it come right. You're only straightening out something that you thought was straightened out a long time ago. Don't—don't worry, Sue. It couldn't be wrong, you know, and mean so much happiness to Terry. He's so good. He's always been such a wonderful person. And you and he seem to me to have been simply made for each other."

"Seeing him—seeing Alec yesterday," Susannah said, "has shattered me, somehow. I feel as if I'd lost all my bearings."

"I suppose there's no help for that," Anne said thoughtfully.

Susannah suddenly kissed her good night. They did not often kiss each other, but somehow the touch of Anne's sisterly cheek, the brace of her arm, helped Susannah tonight.

"I think I'd rather have you say that than to tell me it wasn't anything," she said, going away into the dark.

When she got home, breathless from the walk that a little feeling of fear had made swift, 'Liza announced a telegram.

"In the parlor there, on your desk, Mrs Hazeltyne."

Susannah's hands shook as she opened it. It was signed with Alec's initials reversed, a little cipher he had often used in messages to her when he wanted to be surely protected from identification. It read:

"Dear Sanna, I am very anxious to see you before you start West. Can you arrange this tomorrow at my mother's when you bring Phil there? I will be there from four o'clock on hoping to hear from you."

Slowly, the yellow paper in her hand, Susannah mounted the stairs to her room. A great peace seemed to envelop her. Peace, after all the tumult and strain of the day and the night that had gone before. It was like the utter wearied relaxation that follows pain; it was like the relief when a feverish gathering of poison in sensitive flesh has at last broken. She felt a little dazed by it, and very tired. She would sleep now, sleep deep, like a spent child.

Once she thought of Terry, kindly, gentle Terry with his red hair and his long fine hands. He would be a comfort to them in that dignified old Boston house that accident had stricken. He would hold smiling, courageous consultations with all the aunts and uncles and cousins. They all adored him. The moment they were in trouble they all wanted him.

She would be on the train with Phil tomorrow night, but she could write Terry, mail him a long letter in Chicago. She would not tell him of that hour in old Mrs Hazeltyne's house tomorrow when Alec would come forward to meet her. . . .

How would they meet? What would they say? She need not think. It would be enough that they would meet, would have one more talk together before the last parting. The thought of it flooded her senses; she went through the intervening hours like a woman in a trance. She would engineer little Phil into his grandmother's stately, over-furnished, dark, big, elegant apartment, and Alec would be there. Or she and Phil would get there first, and she would hear the subdued buzz of a bell somewhere, and see Mollie in her gray moiré and saucy apron and cap going sedately across the hall toward the door. . . .

And her heart would beat fast and her hands grow cold at the mere thought of it.

CHAPTER XXXIV

It came about quite simply on the day following, almost exactly as she had fancied it. She had gotten little Phil into his grandmother's presence and was helping him off with coat and gloves and cap when the buzzer did actually sound, when Mollie did actually go toward the door in response to it.

"That's Alexander," said his mother, in her rather harsh old voice. "I told him not to come. I didn't know how you'd feel about it."

"He probably wanted to see Phil," Susannah said faintly. She stood up, turning toward the door, one hand on the child's shoulder, her furs loose on her own shoulders, her close little velvet hat with its curling plumes framing her russet hair and darkened eyes and paling face.

And after all, it was only Alec, pleasant and quick in movement, throwing his hat and gloves to Mollie and coming straight toward his child. Susannah freed Phil and stepped back, watching them.

"Hello, Phil. Remember Dad?" Alec said. And she saw that he was deeply stirred.

"Yes, sir'r'r," Phil said, standing erect in military fashion. He held out a small arm and hand, but Alec knelt and encircled him with his arms. He was still holding to the child's shoulder as he stood and turned toward Susannah.

"Sanna, I'm very grateful to you for this. Come over here, Phil, I want to look at you and talk to you."

He drew the child away to a quiet corner of the room. Susannah took a chair beside his mother, and they talked quietly.

"I was so glad to hear that you'd seen Alec, Susannah. I didn't know just how you'd feel about all this. He said you were magnificent. That was the word he used."

"It's an unfortunate situation," Susannah said reluctantly.

"It's exactly the sort of thing you'd expect that Russian woman to get herself into. Brazen!"

"As a matter of fact she didn't have much to do with it. It was Carter not telling Alec what the conditions are."

"You may believe she put him up to it!" the old woman grumbled.

Alec came up to them, still holding Phil by the hand.

"Sanna, may I take this boy off with me for exactly two hours? There's a picture he hasn't seen that he wants to see."

"Please, Sanna, please!" Phil pleaded, his dark little face pressed tightly against her own, his arms strangling her.

"But of course, Alec." How could she say no? It was the child's father who held his hand.

"Then he'll have supper here with Mother, if you'll let him," Alec said. He had it all arranged, of course. "And afterward," he went on, with a quiet glance that set all her senses afloat, "I'll take you to dinner. I have to talk to you."

"Now, Alec, this girl is catching a train tonight," his mother protested.

"My dear Mother, the train leaves at twelve twenty-five. We'll be back at half past nine." Alec and Phil went off, and Susannah went to the guest room to rest and to write a long letter to Terry. But she did not tell him where she was sitting as she wrote, or what the exact plan for the evening was.

"Sanna," Alec said to her, while they were dining, "I want to ask you not to leave for Reno tonight. I want to ask you to let these reservations go, and use your tickets a few days from now, perhaps a week from now."

"To what purpose, Alec?" she asked, looking at him steadily.

"Because," he answered simply, "I can't let you go. You belong to me. You belong to me, my dear," he went on quietly, as she only looked at him with eyes that dilated and darkened and seemed to brim with strange light, "just as I belong to you, as we've always belonged to each other! I've been on fire since that moment when you walked into the office—the same dear, beautiful woman who was married to me, the same voice, the same eyes! It's stronger than we are, and you know it—all that we two remember! There isn't a beautiful inch of you that isn't mine. While I live you can't give it to any other man, Sanna! I couldn't give it to any other woman. I tried to; it was all a farce; I hated her, sitting opposite me at the table, going out with me in the evenings, lying asleep in the bed next to mine. It wasn't *real*. And she knew I knew it wasn't real.

"Sanna," he added, as she did not speak, "try to marry your Terry, if you like. But I'll always be there. Not that you love me any more; I know what you feel for me! I destroyed your happiness, and that's no little thing to do in a world where most of us don't find it twice. You went through terrible hours without me to help you; all I ever brought you was humiliation and sorrow. I know that!

"But, Sanna, the thought of what we've been to each other, those days when I came early to Easthampton and we rode along the beach—those days when we first went to London and I bought you the doll at Swan & Edgar's—those are the days, my dear, that are filling your veins with me now, and mine with you! Go away tonight if you like, put me through the mill if you must, but we're destined for each other—we can't escape!"

His arms were crossed, his elbows on the table. Beautiful and serious and silent, she had listened to him. Now quite simply she said:

"But you see, I agree with you. That's all true, Alec. Nothing you ever did before, or I ever did, really destroyed my life as this will destroy it," she went on. "But that doesn't change it. It's all true! God knows I wish it weren't!"

"What do you mean?" he asked quickly, in a changed voice.

"I mean just what you say—just what you've been saying. I mean that I have to go back, tonight or tomorrow or some day, and tell the finest man I've ever known—the man whose way of doing and thinking things is my way, the man who was kind to me when nobody else could help—I've got to go back to him and tell him that, in some way I don't understand, I belong still to you. That I always will. That from the moment we met five days ago I've not been able to possess myself—you've possessed me. I've been wherever you were, hearing you, seeing you, bound to you for the rest of my life!"

It was said quietly, unaffectedly, but the tone was one of despair, and at the end she put her elbows on the table and her face in her hands. Alec watched her for a moment in silence.

"You mean that the love is all dead?" he finally asked.

"Oh, love!" Susannah echoed, in an impatient whisper. "What does that word mean? My whole life was wrecked on it a few years ago. I comforted myself with my child and books and working in my garden and making over my old farmhouse. And then Evelina was taken away from me and there was nothing, and I had to begin all over again.

And it was then that he—Terry, stood by me, never failed me, thought what I was thinking before I could think it, never said a word too much, never hurt me—never hurt me!

"And I was fool enough to dream," she went on, after a moment's silence, and speaking now in a low tone without looking at him, "I was fool enough to dream that a woman could go on from the past into a new kind of future, forget everything that had happened, forget what she herself had been. It can't be. I know that now. I know that I am as much married to you as I was in the beginning. And where," Susannah ended, looking up with haggard eyes, "where do we go from here?"

Alec spoke slowly, his troubled look upon her.

"I think I never quite understood all this until now, Sanna."

"Nor I; nor I," she said. "If I understand it at all. All I understand is that when a woman has belonged to a man, as I belonged to you, and when that man, free again and loving her again, comes back and wants her, something stronger than love comes into it. She can't help herself then. She can't reason. She only knows that while that man is alive she can't be wife to another man, she can't plan with him and travel with him and sleep at night in his arms. Terry and I," she went on in a musing, absent tone, as if she spoke more to herself than to him, "never thought that any echo of all this would ever come to us. We thought—if we thought of it at all!—that it was over. You see, that's a different world, Alec. It's like stepping back a hundred years to live there in Pemberton where women still put up three hundred glasses of jelly every summer, and boys shovel snow off the sidewalks and slide with their tippets blowing out behind them. One forgets up there."

Alec was watching her steadily. Now he said:

"Sanna, I won you once. I'll win you back."

She was not listening.

"And I'll have to tell him!" she said in a whisper. "Tell him that just going to Reno, just coming back with a paper in my trunk, isn't the answer."

"Sanna, I'm sorry," Alec said. "Listen to me. Try to see it more calmly. It *is* the answer. I'll help to make it the answer. You're all wrought up now. Seeing me again, so close to the time of the other plans, has upset you. But let me help you—let me help you. I'll not see you again, I'll not trouble you. Go on to Reno tonight with Phil, come back in six weeks with the whole thing cleared up and finished, and within a few months you'll realize that I *haven't* any claim on you. It *is* all over. Believe me, dear, I'll do nothing—nothing to bother you again as long as I live!"

"It isn't anything you can do or won't do, Alec," she said, looking at him with hard bright eyes. "It's something I've discovered just in these last few days. Something that you can't change and I can't change. That certain feelings——

"Oh, it's not love!" she broke off to say in an angry whisper, as if she spoke to her own thoughts. "But it's something that ties me to you—something that my soul and my mind aren't strong enough to break. And so I'm not going to Reno. I'm going home. Terry 'll be in England; I'll be here. I'll not try to give him what belongs to you—all the memories, all the hours I can't forget! I'd far rather hurt him, as I'm going to hurt him, by saying good-by. You see, Alec," Susannah went on, with a brief smile that instantly faded and a look straight into his eyes, "you've always had everything you wanted. He's never had any of those things—trips on yachts, women making love to him, races in Havana and at Paris, clothes from Regent Street, clubs and bridges and golf and first nights—none of that. He's simple. He finds everything he wants in his own mind. It takes much less to make him happy than it does to make you. Just—just its being April and the frogs peeping will do it for him. Just a new book in a worn old cover from London. But he wanted his wife," she finished in a half-whisper, looking away. "He wanted me beside him in everything he did. And I think a child—I think a child, to Terry——"

She stopped, and there was a long silence.

"What can I do?" Alec asked simply, ending it.

"Nothing. And I can't do anything, either. The claim you have on me would come between us, Terry and me, on our very wedding night. So you see you win again, Alec. I'll go back to Pemberton tomorrow—some day—I don't know when. I'll tell him."

"Don't tell him," Alec said, frowning in pain and sympathy. "For God's sake, Sanna, carry out your original plan, go on to Reno tonight. You won't go on feeling this way; in a few weeks, in a few days perhaps, you'll feel differently. If there was anything in the world I could do, you know I'd do it, rather than feel that I'd wrecked your life again! I love you, Sanna; I suppose you can't help feeling it. But I've no right to, and if you have the feeling that you owe me the slightest shred of consideration in the matter, I beg you——"

"I haven't," she said in an almost absent tone as he paused. "It isn't that. It isn't you at all. It's in me, somewhere inside me—the knowledge that I can't give him everything, and that I won't give him less than everything; that you're somewhere, perhaps remembering me as I remember you—isn't fair to him. And I have to be fair to him. He's too fine to be —cheated."

"Sanna, after a while, when it's all quieted down a little, might there be a chance for me again?"

"I don't know," she said, looking away with darkly musing eyes. "There again, Alec, *he* would be. I'd want you to give me what he gives me—I'd want to trust you as I trust him——"

"And you couldn't," the man said simply, finishing her sentence for her.

"No," she answered quite honestly. And after a moment she gathered her furs about her and reached for her gloves. "I think if you'll take me back to your mother's, Alec . . ." she said. "I'm so horribly tired."

"Let me think about this," Alec said, frowning.

They went back to his mother's apartment and into the little library off the big drawing room. Philip, half undressed and lightly covered on a couch, had long been asleep; Mrs Hazeltyne was reading in the larger room, her beautifully dressed white head illumined in a ring of lamplight. Everything else was in semidarkness at nine o'clock. Alec lighted a lamp.

"Sit down a minute, Sanna," Alec said. "Is it because of Phil that you won't make the break?"

"No, not Phil. I know you'd leave him with me," she said. She sat on the edge of a high-backed brocaded chair of carved black wood, her furs hanging from her arm, her gloves and bag still held in her hand.

"Of me, then?"

"No, not that, either. It's something in me—something I can't help—something that means that as long as we two are alive and our memories are alive, I'm not free."

There was a silence.

"Then you belong to me," Alec said, ending it. "We are legally still man and wife. Sanna——"

"No," she said, staring into space with narrowed eyes, speaking as if to herself, "it's not that. But it's that you might at any time remind me of that," she went on. "It's that in the background of my life—the new life with Terry in England, or back there in Pemberton—there'd always be the feeling that something, anything, might come up to remind me of it all, to make me feel bound to it all."

"Other women do it."

"But not with men like Terry!" she countered quickly. "I have to think of him. His family. I know how ridiculous

considerations of family sound to all of us in New York.
Most of your friends haven't any families. They started as
actresses or newspapermen or freelancers of some sort; they
broke away from their families back in Nebraska or Oregon
or Kansas. Half of them have been divorced and remarried,
sometimes in the same little circle of intimate friends.

"The Duquesnes aren't like that. I don't mean that they're
prigs. I don't mean that they go to meeting and eat cold
lunch on Sundays! I've never laughed so much in my life as
I have with Terry and Anne; I've never heard such thrilling talk as there is sometimes at their house when people
come from Boston or Montreal or Baltimore. But their
feelings are different—so different that one feels somehow
—well, what shall I call it? One feels *good,* the old-fashioned
goodness that—that doesn't get intoxicated and cheat on
marriage and gamble all the time. It sounds dull, but it isn't.
I think it's the way I've always wanted to live. But one
doesn't live that way in Shanghai—nor in New York nor in
Palm Beach!"

She stopped speaking and brought her tired eyes to his.
Alec was sitting at a little distance from her, his arms folded
on his chest, his half-frowning look fixed upon her.

"Suppose I told you that I never, under any circumstances,
would bother you any further, Sanna?"

"Ah, but you couldn't, you see. There 'd always be Phil,
your child, not mine. You might marry, and want him.
There might be other children some day, and I'd have to
tell them that I had been married to Phil's father before I
was married to their own. It wouldn't matter in your crowd,
Alec. But can't you see that it would in theirs—to him and
to me, too?"

"But, Sanna, things haven't changed so much since you
did plan to do it."

"No, not actually. That is, although we weren't divorced,
I could get a divorce, and in a month or two everything

would be as I thought it was. But this last week has changed everything just the same, Alec. I'd let myself think that I had left all the past behind me, I'd been through such——"
She stopped, began again on a lower key. "I'd been through so much," she said quickly, hurrying past the thoughts that the words brought up in a rush, "that I seemed to myself a different person. We never are, I suppose. We're always the same persons. Your writing me what you did, my seeing you, the whole thing coming up fresh again—awakened me from the dream."

"Does *he* see it so?" Alec asked with a keen look.

"Terry? He's a very quiet, very intense person of thirty-five," Susannah answered, "and he loves me. He was a long time discovering it, I think. Perhaps he'd rather put that sort of thing out of his life—or let it drift out. But when such a man loves——! I could make any conditions with him; there's nothing that would matter. What his people would think wouldn't bother him!"

"And if I went away, and promised never to communicate with you again?"

"No, that wouldn't do it," she said almost absently. She stood up. "I think we won't start West tonight," she added. "I'll go tell your mother."

"She'll immediately think that that means that we are reconciled, Sanna."

"Well, if she likes to think that . . ." Her voice trailed off indifferently. "But we know that there's no question of —reconciliation. It isn't quite so simple."

"And what are you going to do?"

"Why, tomorrow 'Liza and Phil and I'll go back to Pemberton. Terry will probably be there until they get his uncle's estate straightened out, but that only means a few weeks, and then he and Anne and her children are going to England —for a long time, perhaps. I may take Phil and go to China. Mother's playing with the idea of marrying an old

sweetheart there; she's past fifty, but you know her! I
don't know what I'll do. It's all—mixed up, and no matter
what I plan it doesn't seem to straighten it out. But a few
weeks of quiet, of thinking, will make it all seem clearer,"
Susannah ended, in a more courageous tone. "I'll have a few
talks with Terry; he'll understand. And if I do come to any
conclusion I'll write you."

Alec was standing close to her in the dim shadows of the
luxurious little library; he looked down at her with the kindly
protective expression she had once so loved in his handsome
eyes.

"And will you remember that if you can bring yourself
to give me another chance I'll be ready and waiting, Sanna?"
he said. "Will you remember that I've—I've changed, too?
That I'm sorry, that I'll give all the rest of my life to making
it all up to you, making you happy? We'll live where you
want to live, and the way you want to live, and for every
unhappy hour I've caused you I'll repay you with a hundred
other hours. Everything's different with me now, Sanna.
Half the old crowd are down and out; we don't know how
long Hazeltyne & Bowers can keep this up. We might *have* to
live the way you like to live; we mightn't be able to afford
the apartment and the Easthampton place and all the rest of
it. Although," Alec added, narrowing his eyes, speaking half
aloud in answer to his own thoughts, "I can't see how—
even with this market—Schwabacker was talking to me
about it today—it's bound to——"

Susannah laughed in spite of herself.

"Alec!" she said, faintly shaking her head.

"But I mean it's *there,* Sanna," he said. "America's wealth
is there. There's no counting her resources! I could always
take care of you and the kid."

"I'm afraid never that again," she answered him slowly,
beginning to walk toward the door.

"But then, what *is* your life going to be, dear?" he asked.

stopping her. "You're not the sort of woman to travel with a little boy, never to be loved and cared for by someone ever again!"

"No, that doesn't seem like my life, either, Alec."

She moved on, and he put an arresting hand on her shoulder and turned her about, and held her for a moment, looking straight into her eyes.

"Will you forgive me?" he asked very simply.

She felt tears thickening in her throat and stinging behind her eyelids.

"Alec—it isn't that——" she said with difficulty.

"But will you forgive me?"

"You gave me the happiest years I'd ever known," she said in answer. "They were such proud years, such full years! And I had Evelina. There never will be any talk of forgiveness between you and me. I loved you—perhaps I love you still, Alec. I don't know. That's one of the things I have to find out. I have to find out if this feeling of not being separated—being still a part of you as you are a part of me—might be something like loving.

"You must leave me alone to think it out. To think it out," she repeated wearily, pressing her free hand against her forehead as if it ached. "I've got to go now and tell 'Liza we aren't leaving tonight. Poor 'Liza; she was very much excited about the Rockies! And I'll have one of the girls help her get Phil to bed in the spare guest room. Then I'll talk to your mother, Alec, and after that turn in myself." She shifted furs and bag and gloves and offered him her hand. "I'll not see you again," she said. "But I'll write you if anything happens that we—we ought to talk about."

"May I kiss you good-by?" the man asked, a little huskily.

She did not answer in words. But she lifted her face as a child might, and her honest eyes were on his for a moment. Alec put his arms about her, and she heard what might almost have been a sob.

"And you do forgive me?" he said.

"Oh, Alec, always!" she whispered, the tears she had been holding back coming in a flood.

"No, don't cry," he said. "I'm not going to make you cry any more. Not ever!"

He went with her to his mother, and kissed the older woman good night, and with only a perfunctory word of good-by to Susannah, was gone. For a while she sat talking to his mother with what self-control she could command. Susannah felt tired to the point of exhaustion; her mind was a whirl of distressed and confused thoughts. But under them all there was a strange feeling of triumph and of peace. Somehow she knew already that she had encountered one of the dragons in the path of life and had passed him by unharmed.

❧ CHAPTER XXXV ❧

It was on the following Monday morning that Susannah crossed the lane and went down past the Millers' barn and the Hicks's long fence, and so into the Duquesne orchard by the back gate, and to the old toolshed where Terry, in faded blue shirt and worn cords, was fussing with an old pony harness decorated with dulled red tassels, a bowl of dirty suds, some rags and a soft old chamois skin. Soft pale sunshine was filtering into the shed, sending bars of light across the heterogeneous collection of tools, ropes, axes, leaf rakes and broken shallow boxes of nails; this place was Jerd's and Phil's delight; Susannah was familiar with every inch of it. She stood in the doorway, and Terry looked up to see what suddenly had blocked the light, and came toward her. She saw his color change.

"Sue! Good heavens, I thought you were in Nevada by this time!"

"I know you did." Susannah spoke carefully, like a child repeating a lesson. She tried to smile.

"When'd you get back? What's happened?"

"We got back last night, quite late, Phil and I. We came in Mrs Hazeltyne's car. He went off to school this morning."

358

"You're not going to Reno?"

"No."

Terry stared at her, uncomprehending. She was half leaning against, half sitting on a high stool now. He put his handful of damp rags down and leaned back against the table, waiting for an explanation.

"Tell me, dear," he said. "Don't look that way. I can see that—that it's all gone wrong. But don't worry, Sue."

"Oh, *worry!*" she repeated, breaking. She groped in the pocket of her sweater for a handkerchief, put it to her eyes. Terry came to her and put an arm about her, and she dropped her face against his shoulder. She felt his cheek against her hair for a second; then he went back to his old position, and Susannah gulped and began, with what self-control she could muster, to tell him about it.

"Friday night, just before train time, everything changed. We didn't go."

"You didn't let me know."

"No use. You see," Susannah said, forcing her way, "you see that what I didn't understand was that—that there was Alec."

"Alec. He wants you back?"

"It isn't that. It's my side of it. It's my side of it!"

Terry took up a strap, polished it, his eyes upon it as he said:

"You mean that you like him better than you think you did?"

"Oh no, not that! How could I, Terry?" Susannah asked. "I'm not an utter fool! He failed me when I needed him; he went away with another woman when I begged him—when I cried for days and days——"

"Don't!" Terry interrupted her briefly, not looking up from his work.

"He's always had everything, taken everything he wanted, never been stopped, never been made to think what other persons are feeling, never thought of anything but just amusement—good times—poker one night and a prize fight the next and a house party after that, and always women and cocktails and food and music and white shoes or evening dress—just what he wanted—always what he wanted——"

"Well?" Terry asked, clearing his throat.

She let the silence last for another few seconds.

"Well, what I feel can't be love," she said somberly, after a while.

"What is it, then?"

"I don't know. It's so ridiculous," Susannah went on, frowning, finding her words with difficulty, "for anyone who has been through what I have been through to talk of love! There are other things stronger—there are ties one *can't* break——"

"He said so?" Terry asked quietly. But there was a hint of grimness in his voice that was new to her.

"No. Or if he did, I knew it without anything he said. Oh," Susannah said, "if I'd gone on in that sort of life, if Alec and I had had six—seven—ten years together, as so many of them do, and then had gotten divorces and re-married each other's friends, that might have seemed normal enough to me! One breathes a different air; one's on a quite different level there. But I can't divorce him and come to you, Terry, not with your background, not with what your life is here—reasonable and dignified, with the line of magnificent men and women, and samplers and Copleys and silver and chairs, behind you! What's gone before will prevent me from being Mrs Terence Duquesne of Pemberton, superintending spring cleaning and managing the village charities and putting up sweet tomato pickle, living a woman's life that is honest and real, with boys and girls growing up, and family gatherings at Christmastime, and long summers down here. I can't do that, not while he is in the world, he who was all my life for three long years!"

There was a silence.

"Then what are you going to do, Sue?" Terry asked presently, patiently, watching her.

And again she answered forlornly, "I don't know."

"You'll go back to him?"

"How can I? It's the same old thing. It would be dinners and cocktail parties and late nights again. And if I couldn't stand it before I knew you, how could I bear it now!"

"He threatened to take Phil away, I suppose?"

"Oh no. Alec's not like that. There's something—grand about him. Something almost—royal," Susannah said.

"I can imagine," Terry commented with such obvious irony that she laughed a brief, sad little laugh.

"I mean that what he does he does with an air that makes it seem the only possible thing. There is a sort of—of *force* about him," Susannah explained, looking eagerly at Terry for understanding. But Terry had resumed his work with the strap, was rubbing short bits of it briefly, holding them off to study them, avoiding her eyes. "I felt it the instant I saw him last week," she went on. "The fact that to have been his wife was a definite thing, like losing an arm—or having been born a mulatto—— I'm not expressing it as I want to," Susannah interrupted herself, breaking off short.

"It means so much unhappiness for me," Terry said mildly, as if he spoke to himself.

"Yes, and for me."

"Isn't it a pity, Sue?"

"So much of life seems to be just—stupidly twisted."

"And what are you going to do?"

"I had to talk to you first, Terry. I came down the orchard way hoping that I'd see you alone. What are *you* going to do?"

"Go to England as soon as I can, I suppose, with Anne. I can't stay here if you're here. Once I might have, but not now. My uncle's estate will take a few weeks, but he left everything shipshape; it isn't going to be any trouble. And then I'll get off. You'll—you'll go back to him some day, Sue."

"Not now. I'm more married to you now than ever I was to him. He keeps me from you, Terry, but not any more than you keep me from him!" Her smile was sad enough, but he made his own smile meet it more cheerfully as he said:

"But look here, you're not going to be the only one who faces this! Life takes queer twists and turns sometimes. I'll have my wife yet, and all those brown little girls and boys will be charging about this orchard scaring us to death in spite of everything! Perhaps you'll go to Reno after all, Sue, when you've thought it all over quietly. Perhaps some day I'll go down to Southampton to meet a lady in a blue suit——"

"My wedding suit! Still in its tissue papers," she said in a whisper as he paused. Her smiling eyes brimmed; her smiling mouth trembled.

"And we'll send Phil off with 'Liza and have our wedding supper—well, where? Some place that not too many people go. And then we'll walk along the Embankment in the moonlight and hear Old Ben ringing in our marriage!"

"Oh, Terry, let's *think* it!"

"Meanwhile, let's enjoy what we know we have," Terry said, laying down his sponge, wiping his hands on the chamois skin, reaching for his shabby old coat. "We have today and tomorrow and a few more days when I can come over and have breakfast with you, and we can lunch with Anne, and have supper at your house. And if I have to go to Boston, perhaps you'll come along in my old car and we'll buy books and take walks. And let's talk, Sue, as if it *were* all going to come right, let's plan for England next spring, if not now. And even about divorce, my dear," Terry said, walking beside her now past the old barns and fences toward the house, "let's not be adamant. It's being done all the time. Perhaps after a little he might want to marry someone else; that would make you feel differently, wouldn't it?"

"Ah, it would!"

"Well, you see!" They went into the house, under the thinned maple shadows, together. The table was spread for luncheon, the three children leaping about with the usual vigor of school children in luncheon hour. Anne greeted Susannah unsurprisedly. Phil had already told her the little he knew of the change and the reasons for it. The good home odors of chops and baked potatoes and baking gingerbread were in the air. Susannah cut up Phil's meat; Anne busied herself with Jerd's. Nancy launched forth upon a vivid story of a little girl in school and how she had cried like a *baby* when her bloomer elastic broke.

"Girls cry all the time," Jerd observed, his mouth full of buttered potato.

"Oh, Terry, I didn't tell you!" Anne said suddenly. "Gus Trimler's waiting to talk to you in the old laundry. He's in some sort of fix. Come out with me and speak to him just a minute."

"Anne, you're terribly pale. Move your face," Susannah said, struck, as Anne stood up. "No, it's not the light, either. What have you done to yourself? You look sick!"

"I—my head aches," Anne said, going to the door. Terry followed her with a quick anxious question:

"Since when, Sis?"

They went out together. When they had reached the side porch, out of hearing of the lunch table, she caught at his lapel.

"Terry!" she said, her face colorless. "Minnie Brock just

telephoned. She'd a telegram for Sue, but she didn't want to send it by the Trimler boy. She telephoned here to ask if you'd go over and tell Sue."

She crammed a paper into his hand.

"I copied it down," she said. "Read it! He's dead."

"Who?" Terry said, in a whisper, steadying his eyeglasses on their black ribbon. "Hazeltyne!"

"Read it! It says he was cleaning his gun. He'd gone up to Canada, hunting, with two other men."

"My God!" Terry said, reading the scribbled penciled lines. His eyes met his sister's eyes. "Suicide?" he said.

"Do you think so?" Anne's eyes never left his face.

"Cleaning his gun, eh? And 'apparently in best of health and spirits.' Ah, well, we'll never know," Terry said, studying the telegram again. "She told me that he had been worried about his business affairs. He wouldn't be the only one who'd taken this way out. They'll call it accident, of course. Dead! Hazeltyne dead!"

"How can we tell her, Terry? And poor little Phil! He's just been telling me that his father took him to a movie and is going to send him a shotgun. But oh, Terry," Anne said, holding tight to his arm, "it's a merciful solution for us all, isn't it? Oh, my darling, think what it means to you! I can't be sorry. She'd come back to tell you that she couldn't go through with the divorce, hadn't she? 'Liza came over to say their telephone wasn't working half an hour ago, and she said to me so dolefully, 'We aren't going West, Mrs Lambert, nor to England, either,' and I knew then that it was all wrong! Terry, will she take it very hard?"

"At first. It 'll be a terrible shock to her. He had a great hold over her—she doesn't love easily, Sue, and she loved him. It can't help shaking her. But in the end she'll see— she's bound to see—that it's the solution. Anne——" Terry said. In one of his rare revealings of deep emotion, he gripped her shoulder with his arm, put his hard cheek against hers for a moment. "My God," he said, "what this means to me!"

"He must have seen what a position she was in, Terry."

"There must have been something generous in him, whatever he'd done to her," Terry said, "if he really did do this—if it wasn't an accident—if it occurred to him that this would clear it up, once and for all. Poor fellow!"

"Let's go back, Terry, we mustn't be gone too long. We can wait until the children go, and then I'll slip out, and you tell her."

"Perhaps you're the one to tell her, Anne?"

"No; you. I'll be round somewhere near if you need me. Poor Sue, how many storms and shocks she seems to have to take!"

"Let's hope this is the last, Anne."

They went back to the dining room. Susannah glanced up at them casually, glancing back at the second potato that she was mashing and seasoning for Phil.

"I begin to feel rested and quiet and *right*," she said. "It's good to get home!"

"It seems 's' if we sorter b'longed here," said Phil.

A door banged somewhere in a sudden onslaught of warm autumn wind; red leaves went down past the window; the light curtains streamed into the room. Then there was quiet again at the family lunch table, and the mellow harmony of its two-hundredth summer reigned again in the old Duquesne house.

THE END